The forbidden
Summoning

The Forbidden Summoning: Book 1
Copyright © 2024 by Tim Rayborn

All rights reserved under the Pan-American and International
Copyright Conventions. This book may not be reproduced in whole
or in part, except for brief quotations embodied in critical articles
or reviews, in any form or by any means, electronic or mechanical,
including photocopying, recording, or by any information storage
and retrieval system now known or hereinafter invented,
without written permission of the publisher, Thousand Acres Press.

Library of Congress Number: 2022951719

ISBN (paperback): 978-1-963271-33-1
ISBN (eBook): 978-1-963271-34-8

Cover Illustration by Laura de Antonio | Ldeag_Art
Map by Daniël Hasenbos | danielsmaps.com
Cover Design by Piere d'Arterie | instagram.com/piere_d_arterie

For further information, contact:

THOUSAND ACRES

Thousand Acres Press
825 Wildlife
Estes Park, CO 80517

The Forbidden Summoning

BOOK 1 OF *THE DARK RENEWAL*

Tim Rayborn

For all those still searching for their own music

RILNARYA

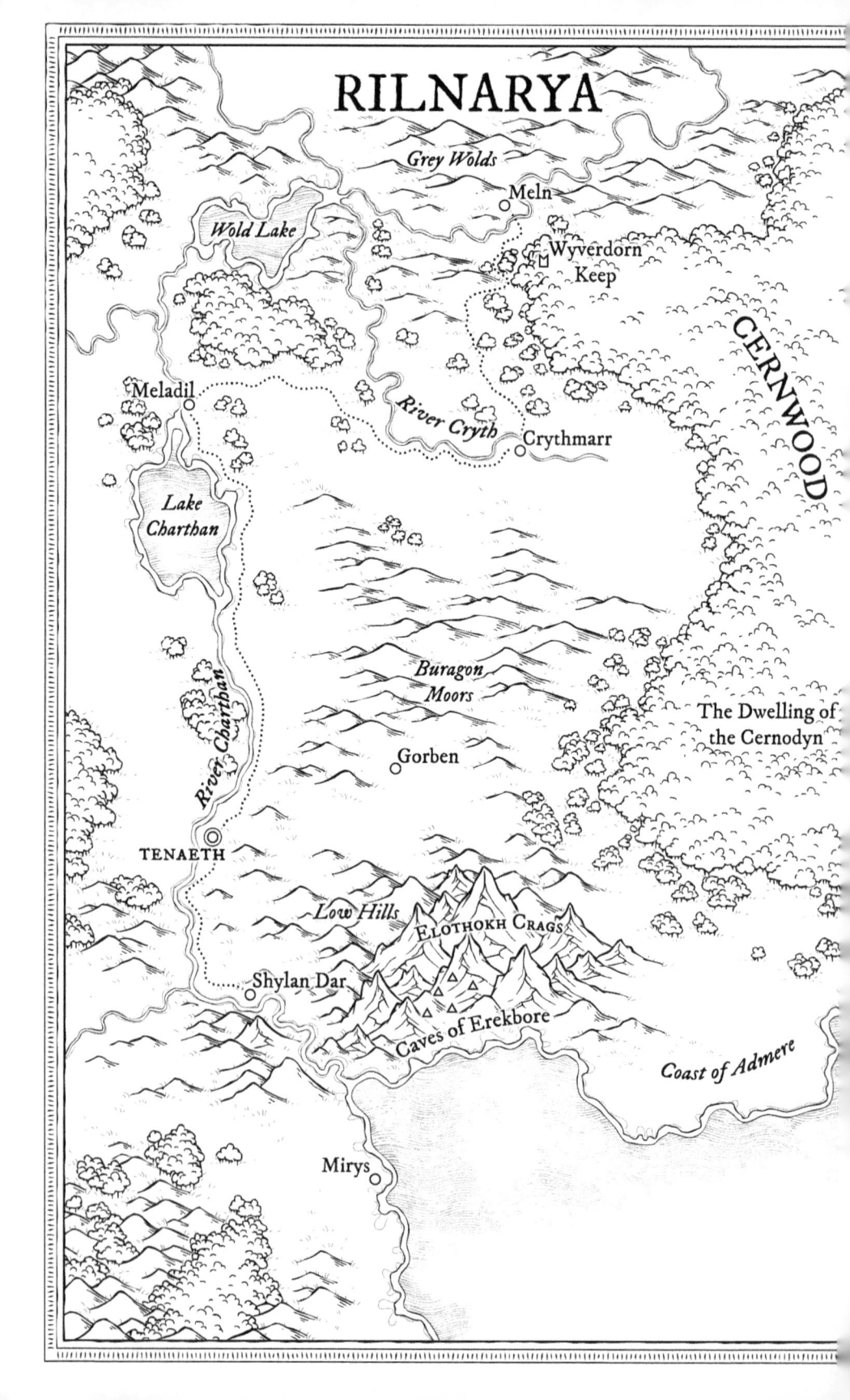

Grey Wolds

Meln

Wold Lake

Wyverdorn Keep

Meladil

River Cryth

Crythmarr

CERNWOOD

Lake Charthan

Buragon Moors

The Dwelling of the Cernodyn

Gorben

River Charthan

TENAETH

Low Hills

Elothokh Crags

Shylan Dar

Caves of Erekbore

Coast of Admere

Mirys

Part One

Earth Ravage

"The earth bleeds."

In a dark and cold stone chamber, a figure sat in mid-air, his legs crossed, his long grey robe trailing to the floor. With cruel eyes, he gazed into an orb of pulsing light floating above his outstretched palms.

Scrying into its center, he beheld the rumbling that shook a far-away barren landscape, its ground splitting open along the seams of ancient land-wounds. Primal energies born of a loathsome magic disgorged, stinging the surface of the ruined plains. Shadowy, swirling mists poured forth, free after centuries of imprisonment.

"It lives."

Ghostly shapes writhed within the darkness below, seeking to expand and destroy, seeking only to do Its will. Spirits of beings long dead and banished churned and pulsed in Its hateful core, feeding It with their essences, their identities molded and twisted into Its own.

"And yet, Its will is now bound to that of the Four."

Thunder roared overhead. The air rippled and distorted in the blasting heat, as howling winds whipped about with sentient malevolence.

"The earth ravage has begun."

Misshapen wraiths clawed their way upward with bony, decaying fingers through crumbling rocks, emerging from the splitting chasms of their imprisonment, their lifeless forms ravenous and wretched. These creatures would soon seek sustenance in the energies of the living, far from this desolate wasteland. For It needed to feed.

He bowed in grim satisfaction, holding a reverence for the horrific forces unleashed. That which he'd anticipated for so long would soon arrive.

Dismissing the orb with a wave of his hand, he descended gently to the floor. Drawing his hood over his head, he clasped his hands together. He bowed again, not to some higher power, but to his own ability, his own discipline.

He walked into the shadows, leaving only the echo of his footsteps.

One

"What do you mean it's not here?" Shaking, seething, and horrified, Dorinen stopped to catch her breath.

She scanned the forest clearing, but apart from trampled grass and a few broken tree branches, Cardwil spoke the truth. The hideous creature had somehow evaded them. She kicked at the ground in frustration and reached for the sword at her belt, her hand trembling as she clasped the grip, but not drawing the blade. Not yet.

"It's just gone. I don't understand how." Cardwil stumbled toward her, his breathing labored. "We saw it. It came right out here, but now…"

She understood his terror, and taking a deep breath to calm her own nerves, she placed her free hand on his shoulder, not that any gesture could comfort either of them. She tried to force away thoughts of what might have happened to their friends, those that the beast had not butchered but had instead taken away. Yet, she needed to ask.

"The others?" She swallowed hard, not wanting to know.

"Gone too." Cardwil's voice shook. "I don't know if they escaped, or if they're dead." A muffled whimper engulfed his words. "I'm sorry."

Dorinen would have given anything to deflect the rising tide of desperation, the sickening sense of loss. She took another breath, trying to remain composed, but she didn't know how long she could hold herself together.

The frigid, damp, pre-dawn air filled her nose, but it seemed off. She sensed a foulness, like burnt hair and scorched flesh, weaving through the aromas of dew and moss, leaf and wood. She paused and committed this pungent stench to her memory.

"We need to get back to the Dwelling," she said, turning to the trees behind her, her anger welling up again.

"And leave them out here?" Cardwil took a step back.

She shot him an exasperated glare in return. "They're not here. You said so yourself. But they might yet be in the forest, somewhere. I'm going to try to track this thing, but I need to be prepared."

"The Daatha won't like that idea."

"I don't care what the council thinks!" she snapped, storming off. "We might yet have a chance to save them, and by the Five Hallowed Oaks, I'm going to take it."

* * *

"This is unwise," Efral said, her voice almost too calm in the face of the Dwelling's horror.

"We have no other choice," Dorinen protested, clenching her fists and glaring at her elder. "You know what I can do. If it's still out there, I can find it. I can find them!"

"And that is exactly the problem," Efral replied. "We do not need another death today."

Dorinen scoffed and started to answer, but another council member, Sheyna, raised her hand, gesturing for them both to be silent.

"No, Dorinen is correct. We will permit you to search for this creature and our people," she said, "but you must not engage it. Track the beast, find where it came from, if you can. Do not act impulsively. It's far too dangerous." Sheyna faced down Dorinen with a demanding expression.

"Now, when have I ever disobeyed you or any of the council?" Dorinen held out her hands in mock submission. She observed all four members of the Daatha, assembled in haste in their meeting chamber to consider the night's horrific events. Flickering candles in the long shadows made their expressions appear even more dour than usual.

"This is not a time to jest, Dorinen," Sheyna said, her eyes narrowing. "We have lost three of our own, and two others are missing. The danger cannot be overstated. Do as you are told and return as soon as you learn anything. We will decide what to do then."

"I'm well aware of what's happened," Dorinen snapped. "I saw what it did, I..." She choked back a sob, and a numbness ran down her back.

Harl. I'm so sorry. I failed you.

"There will be time for us to grieve, all of us," Calan offered, seeing her distress. "But we need you, Dorinen. We must find out what this perversity is, where it came from, and if it might return. I shall call a gathering at mid-morn. We'll do what we can to calm the Dwelling, but we need answers. You are our finest tracker, but you must do as Sheyna asks. Can we rely on you?"

Dorinen clenched her jaw and stared at the floor. At last, she composed herself and nodded. "Yes, of course. I'll gather my things and be off at sunrise."

* * *

Forest mist rose in the waning afternoon sun. Shafts of dwindling golden light streamed through ancient trees, dancing in the swirling fog, while the foliage of midsummer grew thick and lush. In different circumstances, Dorinen would welcome the sight, but today it obscured her view.

She moved silently through the underbrush, aware of every sound and sensation in the approaching dark but focused only on her mission. She picked up a faint trace of the one scent that stood out from the rest of those of Cernwood: charred, unnatural, violating the sacred domain of the forest, its very existence an abomination.

No paths pointed the way here, only occasional markers set by her people as guides, and recognizable by them alone. And though the creature left no obvious trail, it couldn't hide from her.

Remember your task, she reminded herself. *Don't engage it, and don't act impulsively. It's far too dangerous.*

The words of her elders played over in her mind. Impulsive?

That's why they gave you their leave. They're quietly hoping you'll slay it.

Though not yet thirty summers in age, the council took pride in her skills, as did she, and she wouldn't let down them, or herself. She scanned for footprints, broken branches, signs of struggle, anything that her well-honed senses might offer to give her an advantage in pursuit.

As she moved, her mind turned over the horrific events of the day. The silence of the pre-dawn shattered by unearthly screeches. The screams of her people. Terror, blood, death. It struck and then vanished as she and Cardwil pursued it into the treedark. Her people could only pray it wouldn't return.

No, it's still here, nearby.

She slid down a small bank to a rippling stream, dotted with rocks and forded by a fallen tree. Pausing, she took a deep breath. The air's earthy richness calmed her, though now it also smelled tainted. She stopped again, listening with intent, but hearing only the sound of trickling water. No animals stirred, not even in the distance, as if the forest were suspended in time. She darted her glance in all directions, fearing a growing sense of exposure.

You'll not fight it unless you must. But neither will you be caught unprepared.

Tying back loose strands of her long brown hair, she drew out and strung her bow, readying an arrow.

Stay focused.

She made her way across the stream and up the other side of the bank with light and deliberate steps. Taking cover in a thick patch of ferns with her back to a large oak, she waited, studying the thick canopy of trees and the undergrowth. Little light penetrated through the tangle of branches and leaves overhead, creating a premature twilight.

The awful scent now permeated the air, and she recoiled, sensing an almost tangible evil close by.

Yet she sensed something else. A strange and unfamiliar quality of vitality, as if the forest lived in a deeper way than she'd suspected, as if it also knew of her and watched her. The creature's darkness mingled with this contrary presence, something greater that surrounded her and almost calmed her. The hairs on the back of her neck stood up.

But she had no time to consider this mystery. She quieted the sound of her breathing, focusing on the long shadows of the coming dusk, yet her fine vision revealed nothing. She gripped her bow with conviction, even though her hand trembled.

A crackle sounded to her left, and a claw swiped out of the brambles. She ducked away before it could tear across her face, in time to roll away and behold the horror in front of her.

It stood taller than a man, with dark grey, leathery skin. It twisted its bat-like face into a glower and bellowed a horrific cry, hurting her ears.

Shaking off the ringing, she let her arrow fly, but it bounced off the creature's chest.

"By Urkera! What?"

The beast lunged for her with its over-long arms. She leapt

backward, again avoiding its attack, and managed to release another arrow, this time hitting it straight in the neck. It growled and pulled out the shaft, which had hardly penetrated its flesh. Only a thin trickle of grey blood oozed from the wound. It snapped the arrow in two and made a leering face resembling a grin.

"What in the name of the Five Oaks are you?" she gasped.

With remarkable speed for its size, it lashed out at her again. As she tried to dodge the attack, a talon caught her left wrist, slicing her skin and sending her bow flying into the darkness.

She drew her sword on instinct but stumbled. Worse, a numbness started in the wound, just a tingle at first, but it soon began to spread to her forearm and into her fingers. She cursed again. Venomous talons.

She pointed her sword at it as a warning, but it merely hissed in response, as if toying with her.

"So much for a show of bravery," she said. Impulsive, indeed!

Still, she made a daring lunge forward, swinging her sword across its chest. Instead of tearing its flesh wide open, her blow only scratched the top layers of its thick hide. She crouched in haste to avoid its claws, and flipped out of harm's way, holding forth her sword with shaking hands as she scrambled to her feet.

She took a deep breath and tried to calm down, but her heart pounded, and her breathing became shallow. The beast reveled in this standoff, and snarling, it crept toward her, a predator stalking its prey. Dorinen slid to one side of the tree behind her, taking note of the nearby stream bank, but she had no plan and her options dwindled.

The numbness oozed up her arm, in a slow but steady advance, cold and swollen, now rendering her fighting hand useless. She transferred her sword to her other hand and tried to find her balance with the blade.

The beast's eyes glowed a hideous yellow in the growing dusk, as it spread open its fleshy bat wings, blotting out what little sun shone beneath the forest canopy. Dorinen managed to evade another attack by leaping to one side, but she misjudged the distance, and tripping, tumbled headlong over the edge of the bank. She crashed into the stream, her head colliding with the rocks in the water. Her ankle twisted and she cried out in pain.

Reeling from dizziness, she struggled to pull herself up and shake off the darkness threatening to claim her. Blood trickled from a forehead wound and stung sharply, enough to bring her mind back into the present moment. She looked back to where she'd fallen from, but the creature had vanished.

"It's so fast," she panted, fighting the spinning sensation in her head. "How does it move so quickly?"

Retrieving her sword, she shook out her hands, but the venom's numbness now crept into her shoulder, rendering her arm all but useless. Worse, her ankle throbbed. She staggered upstream to take cover in the undergrowth, her dread giving way to resignation.

"I can't win. I can't even..."

A burning sharpness seared through the back of her leg, and she crashed face first into the water again. She cried out and scrambled to turn herself around, fumbling for her fallen weapon.

The creature loomed above her, a twisted grin on its face. Opening its mouth to reveal blood-stained fangs, a viscous drool rolled off of its grey tongue, splattering into the water.

Terror took hold of Dorinen, and she choked back tears of agony, stifling a scream. Somehow, it had appeared right behind her without her even knowing. She knew she would be dead now, if it had wanted her to be.

In desperation, she pressed on the gaping wound in her leg, her hands soon covered with blood, while nausea and light-headedness threatened to send her into blackness. She tried to stand, but fell back into the water, crying out in agony. And the numbness began to take her knee.

"It's over..."

She feared more than anything that it might torture her out of sadistic pleasure. Fighting back tears, she resolved not go quietly.

As it gloated over her, snorting and cocking its head, she focused on standing, an effort her wounds now made all but impossible. Drawing in her right knee, she shifted her position, gasping to exaggerate her pain and fear. The creature snorted in obscene delight, its heavy breathing and hissing growing ever more intense. She prepared to strike, transfixed by its horrid visage, not daring to breathe.

She let fly a kick, her heavy-heeled boot landing directly on its knee, breaking the joint with a sickening crunch of bone. The creature stumbled back, howling, and fell into the stream with a tremendous splash.

Determined to take the advantage, she limped forward, reeling in waves of unbearable anguish. With her good arm, she thrust her sword against the creature's gut, the blade meeting with great resistance. She pushed harder and at last, the point pierced its hide. With her waning strength, Dorinen forced it in as deep as she could. If these were to be her final moments, she was determined not to go without a fight.

It howled again and thrashed about, as thick, grey blood spurted from the wound.

She twisted her sword into the wound to inflict as much damage as she could muster, nearly vomiting as horrid ichor sprayed her face.

The creature flailed and swiped at the side of her head, the force of the blow sending her rolling away onto the stream bank. As she fought the darkness swirling about her, she saw it struggle to its feet. It shrieked as it wrenched her sword from its stomach and stumbled to where she lay, prone and defenseless.

Concussed, exhausted, Dorinen surrendered and awaited her end.

The creature rocked its head back and screamed, a horrific howl resembling a laugh. It raised its claws and prepared to plunge them into her.

But instead, it froze, eyes wide with something like fear.

With what strength and will she had left, Dorinen seized the chance to edge herself away from the creature, but still it didn't move.

The earth rumbled beneath her and that otherworldly presence intensified. The ground and the trees, the water and undergrowth, all shimmered with vibrant colors. Tiny globes of gold and green light manifested from deep within the foliage, as if the very soul of the forest was revealing itself. Like an army of fireflies, these lights poured forth from trees and plants, from rocks and the water. They danced about one another, swirling and crackling in a magical choreography.

All but forgetting her plight, and certain she hallucinated as she lay dying, Dorinen watched transfixed as these globes came together, drifted apart, and spun about one another in spirals, as if controlled, as if intelligent. They fused together, first forming a vague outline, then a more definite shape. Green and gold transformed into a brilliant violet as a figure appeared in the pulsating chaos.

In her near delirium, Dorinen watched in disbelief as a tall man stepped out of the light, dressed in purple and blue velvets, breeches and a waistcoat, with knee-high purple boots, and a long silvery-grey cloak.

The lights faded, and the encompassing presence now seemed to settle in him alone. He strode toward the frozen beast, grim intention in his expression, though Dorinen could have sworn she saw a smirk on his face. With a wave of his hand, the creature could move again, and it struck out at him. For a moment, she feared it would tear through this newcomer, but he deflected its attack by holding out his other hand. Its claws never came anywhere near him.

He waved his hand again, and a swath of purple light surged forth from the arc of his swing, burning a deep gash across the creature's chest. Crackling violet lights slithered all about the wound in random directions, sending out wafts of grey smoke. Screeching, the beast stumbled away, not retaliating, but only hissing at this new opponent.

The man swaggered forward. Another wave of his hand and purple light again shot forth, burning away the creature's injured leg.

It stumbled and fell, clutching at the charred and smoking stump, and screaming as it writhed and splashed in the stream.

"I do suppose that was a bit unfair of me, eh lad?" the man remarked in a dry, sarcastic voice. "Well, you win some, you lose some. I'm only playing by your rules, after all."

He clapped his hands together twice, and a bolt of lightning shot forth from them, hitting the creature in the face and tearing its head clean off.

Dorinen gasped, and a convulsive pain surged through her head, lapsing into a bloody cough.

He sighed and turned to her, one hand flicking back a lock of his long, fair hair. "Tiresome creatures, really. They don't even have the decency to stop drooling, did you notice? And if you get that vile grey blood of theirs on your clothes, well." He shook his head in disapproval.

Dorinen gave in to shock. Poisoned, bleeding, dying, she'd just watched a colorful dandy destroy the creature as easily as she could snap a twig, yet now he complained about his sartorial state. His foppish countenance seemed utterly out of place with both the forest and the unearthly spectacle she'd witnessed. As he approached, she couldn't find the strength to say anything at all.

The man doffed his wide-brimmed hat, its long white plume fluttering behind it. He bowed and knelt beside her, but stopped her before she could even try to form words. "Come now, you're injured. You put up a good fight, I must say. Showed the damned thing that its supper would not be easy to come by. What do you suppose it wanted to eat first? No, don't answer, it's not worth ruminating on."

Winking at her, he placed a velvet-gloved hand on her leg. The sparkle of jeweled rings worn over the glove only made the scene all the more unreal to her.

Certain she imagined it all, she said nothing, reduced to being an unwilling player in an impossible farce. She could barely raise her head as the man gave her a wry smile and turned his attention to her wound.

He closed his eyes, and a vibrant blue light glowed from his hands, passing into her. At once, her bleeding stopped and the gash began to heal. After a short time, it was like her injury had never been there at all.

He next took gentle hold of her wounded wrist and did the same. The feeling returned to her arm in prickling pins and needles, as if revived from a long sleep. She shook it with vigor, trying to hasten her recovery. He held her forehead and then her ankle, and soon, the pain in both also dissolved.

Her mind cleared enough to get a sense of the whole bizarre situation, and she sat up.

"I was... I was dead, or nearly. I don't understand."

The creature's corpse disintegrated into ash in the distance. Nothing made sense.

Offering no explanation, this mysterious man retrieved her sword, handing it to her with a courtly bow and another silly grin. She gave him a weak smile in return as he helped her to her feet. The soft sensation of his glove astonished her, its texture smoother and purer than any fabric she'd ever touched.

"Unchecked, memories of such an appalling creature could haunt you for a long time," he said, "so I have also arranged for them not overly trouble your thoughts or your sleep. You'll note your garments are repaired and the blood washed away, as well. You're quite welcome."

"Thank you?" she managed to say.

"I do believe you've lost your bow," he said with an air of concern but also a flippant twinge. He snapped his fingers and at once, Dorinen's bow flew from the underbrush and landed at her feet in a flash of purple light. She stared, first at the bow and then back at him, struggling to make sense of it.

"I hope you're not expecting your arrows, as well," he added in an irritated tone. "I mean, honestly, there are limits to what even *I* can do."

Dorinen finally found her voice. "Who *are* you?" she stammered, worrying at once that she must have sounded ridiculous and even rude.

"Oh, lovely!" he said with a bit of a chuckle and a clap of his hands. "I did worry you would *never* ask! Now then, who shall I be, eh? Who would you want me to be? A dastardly Darrowrath magic-caster from Gavalahorne? No, no, they're always going about in those drab black robes, aren't they? I daresay I couldn't pass for one, not that I'd want to! Well, what else? A wealthy merchant from Mirys? A scholar of Tenaeth?" He tapped a finger on the side of his face and rubbed his thinly bearded chin, as if truly pondering the conundrum of his own identity.

Bewildered, lost, shaking her head, Dorinen couldn't understand.

But the man's sarcastic demeanor faded into a serious and concerned expression. "No, you deserve better than such frivolities. You have fared remarkably well today and shown much courage. Very well, Dorinen Elqestir."

"How, how do you know who I—"

"I am known by too many names, I must admit," he interrupted. "I am Enwyonn, Teuvell, Eladra, Koliserr, and many more besides. I am earth and air, tree and river, the ice of a bitter winter, the rays of the hot summer sun. Your people know me as Urkera, the Soul of the Earth Heart. I am Ramwin Roakthone, Embodiment of the Land Spirit. Or rather… one manifestation of them, anyway. Embodiments, that is. I believe the correct term is a Sarvethar?"

Dorinen's stomach tightened, and she grimaced in irritation. He'd just made a proclamation as absurd as it was blasphemous. This foppish rake, however powerful he might be, claimed to be nothing less than an incarnation of the Creator and Sustainer, the very soul of the world and all in it.

She didn't hide her suspicion or her dislike for his words. "A Sarvethar? Forgive me, but I don't believe you, sir. You're probably a powerful, if deluded magic-caster, kind in intent, but obviously mad."

He stepped forward and said with authority, "Look at me." She tried to avoid him, hoping her ire would subside. But she knew his will was stronger, and she resisted only for a moment more.

And when she met the gaze of his piercing blue eyes, something stirred in her that she'd never felt before, as if she could see the entire cosmos in them: past, present, and future merging into a single point. All that was and ever would be coalesced in one moment, the embodiment of the pervasive presence from before. Ramwin enveloped her, cloaked her in a shield of loving protection, and told her without a doubt that she indeed belonged to the glory of everything around her.

And in that moment, Dorinen knew. The Land Spirit revealed itself to her, however briefly, and showed her the truth of this colorful being's claims. The glory already began to fade, and her mind couldn't hold onto what she'd seen, but it sufficed. The tears she'd forced back before came to her as she averted her own eyes. In reverence, she knelt at his feet. She couldn't form words as she hugged herself; how could she address her sustainer, her soul?

"Really!" he exclaimed. "All this fuss! I'm flattered, of course, but there is much to be said and done. Please."

She kept her head bowed, quietly sobbing.

He blew out a short puff of air and tapped her on the top of her head gently, almost teasingly, before offering his hand to help her to her feet.

Questions flooded Dorinen's mind. She voiced her first: "How is this possible, my lord?"

"Oh, call me Ramwin, please," he insisted, and the sincerity of his plea, combined with a mildly annoyed but jovial expression, reinforced to her that he would not suffer any subservience.

Dorinen couldn't comprehend his behavior; nothing she'd learned about Urkera had prepared her for this experience. "Why are you here?" she almost demanded. "Why have you come to me? What was that creature?"

He held up a hand to request her silence. "So many things to explain, but one question at a time, I beg you. I wouldn't be much of a host if I simply confused you with a jumble of overlapping facts and confusing histories."

"Host?"

"Of course. You have entered my domain. Well, of course, it's *all* my domain. I do recall once receiving a delegation of Chtai priests in the Frozen Knolls. They never could understand why I was wearing velvet in the middle of a snowstorm." His expression turned comically quizzical. "Come to think of it, neither could I! I mean a bit of rain is fine, but ice? Snow? My word, I was in a terrible state, I can assure you!" He paused and bowed his head. "But, my humblest apologies, I do digress!"

He pulled out a small silk handkerchief to polish a large blue stone on one of his rings, as if it were the most important thing to do then and there. "You are in a place that I hold particularly dear, and your people are beloved to me," he continued, concentrating on his new his task.

Dorinen's heart swelled with pride at his approval. She gave a slight bow of her own in thanks and respect. Ramwin shook his head, almost in mock annoyance.

"Ever since they turned away from the world, the Cernodyn have cared for and protected this great forest, and they have done so well and wisely," he said. "But something has happened, something terrible that should not be. That creature was a part of it, and necessitated my coming here, to this place, and to you, apparently. Congratulations are in order, I suppose!"

"What do you mean?" Dorinen asked, but a bout of dizziness struck her, and she slumped to the ground, the weight of her ordeal becoming too much to bear. Ramwin caught and steadied her.

"You are weak from your travails," he said. "It's growing dark. Come, let me offer you a more fitting hospitality."

He snapped his fingers again. A purple mist encircled them, and with a flash of light, they were gone.

Two

Andra Illindrien sat on the carpeted floor, her red gown stretched out about her. The delicate sounds of her kenlim echoed off of the stone walls of the empty *Mirithnaa*, the Hall of Song, her college's temple. She held her beautiful lyre close, playing a gentle melody she'd composed earlier. The strings flowed through the silence like liquid, the melody cascading about her in a gentle echo. No words yet came to her, though she knew they would.

With the sun now set, only golden lantern glow illuminated the main hall. Sweet-smelling incense burned in the distance, its aromas of amber, rose, and musk ever present in this holy place. Andra closed her eyes and allowed the sensations of sound and scent to take her. She swayed back and forth as she played, and a smile came to her face. The Lady Teuvell's magic wove its way through her song, embracing her, uplifting her. Andra's smile broadened as she reflected on her first commencement from the Artisan's College earlier in the day. She had much more to learn, but for now, she could allow herself to be proud.

"And," she said, opening one eye, "this calls for a celebration. Perhaps one of those old bottles of Mirysian wine from today's ceremony?"

With the melody firmly established, she began to improvise, all while concentrating on the object of her desire. Visualizing the old glass container that sat in a nearby kitchen chamber, she let the Lady's power flow through her and directed the energy needed to bring the precious indulgence to her. She willed the bottle to rise and move through the air, following its path in her mind's eye. So delighted was she when it gently floated into the chamber that she risked losing her concentration and letting it crash to the floor. But she kept her composure and, focusing once more, brought the fragile vessel to rest next to her.

"Splendid, and well deserved!"

She set aside her instrument and picked up the bottle, dislodging its cork and taking a deep whiff of its well-aged contents. "A perfect balance of dried fruits and wood, with notes of old leather and Maradhoorian spices, and… a bit of barnyard… though in a good way. It will do nicely."

She took far more than a delicate sip, reveling in a generous gulp that would have made experts and fanciers of such rare libations recoil in horror.

"Ah," she whispered in satisfaction. "My apologies, Lady, for using your blessed magic in such an unrefined way. But tonight is a time for celebration, after all. I won't help myself again… at least not too soon."

As she relished in quaffing a bit more, she became aware of not being alone.

She knew the intruder, despite the care he'd surely taken to enter the Hall in silence. She let out a quiet chuckle and set down the bottle.

Without turning around, she said, "I know you're there, and you know you can't hide from me. You won't stop testing me, will you?"

She glanced back at the man standing at the main entry to the temple, dressed in a grey robe elegantly trimmed in scarlet embroidered floral patterns, its hood hiding some of his features. Andra detected the faintest hint of a grin on his red-bearded face.

"Your music ennobles this Hall," he said in a serious tone. "You honor the Land Spirit and the Lady Teuvell with your transcendent melodies and words... oh, Mistress of Assonance."

Andra burst out laughing and almost fell over.

The robed man joined in her merriment and strode forward, offering her a hand up. She took it and stood to face him, snickering at his splendid parody of the words spoken to her at the Passage Ceremony earlier in the day.

They paused for a moment, trying to regain their composure, but both cracked and dissolved into fits of laughter again.

Finally, she said, "Did you see the old prelate at the ceremony? He seemed completely miserable the whole time. I'd swear his frowning face was a mask!" She mimicked him, drawing her mouth downward in an exaggerated manner, and promptly lapsed into a new bout of giggles.

"His dour manner must surely be a wicked enchantment or a punishment for some priestly misdeed," her companion said, his voice becoming increasingly falsetto before finally trailing away into a fresh round of guffaws.

The artificial solemnity of the ceremony had been more than this jovial duo could bear.

"I know it's meant to be a reverent affair," Andra managed to say, "and I tried to give it proper respect, but I'd expected nothing so extreme. The whole thing was absurd, so serious. I've never seen anything so ridiculous in my life!" Through her laughter, she sputtered, "And the title: 'Mistress of Assonance.' I swear I revert to being twelve summers old every time I hear it!"

It took some time before both recovered sufficiently to continue conversing. Andra threw her arms around the man and gave him a warm hug, to which he responded with equal warmth.

"Oh, Narick, I'll miss this place and you so much!" She wiped the tears of mirth from her eyes, fearing that tears of sadness would soon replace them.

She looked up at him, his hood fallen back from his vigorous laughter, revealing his short red hair and neatly trimmed beard. Narick Yerral, a monk of the Shylan Dar order, and her best friend here in the capital city of Tenaeth. He and his brothers devoted themselves to Enwyonn, patron of learning and wisdom, bringer of harmony. But Andra loved that he enjoyed a good laugh whenever he could.

These happy times reminded her of how he'd befriended her in her early days in Tenaeth five summers ago, when she'd arrived to begin her studies at the college of Teuvell. Now, she regarded him with a sibling-like affection and wrestled with her mixture of admiration and sadness.

"What is it?" he asked.

"Do you remember how you promised my parents that you'd keep a protective eye on their 'gifted' daughter?"

"How could I not?"

"I've so appreciated it. I'm just sad to leave. I wish your Mother House weren't so far away."

"I'm here at the Daughter House whenever I can be. They need my skills."

"Those of the mind, or the deadly fighting arts you all like to indulge in?"

He chuckled. "Both?"

"And you're here more often than you should be!" She swatted him gently on the shoulder. "In any case, you must promise me you'll come to Meln and visit. My mother and father dearly wish to see you again."

"Nothing will keep me away, I do promise you!" He spied the illicit bottle still sitting on the floor. "Been celebrating on your own, I see?"

"Testing my abilities, thank you very much! The Lady has blessed me with Her presence when I create, so who am I to deny Her gifts, especially when there's pleasure to be enjoyed?" She winked at him.

"How can I possibly argue with such sound metaphysical reasoning?" He paused, his expression becoming more thoughtful. "But there's something I need to talk to you about. It concerns your journey, in fact."

Andra raised one eyebrow. "Whenever you sound too serious, I get worried. Should I be worried?" She tugged at one of the sleeves of his robe.

"Probably not."

"Probably not?"

"I understand," he continued, "you've not heard from your family for almost a moonspan, and that the arranged escort hasn't arrived. Is it true?"

She looked away, releasing his sleeve with an exaggerated sigh.

"Is it true?" he repeated.

She grudgingly nodded. "It's not so unusual," she deflected, turning her attention back to him. "My father is a busy man at this time of year, which is why he hasn't come here himself. Maybe the escort got delayed. And messages go astray all the time. I can make the journey to Meln myself. I'm not a child, Narick."

"I didn't say you were." The calmness of his tone irked her.

"And I don't need the services of Tenaeth's hired guards, if that's what you're going to suggest." She stepped back and pointed an accusing finger at him. "They're expensive, boring, and poor company. Also, hiring some of them would mean waiting for several days until they're available."

"There are many dangers on the roads now, my friend," he said. "One does not need to set off across the countryside to meet with trouble. The Gro'aken have become bolder lately. Some are even attacking travelers along the main routes. There aren't enough patrols to keep all of them at bay. And the Iron Rose have caused many problems for Tenaeth and Rilnarya over the past many moonspans. I fear their presence is becoming stronger. They target everyone from lone travelers to large merchant parties. The ransoms they demand for the kidnapped grow ever larger, and they don't treat their prisoners kindly."

He paused again, his solemn countenance eclipsing the mirth he'd shown a few moments before. "And there is… another worry. Something is stirring. My own order has sensed it. We don't know what it is yet, but it's wrong, out of place. Dreams of death and foul creatures haunt our mystics and seers. Our prayers and meditations have so far yielded nothing. Enwyonn is silent for now. Our best scholars are pouring through ancient tomes in search of further insights." He grimaced. "We've even considered going to Xalphed Gornio for assistance."

"Is that a problem?"

"Tenaeth's great sage, though popular and wise, is, shall we say, something of a rival to us for the role of the city's chief guardians and keepers of knowledge. Yes, it's childish and petty, but it's true. And that's how concerned we are."

She wrinkled her brow. "Why haven't you told me about this before?"

"It wasn't the right time. And with your ceremony approaching, you didn't need anything else to concern yourself with. It will be best for you to return home. And speaking of concerns, is your sleep still troubled?"

"A little. I'm having that recurring dream."

"With the figure shrouded in shadows?"

She nodded. "Only, I'm beginning to see her now."

"Her?" he said with a slight grin. "Well then, we know what kind of dream it is after all."

She shoved him on the shoulder, her cheeks flushing with heat. "It's not *that* kind of dream!"

He chuckled. "Who is she? What do you think it means?"

"I don't know, not yet. But it happens every few nights, and each time it feels more natural to me. Like, she's someone I know, or need to. Maybe I'll learn more the next time I dream of her, if I do."

"Keep me informed. It might not be a coincidence if you are having some kind of sleep vision now."

"But why? I'm not important."

He smiled. "You're wrong, my friend. In the meantime, the order and I must be vigilant."

Andra took his hand. "Will you be going back to the Mother House to assist them?"

"After I return to Tenaeth, yes," he answered.

"Return from where?"

"From Meln. You won't accept hired guards, and I won't accept that you travel alone. Therefore, I'll accompany you."

She started to protest, but he held up his hand. "I've received leave from my House, and you did just make me promise to come and visit, did you not? Why not right away? We can leave tomorrow."

She hugged him again. She trusted no one else as much, and it would make the often-dreary journey to Meln pass more quickly.

He stepped back and peered over her shoulder. "But first, you should put that bottle back where it belongs."

"Excuse me, I'm not finished with it yet!"

* * *

Morning came too soon, as mornings all too often do, and a loud knock on Andra's door startled her awake to the unwelcome sight of sunlight shining through her window. She groaned and pulled the blanket over her head, trying to block out the world and imagine that dawn remained far off. Mornings never failed to remind her of why she'd never been an early riser. Surely, the worst part of her studies and training had been the obligation to be awake at sunrise, or even moonset, for certain exercises and meditations. She'd slept soundly through a good number of lessons over the years.

The knock came again, louder and more forceful, accompanied by a melodious voice. "Andra! Rise my darling, midmorn beckons, and you must prepare for your departure!"

It was the unmistakable voice of Wenn, one of Andra's tutors, self-appointed nursemaid, and a general busybody. Andra could dismiss some of the woman's notions as peculiar and naïve, but she trusted in Wenn's wisdom. This respect led Andra to answer the too-enthusiastic summons with a grudging acknowledgement. "I'll be up shortly!"

Rubbing her aching head, she turned her gaze to her left. "Oh, Teuvell's tits!"

"That knock, is it bad?" the young woman lying next to her whispered.

"Well, yes. You're not supposed to be here!" Andra whispered back.

"Oh, thank you for telling me this now." She propped herself on one elbow.

"Look," Andra said, sitting up. "I need to get you out of here, without being seen. That's the Hall Mistress, Wenn. She means well, has a good heart. But she has old-fashioned views on a lot of things, and she won't be pleased I brought a young lady I only met yesternight in a tavern back here to—"

"It was rather nice, wasn't it?" Her companion gave her a dreamy smile.

"It was, very, even if we were both well into our cups. But listen... um, sorry. What's your name again?"

Her companion glared at her. "Vanari."

"Right! Vanari, of course. Sorry. Come on, get dressed."

Vanari did as Andra asked while Andra scrambled out of bed and opened her door a crack to peer out in both hallway directions, relived to see no one else about.

"This is good," she whispered and pointed out the door. "Now, go that way, and you'll come to a staircase on your right. Take it down three flights, not four. The last goes to the cellar. Enter into the hallway directly before you and take the second left exit. You'll come to the courtyard, and from there, you can stroll right out of the college with no worries. All clear?"

Vanari seemed unconvinced as she tightened the belt around her skirt. "Uh, I think so."

"You'll be fine, just do as I've told you. And keep quiet!"

She opened the door a little more. Vanari stopped in front of it. "Will I see you again?"

Andra exhaled. "I'm leaving Tenaeth today to travel home, so it might be some time, but, um, I'll inquire after you when I return, yes?"

Vanari smiled and kissed Andra on the lips. "Good! Take care of yourself... Andra." She crept into the hallway. Andra watched until she turned the corner and made for the stairs.

Closing her door and flopping on the edge of her bed with a relived sigh, she noticed herself in the little mirror set on her small table. Her long, wavy golden hair was a mess, and drink woe knocked at her head, worse than Wenn's wake-ups. She swore there were bags under her eyes and couldn't believe both Narick and Wenn had described her as "beautiful" at yesterday's ceremony.

Fortunately, she'd already packed, knowing it would be well near impossible to do so this morning. Maybe she'd indeed attained some wisdom over the past few years.

She blew a stand of messy hair out and away from her face. "Not likely."

The next stage of her training awaited her. But for now, she wanted to be home in her village, a place she'd not seen for nearly two summers.

"The peace of the Grey Wolds and ambles in Cernwood are calling," she said with longing. "Hm, that was quite poetic!" She sighed. "I'll miss this place, but I'm tired of the crowds, the commotion. Fine for a capital city, I suppose, but I need open space, freedom from small streets and cramped buildings."

She held out one hand. "The scents of country air and fresh meadow flowers, the sounds of farms and the gentle wind rushing through trees, these are sweeter to me than Dalaethrian honey wine." She cringed. "And now I'm just creating bad poetry!"

She glanced in the mirror again, this time with some despair. She'd have no chance to fix her atrocious dishevelment, so she settled for brushing her hair and tying it back. The only problem with this solution was that now the bags under her eyes became even more visible. She groaned again and got dressed, throwing on undergarments, a voluminous white shirt and a fitted red waistcoat, woolen traveling trousers and a pair of short and sturdy boots. Today was not a day for being glamorous, anyway.

She packed her kenlim and fine wooden fipple flute in their leather cases and gathered them along with her cloak. Taking hold of her traveling bags, she made for the door. She paused, looking around her room, recalling with fondness the memories it held for her. It would be hers again upon her return, but she couldn't help feeling like she was saying goodbye to an old friend.

She recalled those many nights when she'd snuck her fellow student Emyrith in here; Wenn would certainly not have approved of their amorous exploits. But Em, a young song-maker with an attitude and ambitions of her own, left the college two summers ago, and Andra hadn't heard from her since. A twinge of sadness tugged at her as she closed the door.

Andra wondered again where Em had ended up and how different her life might be had she gone with her. "Oh, what am I thinking? Em left me." She found herself annoyed that their parting still pained her to dwell on for too long. She thought instead about last night with Vanari, a final drunken carousal before leaving.

Those happy memories were interrupted by the sound of footsteps. She turned to see a large woman of about fifty autumns—Andra had never dared ask her true age—half-skipping down the hallway, arms open wide.

"Good morning, my darling! I feared you would never wake. But that's always been your problem, hasn't it? Have you not used the decoction I made for you? I've told you, my grandmother would prepare it when I needed to sleep, which was often on our farm, and—"

Andra cut her off by giving her a big hug, surprising herself almost as much as Wenn. But it produced the desired effect. For once, the older woman was speechless.

"I'll miss you so much, Mistress Wenn," Andra said, relieved to take control of the situation. "And thank you for your concern, as always. But I must hurry now if I'm to make a good start to the day. Narick will be waiting for me."

She made to leave but stopped when she beheld the silent Wenn's face, her large brown eyes filling with tears. Andra had a sudden rush of guilt, realizing this must be a painful parting. For all of Wenn's annoying fussing, Andra enjoyed the attention. She hugged her tutor again.

"I won't be gone too long, a year at most. I will return, and I'll write to you, I promise."

Wenn smiled through her tears. "Go, child, and be granted a speedy journey. I know your family misses you, as I shall. May Teuvell grant you good song until we meet again!"

"And you as well," Andra replied, holding both of Wenn's hands in her own.

They regarded one another fondly for a moment longer, and then Andra turned and made her way down three flights of creaky wooden stairs and across the college's cobblestone courtyard to the public entryway. No sign of Vanari.

"Good."

She half expected an entourage of masters there to see her off, but realized her vanity; most had made their farewells at yesterday's ceremony.

Only the old tutor and harper, Izznil, stood near the front gate, clothed in the traditional dark green robe of a cleric of Teuvell. Stringy white tufts of hair clung to the side of his otherwise bald head, and his wizened features showed a man of considerable age, eighty winters or more. But he remained as agile and sharp as a man half his age. He greeted her with a brief embrace, and they exchanged pleasantries. He then held out a small leather pouch to her, bidding her to take it.

Furrowing her brow, Andra did so, opening the drawstring to reveal a multi-faceted purple gemstone inside.

"What's this?" she asked, certain its value must be far too great for Izznil to part with, whatever it might be.

"Do not ask questions now. Just take it with you, my young friend," he answered with assurance. "It will strengthen the potency of the magic the Lady grants you. It is most powerful, so have a care in using it, as I know you will."

"But," Andra countered, lowering her voice, "what's it for? I don't understand."

"There are many rules and regulations in this college," Izznil said, "and they exist for a good reason. They protect and ensure that our sacred arts are not misused. But sometimes these rules are too rigid and must be bent, if not broken. You are ready, Andra Illindrien, and I believe you will need this gem, before you can ever to return to these halls. Take it, with my blessing."

Andra stared at him, perplexed and at a momentary loss for words. "But why will I need it?" she demanded at last. "I mean, I can do some tricks with melodies, but I can't fully channel the Lady's energies, not yet. I might never."

Izznil held up his palm and shook his head. "Enough for now. The designated must be prepared for what is coming. Brother Narick has spoken to you of his concerns, has he not?"

Andra stepped back, her eyes widening. Izznil had an uncanny ability to intuit things he couldn't possibly have known. "Yes."

He gave her a single nod in reply, his hunch confirmed. What was coming? And who were "the designated"?

Before she could ask, he bid her farewell and walked away in haste. Andra knew better than to go after him. If a senior master of the college offered such a gift to her, she could only trust in his well-founded judgement. Putting the pouch away in a larger bag, she made for the stables, where Narick would be waiting.

* * *

By the time Andra arrived at the stable yard, Narick had already secured horses for their journey and appeared well prepared for it, being dressed in traveling clothes, wool trousers, and tall boots. Only his grey shirt trimmed with scarlet hinted at his monastic affiliation.

He eyed her for a moment. "Well, you clearly didn't get enough sleep last night. More than a little drink woe from the wine? Or did you sneak a special someone into your room for a final farewell? I hope she was worth it!"

Andra shot him a dark look which only made him laugh. She packed her possessions on her horse and considered the gem again. Should she tell him? At some point, but not now.

They set off, leading their horses down one of Tenaeth's main streets and heading for the northern exit. They passed through the gate of the first stone wall, the second, then the third—the tallest of them—all built in an earlier and more violent age. Would the danger soon return?

They followed the hill, sloping downward toward the River Charthan.

"We'll journey to the town of Meladil," Narick said as they entered the verdant countryside. "And from there eastward."

"But isn't that way less safe than following the river to Wold Lake?" Andra asked as she settled on her horse's saddle.

"The roads between Meladil and Crythmarr have been peaceful enough lately," he answered. "Once we're into the foothills of the Grey Wolds, I'm sure all will be well. I hear your village has grown even more prosperous in recent seasons."

"We're more a town than a village now, honestly," she answered. "Our skilled merchants keep the money coming in!"

"Well, be glad the Tveor up north protect you all from Gro'aken and other unpleasantness," he replied. "Only the foolish engage them in battle. The denizens of the Mountains of Sorrow learned that painful lesson long ago."

"I've never thought much about it," she answered. "That's the problem with prolonged peace, I suppose. We tend to forget about the bad times, which maybe allows things to become dangerous again, if we're not careful."

Narick's expression darkened a little, but he didn't answer. In contrast to his mood, the summer sun grew hot as it edged to its zenith in the sky. Andra scolded herself for not being awake earlier, though she knew Narick wouldn't complain.

They rode past fields and farms, where the crops would soon begin to bear their bounty. Andra loved this time of year, high summer, when the Land Spirit blessed all peoples, and many a song in praise for this act of generosity resounded from the lips of Teuvell's Artisans.

"The Festival of First Harvestgift is in a little over one moonspan," she said. "I'm so happy I'll get to celebrate with my family this year."

"As am I." But something about his expression seemed off, almost as if he didn't know for sure if they would be celebrating at all.

They followed the dusty road along the River Charthan for most of the day, before it split in two directions, one continuing north, and one east toward Gorben.

"We'll avoid Gorben, I assume?" she asked.

"I have no desire to go to the last outpost of so-called civilization before the moors. Lately, it's been a haven for the Iron Rose. And the moors themselves are a miserable place. Strange creatures and human outcasts infest it, despite all efforts to drive them out."

She put one hand over her mouth and suppressed a laugh. "Yes, thank you for the geography lesson. I'm well aware of its dangers. I was joking when I asked if we were avoiding that place, since I know how hated it is!"

He rolled his eyes as she chuckled at last.

They continued north. As dusk approached, the pair came to a hamlet offering simple, if satisfactory, lodgings for travelers in a humble religious house dedicated to Eladra, Matron of Peace. Andra noted the simplicity of the wooden structure, and how much it differed from the buildings of Teuvell's Artisans, or even the Shylan Dar monks.

As they led their horses to the grounds of the shrine, she turned to Narick. "Wait, Eladra's devotees have sworn not to use violence, right? And doesn't everyone who enters their shrines have to abide by this oath for the duration of their stay?"

"Indeed, and I'm well aware of that." Now it was his turn to act annoyed with her.

"I know, I know. But given the Shylan Dar's reputation for battle-readiness, you'll no doubt be viewed with at least a little suspicion." She enjoyed teasing him to lighten his somber mood.

"I will gladly respect their wishes and take the oath of peace to enter the house," he said. "I have no intentions of fighting in this place. Besides," he added with confidence, "I'm sure we'll be quite safe."

Andra allowed herself to relax. "True enough. What could happen here?"

Three

When Dorinen opened her eyes, the mist had faded, and the spinning in her head had ceased. She found herself standing in a sumptuous dining room, decorated with exquisite silks and tapestries of a kind she'd never seen before. The dark wood on the walls and floor was well crafted, though its use for such a gaudy and vain purpose annoyed her a little. A table with a cloth of purple presented quite a sight, prepared with polished silver platters, goblets of pewter and gold, and an absurd array of utensils. All manner of foods decorated the setting, some of which she didn't even recognize. Ornate brass candleholders dotted the wooden walls, their candles lighting the room with a warm, golden glow.

Ramwin stood by the table, where his hat rested, smiling that sarcastic and puzzling smile.

"I assumed this might be more to your liking," he said, holding out a pewter goblet to her. "After all, it was getting a bit damp and chilly out there, and you just *cannot* find a fine wine if you're lost somewhere in a forest!"

Dorinen fought the urge to barrage him with a load of questions and accepted the goblet with gratitude, mindful of her thirst and hunger. "Where are we?" she asked.

"Oh, between here and there, not anywhere in particular, merely a place I devised at the last moment. My apologies for the simplicity." He glanced around, an expression of worry crossing his face. "Oh dear, first I didn't retrieve your arrows and now this, eh? You must think I've no concept of decent social engagement!"

Trying to make sense of him, she took a cautious sip of the wine. She raised her eyebrows and her mood lifted. "It's magnificent. I've never tasted anything like it."

"A vintage you will not find in your part of the world, I can assure you. It comes from a far-off southern land. Perhaps you'll journey there someday."

"I've seldom set foot out of Cernwood and have little experience with greater Rilnarya, much less anything farther away."

She wanted to ask many questions, but he reached into his waistcoat pocket and removed a small but highly decorated golden object, a timepiece of some sort. He examined it briefly and announced, "My apologies. You must excuse me for a moment. Please do partake of whatever fare suits you. I shan't be long."

With a shimmer in the air, an ornate door materialized on the wall nearest to him. Before she could say another word, he stepped through, and the door vanished as quickly as it had appeared.

Left without the chance to speak further, she slumped in one of the chairs, its soft, cushioned seat welcoming her. She buried her face in her hands and shook her head.

"This day is nothing but madness," she sighed. "Or perhaps I'm dead. Is this the life beyond life?" She half-expected to awaken from a bizarre dream, or to regain consciousness only to see that vile creature looming over her, ready to strike. Mercifully, no such horror came, and after a short time, she resigned herself to her bizarre situation.

"Apparently, this is all real, and he might truly be the Sarvethar. But how? What is happening?"

Despite what she'd seen in the forest, this experience had to be impossible, and she couldn't shake the doubt from her head. In the legends of her people and indeed, all of Rilnarya, Ramwin Roakthone was a Sarvethar of the Land Spirit, but he'd not been seen in these lands for centuries, *if* he even existed. Those old tales must surely have been mere diversions for children and fables to teach the pious. Was he the true guise of the Spirit who interacted with mortals in this world? She chuckled at what the Shylan Dar monks would do if they could witness what she'd just seen.

But why would the Sarvethar need to check the time? Why would he resort to ridiculous play-acting? And why did he bring her here, wherever "here" was?

Such questions would have to wait. Weariness overcame her, so she leaned back and fell into a doze.

Sometime later, she heard a wind-like sound and snapped awake to see a new door open on the wall opposite of where Ramwin previously exited. Dorinen wasn't surprised; nothing shocked her at this point, and she decided not to bother asking where he'd gone.

Probably to save some city at the outer edges of the known world.

"Terribly sorry!" A woman strode to the table. "And no, it wasn't a city." She took a seat opposite Dorinen. She sported the same hair, same eyes, same clothing, and same sarcastic demeanor as Ramwin, but she was definitely not the entity Dorinen had met before.

"Who, who are you?" Dorinen stammered.

The woman paused. "Oh dear. Yes of course, you were expecting Ramwin." She snapped her fingers, and he reappeared in a flash of white light.

Dorinen's jaw dropped. "How?"

"Well, I can take any form I wish," he said, "because I'm in all things and I am all things, so to speak. Do you not yet see? You *are* me, or rather, a part of me, and I am you, at least in some way. All that lives is a manifestation of Spirit, yes?"

She nodded, though perplexed by his almost nonsensical explanation. Or perhaps it made all the sense in the world. Dorinen couldn't be sure; she wasn't sure of anything right now.

"Well there you are," he continued. "The scriptures of Shylan Dar proclaim the Spirit manifests itself in numerous ways, including as a Sarvethar in many incarnations in many lands, and that all souls are imbued with its life force, and so on and so forth, blah, blah. I am said Sarvethar. I know what you know, or at least what you choose to let me know."

This remark puzzled her. How could he be all things and only know what she permitted him to? She'd never made any decisions of the sort, at least none she'd be conscious of in any case. But before she could ask about it, Ramwin addressed her confusion.

"The will of all living beings is free. The Spirit animates, if you will, but does not control. What you choose to do is your own calling, and it's not for me to take your personal sovereignty away from you. That is how you grow. Indeed, my own essence is enhanced by this freedom of choice. You were curious as to my whereabouts, and you asked the question of me, even if you didn't realize you were doing so."

Her mind reeled as she took in the implications of his words. "I never considered that the Spirit animates life for any purpose beyond its own majesty," she answered, as much to herself as to him.

"Ah, but such a state allows me to truly 'live' through the countless lives touched by me. Besides," he added with a wink, "if everything were a mere reflection of me, it would be intolerable! I mean, would the world truly want untold thousands of Ramwins running about?"

Dorinen stifled a snort at such a disconcerting thought. Ramwin joined with a jolly chuckle and lifted his goblet to her in a salute. He said nothing more, but plucked a few pieces of some small, strange-shaped pink fruit, offering one to her, and quickly tossing the other into his mouth. Her suspicions and fears faded, and she began to relax, even as doubts still lingered.

She cleared her throat. "Forgive me, but why do you assume this role? This..." she asked, gesturing at his attire. Fearing she'd overstepped, she relaxed when he flashed his inimitable smile and lowered his goblet to the table.

"Why, indeed?" He mused in mock seriousness, sitting back in his chair, and raising one boot to rest on the table. "I can and do wear many forms in this world and others, but I suppose if one is to *be* the whole cosmos, one must be expected to take on some of the trappings that such an office requires. Consider the kings and nobles who once ruled your lands. Greedy, bloated old men who grew rich off the labors of their subjects. They did nothing to earn their lofty positions save to be born into them, and they were simply presented a kingdom or a fiefdom when they were old enough. The people were correct to get rid of them. Surely, if these slobs could do nothing but wear opulent robes, count coins, and fall to the floor in drunken stupors, I'm entitled to *some* comforts! Most of them had no sense of fashion in any case, and their color combinations were dreadful!"

Dorinen crossed her arms and leaned back. "But there are no monarchs in our lands, save for Gavalahorne, and they have a queen!" She wanted to press the issue, but stopped short, realizing the bizarre futility of discussing politics with the Sarvethar.

"There are many other lands in this world, my dear," he said. "Besides, if you no longer have monarchs, then surely someone must step in to fill the gap, at least as far as good dress sense is concerned. I rather like the opulent decadence of excessive wealth's trappings!"

Ramwin acted as quite the vain popinjay now, examining the rings on the glove of his left hand. He seemed unlikely to explain further, so Dorinen let out a frustrated sigh and didn't pursue the matter. She'd become so fascinated by this surreal show, she'd almost forgotten that a short time ago she came close to an appalling death. Finding herself reluctant to darken the mood, she didn't want to mention it, reasoning he'd discuss the subject when it suited him. Or not.

As soon as she made this choice, Ramwin, still studying his rings, announced, "The monstrosity you fought is—well, was—a Vordlai. They are ancient and vile creatures, consigned to the endless twilight of their own dimension, Torr Hiirgroth, a realm of the Underplanes."

She blinked hard. Despite this outlandish explanation, with what she'd witnessed today, nothing he could tell her would be too fantastic or far-fetched.

"Their presence in your world is utterly forbidden," he continued. "They were supposed to have been banished five centuries ago."

"Supposed to have been banished? So, what in the name of the Five Hallowed Oaks was one doing in Cernwood?"

"A good question. Unlike its kin, this one and several others remained on this plane, suspended in a magical sleep since the days of the Gharborr War, five hundred years ago, but I suppose they've woken up. The beast who attacked you must have ventured forth to feed. It found the Cernodyn Dwelling a suitable place to begin its cruel harvest."

For the first time since she'd met him, Dorinen saw a hint of sadness on Ramwin's face as he continued to scan his jeweled rings.

"It took Harl." She lowered her head, feeling the sting of tears. "He was kind to me after my own parents were killed, when I was merely five summers of age. He was one of several who cared for me, of course, but I always held a special fondness for him, and that thing…" There was no point in trying to hold back her tears.

"I'm truly sorry for your loss." Ramwin answered with genuine pity, though he didn't look at her.

She took a deep breath and gathered herself together, wiping her eyes. "But how is it even possible for these Vordlai to be free?"

After an uncomfortable silence, he finally turned his attention to her, gazing at her with soulful purpose. He lowered his boot from the table and sat up straight.

"I suspect someone has stirred them. And worse, an even greater disturbance in this world has called to me. In the north, in the Wastes of Yrthryr, an earth ravage has begun."

Dorinen leaned forward, not believing her ears. "Wait. An earth ravage? But that's just a tale we tell children so they'll listen to their mothers, or perhaps to scare each other."

"All myths have their roots in the truth, do they not?"

"But the earth ravage can't have actually happened, surely," she insisted. "How could such a force destroy the land and kill every living thing? It's not possible."

"Sadly, it is. Do you know what happened during the Gharborr War in Yrthryr?"

Before she could answer, he continued. "Yrthryr and its neighboring nation, Escarin, went to war, for all the usual reasons that such atrocities happen: corrupted power, disputes over resources and territories, misplaced national pride. But after a time, things went badly for Yrthryr. A magic caster named Ananbrom took desperate measures to save his nation from total defeat. Hoping for supernatural aid, this foolish young man succeeded in summoning the Arltorath."

"The who?"

"The Arltorath. Four ancient sorcerers whose countless lifetimes of devotion to necromancy and the black arts utterly corrupted them. They had lain banished and dormant for years beyond counting. They cannot be destroyed, you see, only contained. When Ananbrom summoned them back from their exile, they brought with them utter catastrophe. Their darkened conjurations called forth the Eral-savat, a formless, hate-filled monstrosity long buried deep in the earth. It wanted only to destroy, and when freed, it erupted from the depths as the earth ravage, killing everything it touched, scouring the land itself.

By freeing the Four, Ananbrom unwittingly precipitated the massacre of his own people and the destruction of his realm."

Dorinen rubbed her chin. "But someone defeated it, surely? Defeated them? Otherwise, we wouldn't be sitting here now."

"Indeed. Other workers of arcane magicks contained the Eral-savat. They even banished the Four once again, for the twentieth time at least." He rolled his eyes, almost in annoyance. "And for centuries it was so. Indeed, the matter should have ended there. But such wickedness cannot so easily be put to rest, I fear. There are souls of the dead still in those forbidding depths, trapped between two worlds, still subject to the Eral-savat's influence, ever hungering for destruction. By your own mortal perception, they have lain there for centuries, their existence unnoticed and unhindered. But what is time to the dead?"

Coldness seized Dorinen, and she shivered, hardly believing his words. Of course, she'd heard of these ancient battles, though she brushed them off as mere legends. But here the Sarvethar was telling her with all solemnity and seriousness that these events had truly transpired.

"I'm quite sorry to say," he continued, "that the terrible power of the Eral-savat is again free in this world. As we speak, it is razing and twisting the landscape of Yrthryr once more, re-animating the dead within it."

She sat back, trying to take it all in. "All right," she said after a moment, "but what about those Vordlai? Where do they come from? How do they figure into this?"

"The beast you tracked in the forest comes from the same substance as the Eral-savat. But it and its kin were imprisoned in a place deep underground, where those who sought to sow disruption long worked to bring such appalling entities from the Underplanes into this world. A sealed portal there acts as a gateway between Torr Hiirgroth and this world. I believe whoever has succeeded in awakening the Vordlai has something to do with the reemergence of the earth ravage and is more than likely trying to open the portal, as well."

Dorinen's eyes narrowed. "I'm not sure what this has to do with me."

"The earth ravage must be stopped, of course," he answered with gravity in his voice. "But first, the Vordlai have to be destroyed or subdued, and the portal secured. That will purchase some time."

"Time? Time for what?"

"It will slow the advance of the earth ravage, and also... well, that's not important at this moment. Now—"

"Wait," she snapped, frustration and confusion beginning to weigh on her. "If you *are* who you claim, and I'm starting to believe it, why haven't you confronted these horrors and destroyed them yourself? I saw what you did to that thing in the forest. It didn't stand a chance against you. You could easily remove this menace from our lands."

Ramwin rested his face in his palm, as if searching for the right answer. "Despite what the Shylan Dar proclaim, I'm afraid I am not all-powerful, certainly not now. Yes, I inhabit the land. Yes, I am in all things, but I am not the only force here. Other powers dwell in these many dimensions, and while I encompass them all, they, like you, have their own freedom of choice, and I cannot interfere with that choice, even in the face of destruction. To do so would be to deny an aspect of myself. Every being must take the course of its own choosing, no matter how despicable or harmful. It is a cosmic principle by which even I am bound."

Dorinen slumped back in her chair.

Ramwin also sat back. "The Eral-savat is a most strange phenomenon. While all things in your world are in some sense components of me, sustained by me, the Eral-savat is instead the sum total of its components, the spirits of countless unfortunate dead trapped within it, and in turn, it is sustained by them. It ultimately devours their individuality. It is a perverse mockery of life essence and seeks to undo all I have done. I enrich and bless, but the Eral-savat enslaves and annihilates. There's... more to the whole tale, but that is all you need to know for now."

She shifted in her seat. "I fear that 'all I need to know for now' is already far too much."

He leaned forward with intent. "I cannot battle these evils directly, but the living of this world can. Choosing to stand against them would be the enacting of my will in a manner that allows for my non-interference and the continued freedoms of all beings."

Dorinen slapped the table, spilling some wine out of her goblet. "But you *did*. If you hadn't 'interfered,' as you put it, I'd be dead by now, horribly so."

His face softened. "I took a necessary step to ensure your safety. One Vordlai means little in the grand scheme of things, but I must have a care in the future. I cannot accompany you or provide assistance beyond knowledge for your benefit. You must find your own way, and in doing so you will defeat this abomination."

Dorinen could hardly believe what he was saying. "Wait, you're suggesting *I* confront these creatures? You saw what one of them did to me! And what about *my* free will? What about my choices? You speak as if I've agreed to this, but I have not! Am I being forced into this conflict without my consent?"

"I cannot and will not force you to do anything," he said with a deep sincerity.

He reached out across the table and gently took her other hand. His touch was soft yet strong, as in the forest, and the feeling of absolute love and trust surrounded Dorinen again.

"When the Vordlai woke and began their bloody foraging," Ramwin said, "I was aware, but I needed to wait to see what they would do. I mean, I *knew* what they would do, but I could not act until they'd done so. Sadly, the nest of sleeping Vordlai is within the boundaries of Cernwood itself, so I suppose that's why it attacked your people first."

Dorinen gasped and jerked her hand back. "What? These foul creatures are a part of our sacred wood?"

"Their lair is in the north of the forest, as I said, far below the ground," Ramwin continued. "When the Vordlai attacked your home and you were sent after it, I was also aware. I'd presumed there would be one among your people who was up to the task, and I was not disappointed. Your skills are remarkable. Few others could have tracked the beast as far as you did."

"I did well enough to nearly end up in the thing's belly," she countered, adopting a bit of his own sarcastic expression. "But why not raise an army to fight such a threat? The combined forces of Tenaeth and the Tveor could surely defeat this evil."

"Wars have been fought against such foes," Ramwin answered, his voice more somber, "but always with a terrible cost to both people and lands. The terrors unleashed by those conflicts must not be repeated, or else all will be plunged into darkness and barbarism. Those who might die fighting would potentially provide the Eral-savat with more life-essence, more souls, more 'food' if you will. So too would the fear that would sweep across the land should the people know, giving the Eral-savat even more strength. It is… a dangerous age, and secrecy is important in this endeavor."

She crossed her arms. "So, send some priests to confront it, or those Shylan Dar monks."

He paused, smiling like an admiring parent. "Ah, the most sensitive of the Shylan Dar already know of the Eral-savat's re-existence, and of much else. They've always been too clever for their own good!" Ramwin chuckled and continued. "But it is your home the Vordlai have defiled, and they will do so again. So, one from among your people is the best choice to confront them. And as you faced the Vordlai with remarkable courage, you revealed yourself to have great potential."

"But I cannot fight them!" Dorinen leaned forward and gripped Ramwin's hand. "I have a better idea. Return with me to the Dwelling of the Cernodyn. My people will fortify their defenses, and with the knowledge that you've come to them, their faith will be strengthened. And your power will be enough to defeat them!"

"I cannot," Ramwin answered, his face pained. "And you must tell no one what I've said, even if you refuse my offer and return to your home. The people of these lands must not know of this threat, not yet. Perhaps not ever."

Dorinen's heart sank. "So not only can I not warn my kin, but you're also asking me to go on a journey into certain death. How can you possibly believe I can do what you're asking?" But how could she say no to him?

As if reading her mind, he said, "I will return you to your people if you wish."

A crisis of conscience and belief crashed like a wave over her. She shivered, almost sickened by the thought of it all, and let go of his hand.

"Before today, I'd never been sure the Land Spirit, Urkera, even existed, and now you're sitting in front of me, pleading for my help to save the world." She ran her fingers through her hair and sighed. "I suppose I should be honored, but all I feel is the weight of a terrible burden. You're saying I must face forces so powerful and evil that no one has ever fully vanquished them in the past? All by myself?"

"I didn't say you would undertake this task alone," he remarked, almost casually.

Her face brightened. "Then you *are* coming with me?"

"No. As I said, I cannot."

Her heart sank and she shrank back into her chair.

"However," he continued, "there is one you can seek, in the Caves of Erekbore, by the Admere Sea. A warrior and magic-caster of power and renown, a half-Dalaethrian named Mylth Gwyndon."

Dorinen furrowed her brow in confusion. "Half... Dalaethrian? Is such a thing even possible? I can't imagine how one of those beings would befriend a mortal closely enough to allow for any kind of union."

"Mylth is rather unique, I assure you," he answered with a knowing wink. "He has served me in the past, though our relationship now is somewhat, shall we say, strained. Nevertheless, he understands a great deal about these evils and has the power and knowledge to counter them. He can act where I cannot. Together, you can locate the Vordlai lair and destroy the ones who have escaped into this world. He should be able seal the portal and prevent further Vordlai on the other side from breaking through, which, as I said, will slow the Eral-savat's spread."

"But does he know where the portal is?" she asked.

"I don't know." He sounded apologetic.

"You said these creatures are in Cernwood, in the north?"

"I can perceive the general location," he replied, "but disruptive forces are now blocking my complete awareness. I told you, I am not all-powerful in this world, certainly not in this age. Not all things are known to me, and my predicament will only grow worse. You must find the portal, for by my actions, I am already dangerously close to unleashing more chaos, and bringing about… the end, sooner than it need be."

He spoke sadly, almost like a dying man, and Dorinen eyed him with concern.

"Oh, but do be careful when you find him." His face brightened. "He's been in his *Hyradenn* for sixty-seven summers and will be none too happy to be disturbed from it, especially when he learns that I've sent you."

"His what?" If Dorinen hadn't already dreaded this impossible mission being foisted upon her, she surely dreaded it now.

"A sleep. Well, no. A meditation? It's a little of both, I suppose. The Dalaethri practice it so they can remain immortal. They prefer to persist in such a state for one hundred years at a time."

"And you're asking me to wake this Mylth early." She did not like the idea of having to disturb an immortal being from his century-long rest.

"I think the dire situation will alleviate any annoyance he might have."

"You think? But you just said he wouldn't be happy…"

He flicked his ringed finger, brushing away her concerns. "I can deliver you to the coast, near to the Elothokh Crags, where the caves lie. Two good horses will await you at the crags' edge to speed you on your journey. I will also arrange to send word to your people, informing them that you are well and will return in due course."

"But how will I find him in the caves?" She protested. With each word Ramwin spoke, the more impossible this task became. "How do I wake him, and why should he believe me when I tell him what we're supposed to do? If I even agree to this?"

Ramwin snapped his fingers, producing a small white stone attached to a long loop of leather, which he handed to her. "Wear this. It will guide you to his location and protect you. Dalaethrians make their hiding places well, but I know where they all are." He wagged one finger and grinned with a knowing smugness. "Most of them guard their meditation chambers with powerful magical wards. When you find him, take off the stone and place it around his neck. It will bring him out of his profoundly relaxed state far more gently and effectively than giving him a shake on the shoulder, which would likely cost you your life! He will recognize this little rock, for no mortal being would possess it. As for his dual nature, well, I shall leave it for him to tell you, if he chooses."

Dorinen shook her head in disbelief. "And I simply explain to him everything you've told me, he willingly agrees, and we set out into danger like we're old friends, not even knowing where we're going? We defeat these creatures—who knows how?—and save Cernwood and perhaps the world from destruction?" Dorinen assumed his sarcastic expression and waved one hand in the air with flippancy.

He met her sarcasm with his wry, amused smile. He cocked his head slightly to one side, and with a shrug raised his eyebrows.

"Precisely!"

four

Andra and Narick entered the simple wooden structure of the Eladran shrine, where a mature woman dressed in a plain white robe greeted them.

"Be welcome, weary ones. I am Faehl, first among the compeers of this house. Take rest and nourishment if you have need, but you must forswear all acts of violence on these grounds." She glared at Narick.

Andra leaned in to him. "I told you," she whispered.

Ignoring her, Narick bowed. "Thank you, Compeer Faehl. We are of the Shylan Dar and Artisans of Teuvell, and we gladly accept your terms and your hospitality."

She held out her hands without emotion. "Then be welcome, Siblings of the Spirit."

Andra noted the sparse, if adequate, furnishings of the interior as their hosts showed them to a large room upstairs, a candle-lit dormitory set aside for travelers and pilgrims. When she and Narick were alone, Andra sat on one of the cots and removed her boots, glancing around at the old building, with its exposed timber beams and aged planks.

"I mean, it *could* use a bit of decoration," she cracked, rubbing her sore feet.

"No other travelers are here tonight," Narick observed, clearly ignoring her attempt at humor. "That's good."

"You know, for a member of a communal order, you're pretty fond of being alone," she quipped.

"The emphasis on scholarship, personal development, and meditation all require solitude, which suits me." He sat on his own cot. "I suppose I could go be a hermit on the outskirts of the moors, but where's the fun in that? You're one of the few people whose company I genuinely enjoy. You appreciate my irreverent sense of humor."

She chuckled and set her boots aside.

He scanned the room, nearly empty save for cots and a few tables, and sarcastically sighed with a raised eyebrow at her. "Not even a rose-scented pleasure fountain. How will you survive the night?"

She stared at the floor, barely concealing her embarrassed grin. "Pleasure fountains aid in sleep, prayer, and meditation," she answered with mock indignation.

"I'm sure you have discovered their effectiveness in enhancing the amorous senses as well."

She blushed. If Narick were to tell her father even some of what he knew about her adventures in Tenaeth, she would no doubt never be allowed to leave home again. And Narick didn't know everything.

She looked around again at the room and changed the subject. "This place is definitely plain, though."

"Devotees to the Lady of Peace love the natural world, and their emphasis is on creating beauty outdoors, instead of lavish interiors."

"Well, I'm more concerned with a meal and a lot of sleep at this point." She yawned.

"Just remember, it's customary for guests to view the garden of an

Eladran shrine, usually after their dawn devotions. We wouldn't want to be rude."

Andra cringed at the offer, reminded of how little sleep she'd had the night before. But not wanting to risk offending their hosts, or even worse, a round of mirthful taunts from her friend for sleeping late, she acquiesced.

Once settled, the two returned to the ground floor of the shrine and went to a small refectory lit by candles and a hearth fire. They ate crusty brown bread and vegetable soup with an unimpressive red wine. Yet Andra found this simple fare more than satisfactory after a long day's travel. They took their meal in silence, the Eladran custom, then made their way back upstairs to the dormitory.

Soon, a series of gentle chimes sounded, calling the community's faithful to their nightly meditative gathering before retiring. The soft chanting presented a tranquil beauty, quite unlike the elaborate music of Andra's college's ceremonies.

"It's all so odd," she reflected.

"What is?" Narick asked, preparing his meditation cushion.

"This, the shrine. It's so different from the temples to Teuvell. And not only the design. I mean, our methods, our whole approach to the Spirit is virtually the opposite of the Eladrans'. Teuvell is love, beauty, celebration, music and art, passion, the senses. Eladra seems so austere, so detached. How can we say we revere the same essence?"

Narick settled himself onto his cushion, crossing his legs in a way that would leave Andra's own legs numb if she tried it herself. "You've answered your own question."

She folded her arms. "I'm about to have an academic lecture, aren't I? Should I take notes?"

He chuckled. "The Spirit imbues all things with life."

"Yes, thank you. I learned about it at the age of three."

"Within this world are the things we know," he said, ignoring her, "and each has its opposite to support the balance. It's why the

Shylan Dar revere Enwyonn as the bringer of harmony. The simplicity of Eladra's devotees contrasts with the excesses of *some* of Teuvell's."

He winked at Andra, at which she rolled her eyes.

"But each order exists to complement one another," he went on. "I know the Eladrans sometimes seem difficult and humorless, but we all represent a vital aspect of life. The peace and life-affirming values of Eladra are no less important than the celebrations of the senses encouraged by Teuvell. To us, Enwyonn represents that balance, and the three encompass many of the great values of this world."

Andra flopped on her lumpy cot. "I'm always impressed by how easily you can clarify complex philosophical questions into simple explanations. I'm sure a lot of ink and parchment has been wasted over the centuries, when the Shylan Dar should have employed people like you to make things clearer."

He shrugged and adjusted his seating, recrossing his legs, which still looked uncomfortable.

She pondered these ideas, reminding herself of each individual's differing interpretation of the Spirit. "I always wish for my music to be worthy of the Lady," she offered, "even if I still have so much to learn."

"I've no doubt it is," he answered. "Now, if you will excuse me, I must attend to my own devotions."

He closed his eyes and rested his arms on his knees, palms facing upward, a nightly practice to calm the mind after the day's concerns. She'd once tried to learn the technique from him but found she didn't have the patience to practice it each day, so she gave up after a fortnight. Her own musical explorations sufficed to center her in most cases.

Knowing that Narick would be meditating for some time, she changed into her large nightshirt, lay down again, aware of the gentle orange glow of flickering candlelight.

Outside, trees rustled and leaves whispered, and something brushed against the wall. Andra dismissed it as the wind and drifted off to a much-needed sleep.

* * *

Sometime later, a loud knock from outside jolted her awake. She sat up, straining to see. Moonlight illuminated the room, contrasted by Narick's silhouette by the window. He'd donned his traveling clothes again, meaning he was expecting trouble. He raised a hand to indicate for her to remain silent, and she obeyed, trusting his instincts.

Another knock came from a different location. It sounded accidental, as if someone had stumbled and hit the outside wall.

Without turning to face her, Narick whispered, "Gro'aken."

Andra's eyed widened. "Here? So close to Tenaeth?"

"Remember what I told you?"

She rose and crept over to him, peering out the window, but she could see nothing distinct, only a portion of the garden bounded by trees. She found herself wishing that the pacifist Eladrans weren't so trusting of their surroundings and would build walls around their communes.

A sudden movement in the treedark caught her attention. A shadowy shape emerged and began lumbering toward the shrine. Even in the darkness, she recognized the creature instantly; Narick was right.

"Wretched creatures," she hissed. "Why are they here? There's nothing worth stealing in a community like this." She'd learned long ago about the Gro'aken coveting gold and any trinkets they could claim, and being happy to kill for them; they sometimes even ate their victims.

"Maybe they're seeking treasures in the wrong place," he answered, his attention fixed on their intruder. "Maybe they're just hungry. Whatever the reason, something is giving them courage."

They stood in silence, watching the Gro'ak wander about. It sniffed the air, and let out a gurgle punctuated with insect-like clicks. Andra squinted to get a better view, to no avail. After a short time, it moved on, disappearing from view.

"Thank goodness it's gone," she sighed.

"No, they roam with their band," Narick whispered. "I've counted four so far, and I believe there is at least one more waiting in the trees."

Andra shuddered and began to imagine the worst possible outcomes. Long ago, her mother had told her folktales about these creatures, but she'd never seen one. Yet here they were, and so close to a settlement.

"Come," he said, interrupting her thoughts and turning to make for the stairs. "Get dressed, and bring your kenlim."

"What are you intending?"

"Someone has to deal with them. If they find a way into the shrine, they'll slaughter the Eladrans. You know as well as I that the devotees will offer no real resistance."

"But we can't fight them," she whispered forcefully, as she crept back to her cot. "We're outnumbered, and besides, we've also taken the vow of non-violence."

He gestured for her to lower her voice. "I didn't say we'd have to fight them or allow them to gain any kind of advantage over us, much less enter the shrine. But if the Eladrans are awakened, at least some will go outside to investigate, and likely lose their lives for doing so."

Andra donned her clothes, oblivious to Narick's presence. She paused and reached into her pouch, retrieving the jewel. She turned it around in her hand for a moment, then knelt to pick up her kenlim. Not knowing why, she had an urge to place it beneath the strings, pressing it against the soundboard.

To her astonishment, the gem glowed a vibrant purple for a moment before fading. Panicking, she tried to tug it from the soundboard, but it had fused itself into the wood, as if it had been built into the instrument.

Narick shot her an alarmed look. "What are you doing?" Now his voice was too loud.

"Nothing! I mean, I don't know. It just—"

"Andra, what is that?" He stared at the glowing gem.

"Izznil gave it to me before I left. Honestly, I don't know what it is, but he said I was 'ready' for it, whatever that means. And now it's, it's stuck to my lyre."

Narick stayed silent but bore a concerned expression. Did he know something he wasn't telling her? If so, he said nothing. He simply motioned for her to follow him, and they tried to descend the stairs quietly, a task made difficult by the worn wooden steps under their feet. Andra flinched as she set one foot on what was surely the squeakiest and loudest of them.

Once on the ground floor, they separated and made their way to windows on opposite sides of the entry hall. Andra saw nothing from her vantage point but a part of the garden. A moment later, Narick beckoned her to join him.

Through his window, she saw three of the creatures near the garden's entrance. Two carried swords, the third a spiked club. In the moonlight, she could see their scraps of badly-fitting clothing and armor, no doubt looted from their many victims. One wore a helmet that was too large. Though straining to see, she still couldn't make out their features. She'd read of their ghastly appearance and now wanted to know if they were truly as terrible as she'd been told.

Narick made for the main door.

"What are we going to do?" Andra's heart began to race.

"We'll draw them away from here, back down the road, which is beyond our non-violence oath. We can trap them there and place ourselves between them and the shrine. With a bit of luck, we might be able to scare them off with no fighting and stay true to our word."

Unconvinced, she swallowed hard and took a deep breath as he opened the door and stepped out into the garden. She followed him with more than a little reluctance and quietly closed the door behind her. The summer night was still but for the sounds of insects, though a shuffling sound from the other side of the building startled her, and she almost cried out.

"They're here." Narick's voice was barely audible. "Wait, but be ready to follow at my signal."

Andra nodded, keeping a firm grasp on her instrument, though her hand shook and her mind raced.

Narick took a deep breath, and to her astonishment, extended his arms out to the side, walking straight toward the small dirt road leading away from the shrine. If he'd wanted to attract their attention, he could have done nothing better, short of calling out to them.

What are you doing? She tightened her grip on her lyre and held her breath.

He hadn't even walked twenty paces when she heard grunting and mumbling coming from around the corner. Her heart pounded, but she resisted the temptation to follow him, since he intended to lure them out to the road, away from the shrine.

She gasped as two of the creatures lurched out after her friend, weapons drawn. She wanted to call out to warn him, but forced herself to remain silent, reasoning that he must be well aware of them. Just a few more steps, and he would be on the road. Andra clenched her teeth and tensed, wanting to trust his instincts, but fighting her anxiousness. *They're too close, they're going to attack him…*

Narick reached the road, only a few paces ahead of the first of the two Gro'aken, who now panted, as if eager with anticipation at an easy kill. One raised its weapon to strike.

Still facing away, he slammed his elbow directly into its neck. It clutched its throat and stumbled back a few steps before collapsing to the ground. For a few moments it convulsed violently and then lay still.

Andra almost cried out, flinching at the sight.

The second Gro'ak swung its sword at Narick, but he caught the creature's arm with his right hand before its weapon could get close. He twisted the wrist, making it drop the weapon at once. Before it could howl out, Narick delivered a devastating punch to the Gro'ak's nose, snapping its head back as it fell lifeless to the dirt.

He'd killed both of them in a matter of moments.

Andra looked on in horror, her mouth wide open, gripping her kenlim with white knuckles. She knew of Narick's prowess and skill, but had never seen him kill before, much less with such efficiency and speed.

Before she could react further, two more Gro'aken emerged from the garden. The one with the too-large helmet ambled after Narick.

The other, however, spied Andra and shuffled toward her, swinging its crude spiked club.

With a shriek, she froze for a moment, before regaining her senses. *No, you fool! You have to get it away from here.* Trying to draw it after her, she ran for the road.

Hearing her heavy footfalls, the other Gro'ak whipped around and confronted her with a snarl. Andra stopped, shocked at the sight before her. Though it only stood as high as her shoulder, a horrible visage leered at her, its red and bloodshot eyes widening as it flared its flattened, pig-like nose. She gasped as it bared decaying, sharp teeth from a mouth too large for its leathery, yellowish face.

Worse, she found herself caught between it and its companion, and still on the grounds of the shrine. Stopping short and cursing herself for being so foolish, she played a series of notes on her kenlim in desperation and chanted ancient words to summon a wind to push away her opponent.

"*Eiath, eiathann, demma mey, demma thann.*"

Protect me, Lady.

She'd barely finished her prayer when a bolt of violet light shot forth from the gemstone in her lyre, hitting the Gro'ak squarely in the face, while the force of the blast made her stumble back a few steps. It fell to the ground, a stump smoldering where its head once sat. Andra's eyes widened and her jaw dropped open. "No! That's not what I meant to happen, I—"

Narick startled her as he dashed past, knocking the fourth Gro'ak onto the well-tended green grass. He grabbed it by the collar of the rough shirt protruding from under its rusty chainmail and dragged it out to the road, breaking its neck with a single twist.

Leaving the body there, he started back to Andra, his face enraged. "What have you done?" He didn't even attempt to keep quiet. "What magic was that?"

"I, I don't know!" she yelled back in defiance.

"You've violated the vow and almost got yourself killed at the same time!"

"I didn't mean for it to happen, I swear!"

"You were supposed to follow me." He motioned angrily to the charred corpse nearby. "Not do whatever in damnation that was!"

"One of the creatures came for me. I tried to lure it away, but the other one," she pointed, "it turned on me. I only sought to push it away, I—"

"Well, clearly that didn't happen. I've no idea what magicks you've been tinkering with, but—"

"I wasn't tinkering with anything!" she shouted.

"Well, thanks to you, our hosts have stirred." He kicked the ground. "And we know what's going to happen now. They're going to expel us and be damned sanctimonious about it!"

Sure enough, several Eladrans emerged from the shrine, with Faehl at their head. An older man Andra hadn't seen before accompanied her, his expression even sterner than hers.

Narick approached her, his hands held out as he began to explain, but Faehl held her fingers over her mouth, palm facing outward.

"What?" Andra pressed. "What's she doing?"

"She's telling us to remain silent."

Faehl surveyed the scene with an almost eerie calmness, noting the dead bodies scattered on the road, and the one lying within the shrine's domain.

"We are an order of peace," she spoke at last, with an icy tone in her voice. "You, of all people know this, monk. Both of you vowed to respect our ways in this place."

"These creatures were going to attack you, murder you!" Andra interjected, hoping to mount some kind of defense for herself and Narick. "You know what Gro'aken do!" Though she herself barely knew.

Unmoved, Faehl responded. "The intention of these creatures is not the issue. It is your actions that are of concern. This is a grave transgression."

"But we were trying to draw them away from the shrine," Andra countered, her voice softer, pleading.

"To kill them on the road?" Faehl snapped. "And then what, would you have disposed of their bodies in the forest, and left us tomorrow as if nothing had happened? Saying not a word? I see you obey your vow in a most literal sense, but not in spirit. Your killing is no more acceptable to us on the road than it is here."

Faehl sneered with contempt at Narick. "I expect nothing less from the Shylan Dar, with their clever logic and means of subverting spiritual law when it suits them." She turned to Andra. "It is a pity that you, young songstress, are already so swayed by their ways."

Seething, Narick opened his mouth and raised a pointed finger, presumably to give Faehl a good telling off. But before he could protest, something hissed passed him.

The old man at Faehl's side let out a short gasp and sank to the ground. Several other Eladrans screamed and shrank away in fear, seeing the large and crude dart embedded in his chest.

Narick cursed. "You see what your lecturing has led to?"

But Faehl didn't even seem to hear his words. She wavered by the elder's body, as if numb with disbelief and in danger of collapsing to the ground.

A cry erupted from the garden, drawing everyone's attention.

Narick turned to them. "Get inside, now! All of you!" He hurried off in the direction of the scream.

Andra took Faehl's arm, trying to force her to move, but she would not. Letting the older woman's sleeve go with a frustrated jerk, she resolved instead to search for other Gro'aken who might be lurking nearby. Gripping her kenlim and taking a deep breath to steady herself, she set out to search farther down the road.

* * *

At the edge of the garden, Narick came upon the body of another Eladran devotee, a young man. Peering under the man's torn garment, he recoiled at the gaping hole where the victim's heart had been. Hearing a commotion, he spied the remaining Gro'ak fleeing awkwardly for the trees, clutching the man's heart in its sinewy hand.

Swearing again and gritting his teeth, Narick set off after the creature, oblivious now to any concerns about vows.

At the forest's edge, he caught it by the scruff of its wrinkled and leathery neck, and with a sharp tug, he slammed its forehead hard into the nearest tree. It fell and dropped the heart, blood oozing from the wound in its head.

He hauled the dazed creature up in front of him and stared straight into its glazed red eyes. "Rip your heart out as you did Eladran's, I can," he growled in the Gro'aken tongue. "Killed your kin, I have made so, and should kill now you."

The creature gurgled and gnashed its teeth and hissed. "Monk-man speak so brave, yet save not weakling fools in white this night. Tasty fools, tasty hearts!" It cackled.

Narick clutched its dirty jerkin with both hands and leaned in. "Blood-drunk and weak are you. Run to your battleband and warn them: death visits all who walk close to this place in the later. Do it myself. Understand?"

He threw the creature to the ground. It chittered and cowed

beneath him for a moment before scrambling to its feet and fleeing into the night.

Ending its life would have been a mercy. If it returned to its band having failed to bring treasure, the chief would no doubt kill it. If it chose to run away, it would become an outcast, and its former war kin would hunt it down.

Either fate was fine with Narick.

When he returned to the garden, he discovered the group hadn't heeded his warning and still remained outside. Several Eladrans knelt near the body of the slain man, holding one another, whimpering, muttering, and wiping away tears.

Not bothering to mention the second of their dead devotees, Narick shook his head. "How can they possibly be so inexperienced in the ways of the world?"

* * *

Andra emerged from a cluster of nearby trees to return to the shrine, seeing Narick now standing apart from the Eladrans, lost in thought.

"I couldn't find any others up the lane," she muttered as she approached him, disappointed but relieved to say so.

"You went out there?" Narick snapped, seething. "I took care of the one who murdered that man, but what if there were more? You could have been killed! What in Enwyonn's name were you thinking?"

"Oh, I see," Andra replied in a chilly voice, trying to restrain her irritation. "So, I should have stayed here waiting for it to shoot another dart at one of us while you were off playing the hero."

Narick scowled. "You should have tried to get the others inside. These creatures might be slow and dim-witted, but they're clever enough when it comes to obtaining food and looted goods, and they can see far better in the dark than you." He pointed behind himself.

"Perhaps you should go take a good look at the man in the garden who is now missing his heart!"

Andra swallowed hard, hugging her lyre, the ugly reality of the situation sinking in. She conceded that Narick spoke truly about the danger, but she didn't like seeing this side of him. Shylan Dar monks used deadly force when necessary, but the quiet man with the jolly sense of humor was nowhere to be found now. And Narick acted so intense and angry, it unsettled her.

"We've violated our vow," he said in a calmer voice.

She swore under her breath. "We'll have to leave the shrine right away, yes?"

"Indeed, and we're never allowed to return."

She didn't answer, though she turned over the night's events in her head. The matter of the jewel haunted her now. Her song was only meant to stop the creature long enough for her to get out of its way, maybe shove it to the road. Instead, she'd burned its head clean off. How could Izznil have given such a powerful artifact to her without telling her what it was, or what it was capable of?

Returning to the present moment, she saw Narick walking purposefully toward the shrine's door. But two younger Eladran men stopped him before he could enter, and after some heated words with one of them, he turned away and came back to Andra.

"We're no longer even permitted to enter the dormitory," he explained in frustration. "They will bring our belongings to us, and we must leave straight away."

"Narick, I'm sorry," she replied. "I know you're right. I shouldn't have left the grounds, and…"

His anger softened, and he held up a weary hand. "Honestly, you did far better than some adventurers I've known. You kept calm and didn't panic, a good showing for your first encounter with Gro'aken. You tried to push away the one in front of you, but what in Hiirgroth's foul name happened out there? With that gemstone, I mean. How did you do… whatever you did?"

"I swear I don't know," she answered, holding up one hand. "It's a magic I've never seen before. It completely changed the nature of my spell into something deadly. I didn't mean for that to happen, I promise!"

"You're sure you don't know how you did it?"

"Yes, I'm sure!" she answered with exasperation. "Do you think I would lie to you about something like this?"

"No, forgive me." He placed a calming hand on her shoulder. "Clearly, there's much you need to learn about its powers, whatever it is. Izznil must have given it to you for a good reason."

She let out a frustrated sigh. "I'm probably the last person who should have this sort of thing!" She lowered her voice. "We only tried to help them. The Eladrans might all be dead if we hadn't violated the vow. Would Faehl have preferred they all die?"

"It's an irrelevant question, I'm afraid." Narick glanced back to the shrine in exasperation. "The vow of peace that each Eladran takes is binding and cannot be violated, no matter what the circumstances, even if it means their death. I'm convinced it's quite self-righteous, even if I respect them for what they believe. Indeed, we should strive for peace above everything, and their ideals are noble and well meaning. But this headstrong attitude will ultimately endanger them all. These times are increasingly chaotic and perilous, and I'm afraid of what lies ahead."

Worry tugged at Andra again. "It's still several hours till dawn, and I doubt anyone else in the hamlet will let us stay with them. Not after what happened here. So, where will we sleep?"

"Outside of course," he said, as though the answer were obvious.

"But there might be more Gro'aken out there."

"There might, but I wouldn't worry overly about them again tonight. I spoke with one. They know they're beaten here, and any others will have fled by now. They won't be back."

Andra couldn't believe his words. "You can speak their language?"

"Enough of it."

Even after five years, Andra wondered how much he'd truly told her about himself.

"And if more do come back, I'll break every one of their damned necks!"

Andra took a step back. Narick seemed to enjoy the possibility of more violence, and for the first time ever, being near him made her uncomfortable.

He wandered about, hands clasped behind his back. "Perhaps this attack will alert the Eladrans to the dangers surrounding them, old and new," he said, more to himself than to her. "No, a thousand years of tradition will not bow before any threat. There will be more attacks on their houses, and they'll do nothing. Just allow themselves to be slaughtered."

"Maybe the others living nearby will help them prepare," Andra suggested.

He turned to her. "Well, this community will have to deal with its own damned problems."

At that moment, two Eladrans approached, bearing Andra's and Narick's belongings, which they placed on the ground. Without saying anything, they turned and made their way back to the shrine. Another devotee retrieved their horses and led the animals out onto the road. He too turned away silently and walked back to the garden.

After securing their possessions, Andra and Narick mounted, drew their cloaks about them, and swiftly rode away from the shrine without speaking another word to their former hosts.

five

Dorinen stood before the towering grey rock formations of the Elothokh Crags. Somewhere within their maze of innumerable caves, Mylth Gwyndon slept.

Ramwin delivered her, as promised, to a place outside the crags, providing two fine horses, saddled and equipped with provisions for animals and riders alike. And he'd done it with a simple snap of his fingers and a flash of white light. Though it must have been nighttime when she left him, a new day now dawned, yet she felt no ill effects or disorientation. In any case, he hadn't come with her, and she'd not seen him since.

Despite the Sarvethar's impressive displays, he didn't match in the slightest the image or majesty she'd heard about him, much less what scriptures attributed to him.

"Why didn't he just summon this man himself? Why am I here with horses? Why am I here at all?"

From her place on a hilltop, she could glimpse the white waves of the silvery Admere Sea in the distance. A stinging wind swept across her face and chilled her, bringing the smell of sea salt and damp air to her nose. Overhead, storm clouds gathered, and she knew they would soon burst. Summer was only notable for its absence here.

"So be it," she said with resignation. "Time to find this place, if that's even possible."

She examined Ramwin's small white stone, now worn around her neck. While he'd assured her she needed it to locate Mylth, it had done nothing yet to help her.

As she considered how she would lead two horses into this tangled mess of rocks and jagged peaks, each animal nuzzled her in turn and set off at a slow gait along the gnarled path before them, as if knowing where they should go. She watched them in disbelief for one long breath and hastened to make her way to walk in front of them, not even needing to take the reins of either animal. She began a gradual ascent upward; at least the path was where he said it would be.

After a time, the narrow ravine widened to reveal high cliffs towering over her, and several other paths leading to places Dorinen could only imagine, but didn't want to. No sounds intruded here, save for those of sea birds making their nests in the cliffs, and the howling wind filtering through the rocky passageways with an eerie whistle, like a chorus of ghosts.

She came to a halt and pulled her woolen cloak about her. The horses paused, as if waiting for her lead.

"Please show me the way," she said, one hand clutching the stone tightly. Almost at once, she wanted to turn south, to one especially narrow canyon. She held out the stone.

"I don't know if you're speaking to me, or if I'm imagining it, but I'll trust you and go with my instinct. Oh, by my ancestors' blood, I'm talking to a rock!" It bothered her that this wasn't the strangest experience she'd endured in the past day. Weary of trying to understand it all, she instead focused on the task at hand.

As she followed the trail into the new canyon, it narrowed to the point of barely allowing room for the horses to fit single file. The path became steeper as it wound farther up into the crags. She trekked on, sometimes through short tunnels, other times along a cliff's edge, all the while trying to convince herself that she'd made the right decision by coming here. Occasionally, she'd encounter trails branching off in other directions, but she resolved to stay on the main way. As she approached a fork, the first drops of rain hit her face, and her certainty faltered.

"By the Oaks, which way now?"

She chose one path for no particular reason, or did some force truly guide her? She and the horses followed it for a short time, before it ended at the mouth of a cave wide enough to accommodate the animals. The rain now pelted down in force, so she led them under its shelter, hoping they wouldn't wander off.

She turned to face the dark, with more than a little trepidation. Such a damp, unpleasant place seemed an unlikely abode for a sleeping Dalaethrian, one of those legendary beings of ancient history.

She almost laughed. "I suppose that's why they're not disturbed here, but I'll wager some of these caves must have things far more unpleasant in them."

As she took her first tentative steps, the stone around her neck emitted a faint golden light, as if confirming her choice. She clutched it in relief, even though she could barely see more than a few feet in front of her.

The passage descended slightly, and the soles of her boots slipped on the loose rocks beneath them. She put a hand out to the cave wall, cursing herself for her fumbling steps. Ahead of her, the dark only deepened, and she began to worry she'd been mistaken after all. Was Ramwin playing some horrid joke on her?

But soon she glimpsed an orange glow in the distance, which became more defined as she approached, and squinting, she saw the entrance to a larger cavern. The stone around her neck shone brightly in hues of gold and white, and it began to vibrate ever so slightly. She crept forward, her hand finding the hilt of her sword.

When she reached the entrance, she peered in to behold a truly remarkable sight: a large, natural stone grotto, where a smokeless fire burned in a golden brazier set along the wall. She breathed in a rich perfumed aroma of spiced wood and resin incense. Lavish white and golden silks hung tent-like from the walls and ceiling, adorned with dangling bells and chimes. An elaborate crimson carpet covered the floor, woven with arcane lettering and floral knotwork patterns.

In the center of the cavern sat the most beautiful being she'd ever seen. Resting cross-legged on a scarlet cushion, he wore a white silk robe with gold trim, his hands clasped together on his lap. His long golden hair hung freely and loosely to his chest, framing his slender features and clean-shaven face.

His eyes were closed, or nearly so. He didn't appear to be breathing and showed no signs of life, as if he were in a kind of stasis. She noticed that the air here oddly resembled Cernwood's before Ramwin appeared, and she hesitated to step into the room. The warm atmosphere made her movements slow, like being underwater.

With a deep breath of resolve, she crept in, her hand moving away from her sword hilt to clutch the strange stone again. Its vibration grew stronger.

While mindful of Ramwin's instruction to place the stone around Mylth's neck, she became distracted by the décor and trappings of this unique place, something she imagined that few, if any, humans had ever seen. Surely, she beheld something almost forbidden.

She worried about how to proceed. Ramwin said he and Mylth weren't on the best of terms, so how would he react to being interrupted from his restful state, particularly at Ramwin's request? Would he awaken right away, or would it take time? And would he see Dorinen as a threat?

She exhaled to calm her tension and readied herself.

Nothing else to do, I suppose.

As she moved toward him, she accidentally nudged one of the small hanging bells. It rang loudly and clearly, more so than it should have for its size. She cursed and jumped back with a start. Was it an alarm? She nearly drew her sword but thought better of it.

Yet Mylth didn't react. In fact, nothing happened.

Dorinen struggled against a sudden spell of dizziness as she approached him from behind. Shaking it off, she came around to face him. The stone hummed softly. She removed the cord and held it out in front of her, her hands quivering and her throat tightening. It glowed brightly and swayed back and forth on its own. Even though her heart pounded, and her mouth went dry, she found the determination to place it about his neck.

It ceased to glow and hum, its golden light passing into and coursing through his whole form, outward to his arms and legs. It dissipated, and he began to stir.

She held her breath, not knowing what to say or do, not daring to utter a word. For a short time, he did nothing. With no discernible expression, he turned his gaze to her. His emerald green eyes caught hers, and she froze. Perhaps he could view into her soul; regardless, she sensed a deep wisdom within him.

In a calm voice, he addressed her. "Why have I been awakened?" There was no hostility or accusation in his words, but she faltered and couldn't bring herself to answer right away.

"You are needed," she replied at last, unsure of her choice of phrase, and fearing he'd sense her nervousness. Apprehension in the presence of a being of great power had become all too familiar to her.

"Who calls me?" he asked with equal tranquility.

"I am Dorinen of the Cernodyn, from the Dwelling in Cernwood. I've been sent to contact you. It, it is a time of great danger and need."

Mylth regarded her with a vague expression of suspicion. "You could not know of my resting place, Dorinen of Cernwood, which my elder enchantments have kept hidden and well-guarded. Yet here you are, unharmed. I sensed you the moment you entered the chamber. Your people, fine though they are, do not possess the means to wake me." He took hold of the white stone and examined it. "How did you obtain this? Only the greatest magic workers or my own people can craft such an artifact."

Dorinen hesitated. She suspected he already knew the answer.

"It was given to me… by Ramwin Roakthone. He sent me to wake you and gave me the stone to, to do so." She found herself wanting to leave immediately.

"Ramwin," he whispered, closing his eyes. "Of course. He will not let me rest, will not cease to pursue and torment me." He let go of the stone with an angry jerk.

Dorinen remained motionless, regarding him with a mixture of wonder and apology.

He rose to his feet with irritation and astonishing swiftness, a decided change from his initial demeanor. "What is the year?"

"By the Reckoning of Ilrath, 2,370," she answered in a broken voice, now glancing at the floor.

"Sixty-seven summers!" He scowled, turning to the cave's entrance. "The Sarvethar could not let me rest in peace for even a full hundred-year." He turned to her. "Tell your lord I have no interest in his affairs. He parted from me long ago and I from him. You may leave as you came and will suffer no harm." He waved her away and prepared to sit again.

"But you don't understand," she protested. "Ramwin said you are the only one who can help. There is a great danger in the lands."

"The all-powerful Land Spirit does not need the help of mortals or Dalaethrians. It is all part of the cosmic jest that the Sarvethar loves to engage in. Nothing we do is of any consequence to the outcome."

"That's not true! He told me he cannot intervene, because—"

"To do so would violate the Spirit's charge to grant all beings their freedom and would potentially rip the 'fabric of realty,' or some such, yes?" Mylth's sarcastic demeanor led her to believe he already knew everything she was going to say.

She feared her mission had already been for nothing. "There's more. He told me those things, yes, but he appears weak, worried, as if he fears something far worse?"

"Doubtful," he retorted. "More likely his velvet doublet is out of fashion, and he's at a loss as to what to do about it."

"Yes, he was silly and foppish," she concurred, "though I would never have believed who he was had I not seen his power."

Mylth smiled without humor, his annoyance plain to see. "Few people do."

"There was an urgency to his words," she continued. "He insisted I find you. He said you are capable of stopping the evil that's returning."

Mylth raised an eyebrow. "Does he suppose that base flattery will make up for his wrongs against me? That I will simply forgive him and do tricks for him like a lap dog? I do not follow Ramwin's wishes, and I do not do his bidding."

Dorinen stared at him blankly, having no clue as to what he spoke of.

"My restoration is not complete." Mylth rubbed his forehead. "I am not at my full strength, and I am not interested in the current ills of the mortal world, which rise and fall like the tides of the great sea beyond these caves. Please leave me now, and tell him to find someone else to play his games with."

He sat on his cushion again.

Dorinen's heart sank. There was no convincing him. *I've failed. Ramwin was wrong.*

But instead of accepting his decision, anger welled up in her, and she made one last attempt to convince him. She knelt to look him in the eye, determined to say her piece.

"When the Vordlai return to my Dwelling and slaughter more

of my people, I hope you will think long about what you've said and done here."

"Vordlai?" he snapped.

"Yes. Your magic may protect you in here, but when you reawaken thirty-three summers hence, there may not be a world out there to return to!"

"How do you know about the Vordlai? When was this?"

At last, she'd gained his attention. "One attacked my people and then me in Cernwood, no more than a day ago. It nearly killed me, but Ramwin saved my life."

"Damn it!" He pounded his fist into his palm. "And no doubt with all of his usual flash and flurry. Did he complain about soiling his clothes with the creature's blood?"

Dorinen again found herself at a loss for words. Clearly, he knew Ramwin well.

Mylth shook his head. "That's not important, of course. My apologies to you. This is indeed serious. If the Vordlai have returned to Cernwood, I can almost forgive the bastard in this instance."

"You know of these creatures?" Dorinen asked.

"Oh yes, my lady. I helped to fight against them in the War of Gharborr."

"What? How? That was over five hundred years ago."

"Indeed. By appearance, I have the body of a man of some thirty-five summers, but I am over six of your centuries old. He must have told you it's why we engage in our hundred-year meditative solitude."

"Even though you're half human?"

He frowned and took in a sharp breath.

Dorinen regretted her words. "I'm sorry."

He paused for a moment before answering. "I can still partake of the *Hyradenn*, though I grow more weary than my kin at times. When I am in the mortal world, I must eat and sleep just as you do. I do not know if I will age and eventually die. Perhaps so, but it wouldn't be for several thousand years."

Dorinen wanted to ask him a dozen questions about his parentage, his life, how he'd known Ramwin, and why they were at odds. But her curiosity would have to wait. Besides, he might not be inclined to answer such personal questions from a stranger.

Mylth stood again and scanned the cavern. "Good. Everything is as I have left it. Thank you for not disturbing anything. Normally, my magical wards would have killed you before you got this far. Even if you had made it to the cavern, the tones of the bells would have driven you mad if not for the stone you wore. I heard when you disturbed one of the chimes earlier."

"How did you know?"

"We do not slumber in the way you might imagine," he explained. "We are conscious of our surroundings but focused on a deeper level of awareness, as you might experience when you begin to fall asleep. That you are not dead proves you are who you claim, and that Ramwin protects you, irritating though it is to admit. No evil force could have entered here."

Though intrigued by his answer, her mind returned to what he'd said about fighting in the war. "You said you confronted the Vordlai in the War of Gharborr. How were they defeated? The one I battled nearly killed me with ease."

"They are not easily beaten, I can assure you. Mortal weapons do them little damage."

"So I noticed." She crossed her arms. "I should not even be standing here before you."

"Hm. And I imagine it taunted you," he replied with a knowing nod. "Perhaps gave you some false confidence before it descended for the kill."

"I did it some grave injury," she hastened to add with pride. "Broke its knee and drove my sword deep into its belly!"

Mylth raised an eyebrow again. "Few can damage their enchanted hides. Even great warriors of the past fell quickly before them. Perhaps Ramwin did choose his new lackey well."

She bristled at the insult but held her tongue.

"I assume Ramwin made quick work of the beast and saved you?"

"He tore it apart like an old toy." Dorinen ignored his rudeness to keep the conversation going. "I've never seen such power."

Mylth nodded again. "And it will take such power to subdue the creatures once more. Where are they coming from?"

Dorinen noted with some dismay that he hadn't actually answered her question about how the Vordlai were defeated. "He didn't know the location of their lair. They're somewhere in the north of Cernwood, in what Ramwin said is a kind of nexus between worlds?"

"Banished after the war. Locked away for all time—we assumed—but only a few knew the exact location. How many of the creatures were there?"

"He didn't tell me, but he assured me that eventually others would venture into the forest and elsewhere, seeking to feed. He said further knowledge was being blocked from him."

Concern shadowed Mylth's face. "Why?"

"He said a new earth ravage has arisen in the Wastes of Yrthryr, driven by the, um—"

"The Eral-savat," he answered. "Damnation!"

"Yes, that's it," she answered, grateful he'd begun to acknowledge the danger. "It's already growing. At the same time, someone has awoken the Vordlai, and is drawing on powers from Torr…"

"Torr Hiirgroth." Mylth rubbed his temples, as if in pain.

"How did this really happen?" she demanded. "This earth ravage? Ramwin didn't offer many details."

He paused for a moment, as if lost in thought. "The incursion always needs a catalyst. No matter how much the collective spirits of the malevolent dead wish, they cannot easily enter our dimension.

Someone in this world has used powerful and ancient magic to awaken the Eral-savat, though I very much doubt they can control it, at least not for long. They're either mad or so evil that they cannot care about what they have wrought. I would wager whoever endeavored to enact the earth ravage is also responsible for freeing the Vordlai."

"Ramwin though so, too." Dorinen shivered, as the reality of her experiences struck her again.

"So, what does the insufferable jester want us to do?" He held up his hands, as if waiting for all to be explained.

She hesitated for a moment, until she realized he was referring to Ramwin. "Um, he said you would know."

Mylth's face sank into his palm, and he shook his head. "I knew it. The fool has no plan, no advice, nothing. He just appears, tells you the world is ending, and can you please do something about it, if it's not too much of a bother. Oh, and have some wine and cake."

Ignoring his sarcasm, Dorinen tried to recall the Sarvethar's words. "He said something about finding a portal, which is failing, and securing the seal. That will prevent more Vordlai from entering into our own world. And he said it would buy more time?"

"Indeed. The place containing the dimensional gate has undoubtedly been a location for worshippers of dark forces in the centuries after the war. It's possible that whoever raised the Eral-savat did so from this place. If we can find the portal, we might also learn who undertook this forbidden summoning. And if we can stop whoever did this, we might then be able to banish the Eral-savat again before the earth ravage grows too large."

"What happens if it does? Grow too large?" She didn't want to know the answer.

"The end of all things in this world."

Dorinen shuddered. "What did the earth ravage do during the war?"

"Before those dark times, Yrthryr was a lush country, abundant with life and a great civilization. The Eral-savat destroyed it, and it has never recovered. We were able to subdue the force before it grew too large, but the destruction it caused has never been reversed."

"We?"

Mylth stepped away from her. "That's not important now. If this madness is to be halted, you and I don't have much time. We must discover the location of the Vordlai lair, and quickly." He stopped at the table, as if reminiscing. "I have an old friend in Tenaeth who will be of help in that respect. You have mounts and supplies?"

"I do."

"Good. Let us prepare. I will go with you, but I can assure you, Ramwin and I will have words after this affair is completed. He will be in my debt in a way he never imagined possible."

Without another word, he took hold of a magnificent sword on a table by the wall, its elaborate hilt set with a smooth blue jewel. He next ran his hands over a beautiful bow of dark wood, trimmed in gold.

"That bow is exquisite," she remarked.

"Indeed." He didn't turn back to face her. "Among the finest you'll ever see."

Finally, he inspected several neatly arranged jars and bottles made of multi-colored glass, each containing different liquids, plants, and powders. Dorinen could only speculate about their uses. He began to gather up some and set them into small pouches, placing these in a larger leather shoulder bag.

"We use elements of this world to create magic," he said as an explanation, "unlike, say, the Artisans of Teuvell, who channel the Spirit's power via their arts. So, I'll need some of these items. Unfortunately, I cannot bring everything."

She offered to leave while he changed his clothes, but he paid her no heed, so she quietly exited the cavern and made her way back to the mouth of the cave. Whatever the outcome, she understood she'd now committed to this task.

Outside, the rain and wind began to subside, and she stood

watching the elements for some time, pondering what Mylth and Ramwin had told her. She wrestled with fear? Doubt? She'd long believed herself incapable of them. Yet she'd come face to face with a terrifying and brutal death, received confirmation of the Sarvethar's existence, and been burdened with the responsibility of trying to save her world alongside an ancient being whose people were more legend than fact to many. How could anyone take all of that in?

She hugged herself as a chill from the air swept through her, though dread of an uncertain future was surely as much a cause of her discomfort as the frigid gusts. For the first time in her life, she didn't know what to do. She frowned and looked at one horse, as if it might have an answer, and cursed herself over her indecision and uncertainty.

Something about Mylth perplexed her as well, but in a good way. He appeared powerful, wise, and calming; she was almost soothed by his presence. His face spoke more to her than his words, and she beheld a sense of knowing, perhaps recognition on a deep level. She welcomed that feeling.

Her mood changed again the more she considered the danger ahead. They'd been charged with an impossible task, one which they would likely not survive. She could only pray their efforts would not be in vain.

Mylth emerged from the shadows a short time later; she hadn't even heard his approach. Dressed in unassuming traveler's clothes, save for an ornate gold pin holding his grey cloak in place, he carried the sword and the bow, and placed his bags on one of the horses, perhaps knowing which one preferred him. He whispered something into the creature's ear, and received a nuzzle in response.

As the wind caught his hair and blew it back, she saw that his ears ended in short points, not as long and prominent as those of a full Dalaethrian—or so she'd heard—but enough to mark him as something more than human.

He halted for a moment before the cave entrance and spoke some words in a language she didn't recognize. At once, a sheet of green light materialized, transforming into an illusionary rock wall. "My haven must be kept safe and private," he said. "Once this affair is finished, I shall return here to finish my rest."

He mounted the horse. "We must pass through the crags and cross the Low Hills to the northwest. It's the quickest route to Tenaeth. There's a way through the canyons that will allow us to leave this place safely. I've used it many times. Follow me."

In haste, she mounted her own animal. Mylth rode at a brisk pace, and she followed, wary of the narrow trails ahead. She needed to trust him, it seemed, in all things.

"I hope you're right about finding the answers in Tenaeth from this friend of yours," she called out to him. "I don't like cities and don't want to stay there longer than absolutely necessary."

If he heard her, he didn't respond. Once again, apprehension and doubt seized her, and once again, she struggled to banish them from her thoughts. The sullen skies above mirrored the foreboding fear in her heart.

Six

After their expulsion from the Eladran shrine, Andra and Narick rode north along the main road paralleling the River Charthan for two days.

Since their encounter with the Gro'aken, the mood between them grew more somber. What had begun as an exciting adventure for Andra had deteriorated instead into a tedious and even upsetting journey. She'd not yet come to terms with the ease and efficiency with which Narick had killed those creatures. Not that she felt sympathy for them, but he'd exhibited a disturbing coldness she'd never seen before. Worse, in an instant, his actions had altered the image she'd built up of him over the past five years.

She struggled with her hurt feelings, disappointed in him for reasons she didn't yet understand, and couldn't bring herself to say much to him. So, they traveled in silence, and she preferred to ride ahead of him on her own. For his part, Narick kept his attention firmly on the road, and he often acted as if she were not even there.

She also wrestled with the implications of the power of the gem now affixed to her kenlim, turning it over and over in her mind.

It shouldn't have ripped that creature's head off. What has it done to my lyre? What has it done to me? What if someone gets hurt because I don't know what I'm doing? Why did Izznil give it to me? He must have made a terrible mistake. I'm not nearly as responsible as he thinks I am!

And yet, she'd known Teuvell's touch in the past; the Lady's power had spread through her, even in simple magical workings; knowing this eased her mind a little. In any case, she eagerly anticipated a proper night's rest in a town.

When we're settled, I'll call to Her again.

As dusk approached, they entered one of the many fishing communities along Lake Charthan. They chose a small inn, where the innkeeper received them with a kind welcome and offered them their first proper meal since they'd left Tenaeth. He typified his profession, being generous of build, with a bushy mustache, a balding head, and a boisterous and jolly nature. Andra enjoyed the convivial air of his common room as she and Narick eagerly devoured the food and drinks he set before them.

Only after she retired to her room and lay on her bed did she realize the extent of her weariness. She hadn't slept well, and being on hard ground and wary of more Gro'aken attacks just worsened the whole experience. Her fatigue made her ever more fractious, contributing to her tension with Narick.

Even though she craved sleep, she nevertheless sat up and removed her kenlim from its leather case, holding it in her arms, joking to herself that it was like cradling an infant. She tried to focus on the strange purple gemstone now attached to the sound board.

This is hardly the best time. But curiosity got the better of her, and she'd not had the chance to be truly alone with the instrument before now.

Keeping her mind focused on the stone, she once again began to pluck the melody she'd played in the *Mirithnaa*. After a short time, the gem began to glow. She continued to play, improvising variations. The light remained constant and didn't respond to her changes in mood, tempo, or volume. In fact, nothing out of the ordinary happened. She played on for a short time longer, but finally, exhaustion overcame her.

"So much for learning anything else," she sighed. She stopped playing, and the glow faded. With some disappointment, she put the instrument away, fell onto her bed, and curled up into a deep and much-needed sleep.

* * *

Next door, restlessness disturbed Narick.

"Three nights now, and I can't concentrate," he whispered in frustration, "and it's getting worse. It's like being a novice again. By Enwyonn, what's wrong with me?"

The encounter with the Gro'aken and the consequences of the fight had been unfortunate, to be sure, but such a skirmish wouldn't normally cause him any true distraction. This kind of turmoil had only burdened him once before.

"The loss of your old mentor was worse," he assured himself.

Still, he couldn't convince himself all would be well, and no matter how he tried, he couldn't silence his mind. He didn't know what disturbed him so much, and worse, he couldn't guess how long it might continue.

"And what about Andra and that jewel of hers? That kind of power is dangerous. Why did Izznil give her such an artifact? She might be capable of greater magic, but is this the proper way for it to be brought out? Is it too soon?"

Dwelling on these problems would solve nothing, so he stood and exited his room, hoping a night walk would be better than staring aimlessly at the floor.

He departed the inn and made his way to the lake to be alone. He gazed out into a clear night, the waning moon shining brightly over the surface of the water. Standing on the rocky shore, a slight breeze rising around him, he welcomed the chill of the air.

He was aware of someone behind him before the sound of an approach. He remained still, his hands ready to defend himself if need be. He saw from the corner of his eye a man dressed in a long grey cloak, the hood drawn over his head. The stranger wandered to Narick's side and stood beside him. Narick made no sound but remained alert and ready.

After an uncomfortable silence, the man spoke. "As good a place as any for a restless night, I should imagine. You were right to desire to be alone at this time."

Narick turned his head a bit. He couldn't make out the man's features but saw that he was tall and wore fine clothing of purple and blue velvets. A gloved hand adorned with rings held the cloak about him, hiding the rest of his form. Narick knew at once that this was no ordinary traveler taking a moonlit stroll. He sensed vibrant life in this man, as if an abundance of creation were here in this time and place, however fleeting, for as long as the stranger stood near him. But as he considered it, the idea seemed absurd.

His years of training had not prepared him for such shocking exhilaration, but he couldn't doubt what he perceived, even as his rational mind fought against it. Light-headedness threatened to submerge him at the very prospect. As a truth dawned on him, he was able to whisper, "You!"

The hooded man did not turn to him or give any sign confirming Narick's intuition. He merely stood silently for a time.

Finally, he spoke in a calm and soothing voice. "A great danger is coming to this world. Vordlai have been loosed into Cernwood. A resurgent Eral-savat lives, and the earth ravage has begun again in Yrthryr. You and your order are correct in your suspicions. Complete your journey quickly, for you will be needed. There are others who will come to you, and you shall help each other. Guard young Andra Illindrien well. Her potential power is great and may offer true hope to save everything. The one she dreams of will soon find her."

Narick stood in stunned silence, not comprehending. Slowly, however, realization entered his mind. With these few words from the Sarvethar, he understood his recent fears, his restlessness, and the sense of disturbance plaguing him.

"Why? Why me?" he managed to stammer in a half-whispered voice.

"You are good and wise, Narick Yerral, among the greatest of devotees in the Shylan Dar order. You are worthy, and I am honored by your dedication. Stay true to yourself and have no doubts. You can do much in the dark days to come, and you will need to."

These words overpowered even the highly disciplined monk. He surprised himself as he faltered and slumped to the ground. The man reached down and gently helped him to stand again. For a brief moment, Narick glimpsed his face and his shining, soulful eyes beneath the hood. They were an eternity enshrined in a heartbeat, and as he stood again, tears of joy welled up within him.

The Sarvethar gently touched Narick's cheek. "Go now, my friend, and sleep. Rest well. We shall meet again when the time requires."

Drowsiness swept through Narick, unlike any fatigue he'd experienced for ages. As his mind slipped into the peace of sleep, he heard the snapping of fingers and felt himself falling into his bed at the inn.

* * *

The dream had visited Andra again last night, clearer and more insistent than ever. Who was this woman who beckoned her while she slept? What did she want?

Outside, the clear sky revealed midmorn, and bright sunlight streamed through the window into Andra's room. She questioned why Narick had let her sleep so late, since he always preferred to be awake and on the road at an uncomfortably early hour. Andra rejoiced in the extra sleep, but his absence worried her. Whatever tension there might be between them, it wasn't like him to break with routine.

What if there'd been another Gro'aken attack? Surely, Andra would have heard something, and Narick would have woken her to assist the villagers in fighting back. Maybe for once, he just needed some extra sleep.

Convincing herself that they'd both simply craved more rest, she decided to luxuriate in her first proper bath since leaving the city. After wringing out her wet hair and finding some clean clothes, she made her way to the inn's common room. Deserted except for two merchants eating bread and cheese quietly at a corner table, the woody and sweet aroma of their herbal tea filled the air and tempted Andra to stay for a meal. She'd always preferred a slow and quiet morning, something neither her family nor her college ever appreciated.

She broke her fast with similar fare to the merchants', and since she still saw no sign of Narick, decided to go for a brief walk, returning to her room and putting on her boots. She paused for a moment before leaving, retrieving her wooden flute and tucking it securely into her belt, not yet sure why she did so.

The village was a bustle of activity. Food vendors sold their wares on the dusty main street, and the welcoming smells of cooking food and burning wood filled the air, reminding Andra of home. A fish monger thrust an odorous trout in front of her face, perhaps trying to make a quick sell. Not quite so welcome! She recoiled in disgust. It smelled several days old, and she graciously declined his offer, even at half-price.

She considered wandering to the docks, but the lakeside already teemed with people and boats, and she didn't wish to be immersed in a crowd this early in the day. She glanced in the opposite direction of the lake, to where a forest grew right to the village's edge. Feeling drawn to the trees, she set off, escaping the commotion of commerce to embrace the quiet of the woods.

Wandering for a short time under a canopy of branches and shade, she found a suitable old oak and sat before it. The chaotic sounds of the village faded into a welcome chorus of birds and insects. She took out her flute, and began playing on a whim. Her melody opened with only five notes, repeated more like an exercise than a true song, but she expanded the tune upward and downward, adding embellishments and ornaments at her leisure. The tune took on a life of its own, and Andra found herself drifting into a trance-like state even as she focused on playing.

Lady, hear me. Andra prayed for some sign, some guidance about the gem, her dreams, the peril of her world, anything. Yet nothing but the sounds of nature answered her plea, and even in her relaxed state, frustration tugged at her.

Just as she decided to stop, she saw in her mind's eye mists swirling in twilight and a path leading away into them. She flinched, fearing something had gone wrong, and as with the jewel, that she might release some terrible power without intending to. A presence invited her to go forward, so she imagined herself walking along the path, into the fog, into the unknown.

Who's there?

She heard a whisper in a language she didn't understand, arising from the edge of her perception, always out of sight.

Who are you?

The voice sounded again, as if pleading.

Are you the one from my dreams? What do you want of me?

She saw movement in the mists, there for a moment and then gone again.

Please! Help me, speak to me.

The shape of a hand formed in the haze, beckoning her as if in welcome. Andra tried to take it. *Please…*

At once, her eyes snapped open and she was back in the forest, her flute having fallen into her lap. Nothing seemed out of place around her, and no evidence of the murky world of her vision lingered.

She scowled and slumped forward. "I was so close! Why is this happening, and why does it always end before I can learn more?"

She sighed and stood, putting her flute away, conceding that once again, she would have no answers. "That's enough magic for one morning. Narick is probably awake by now and wondering where I am." Her mood darkened at the thought of having to face him.

More days of travel lay before them, and though they would pass other towns along the way, she suspected Narick would prefer to keep their stops to a minimum. The sun already approached its high point in the sky and they'd lost valuable traveling time.

Andra expected Narick to be broody and quiet again, keeping his focus on the road. At some point soon, they would have to break this silence and talk. Her stomach tensed.

After buying extra food for their journey, she went back to the inn and found the common room already filled with people eager for a midday meal, the innkeeper struggling to meet the demand. A loud crash from the kitchen set him off on a stream of colorful curses as he hurried to assess the damage. She suppressed a chuckle, and with Narick nowhere in sight, she hurried upstairs and returned to her room, where she quickly packed her belongings. If he showed, she'd be ready for a swift departure without one of his lectures on punctuality. In fact, the less said to him right now, the better. She almost wished she could make the remainder of the trip alone, but immediately regretted feeling so resentful.

She waited a while longer, but Narick still didn't emerge from his room. The day wore on, and she began to worry again.

With caution, she went to his door and tapped on it. When no answer came, she knocked with a bit more force, but was again greeted with silence. She took hold of the latch, knowing that even though it locked from the inside, she might as well try. To her surprise, it moved, and she pushed the door open, peering around to catch a glimpse of the other side.

She saw him seated on his meditation cushion, wearing his robe with the hood pulled over his head, his back to her. He didn't move and made no sound. Her relief at seeing him matched her guilt for intruding.

She prepared to close the door and leave him be, when his voice, hoarse and faint, said, "Please stay."

He didn't sound well. Andra's mind raced through a number of possibilities about what might be wrong. She entered, closed the door, and stood behind him, swallowing hard.

He motioned to the bed. "Sit."

She did as he said, staying focused on him, though he didn't turn to face her.

Clearing her throat, she tried to speak, deciding on a mundane topic. "It's, it is getting on into the day. We, we should leave soon. If that's all right."

"Yes." His voice was barely a whisper.

"I bought some extra food from the markets. We were getting a bit low."

Still, he didn't move.

"Narick?" she asked weakly, her voice shaking.

He inclined his head slightly toward her, as if in answer.

"Are, are you well?"

He remained motionless for a moment longer before turning to face her, his eyes red and swollen from crying. At once, she knelt on the floor in front of him, taking his hands.

"Please, dear friend, tell me, what's wrong? Is it me? Have I hurt you so badly?" Could their friendship be damaged beyond repair?

With a calm and reassuring grip, he held her hands and smiled faintly, shaking his head. "No, my dear. It's not you. Not you at all."

"Then what troubles you?" she asked, relieved even as she worried.

"Nothing troubles me, nothing at all. Last night," he continued, his voice still faint, "I was restless, as I have been for days. I wandered to the shore of the lake, hoping some time by the water would do my mind good." His expression took on a serious tone, and he edged closer to Andra. "There, I received something, a gift beyond price. When I awoke this morning, I feared it had been a dream, but I knew—I know—in my heart it was real, more real than anything I have ever experienced in my life." His hands closed more firmly about Andra's. "Dearest Andra, it was real, *he* was real, and he was here!"

"Who? Who was here, Narick?"

"Ramwin Roakthone!" Narick's voice was barely audible.

Andra's eyes widened in shock, and she pulled back. "What? The Sarvethar? Are you certain?"

"More than anything. I spoke with him, Andra. He spoke with *me*." He began to cry again. "He said, he said I am one of his great devotees, that I honor him with my service and deeds." He sniffed and fidgeted with his hands. "One of his great devotees? How can that be? I'm sworn to my vows, nothing more. I've tried to live in accordance with them, but I oppose outdated customs and laws. I have a temper, sometimes I'm disobedient, I don't keep the observances properly, so I don't know what he meant! I don't know what any of it means."

Andra gave his hands a gentle squeeze. The friend she adored and admired as a model of discipline and strength was just as human as she, with the same doubts and fears as anyone. The tension and distrust haunting her since the Gro'aken attack began to melt away. Here was no cold-blooded killer, but a good man trying to do his duty and protect his best friend. She only wished she could give as much in return.

Tears rolled down his cheeks. She drew him close to her, pushing his hood away, holding him tightly and letting him sob. She stroked his hair and gently rocked him back and forth, smiling as she herself cried. Far from losing his treasured friendship, fate must have conspired to bring them closer.

After a quiet moment, she spoke. "This is incredible, miraculous, but why? Why now?" If the Sarvethar had come to Narick, it must be for a good reason beyond repairing her trust in her friend.

"My order has sensed that something is wrong in our world for a long time, as I told you. But it's worse than I feared."

Her throat tightened. "Worse how?"

"It has come again. After five centuries, the Eral-savat has been given new life, and an earth ravage has begun in the Wastes of Yrthryr."

Andra drew back and furrowed her brow. "What do you mean the Eral-savat? That old legend?"

Narick quickly recounted the history to her. When she realized the implications of his words, a chill ran down her back and she placed her other hand over his.

"What are we supposed to do?" she asked.

"He didn't say. He told me only we have to return to your home as soon as we can, and that I need to," he paused, as if hesitating to say more, "to guard you. He said you have great power and that you offer hope."

"The Sarvethar spoke about me?" She gasped and gripped his hands tightly. "What can *I* do? You saw what happened. I nearly got myself killed by a single Gro'ak!" She shook her head and looked away; it was too much to comprehend.

"I don't yet know, but Ramwin said we must get to Meln quickly." Narick's voice returned a bit more to his usual confident tone, as if new life and new determination now coursed through him. "It will take us too long if we journey through Meladil. It's a safer route, but I fear we cannot spare the time. Instead, we should turn northeast off the main road and ride for the River Cryth. We must take the risk and trust in the Spirit's power and guidance. If we leave right after midday, we can still make good time today."

Andra didn't answer, but stared out the window, struggling with his revelations, her mind reeling. It seemed the adventures she sometimes dreamed about as a girl were being forced on her whether she wanted them or not.

Seven

From the center of a great hill in the distance, the glistening white and grey stone towers of Tenaeth rose against the azure sky, although, for Dorinen, the city offered no welcome. She preferred the gentle wind blowing from the west and the clouds above casting shadows over the rolling, tree-dotted terrain surrounding the city's walls. After a tiring ride from the crags, she and Mylth descended from the last of the Low Hills to behold the capital of Rilnarya.

"It's impressive," she said as she breathed in the fresh air but tensed in the presence of so-called civilization, "even beautiful in its own way, but these dwellings feel wrong to me, almost at odds with life itself. I don't understand why anyone would forsake the natural world to live in dark piles of clay and stone, crowded together."

"For many it's a question of safety," Mylth answered.

"Safety? There's so much crime, disease, even impoverishment of the soul."

Mylth shrugged. "Some simply like the excitement, I suppose."

"Well, I'm not convinced. There are plenty of ways to be excited that don't involve wading through a sea of people. Besides, if a settlement needs three walls around it, perhaps it wasn't a good idea in the first place." She gestured to the formidable stone fortifications standing between them and the city.

Mylth didn't respond. For the entirety of their journey, he'd remained mostly silent. Dorinen understood that he wished to focus on the task at hand and required a great amount of time to himself, adjusting to being in this world again. She imagined how unpleasant it must have been for him to be interrupted from such a prolonged meditation. And who wouldn't be annoyed at being woken up in the middle of a deep sleep?

"Come," he said with a half-smile, interrupting her thoughts. "There is much to look forward to there!"

Surprising her with his sudden enthusiasm, he urged his horse into a gallop, forcing her to keep up as they rode across the tree-dotted plain. Joining the main road at last and dismounting, they arrived at the gate of the first wall, an impressive stone edifice with watch towers on either side. The sight of this structure did nothing to improve her opinion of the city. A short line of people waited to enter.

"Why are the guards stopping people at the gates?" she asked. "Isn't Tenaeth supposed to be a free city, allowing access to all travelers and traders?"

"Perhaps the mood is a bit more tense these days," Mylth answered. "They will probably search carts, bags, whatever they might see as suspicious."

"Suspicious in what way?"

"That is partly what we're here to learn."

As he spoke, a guard raised a cloth covering on a farmer's cart, inspected it for no more than two breaths, and motioned for the driver to move on.

"Well," she said, "it appears they're taking little notice of what they discover, if they care at all."

He chuckled. "Highly trained soldiers they are not. But they'll likely view my unusual appearance and our weapons with some caution."

"Perhaps we should hide our arms."

"No, it will be to our advantage to be open."

"Why?"

"Trust me. I've entered this city often in the past."

"True, but you've not been here for nearly seventy years. And if the mood is more somber now, I'm sure other things have changed since then, too."

He said nothing, but strode to the gate, horse reins in hand.

"Halt!" A middle-aged man with grey stubble and a generous belly held up one palm to stop them.

He couldn't "guard" anything if his life depended on it, Dorinen decided.

"Those are most elaborate weapons you carry," he continued in an urban drawl that Dorinen recalled hearing from her childhood visit to this city. "And you look a bit strange to me. Who are you and what's your business here?"

With a calm demeanor and clearly not intimidated, Mylth answered. "I'm here on a personal matter to call on one of the chief residents of this city, a council member and sage. It's urgent, and we are in a hurry."

"Well, Master Golden Tresses, your 'urgent business' will have to wait," the guard said with some bravado. "I cannot just let someone into this city carrying those kinds of arms. You could be an agent of the Iron Rose, a monarchist from Gavalahorne, or"—the man sneered—"a big Gro'ak with a girl's haircut!"

Dorinen choked back a guffaw.

He pointed to his chest with all due bravado. "Furthermore," he said, "I can summon an entire regiment by ringing the tower bell, so I suggest you hold onto your horse, literally, and let me attend to my task."

Mylth was in no mood. Handing his horse's lead to Dorinen, he stood before this would-be inspector with an icy stare. He grabbed the man by the collar and lifted him to glare at his face. The hapless sentry's eyes widened, and he stammered a few words. Behind them, a crowd gathered, no doubt eager to see what slowed the line.

Dorinen's stood back, shocked by Mylth's aggressive move, and she questioned the wisdom of going along with his wishes. She tensed, worried a swarm of the city's constabulary would descend on them, and fearing they might spend a night in the city's jail, or worse. On instinct, she placed a hand on her sword and tuned in to the movements of those around and behind her, who began to mumble in worried voices.

One arm still holding the guard, Mylth calmly reached into a pouch at his belt. He brought forth a silver circular amulet, etched with several markings and sigils, a round red gemstone set into its center. He held it up to the guard's face, who reacted with astonished realization.

"This is the Seal of Etleth, as I'm sure you already know. You also know that Master Xalphed Gornio has instructed that all who carry it are to be admitted at once and escorted to his tower if they so request. Do you still wish to restrict our passage?"

The man shook his head weakly.

Mylth set him down, still with no hint of emotion on his face. "Excellent," he said. "Oh, and on this occasion, we shall graciously decline the generous offer of an escort beyond the third wall and simply ask to be left in peace."

Clutching at his collar, the guard hastily summoned one of his underlings, a lanky youth with matted brown hair whose uniform hung off his shoulders like an empty grain sack. They exchanged a few hushed words, and the boy motioned for Dorinen and Mylth to follow him to the second gate. Taking his horse's lead again, Mylth flashed a smug expression to Dorinen, and gestured up the path. She led her mount on, displeased at the unwanted attention he'd brought them.

They passed through the second and then the final wall, the youth having anxious conversations with the guards on duty at both. In each case, the men gave them a wide berth out of either respect or fear; she couldn't tell which. Only after they'd arrived in the city proper could Dorinen no longer suppress her curiosity.

"What did you show him?" she demanded. "Why was he so afraid of it? And damn it, who are we going to see?"

Mylth pointed to a narrow, cobblestone street, whose stone and timber-framed buildings almost touched on either side. "We must go there."

Dorinen scowled but followed on behind him. They came to an open market square, bustling with mid-day trading. Among the throng of people, the scent of roasting meats and baking bread mingled with spices and perfumes, while the sounds of hawkers and merchants, laughter, and street musicians filled the air. The sun blazed overhead; no breezes found their way here from outside the city walls.

Dorinen shuddered again at this place's oppressiveness. But she saw on Mylth an expression of contentment, not exactly what she'd expected from one who had been so joyless until now.

"Eleoton Square," he said to her, taking in the market. "Where you can find anything in all of Rilnarya for sale, and much from other lands as well." He took it in with satisfaction. "At least some things haven't changed."

But she couldn't share in his fondness and nostalgia. As a child of five autumns, her father and mother visited this city on a diplomatic mission, and even at such a tender age, she hated the large crowds and non-stop noise. On the return home, Iron Rose brigands ambushed their traveling party. Several of the Cernodyn managed to drive away their attackers, and they carried Dorinen to safety, but the Iron Rose killed both of her parents. Being here now brought that pain back.

Ahead, she saw a merchant's booth adorned with an abundance of children's toys. She closed her eyes as she remembered her father carrying her in his arms through crowded streets, and of seeing a smiling toy maker in vibrant red clothing selling small, wooden dragons. Her father traded to obtain one for her, and she delighted in the colors of its painted green body and golden wings. She'd managed to hold on to it during the chaos of the attack, and kept it to this day, locked away in a wooden box back home. She shook off the slight burn of tears and swallowed hard.

"Dorinen?"

Mylth's voice brought her back to the present. She turned to him.

"Are you well?"

"I'm fine," she lied with a sniff. "I was just remembering being here. Long ago. I'm sorry, what did you say?"

"The place we seek is down the main throughway and to the left. See that?" He pointed to a conical tower, rising above its neighbors to pierce the blue sky.

Shaking off her painful memory, she nodded. They set off across the market, leading their horses with some awkwardness through the waxing and waning crowds. Ignoring the invitations and approaches of a dozen and more hawkers, sellers, and con men, they came to their intended street and soon stood before a splendid mansion of grey stone, set amid a walled garden, its tower even more impressive up close. Entering the garden through a black iron gate, they found themselves surrounded by lush and unusual vegetation, flowers of exquisite perfume, fruit-bearing trees and two small fountains, whose silvery water glistened in the early-afternoon sun. Dorinen welcomed the quiet, and how this whole area seemed to be unguarded.

As if anticipating the question that she was about to ask, Mylth said, "Oh, it's protected, I assure you. The seal I carry allows us to enter. Intruders would not be so lucky."

They hitched their horses to two of a row of metal poles nearby with elaborate horses' heads carved on them, threading the leads through the rings held in their mouths.

Mylth strode to the manor's large wooden door. As he was about to lift the brass star-shaped knocker, the door swung inwards to reveal a short and rotund woman clad in a long, white and tan dress. She wore her dark brown hair tied back, making her ruddy face appear wide. She eyed the two visitors suspiciously for a moment and then smiled broadly and threw her arms open.

She squealed with delight as Mylth hugged her and swung her around in the air, and both laughed joyously.

"I didn't think to see you again for a good long while, my darling Mylth!" the woman said with a giggle as he set her on the ground.

"Nor I you, dear Wyath." He kissed her forehead, resting his hands on her shoulders. "He knows I am here, of course?"

"Of course! The moment you flashed that fancy amulet at the gate. Figured you'd do it with a bit of flair. I bet your old adventuring companions would never have been so bold!"

"Indeed not," Mylth answered. "Marcus would have tried to cut a deal, and Tryne would have just punched the guard in the face!"

They shared another hearty laugh.

Dorinen waited in the distance until Mylth motioned for her to come forward.

"Dorinen," he announced proudly, "this is Wyath Algrenn, a dear friend of mine, for a long time."

"I'm charmed," Dorinen said, offering her hand to clasp Wyath's.

"Be welcome," Wyath said warmly, bowing her head. She turned to Mylth and winked, as if communicating in some secret language they alone shared.

Mylth shook his head. "You've not changed at all Wyath, and I'm glad." He turned to Dorinen. "Wyath keeps this home in order and assists its master in many ways. She also maintains this stunning garden."

Wyath beamed. "Master Gornio needs me, you see."

"It's true," Mylth answered in jest. "The runt couldn't tell his ass from a chronicle without dear Wyath's help! Is 'the master' about?"

"Indeed, he is," came a gravelly but gentle voice from behind them. "Just finished putting his ass on a bookshelf and finding a suitable cushion to rest his chronicle on!"

A short, dark-skinned fellow emerged into the sunlight, dressed in a comfortable-looking white shirt and trousers. Dorinen recognized him at once as one of the Enanim, the southern cousins to the Tveor of the north. She'd heard they were a contemplative people, given to learning and history, differing from their more battle-eager northern counterparts. Mylth described him as a "sage" at the gates, and that description suited him. A broad and warm smile sat well on his bearded face.

Mylth pointed at him. "And I shall tell you what to do with your chronicle!"

He knelt and embraced the small man with a warm hug, the two erupting into laughter and patting one another firmly on the back. Wyath stood nearby, beaming.

"Well met, my friend," Mylth said as they parted and beheld one another. "I see that Wyath is keeping a good eye on you."

She fairly glowed now, basking in him giving her credit for her good Enan-keeping.

"You look like you haven't had enough sleep, man," the sage said with a chuckle. "Must be a good reason for you to be up so early."

Mylth's face lost some of its cheerful expression and he nodded. "Indeed, but I suspect you already know something of what's amiss."

The shorter man ran a hand though his long black hair, his expression becoming more solemn. "I've suspected. To be honest, I wasn't entirely surprised when I learned you were at the gates. I hadn't thought to see you again for quite some time, but this confirms my fears. I wish we were meeting again under happier circumstances."

"As do I, old friend. There's a tension in the air here. Even the city guards are being especially nettlesome. But, forgive me." He motioned to Dorinen. "I'm completely lacking in social grace."

He sounded like Ramwin, and an amused Dorinen considered that the two of them were more alike than Mylth cared to admit.

"This is Dorinen Elqestir of Cernwood," Mylth said, "who woke me and apparently, has been charged with the same task as I have." He presented her with a florid gesture of his arm, perhaps meant to mock Ramwin kindly.

She approached, unsure as to how to address the sage. Her discomfort was eased when he simply extended his hand.

"Xalphed Gornio, at your service, my lady. I'm always honored and delighted to make the acquaintance of one of the Cernodyn. Good souls, those. Please, be welcome here."

Taking his hand, Dorinen bowed awkwardly, still feeling out of place despite his friendliness. "Thank you, sir. It's I who am honored to be in your presence."

"Nonsense," Xalphed said with a shake of his head. Dorinen took this to mean she'd been too polite, but he said nothing more, so she let it pass. She noticed that among these outsiders, even with Ramwin, they easily dismissed formality and ideas of rank, unlike her own people. She struggled to make the adjustment in this different world.

"Come," Xalphed said, "let's retire to my sitting room to discuss matters further. Wyath, my darling, would you be so kind as to tend to my friends' horses?"

"I'm not your servant, you know," she called back with annoyance as she strode out to the garden to take care of the animals.

Dorinen found herself speculating on their relationship and the woman's true nature. She and Xalphed sparred in a jovial manner like a long-married couple, deeply devoted to one another and able to take liberties with their comments. Wyath appeared to be human, yet she'd also known Mylth from the time of his last wakening. What kind of magic permeated this place?

She pondered the mystery while Xalphed led them into the entry hall of the home, which seemed far larger on the inside than on the outside. Fine tapestries hung on the walls, with the floor partially covered by a beautiful ruby-red carpet, woven with geometric patterns along the edges. When Xalphed raised his hand, the door at the far end swung open.

Magic indeed.

"Please my friends, sit, and help yourselves." Xalphed motioned to the center of the chamber beyond.

For the second time in only a few days, Dorinen found herself seated at a table with luxurious foods, this time consisting of bowls of fruits and nuts, plates of bread and cheese, and two amphoras of wine next to several pewter goblets. The setting reminded her of her hunger, and that she'd not eaten properly for a few days. As she ate—trying not to stuff her mouth and appear rude—fragrant smells from the garden drifted in through an open leaded glass window.

For a while, the talk was light, much of it involving Mylth and Xalphed catching up on events over the past six decades and recalling earlier times, though both tried to include Dorinen as much as possible in their conversation. Mylth also seemed to understand the potential awkwardness of the situation and apologized to her.

She swallowed a generous bite of cheese. "Please, there's no need. It's been some time since you two have shared conversation, so take no account of me. Besides, your tales could entertain me for hours." She was grateful to forget her worries, even if only for a while.

After they'd satisfied themselves with refreshments and reminiscences, Xalphed leaned forward, more serious now.

"Tell me what you know."

"You should speak first," Mylth said to Dorinen, who found herself sorry that the moment of enjoyment had now passed.

She recounted her ordeal in the forest, her improbable encounter with the Sarvethar, and how she'd been directed to Mylth. When she'd finished, he added his own points to expand on her tale.

Xalphed listened intently. He absorbed every word they said, storing it away for future reference, as if he were a chronicle unto himself. When they'd finished, he sat back and folded his hands together, gazing past them at an open window. At last, he rubbed his bulbous nose. He took a long sip from his wine goblet. "It's all a bit of a problem," he said, stroking his black beard.

That's it? Dorinen shot a pained, questioning look to Mylth, but he ignored her.

"A great problem, indeed," Xalphed continued. "I'd suspected some planar disturbance, but nothing of this magnitude. No doubt by now the Shylan Dar monks are aware of what's happening and wisely have said nothing publicly. They can be reasonable on occasion."

Mylth chuckled at this last remark. Dorinen didn't get the humor, considering the topic of conversation.

"Suffice to say that Xalphed and the Shylan Dar order are... friendly rivals," he explained to her.

"Now," Xalphed said, ignoring him. "The question we must answer first is: where is the location of the portal to the Underplanes? If it is in Cernwood, we face a great difficulty, since the dense forest is all but impenetrable in many places. Correct, Dorinen?"

"Even more so in the north," she answered. "My people don't journey there often, so it's not well known to us. We've preferred to leave it entirely to the Wild and not disturb it."

"Which means I may have to consult several tomes on the history of the War of Gharborr. Perhaps I can glean some information about the location of the banishment." Xalphed's brow tensed. "The only problem is that I must soon take my leave. I wish I could stay and assist you further, perhaps even join you, but this matter cannot be avoided. There are problems arising in Maradhoor, which might well be related to what you've told me. Dovex and I must depart when he returns in two days and make the journey south."

"Dovex?" Dorinen asked, wondering what could be so important about two days from now.

Mylth leaned back in his chair. "He's a... most unusual friend of ours. With luck, you will have the good fortune to meet him."

Xalphed added, "I'm sure he will be delighted at that prospect."

They spoke no further about their mysterious associate, so Dorinen let the matter rest.

"But how will we find the answers we need in only two days?" Mylth asked. "I'd hoped that we'd need go no further than to you, my friend. But I fear if you depart soon, there will nothing else for us here."

"I must admit," Dorinen said to Xalphed, mustering the courage to speak, "I hadn't considered the idea of you joining us. I'm sorry to hear you cannot."

"Alas," he answered, "I do what I must, but I shall try my best to solve this puzzle. You'll simply have to trust me." Xalphed flashed a grin of confidence at Mylth. "Have I ever failed us before?"

"I'm not going to answer that question in polite company," Mylth quipped.

Xalphed mouthed a mild swear word at him in response and stood. "If we're to find where those damned Vordlai are lurking, we'd best get on with it!"

* * *

Dorinen gazed awestruck at the library, each room lined with shelves for both books and scroll cases, and each shelf seemingly holding more documents than the last. The rich scents of leather and parchment, paper and dust, filled the air, and she found herself enjoying being here more than she expected.

"It's immense," she remarked, turning about to take in the whole of the first chamber.

"Six rooms on two floors," Xalphed declared with pride.

"Yet you know where everything is, I gather?"

"Ah, well, that's all due to the detailed record-keeping system Wyath devised."

Dorinen folded her arms. "I suspect you also have a remarkable memory."

"Well, yes, there's that, too," he conceded, holding one hand over his heart and accepting her compliment. He flashed her a wink. "But I wouldn't want to appear as if I'm bragging."

"That would be a first," Mylth joked.

Wyath rejoined them, and for the rest of the day, they pored over books in Xalphed's library.

"I've never even seen some of these languages," Dorinen said to their host at one point, leafing through a few books. "But you know them all."

"If you live a long time, you acquire many gifts, most of them intangible," he offered as an explanation.

Mylth said little, devoting his time to several tomes also written in archaic tongues, presumably not spoken for centuries. She could only wonder about what the two of them must have seen in their long lives.

Daylight began to fade, and shadows grew across the room.

"I imagine it will be a long night for us all," Wyath said, trying to sound encouraging as she lit more candles.

Dorinen grew weary, though since the others seemed unaffected by fatigue, she resolved to push on. "I'm curious," she said to no one in particular. "Why would the Vordlai be banished to a magical sleep in the same place containing a portal to the Underplanes? Wouldn't it have been far more sensible to try to send them back to their own dimension rather than lock them in that place? Or if not, at least keep the two as far apart as possible?"

"A good question," Xalphed replied. "If I recall, the magic-casters decided the banishment spell would act in a two-fold manner. No one could send the Vordlai who remained in this world to Torr Hiirgroth without more power. Those who opposed the creatures simply did not have the strength left for the task. However, one spell-worker, Denderath, conceived of the idea of drawing the creatures back to their entryway into this world, and creating a kind of stasis to weaken the inter-dimensional portal. In effect, he put it and the remaining beasts to sleep. Thus, he nullified the Vordlai, and disabled their way in."

Mylth set aside a particularly thick tome. "Denderath decided that for the safety of all, only a few would ever know the gateway's location," he added. "He wanted this knowledge never to be shared widely, and for it only to be given to the most trusted and powerful of magic casters. Perhaps with the passage of centuries, the threat diminished, and the knowledge was forgotten, or recorded in books now lost to us. That's why we're seeking clues here."

Dorinen had never overly concerned herself with the history of the world beyond Cernwood, but now she found herself burning with curiosity to know more. She returned to the book she'd been flipping through, a history written a mere forty winters ago according to the date on the frontispiece, and she doubted there was anything of interest to their search. Indeed, she suspected Xalphed and Mylth had simply given her a pile of books in the common language so she'd feel included. She couldn't decide if this gesture was thoughtful or insulting.

But one passage caught her attention. She read it again to make sure she'd understood it correctly. Her tired eyes widened.

"I might have found something," she announced. "I'm surprised I didn't recall it earlier. My people have a story telling of a night beast that would steal children away from the dwelling, taking them to the north to devour them. It was the sort of tale young ones tell to frighten each other around campfires, daring them to walk out into the woods after dark. We never really took it seriously. In our stories, the beast was called the Wardess. It was said to dwell in a dark cave far under the ground. And here it says, 'The wicked beasts returned to Vordiss to lie in wait.' Wardess, Vordiss: that's too close to be a coincidence." She showed the others the page.

"I know of no place in Cernwood or outside of it with such a unique name," Xalphed replied, deflating Dorinen's optimism. She expected him to dismiss it. "However…"

He reached for a particularly old tome that appeared to have been unopened for decades. Blowing dust off the cover, he perused the table of contents with great interest, finally deciding on a selection about halfway through the book. Dorinen and Mylth moved in to examine the contents.

"I don't recognize the script," she said.

"Nor I," Mylth said to her surprise.

"It's an archaic mages' script from Gavalahorne rarely seen these days," Xalphed explained. "This volume is almost a hundred autumns old, and even back then, the tongue was not in common use. This section details part of the ritual for the Vordlai's banishment. I've skimmed through it before, and if I recall correctly, there is something about… here!" He pointed to the middle of one page, a triumphant smile on his face, as if he'd solved the whole mystery.

Mylth's face became impassive. "Well done, sage. I'm most impressed. Perhaps after you've finished gloating, you would care to tell us what you're pointing at?"

Xalphed scowled at Mylth, his moment stolen. Clearing his throat, Xalphed translated, "For in blackness they shall dwell, until the time of the dying of the eternal. The dark caverns of Vordiss shall hold them in timeless sleep and the gate to Torr Hiirgroth shall be sealed. Behold, deep within the earth is this damnation, sealed by trees and stone below the grey lands. And justice shall reside over it, with steady guard and watchful eye."

Xalphed paused for a moment. "I wonder. I assumed the words 'justice shall reside over it' were simply a statement about the restoration of order to the lands in the aftermath of the war. Perhaps it refers not to the state of the world, but an actual structure, a place. What if something was built over the site to act as a guard?"

"It would be a logical defense," Mylth agreed. "A location in Cernwood hidden among the thick forest would allow for the construction of some kind of tower or building which would attract little attention."

"The part about 'sealed by trees and stone' could mean that, as well," Dorinen added. "A building hidden in the forest, I mean. But what about 'below the grey lands'?"

"The Grey Wolds?" Wyath offered.

Xalphed snapped his fingers. "That might well be it. So, what we seek is indeed in the north of the forest, probably near the Grey Wolds."

"Ramwin implied as much," Dorinen said, "though I don't know of any ancient structures or even ruins there." She hated to spoil the moment and tried to offer some encouragement. "But I'm not familiar with the area, none of us are. The woods in places there are virtually impassable, even by us."

"All the more reason why what we seek may be there," Mylth said. "The forest has retreated in the region over the centuries," he added after a moment, "which would be of help."

Dorinen bristled. "The woods didn't retreat," she objected, "people cut the trees down and cleared the land."

"My apologies," Mylth offered, holding one hand to his chest and bowing his head. "I simply meant that the site might be easier to find as a result." His gesture didn't quell her irritation, even though she knew he'd meant no harm.

"There will be no need to search for anything, if I'm right," Xalphed interjected with a sly grin as he stood and strode toward the adjoining room. "And let's be honest, I almost always am!" He disappeared through the doorway. Wyath rolled her eyes, amusing Dorinen.

A short time later, Xalphed returned with a large book and a scroll. Without explaining, he flipped through the pages of the book, both a chronology and an inventory. He muttered to himself for another moment, leaving the others to exchange puzzled glances, though Mylth seemed to understand this behavior. Perhaps he'd seen a lot of it.

Finally, Xalphed looked up. "Of course! How foolish of me. I should have realized this right away!" He unrolled the scroll on the table before them, revealing an old map. "The location of the portal and the Vordlai lair must be under Wyverdorn Keep, not far from the trading village of Meln."

"Isn't Lord Wyverdorn the governor of that region?" Wyath asked.

"Indeed, and he's a good and just man," Xalphed answered. "If this is where the Vordlai have come from, then I fear something terrible might have happened to him and his household. In fact," he paused, "I've heard the people of Meln have acted most oddly around groups of well-to-do merchants, as recently as a fortnight ago. Apparently, they were disinterested in business, engaging in no serious barter and sale, most unusual for a town with a reputation for driving a hard bargain."

"But if the Vordlai have awoken," Mylth asked, "why have they not simply devoured the villagers in Meln and everywhere else?"

Dorinen glared at him, concerned about his potentially callous remark.

"It is their way to seek out the nearest flesh," he added in explanation. "So why would one of them venture south to the Cernodyn Dwelling when an easier target lies so much closer to them?"

"I don't know," Xalphed answered. "Perhaps they've been prevented from feeding close by. Perhaps someone is controlling them." His brow furrowed with worry.

"Ramwin was certain someone has summoned both the Vordlai from their sleep and the Eral-savat from the depths," Dorinen offered.

"To subjugate the Vordlai would be no easy task," Mylth said. "Only a great magic caster or sorcerer would have such power. A few among my people could accomplish it, perhaps, but they would never."

Xalphed concurred. "The mages of Gavalahorne—the Darrowrath—could possibly achieve it, but I am not aware of any of them troubling Rilnarya, and I doubt even those less inclined to do good would seriously consider such an act. There are also some among the Shylan Dar who might possess the training and mental discipline, but again, I know of none that would willingly do so. Of course, the monks are not particularly inclined to tell me of their activities." He let out a sigh. "Whoever might be controlling the Vordlai is probably connected to their presence beneath Wyverdorn Keep. Perhaps our enemy might still be there."

"And not at all inclined to be disturbed," Dorinen said.

"True enough. It appears we have found our direction," Mylth said, turning his attention to her. "We must make for Wyverdorn Keep and try to find the answers there."

She exhaled with resignation, but the grim reality of their plight began to dawn on her. Their discoveries made the task before them all the more real and all the more daunting.

"One thing puzzles me," Xalphed said, drawing back her attention. "Wyverdorn Keep isn't more than a century old."

"It might have been constructed on the site of an earlier keep or tower," Mylth said. "Perhaps whoever built it did so innocently, knowing nothing of what was beneath?"

"Perhaps." The sage stroked his beard, not appearing convinced.

"Xalphed," Mylth spoke again, "is there no way you can come with us? I would be far more at ease with you and Dovex at our side."

Regret crossed Xalphed's face, as if he were torn.

"Quite impossible, I am afraid," a resonant voice sounded from the doorway. "We are needed urgently in Ashyzym."

A tall man dressed in black strode into the room, his shoulder-length hair a mixture of gold and copper, with eyes of a rich amber in color, and a sun-bronzed face.

Xalphed leapt out of his chair and greeted the stranger with a warm hug. "Welcome back, dear Dovex! You're early!"

Another Dalaethrian, perhaps? Dorinen admired his striking countenance, almost overwhelmed at being in the company of so many unfamiliar and wondrous beings.

Dovex turned to Wyath, who hugged the man and kissed his cheek, then strode to Mylth, who'd waited behind her for his turn.

"I had not expected to see you again for some time," Dovex said, embracing him.

"Nor I you, friend," Mylth replied, "but circumstances demand it, I'm afraid."

Mylth informed Dovex of the situation, but as with Xalphed before, he knew something of the peril already. If Ramwin wanted to keep this whole matter a secret, he wasn't doing a very good job.

Xalphed gestured to Dorinen and turned to their new visitor. "Please, do excuse me. I must introduce you to Dorinen of the Cernodyn. It was she to whom the Sarvethar revealed himself, after she fought one of those wretched beasties single-handed."

"You are most welcome here, brave lady of the forest." Dovex bowed.

She waved him away, embarrassed. "Until today, I didn't know how highly regarded the Cernodyn are by some in the greater world."

"It has long been so for those who appreciate quality and nobility of heart," Dovex answered.

"You flatter us, sir." She squirmed a little at his praise.

"Not to disrupt the introductory pleasantries," Xalphed said to Dovex, "but are the circumstances of our planned journey truly that dire?"

"Indeed," Dovex answered. "Tynantri, my blade-sister, informs me of a most worrying development beyond the Bone Sea. We must leave by tomorrow at the latest. Having heard your accounts, I wish we could accompany your friends, but it cannot be so."

"What's the nature of your journey?" Mylth asked.

"I'm sorry, but I shouldn't speak more of it now, not even to you, good companion," Dovex answered. "Perhaps when we have all completed our tasks and returned, we can tell one another of the great deeds we've performed, as in the old days!"

Mylth offered only a slight shake of his head. "Typical dragon, always secretive, yet always boasting!"

Dorinen's eyes widened. "Dragon?"

Dovex gave her an affirming nod. "Indeed, my lady, though I wear a man's form, it is not my only state."

"The question is," Xalphed interrupted, holding up one finger, "are they dragons who take the shape of humanity, or are they humans who are gifted with a remarkable form?"

Dovex shrugged. "I'm not sure we even know anymore."

"Dovex is a Kyrminion, a Flamedrake," Xalphed added with admiration, and more than a little delight at Dorinen's shocked expression. "The Kyrminion dwell in the mountains of western Maradhoor and are among the rarest and oldest of their kind in the world."

Dorinen's mind again reeled at what Xalphed and Mylth must have seen and experienced in their lives. "We could certainly use you on this expedition," she added, a pointless declaration that again made her want to hold her tongue entirely.

Dovex patted Mylth on the back. "I trust Gwyndon here can take care things, and I have no doubt you are a most capable warrior. You shall do well."

"I wish I shared your confidence," she replied. "After my misadventure with the Vordlai, I'm not so sure anymore."

"It is as it must be," Mylth said after an awkward silence. "We'll leave tomorrow morning, once we've equipped ourselves properly. The sooner we can reach the keep, the better."

"I'm sure we can provide most of what you will need," Wyath offered. "It will save you the arduous task of seeking out merchants and vendors tomorrow, and having to bargain. Not a luxury for those in a hurry!"

Xalphed concurred, and Dorinen and Mylth accepted her offer with gratitude. After Wyath announced she would go to the storage rooms to gather said supplies, Xalphed offered to accompany her and help. She would have none of it.

"You have your library to attend to and clean up," she said with mock annoyance, waving him away. "Leave me in peace!"

Scolded, the humbled sage yielded, and Wyath went on her way.

But something still nagged at Dorinen, and she decided to speak her mind, afraid that if she held her tongue, she might never resolve it.

"Master Gornio," she said as he and Mylth cleared away the books and scrolls. "Why does Ramwin, or that form of the Sarvethar anyway, appear as such a, well, a foolish fop?"

At once she regretted her words, fearing she'd offended the sage, and possibly all of creation. To her surprise, Xalphed let out a great guffaw, and Dovex joined in. Mylth, however, scowled, gathering a few books and exiting the chamber. She worried that her question had upset him.

Xalphed cleared his throat. "Let's just say the cosmos has a sense of humor, one we may not always understand, or even appreciate, but it's there, nevertheless. You know how sometimes it seems like things were meant to go wrong? Or some bizarre coincidence happens that must surely be impossible? Ramwin embodies that chaotic, random, even silly element, perhaps to an extreme, but as such, he is as important as Enwyonn, Teuvell, Eladra, Koliserr, Doa, Ayssa, or any other aspect of Spirit that the peoples of this world have perceived and venerated. I assume you've met Rowana?"

"Rowana?"

"Ramwin's feminine form?"

"Oh, um, yes, I did, for a brief moment. He, er, she, transformed back at once, though."

Xalphed chuckled, quite pleased to hear it. "Well, without that spark of mischief in life, what would be the point?"

Dorinen didn't see the humor. "But why do none of the scriptures and chronicles speak of him being so… ridiculous?"

Mylth returned, gathering more books and ignoring their conversation. His obvious irritation distracted her.

Xalphed let him be and continued. "All too often those ancient tomes were written by tired, grumpy old souls who forgot how to laugh, or were so filled with deluded reverence that they feared their own shadows as much as offending the Land Spirit, and so they idealized Ramwin. But one cannot 'offend' the land except by desecrating it, as the Eral-savat does now. You've been blessed by meeting the Sarvethar, in whatever guise it chose to appear to you, and you have seen beyond to a portion of reality most mortals never get to behold. You're one of the lucky ones."

Mylth tensed at these words as he gathered together a collection of scrolls. He left the room again with them in hand, his determined expression betraying something far darker than the good humor of Xalphed's declarations. Perhaps anger, or even grief.

Eight

"It was no coincidence that Izznil entrusted you with that gem and its power, whatever it may mean or what it actually does," Narick said as he and Andra watered their horses in the rolling countryside east of Lake Charthan. "Somehow, he knew you would play an important role in what is to come, and the Spirit has proven this by Ramwin's words."

After leaving the inn, they rode for as long as they dared, stopping only when their horses needed rest and they were both too exhausted to continue the journey. Since Narick's remarkable encounter with Ramwin, the mood had lifted, yet the more Andra heard, the more she worried, especially if the Sarvethar considered it important enough to manifest directly to a mortal.

"I want to believe I need this gem, whatever it is," she said, "but I'm not convinced. It feels like an enormous responsibility, and it's weighing heavily on me. Right now, all I want are the comforts of my home. I miss my parents, as much as they can annoy me, and I just want to see my village and forget about everything else."

"It's easy to retreat when problems arise. Believe me, I know," he said. "But we don't have that luxury, I'm afraid. You'll be up to the task, whatever we might face. Have some faith in yourself, my friend."

Andra stood and paced with her hands clasped behind her back. "If something awful is coming," she said, "I need to know my family and friends are safe, and I'll also need their support. Of course, my father won't approve and will try to interfere and 'protect' me, or even forbid me from doing whatever it is we have to do."

"Well, like it or not, that's one of his responsibilities."

She managed a weak smile. "Father trying to defy the Sarvethar to his face would be a sight!" Her smile faded. "Actually, if anyone in the world could do it, he could."

Narick chuckled. "That he could."

She stopped pacing and allowed herself a moment to imagine the amusing scene.

"How has your sleep been?" he asked.

She sat again on the grassy ground. "Reasonable, I guess. But the dream… it's happening every night now, since I played my flute by the tree. She's there. I can almost see her, but each time I'm about to catch a glimpse of her face, she retreats into the mist and shadows again."

"Does she say anything to you?" He offered her a piece of thick brown bread.

She took it and paused before taking a bite. "I hear words, but I don't understand them. And then she's gone again, like she's being pulled away. Who is she?"

"Whoever she is, I do believe she's someone real. But what her intention is, I cannot say."

"She's imploring me to come to her. It's inviting, as if she's surrounded by goodness and love, but she needs my help. Yet the place where she is, it's somehow ancient, unnerving." She finished off the rest of her bread.

"Well, allow yourself to be open to her but alert me at once if you sense any threat." He stood. "We should go soon."

Summer's heat sometimes became oppressive on the journey, though the air began to cool as they pressed farther north, staying far from the Buragon Moors. Once, Narick detected a band of Iron Rose brigands when scouting ahead, so the pair rerouted to avoid them, leaving the road and traveling directly across the countryside. But taking a more clandestine route overland meant they found themselves at the banks of the River Cryth without safe crossing.

"The river is too swift, deep, and wide to ford safely, even on horseback," Narick grumbled, glancing downstream. "I hadn't considered this before."

Andra assessed the rushing water and the river's width. As an idea dawned on her, she drew out her wooden flute.

"What are you doing?" he asked.

"I have a hunch."

He raised an eyebrow. "A hunch?"

"Do you remember when I helped myself to that bottle of fine wine back at the Hall? I used a new melody to bring it to me."

"Yes, and you played your lyre, correct?"

"I did, though I'd rather not use it again until I know more about what the gem does. But I can duplicate the melody easily enough on the flute."

His eyes narrowed. "To what end?"

She shrugged, recalling the tune, and working out the finger placement on her instrument. "I'm reasonably sure this will work."

"Reasonably sure of what?"

Ignoring his question, she put her flute to her lips and played the melody she'd perfected in the Hall of Song, repeating it a few times to get comfortable with it. It sounded lighter, more uplifting with a woodwind. And uplifting was exactly what she had in mind.

Lady, please let this work.

She focused on Narick with a soft gaze. As she increased her concentration, Narick and his horse floated off the ground.

"Damn it!" he cried out. "What are you doing?"

She ignored his misgivings and stayed with her song, willing them both across the river to set down safely on the other side. The expression on his face gave her more than a little satisfaction, but at least his horse appeared unbothered by the whole affair.

Once she settled them on the far bank, Narick too stunned to say anything, she proceeded to bring herself and her own mount across. After a successful landing, she put her flute away nonchalantly and grinned at her dumbfounded friend.

"It's a simple magic, really," she explained. "I did learn *some* things in my time at the college! As long as I play the tune and focus, the objects of my concentration will remain in the air and go where I will them to. I used the new melody I wrote, but with the same intention to move us. I assumed that would be enough to move much more than a small wine bottle."

"You assumed?" Narick almost choked on his words.

"Of course, with the flute, if I run out of breath..." She grinned, lifting her hand and dropping it in an exaggerated thud to her thigh.

"Then I hope your concentration never wavers," he answered.

"You've never seen me do that before, have you? I mean beyond moving small objects."

He shook his head, patting his horse. "And I'd like not to again for some time."

She mulled over the implications of her accomplishment. "No doubt there's some sacred directive about keeping that spell secret from outsiders or something. Ah well." She sighed with mock guilt, one hand over her heart. "There's *another* rule broken. The college probably won't have me back now!"

Narick shook his head in mild disapproval and turned away.

"It's very useful," she called out to him as they rode from the river. "Once, I fended off the unwanted advances of a drunk Mirysian mercenary in the yard of a tavern. I played a simple song, and the poor fool found himself shoved through the gate and dumped on his backside in the street."

"I'm just grateful you're on *my* side," he called back, urging his horse onward.

* * *

The next morning, they entered a terrain of low rolling hills, the green grass tinged with a hint of silvery-grey. Small forests intermixed with farms throughout the rolling foothills of the Grey Wolds, delighting Andra as she caught sight of them.

"We're only a day and a bit away." She took a deep, satisfied breath. "There's something about this place that always gets to me. The air smells different, and the earth itself… I have a connection with it, and not only because I grew up here. It's like the land *wants* me to be here and misses me when I'm gone. Does that seem mad?"

"No more so than many other things I've seen recently," Narick answered. "A feeling of being bonded to your home is far less remarkable than, say, lifting a man and his full-sized horse in the air with a flute and throwing them across a damned river!" He mock-scowled, and she burst out laughing.

"Look!" she pointed. "Starhold Winery!"

On a hill in the distance, she saw a beloved site: the stone walls of the ancient vintner, towering over the landscape, a fortress not of defense, but of delight. Fruit trees adorned the sloping hillsides, and farmers tended to them, preparing for their upcoming harvest.

"I'm already anticipating my first goblet of Starberry wine," she said, imagining the tangy sweetness she'd been denied for far too long.

"I don't believe I've ever had the pleasure."

"Oh, well, you're in for a treat! The berries grow properly only in these parts, no matter what some people might tell you. I promise you the flavor is unlike anything you've tasted before. Only true Starberry wine from the Grey Wolds can give you drink woe of appalling proportions the morning after."

"I assume you're more than a little acquainted with its effects?" He rubbed one temple as if in pain.

She smiled knowingly and rode on.

"Let's at least take some rest before our task presents itself," he said late in the afternoon. "I'm tired, and I'm sure you are too."

She nodded. "Sleep in a real bed and cooked food will be a blessing for both of us, but we won't reach Meln until tomorrow at midday. I know a lodge not far from here where we can stay the night. We'll just be two of any number of passersby."

The summer shadows hadn't yet grown long when they arrived at the lodge in question. Andra let out a contented sigh. "It's been a while since I've been here. Nice to see nothing much has changed." She dismounted and turned to Narick. "It'll be more than enough for our needs."

And indeed, she spoke the truth. They enjoyed a quiet and simple meal in a side room to the main dining hall and planned to turn in early.

"Believe it or not," she said, downing the last of a goblet of the local wine she so loved with satisfaction, "I want to set off as early as possible tomorrow."

"If I hadn't heard you say so," he teased, "I would never have believed it. And yes, you are correct, this wine is excellent."

"I told you!" She beamed with pride. "But don't let it go to your head, in a very real sense."

"I'm not the one who needs to worry. One small goblet is more than enough for me."

"You monks and your boring self-discipline," she sighed. "But all right, I'll be responsible just this once and call it an evening with only one cup. Alas, what a sad life I lead!" She held one hand to her forehead in a melodramatic fashion.

"No please, have another," he gestured, eyebrows raised. "Nothing would amuse me more than being able to wake you early after a night of indulgence."

"Well, I'm not giving you that pleasure!" She set the goblet on the table and stood, staggering a little. "Damn! I'd forgotten how powerful it is!"

Narick made a motion as if to order a second goblet for her, but she swatted away his arm. They returned to their rooms, and true to her word, she fell asleep early and without the aid of any additional wine.

* * *

As Andra slept, a woman's voice whispered to her.

"Who's there?" Andra replied. "Why do you call to me?"

A shadowy figure appeared, as she'd done in Andra's dreams for so many nights, but she remained shrouded in mist, beyond Andra's perception.

"Please," Andra implored. "Tell me who you are. Tell me what I can do to help you. Are you in danger?"

The woman held out a ghostly hand. On impulse, Andra reached out to try to touch it. She sensed warmth as they drew near, but their hands passed through each other, as if through a stream of water. And yet, for a moment, they connected. In that briefest of instances, Andra embraced something at once ancient and youthful, nurturing and strong, but the sensation faded almost as soon as it arose.

As the woman retreated once again into the mists of this mysterious dreamworld, she whispered.

Mar shokara.

* * *

Andra awoke at dawn, oddly energized and more eager than ever to return home. The words of her mysterious visitor echoed in her mind, but she couldn't fathom their meaning. Rising and preparing herself, she soon found Narick already awake in his own room, but for the moment, she said nothing about her latest dream.

They set off in the stillness and quiet. The chill of the early morning air shook off any lingering wishes Andra might have had for sleep. The eastern sun greeted them with its promise of more summer warmth, creating dazzling displays of color and light on the dew-speckled grass all around them. They followed the main trail over a series of rolling hills, and rode beside farms, whose fields burst with crops coming into bloom.

Finally, well past midmorning, they came alongside the Wold River, winding its way from the Grey Wolds far to the northeast.

"Hmm, that's odd," Andra remarked, almost under her breath.

"What is?" he asked.

"It's nothing, I guess. I'm just surprised there are no boats out today." She urged her animal onward. "We're getting close, keep up the pace!" she called back.

By midday, they caught sight of Meln, set on the north bank of the river and nestled between two low hills. Crossing a nearby bridge, they rode onward.

"It is quite expansive," Narick remarked.

"I know, we still call it a 'village,' though it's far too big now," she bragged. "The locals like their traditions, so 'village' it is."

But as they approached, Andra's excitement turned to uncertainty. "Huh." She glanced around.

"What is it?" he asked.

"There should be at least a few boats filled with goods at the docks, but see?" She pointed ahead. "Just like farther downriver, nothing's there. The river front is usually bustling with traders by now. This is the busiest time of the day."

They dismounted and led their horses along an empty cobblestone street. Occasionally, villagers walked by and greeted them, smiling blankly, with no emotion on their faces, no real life at all.

They passed through the market area, though it might as well have been the middle night, for the lack of activity there. The few sellers present didn't hawk their wares; they simply stood about silently, smiling at Andra and Narick as they passed by, making no attempts to better themselves financially. None tried to woo them with tea or wine or entice them into their shops for friendly conversations before getting on with business. The handful of customers loitering in the market didn't bargain with shopkeepers or haggle over prices for the best deal. Several shops and stalls were closed.

"Something's wrong," Andra said, her stomach knotting. "Meln's vendors have a reputation for making a sale. The more aggressive ones try to entice buyers with offers of generous deals. But there's hardly anyone here to tempt."

She took in the desolate scene, tense and concerned. "It's never like this, never. Meln thrives on its trade. The people are robust and passionate. They don't go about like walking corpses."

Narick murmured in response.

"What? What is it?"

"What you said, 'walking corpses.' It makes me uneasy. Where does your family live?"

"Not far. Three cross streets beyond and toward the river."

They made their way out of the market and into the equally silent streets beyond to Andra's home, a large, three-story half-timber house with a thatched roof, set apart from its neighbors.

She took in a disconcerting sight. "Something's wrong."

The normally lush front garden had started to go brown, with scraggly weeds winding through the once neatly trimmed rose bushes. The topiaries now grew in misshapen ways, tendrils of branches jutting out of what should have been manicured spheres, while short stubs of grass grew from neglected flower beds.

Andra almost gasped in disbelief. "My mother would never allow the garden to become like this. It's her pride and joy. Narick, what's happening?"

He shook his head. "I don't know, my friend. We should speak to your father at once."

Uncertainty gnawing at her, she secured her horse to a hitching post, bid Narick to do the same, and motioned him to follow her in. The front door was unlocked, and led directly to her father's office, with an array of scrolls, parchments, books, and ledgers neatly arranged on the old wooden shelves lining the room.

But he wasn't there.

"This makes no sense," Andra said. "Normally, he'd be hunched over some work, meticulously checking that he'd correctly copied every pen stroke, every punctuation mark." She shuffled though some papers on his desk: tax records, legal documents, receipts for traders as far away as Tenaeth, but they remained unfinished, even messy. His immaculate handwriting gave way to an undecipherable scrawl.

Narick put a steadying hand on her shoulder.

"Father?" she called out. "It's me, Andra! I'm back! I'm home!"

A long moment later, the door opposite them opened, and a thin man with greying dark brown hair, and at least two days of an unshaven face, entered. Andra allowed herself some relief that his quirky, old-fashioned clothes—a waistcoat over a blue-grey shirt with knee-length trousers, long pale socks, and simple leather shoes—hadn't changed since she'd last seen him.

However, his messy hair was far from the immaculately-groomed style he normally sported. His drawn and haggard face suggested he hadn't slept in days.

He observed them for a moment through a pair of gold, wire-framed glasses, his smile absent and insincere.

"Greetings, daughter," he said in a soft voice. He took her hands in his own and leaned forward to kiss her on the forehead. Andra threw a quick headshake at Narick to inform him things were not at all as they should be.

"Father," she answered in an unsteady voice, "you must remember Narick Yerral, whom you met in Tenaeth, all those years ago? He's journeyed with me from the city." She hoped her false cheerful mood might inspire him to react in a more typical manner, perhaps hugging her and expressing his joy. But he did nothing of the sort.

"Odakh, sir," Narick said as he clasped the older man's hand. "It is a pleasure to see you again." Maybe he could shake some sense and life into him?

But Odakh returned his greeting with an absent voice. "A true pleasure it is to see the monk of Shylan Dar again. You are most welcome in my house. All are." He sounded like he'd just woken up, but with no emotion, and even a slight slur to his words.

"Is mother about?" Andra asked, trying to maintain the facade of normality and hide her nervousness. But her heart raced, and she didn't know how long she'd be able to keep up her pretense.

"Soon," Odakh replied. "Soon we will all see her. Soon everything will be perfect. It is so simple, so true. All will be perfect." He looked away, as if enraptured by the support beams in the ceiling.

Andra tried to ward off her tears, knowing she now needed to get away from him. A wave of light-headedness washed over her, and she put one hand on his desk to steady herself. Regaining her composure, she barged past him and up the stairs.

"Mother?" She checked her parents' bed chamber on the top floor, and then her own room on the middle, relieved that at least nothing there had been disturbed. Her bed rested against a plaster wall, as always, though her small glass window hadn't been cleaned for some time.

She searched the rest of the house, but found no trace of her mother: no unfinished needlepoint or half-read books on the woman's bedside table, while a thin layer of dust now settled on her mother's beloved harp. It seemed she'd not been home for some time. Confused and frightened, Andra returned to the ground floor in haste and motioned to Narick.

"Father," she said, composing herself, "I, I'd like to show Narick more of the village. I'll go out with him for a walk, yes? We'll return later."

"Yes, that would be well," Odakh replied, not taking his attention away from the ceiling. "Show the Shylan Dar monk the village. Show him what shall be. The truth is coming soon, and all will be revealed. Show him." His last comments were barely more than a whisper escaping from his lips.

They left her home in haste. She took Narick's hand and led him to a small side street opening into a grassy clearing by the river, shielded by a cluster of tall bushes and a few strong oaks. As Andra eased herself down on the bank, she started shaking.

"Narick, what's happening?" she asked in a trembling voice.

"I don't know, my friend," he said as he sat next to her and held her close. "Something is terribly wrong, and I fear we're the only ones who are aware of it."

"What can we do?" she asked. "Why are they acting this way? It's like some enchantment has fallen over everyone! Where's my mother? Does my father even know?"

"I cannot say, my friend. This may well have something to do with the troubles that lie ahead of us. If the dangers Ramwin spoke of are true, we must consider it as a possibility."

She rested her head on his shoulder.

"However," he continued, "there's something about this situation that doesn't bear the signs of supernatural forces. I'm fairly certain I would sense such a presence if it were here, but I don't. And why would such malevolence choose only one village? It would hardly be content with Meln alone."

"So, what could it be?" she asked, regaining her composure.

Without answering her question, he said, "Does Meln have an official governing chamber?"

She wiped away her tears, unsure what the village governance had to do with her father's altered state. "Yes. Alderman Ternen's house."

"This alderman—does he report to someone higher?"

Andra took a moment to remember. It'd been so long since she'd even considered who oversaw affairs. "Lord Wyverdorn, why?"

"We may find answers with Ternen," he replied.

"But won't he also be under the same spell, or whatever this is?"

"Probably, but if the entire village has been afflicted, why hasn't Lord Wyverdorn done anything in response? My order has heard reports of strange happenings in this region—"

"What?" Andra exclaimed. "And you're only telling me now? You should have said something."

"I didn't want to alarm you."

"Well, I'm alarmed, anyway!"

"But I did ask you about your father not sending an escort, and you not hearing from your parents. Busy or not, that isn't like him."

"True." She dried her eyes.

"This Ternen might also be affected, but maybe we can learn something more from him, or perhaps his documents. Let's pay him a visit, come what may."

Andra's heart sank at his words, and at having to leave her father behind in his muddled state.

They retrieved their horses and led them back through Meln's deserted streets, trying not act suspicious. Soon they arrived at Ternen's house, a two-story square building made of stone, from which hung several banners of office and commerce, brightening the otherwise drab grey exterior.

"There should be a guard outside," she said. "Not that he needs it. I suppose it makes him feel more 'official.'"

They found the door unlocked. No one greeted them as they entered a small reception room. Andra, growing ever more impatient, shoved open a second door and strode into the spacious main meeting hall, its walls draped with simple tapestries.

A moment later, Ternen ambled through a slightly ajar door to their right.

He looked as she remembered him: a large, middle-aged man with a grey beard but little hair. For a moment, she feared he would rush to her and lift her into the air as if she were still six summers old; she hated when he did that.

Instead, he greeted them both with a blank stare, and bid them to sit at the table. When they didn't, he paid no attention.

"Good it is that the time draws near, don't you think?" he asked in a weak voice, unlike his usual jovial and boisterous self.

Not understanding what he meant, Andra nodded in agreement, hoping if she played along, they might gain some information. "Yes, it's good."

Narick risked a question. "Master Ternen, where is Lord Wyverdorn? We expected to see him upon our arrival."

He'd attempted a weak lie, but Andra hoped it might snap the man out of his dreamy stupor.

Ternen viewed them for a moment with confused, glazed eyes. He gave a hauntingly blank smile. "Wyverdorn is with the master, preparing for the arrival, of course. The truth is coming. Stay here, and you shall see. It shall be glorious. With the master. Yes, glorious and wonderful and…"

He trailed off, fixated on some point on the far wall, just like Andra's father. He swayed lightly back and forth, like a reed blown by a gentle breeze.

Narick moved to go, motioning for Andra to follow him. They emerged out of Ternen's hall into the sunlight of early afternoon. A few locals shuffled by, taking no notice of them, and not appearing to be going anywhere in particular. An unsettling, eerie silence permeated the whole village. Only the rushing sound of the river and the calls of birds in the distance revealed that any life remained here at all.

Narick motioned for her to follow him out of Meln, to a path along the river bank. As they walked with their animals, he moved as if he knew exactly where he was going, even though he'd never seen any of these streets before. She could only assume he'd made a mental note of their surroundings earlier to obtain a tactical advantage.

They found an isolated clearing at the village's edge, well out of earshot from anyone. He stopped her and spoke, his voice little more than a whisper.

"I know what has befallen your village. Everyone here has been drugged."

Nine

In a sheltered dell outside the city of Tenaeth, Dorinen found herself staring at a dragon. Like so many creatures, she'd heard stories about their existence, but never dreamed they were real or that she'd one day see one. The longer she stayed away from the Dwelling, the more she found herself face-to-face with these remarkable beings, some terrifying like the Vordlai, and some gorgeous and awe-inspiring like Dovex.

"That was one of the most beautiful sights I've ever seen," she said, finally able to find her words. She worried she might cry, but managed to hold back her tears. Not long before, she'd watched in speechless awe as Dovex effortlessly transformed from a man into a dragon the size of a mid-sized ocean-going ship, his gold and copper scales glimmering in the morning sun.

After his stunning metamorphosis, Dovex stretched his immense wings and roared with delight, flashing his sharp, long teeth. "I don't know how you tiny, squishy, flightless creatures came to dominate these lands," he said in a deep, booming voice. "Why did we ever let you do it?"

"Strength in numbers, boyo!" Xalphed laughed, as he sauntered to his friend. "Too damned many of us, and we breed like Wold Hogs!"

"I suppose that would be a concern for those of you with such proclivities," Dovex mocked. "Happily, my heartmate and I need never worry about such troubles. I am eager to return to him."

"In any case," Mylth said with a broad smile, stepping forward and patting the dragon on his scaly shoulder, "the Dalaethri would turn you all into scurrying little rock lizards if you ever tried to stand against them."

Dorinen found it curious that he said "them" instead of "us." She stood aside as the three continued with their light-hearted banter and familiar teasing, while Mylth affixed a small saddle to Dovex's back. She marveled at how they took such magic and enchantment for granted. It seemed to be just another day for them, while she struggled against the tears of astonishment still forcing their way onto her cheeks.

Mylth fitted a large sack of supplies and travel gear neatly around Dovex's neck.

"Finest pack animal you'll ever see!" Xalphed declared with a pat on the golden scales of his friend's long neck.

With mock indignity, Dovex twisted his enormous head around to glare at Xalphed. "You know, I could eat you all, cooked to perfection with a breath of golden fire." He grinned. "But we must depart, I fear."

"I truly regret you can't accompany us," Mylth said. "We could use your help. Both of you."

"It is unfortunate, but it must be so," Xalphed said. He embraced Mylth, and bowed to Dorinen.

With Mylth's help and Dovex crouching, Xalphed swung into the saddle and strapped himself in. Dovex spread his glistening wings, nearly blotting out the sun, and soon was aloft. Dorinen hardly breathed as with surprising swiftness, dragon and rider became no more than a speck on the horizon.

"Where are they going?" she finally asked, turning to Mylth who watched them disappear into the sky.

"The great city of Ashyzym over the ocean, in Maradhoor," he said, without further explanation.

"And why couldn't they come with us, honestly?"

"The dangers our world faces are transpiring in more than one location, I fear. There are many perils in southlands, so I'm not surprised that something there is trying to disturb the cosmic balance, as well. At the very least, I wish Dovex could have flown us to Crythmarr," he continued, "but their task, whatever it might be, is apparently too urgent. And his presence might have cause quite the commotion for the local residents. We don't need the attention."

He turned to her. "But Xalphed swore he'd make it up to us with a grand feast after all is set right."

Dorinen smiled. "That would be most welcome."

"Provided we all survive, of course," he added.

Her smile disappeared in an instant.

They made for their horses, secured safely in a clump of trees. Dorinen noted that being in the presence of such an enormous and even terrifying creature hadn't spooked them in the slightest.

Mylth untied the lead securing his mount to an elm tree along a babbling stream. "Meladil is too far out of our way if we want to make good time," he said. "So, we'll need to journey northeast to Gorben. Then we'll cross the Buragon Moors as quickly as we can."

"Why quickly?" she asked, untying her own horse, and offering the animal a comforting pat on the neck.

His face became grim as he mounted his horse. "That cold, windswept land offers little in the way of natural protection, save for rocky outcroppings and caves, which are usually inhabited by… unpleasant things."

Mylth didn't explain further what such unpleasant things could be, which made Dorinen pause for a moment. "Shouldn't we go around them?"

"Not if we're going to make the journey as soon as possible." He gave a little nudge of his heels to the horse's haunches and rode ahead.

Dorinen now found herself far from sure about the outcome of their task, no longer as confident in her own abilities as before her ill-fated fight with the Vordlai. And now, having been in the company of true heroes, even living legends, she worried about being woefully inadequate, and again wondered why the Sarvethar had asked her to be a part of such a daunting task. The discomfort of vulnerability ate at her, though she tried to shove it away when it came to mind.

As the two rode in silence, she kept her concerns to herself. She'd seen Mylth open up and exude warmth and humor in the presence of his old friends, but now he closed himself off once again. He was polite enough, to be sure, but he showed little interest in being social, much less being friends.

Frustrated, she rode ahead for a while, on the pretext of scouting the terrain. If he wouldn't to talk to her, she had no reason to ride alongside him.

Sometime after midday, they came to a fork in the road, with the eastern path heading toward their destination.

"I wish we could avoid passing through Gorben, but we have no choice," he grumbled. "It's the last place we'll be able to obtain food and supplies until we reach Crythmarr. I doubt it's changed much in the last seventy summers."

"What's so unpleasant about it?" Dorinen asked.

"Let's just say that during my last visit, several outlaws discovered the hard way that trying to rob and murder a Dalaethrian put them on the wrong side of defensive magic, permanently."

His answer brought Dorinen no comfort.

* * *

After finding a sheltered clearing off the road, Mylth built a small fire with sticks he'd gathered nearby. Sitting on a fallen tree, the two ate a simple travelers' meal of dried meat and hard bread.

Dorinen turned to him after another awkward silence between them. "Thank you," she said.

"For what?" he asked, breaking a bread roll in half and offering a piece to her.

Taking it, she gestured to their surroundings. "For this. It does my heart and soul good to be among trees again. I can draw on their presence, their inner strength. It's like drinking clear water after days of thirst."

"You are most welcome. We won't see any large woodlands before Cernwood, I'm afraid," he said. "It might help you to calm yourself, to focus. You're already at home here, more alive. I can sense the bond between you and these trees. It's lovely to behold."

Dorinen's cheeks flushed and she found herself unsure how to respond. She looked away, and couldn't bring herself to meet his gaze. She shifted about uncomfortably. For a lingering moment, she hoped he might say something, might begin to break down the wall around him, but instead, he stood and retrieved a metal flask from a pack on his horse.

When he returned, he sat a little bit closer to her and offered her a drink. "Dalaethrian honey wine. Rare and expensive in these lands."

"Where did you get this?" she asked, astonished.

"Xalphed offered it as a parting gift."

"I know of it, though I've never sampled it before. Thank you."

She accepted the flask and took a small sip, savoring its sweet spice. She thought it appropriate to indulge in such a legendary drink in a sylvan setting, in the company of such a perplexing and fascinating individual. She handed the container back to him, and he took a sip himself.

"Mylth," her voice hesitated. She wanted to ask the question that lingered in the back of her mind since Ramwin first told her about her traveling companion. Struggling between not wanting to offend him and satisfying her own curiosity, she swallowed and blurted it out. "Forgive my intrusion, but how is it that you are half-Dalaethrian?"

He stared away into the darkness of the trees. Dorinen regretted her question at once and berated herself. She only wanted to know because he fascinated her, but now she feared she'd made a grave mistake.

"Many things are possible in this world," he said after a long pause, not facing her. "The ways of the Dalaethri are unknown to most mortals. It has always been so. And mortals always choose not to learn more than they wish or need to. Such is their nature."

She didn't press the issue any further. Though not angry, his tone suggested he wanted to put distance between them again, he the immortal and she the mere human. She had to assume she had no right to know his affairs and history. He could only have been clearer if he'd told her to leave.

She turned away, their moment ruined. He didn't respond when she stood and announced she would take the first watch. After walking off some distance into the treedark, she glanced back to see him still lost in thought. She sat under a large oak some distance away, alone in her regret and frustration.

* * *

She awoke early. The morning dawned clear and warm, even though the sun lay low on the horizon. Memories of the tense exchange between her and Mylth flooded back to her, but she didn't see him about.

She decided to indulge herself and finding a nearby pond fed by a clear stream, removed her garments and waded in, splashing about in the cool and clear water. She delighted in bathing in the open air again, in being cleansed by natural forest waters. The life force of the water nurtured her, waking her up, and the shivers its cold drops sent through her made her feel more alive and aware than she'd been in days.

That heightened sense of awareness made her jerk around to see Mylth moving into the trees in haste. Had he been watching her? Angry and embarrassed, she finished cleaning herself, and almost jumped out of the pond to throw on her sleeping shirt. She stormed back to their campsite, where she discovered him standing at the edge of the clearing with his back to her.

"How dare you!" she exclaimed.

"Forgive me," he answered, still turned away from her. "Once I saw you were in the water, I immediately left. I meant no offense."

She thrust forth an accusing finger. "What were you doing there at all?"

"I was scouting the area. I decided upon returning to refresh myself by drinking and washing from the stream. Then I saw you at the same moment you became aware of me. I left immediately. I can assure you that I had no desire to cause you embarrassment or discomfort."

Dorinen's anger abated a little, and she blew out a breath to release her tension.

"Go to the pond now if you wish," she said, her initial burning anger subsiding. "I'll stay here."

He gave a curt nod in response and made his way into the trees, never once looking back at her.

* * *

For the next day, they rode in an awkward silence. After Mylth's intrusion on Dorinen's much-needed bath, she'd been angry, but seeing as he'd hardly said a word to her since, she knew she must have offended him deeply with her prying question. She shouldn't have asked. And he shouldn't have ventured near her at the pond, even though he'd sworn he wasn't spying. She let out a long, frustrated sigh as the horse's gait rocked her side to side, accepting that the two of them would never develop any kind of friendship now.

Why is that important at all? she asked herself. *We don't have to like each other. We have a dangerous task to perform, one you chose to take on, and nothing else matters.*

Speculating about what lay ahead distressed her even more, and she half-expected him at any time to politely dismiss her and send her on her way back home. But he gave no such order, and late in the afternoon, almost unexpectedly, they arrived in Gorben.

She found it to be a dirty and ramshackle place, true to its reputation, with no happy hawkers, no bustling marketplace, no children playing in the streets. She recoiled from its infestation of scowling ruffians, assorted numbers of whom watched the pair with suspicious stares from alleys and doorways, eyeing their horses and packs with obvious ill intent. Paint flaked off the sides of buildings, while mold and rot ate at the thatched roofs. One drunken man staggered toward them and vomited into the muddy street after they passed.

She shuddered. "If anywhere could reinforce my opinion about towns and cities, it's this place," she said to Mylth in a quiet voice.

"I can assure you I have no desire to stay here longer than necessary," he answered. "We'll buy what we need at unreasonable prices and make for the moorland tonight."

"Tonight?"

"It's a risky option, but preferable to staying in any poor excuse for an inn here. The innkeeper himself might try to cut our throats in our sleep and take everything we have."

They found what appeared to be the only decent trading post in the town, a stone cottage with no adornment and only a simple sign out in front: "Goods sold and bought."

"Hm," Mylth said, dismounting and eyeing the sign. "It should say 'stolen goods bought and disposed of without questions.' I'll go in and acquire what we need. You stay here and guard the horses. Truly, guard them. There is no town constabulary here."

"None?"

He shrugged. "Who'd want to do it?"

Mylth entered the decrepit building, while Dorinen paced outside. Turning her head to one side, she sensed someone stepping close to her. She tended to the horses, pretending she didn't hear him, hoping he'd go on his way, wherever he was headed.

"Hullo there," a scratchy voice sounded behind her.

She tensed and turned to regard a slovenly man of about forty, his clothing filthy and reeking of stale beer.

"Fine horses ya have there."

She said nothing, taking in her surroundings to sense if any accomplices waited, hidden from her view.

"Be a shame if a pretty young thing like ya were to be… attacked, and those fine animals taken."

"Would it now?" she answered coldly.

"Ya needn't worry, sweetling." The man edged closer, but she held her ground, even as his stench further invaded her nose. "I can provide all the protection ya might need, for as long as you stay in our fair town."

"Most generous of you, but I'm fine, thank you. Good day."

"Now, there be no need for rudeness, lass. We have a system here, ya see: I make ya a generous offer, ya pay me what I'm due, with a little… extra on the side." He chortled, making her skin crawl. "And we all go away satisfied. Well, mainly me, but at least ya keep your life, if not your honor." He rubbed his dirty, calloused hands together and leered. "So, what say ya?"

Dorinen replied with a fast and merciless punch to his nose. He yelped, stumbled backward, slipped on his muddy boots, and hit his head on the old wooden walkway outside the trading post. He groaned and writhed on the ground, but didn't get up.

Out of the corner of her eye, Dorinen saw a few lurkers scrambling away, no doubt to search elsewhere for an easier target. She shook out her hand and remained vigilant.

Mylth returned a while later, scowling and holding two blankets and a few small burlap sacks.

"I needed to pay three times the going rate," he grumbled, almost slamming the sacks into a saddle bag. "I wasn't in the mood to argue, and any threats would have only brought us unwanted attention… what happened?" His eyebrows rose when he noticed the man moaning a few paces away.

"We had a slight disagreement," she said calmly. "And I'd very much like to leave now."

* * *

After a short ride out of Gorben, the moors loomed ahead of them in menacing silence. Dorinen scrutinized the rolling hills, covered with grass and bracken, all of it browned from the summer sun. The winds blew stronger here, though nowhere near as badly as she'd heard they could in the colder seasons.

As the waning moon rose, they were well into the Wild, but the growing darkness made their trek dangerous to continue.

"There," Mylth pointed to an outcropping of rocks with several overhangs that could provide adequate protection. "Far safer to use as a shelter than to risk going into any cave."

She raised an eyebrow. "Was that even an option?"

"Not a good one."

Securing the horses safely near the rock edge, they made a small fire and ate a meal of Gorben's stale bread and poorly smoked meat in uncomfortable silence, wrapping the woolen blankets around themselves for warmth. Mylth offered to take the first watch, and Dorinen willingly let him; perhaps he would stay awake all night. She settled in and listened to the eerie whistling of the moorwind.

Later, the sound of something moving on the rocks above them woke her. The fire had reduced to embers, allowing her to see a clear, star-filled sky. She instinctively retrieved her bow, tightening its string. Mylth crouched nearby and nocked an arrow of his own. He scanned the ridge, but a shake of his head indicated that he saw nothing. The clatter of falling stones made both of them whirl about. Dorinen caught the faintest glimpse of something coal black and oily slithering between the rocks.

Mylth swore under his breath.

"What is it?"

"Scatterlings," he whispered. "I didn't think we'd encounter them this far south. Their food sources must be getting scarce. Take great care, they're vicious, and their tails are venomous."

"I've already been savaged once by a creature's toxin. It's not happening again!" Her heart pounded as she remembered the Vordlai.

Another of the shapes scurried nearby, but she couldn't get a clear shot at it. "Five Oaks! It's too dark, and they move too quickly."

"They know we can see them. But if they're hungry enough, they will strike, regardless. Keep your bow ready." He turned his attention again to the ridge above them.

Dorinen surveyed the dark landscape, hoping to catch a glimpse of one of these creatures. Just in front of her, something hissed and let out a grotesque giggle, like a perversion of a young child's voice. Dorinen aimed her arrow but could find no target. She caught a glimpse of two yellow pinpoints, undoubtedly the creature's eyes. Her stomach tensed and she gritted her teeth.

She heard the twang of Mylth's bowstring. A creature in the rocks above them shrieked and fell back. She almost congratulated him when a shrill, baby-like cackle startled her, this one right behind her.

As she whipped around, the creature rose in front of her, its oily black hide shining in the dim moonlight. It splayed its chubby fingers, revealing sharp, curved claws, and opened its fanged mouth wide, a horrifying contrast to its infant-like visage. The barbed stinger at the end of its tail shook with a menacing hiss.

Dorinen gasped. The Scatterling giggled like a gleeful infant and lunged for her. She staggered back, managing to evade its attack, while Mylth launched another arrow, striking the creature's shoulder. It howled and spat at him. He pulled a dagger from his belt and hurled it with precision. The blade struck the beast in the throat, to a splatter of viscous blood. The repulsive thing convulsed violently and gurgled for a moment before it collapsed to the ground.

Hearing movement behind her, she scrambled to turn, sword now drawn, and confronted another of their would-be predators, sticking out its slender forked tongue as if mocking her. She swung her weapon, grazing its arm. It snickered as it dove for her, but she kicked the monster under its jaw. It tumbled aside and landed hard on the ground. Enraged, the Scatterling yowled like a baby throwing a tantrum, bared its fangs, and sprang up again.

It lunged and swatted at her, its talons catching her jerkin. Before the creature could pull back, Dorinen sliced her sword into its wrist. It cried out and collapsed, clutching the wound and thrashing its deadly tail in pain. Dorinen plunged her blade into its mouth, piercing the back of its skull with a sickening squelching sound.

She heard at least two more of them skittering and wiggling in the dark. As she waited for the next strike, Mylth produced a small block of wood from his shoulder bag. Speaking some words over it, he hurled it outward. It landed in the distance and exploded, showering the air above them with an intense yellow light so bright that Dorinen needed to shield her eyes. Two Scatterlings lurking at the edge of their camp screamed and slithered to the ground, sheltering their faces.

The light persisted, and in a heartbeat, Mylth was upon them.

With a swift arc of his sword, he decapitated one and with a whirl, stabbed the other through the chest.

Dorinen whipped around at the sound of one of the horses yelping in pain.

"You little bastard!"

Another of the loathsome creatures scurried about her mount, its tail upright and dripping with blood. The horse shook and stumbled, the effects of the venom swift and deadly. He quivered for another moment on the ground and fell still. With a hideous titter, the Scattering opened its fanged mouth and bit into the horse's side, tearing away the flesh and devouring it.

Enraged, Dorinen took her bow and shot an arrow at the gibbering horror before it could take another bite. The bolt found its mark in the Scattering's forehead and slammed it to the ground. For a moment it seemed shocked, as if it knew it was dead. Then it slumped over.

Stricken with grief, Dorinen barely saw the effects of Mylth's magical illumination beginning to fade, or noticed as he hurried back to her. He put a gentle hand on her shoulder, but she didn't respond.

"I've scouted the area," he said, catching his breath. "Any others have fled from the light." He hurried to the other horse, which stamped the ground with his hooves and knickered. Grasping the reins before he could bolt, Mylth whispered something into the animal's ear and he settled, coming to a calm standstill.

Dorinen hardly heard Mylth speak, as the sight of her fallen animal sickened her. Her legs shook and she tried to hold back tears, while queasiness bedeviled her belly.

"Some animals must kill others to survive," she said in a shaking voice, "but to see this noble steed struck down by such a foul thing. I should have stopped it."

"There was little you could have done," he said, returning to her side. "We didn't have enough time to anticipate its attack."

"I'm a tracker," she said. "I should have heard it, sensed it, something. And I should have known one of them would make for the horses!" She looked away, cursing herself.

"The things caught us off guard. You'd barely woken up. I was preoccupied with the ones I heard above us." He sounded truly sympathetic, as if trying to ease her guilt.

"It's not just this poor horse," she said, shaking her head as she turned to him. The last of Mylth's magic faded, and she could only see him by the light of the waning embers. "Since the Vordlai attacked me, I've been unsure, off balance. Before, I was confident. I assumed nothing, no one, could best me in a tracking contest or a fight. But if not for Ramwin, the Vordlai would have killed me. The terror of it is still with me, even though he tried ease my mind and take it from my thoughts. I've dreamt about that horror almost every night since. And when the Scatterling attacked, I froze. It's like I lost all my skills. That's never happened before."

"But neither the Vordlai nor the Scatterlings killed you, and you slew two of these things with skill, even courage. Your confidence has been shaken, but you live, and you triumph. In time, your faith in yourself will return. It's often our losses that make us stronger."

Despite his words of encouragement, his voice faltered.

"Come," he motioned, leading her back to their camp. He gathered piles of dried bracken and bid her to do the same. She did so, suspecting what he planned. When both carried large armfuls, they returned to the fallen horse and began covering it.

"Let's not give those wretched creatures a chance to devour our fallen friend," he said. Grasping a small bit of dried plant matter, he whispered something, blew on his hands, and a spark flew from them, igniting the dried brush. A fire grew around the horse and began to consume the remains.

They backed away from the thickening smoke, and Dorinen closed her eyes. "May you flee into the Earth Heart's embrace," she said in prayer. "By the Five Sacred Oaks, may you find your way home to Urkera."

"Those creatures won't return tonight," Mylth said after a while of standing in silence. "The fire will keep them away, and us warm."

He motioned for her to sit. To her surprise, he knelt in front of her and placed his hand on her shoulder.

"I have something that will help you sleep, if you would like it."

She nodded in resignation. "I'll need it after this."

He held up dried flower petals to her nose and said in a half-whisper, "Breathe. Tonight, you will rest well. Nothing will disturb you."

She inhaled the sweet and fragrant scent of roses and lavender and watched as he swayed back and forth. She couldn't find the voice to say anything, but after a moment, a wave of drowsiness swept over her, and she found it difficult to keep her eyes open. She swayed in motion with him, but could no longer clearly see what he did. Soon, the desire for sleep overtook her.

She sensed Mylth laying her down gently and covering her with a blanket. She slept peacefully and deeply, her soundest slumber since before the Vordlai's attack. And for the first time since then, she didn't dream of its horrific claws, the cold flow of venom in her veins, or its evil, piercing glare.

Ten

Andra covered her mouth with her hands. "Drugged?" she whispered, barely audible over the sound of the river flowing nearby.

"A number of potions and powders can leave their victims open to suggestion," Narick said, "but this one is a curious mixture. Someone—this 'master' I presume—is using it to control the people of Meln, but it also renders them docile and emotionless. A powerful combination."

"How could it have affected everyone?" she asked.

He stroked his beard. "How do people get their drinking water?"

"Mostly from wells."

"As I feared. We must locate which wells have been tainted. I'd guess this intoxicant has been introduced slowly for some time, so that no one would notice. If so, the effects would not be readily apparent, at least not until outsiders found they've been trading with 'walking corpses,' as you put it."

Andra shivered and shuffled uncomfortably at hearing her words repeated.

"I want to gather more information and try to learn what type of intoxicant is being used," he continued. "Let's take our horses and secure them away from town. Tonight, we'll return and search Ternen's hall. There may be records or documents there that can give us some clues."

"But what if this 'master' or someone else is here at night?" She flinched even thinking about it.

"You're right. We'll have to prepare carefully. When we go to the hall, bring your instruments. We may have need of them."

"I don't like that idea at all," she protested. "The gem tore off a Gro'ak's head. I won't use that magic against Melnians. They're my people, and they're clearly not in control of their own minds."

"Indeed. We'll only use force as a last resort, or against any dangers assailing us from the outside."

Andra heard his words, but focused on the river. She hugged herself, chilled even in the warmth of the afternoon sun, and wished for this turmoil to be nothing more than a terrible nightmare.

* * *

They remained outside of Meln for the rest of the day, secluding themselves and their animals in a small forest to the east. Night came at last, after a wait she found intolerable. Yesterday, she'd wanted to show him her beloved countryside, to sit by streams, to climb one of the loftier hills and spy the impressive line of trees marking the beginnings of Cernwood to the south.

But those hopes had vanished. She'd come home to a curse that had fallen over everyone she knew. She'd already prayed to Teuvell to guide her to find the answers, but so far, the Lady remained silent. Restless, she paced and wandered, while Narick sat in quiet meditation, preparing for the potentially hazardous undertaking of entering Meln undetected.

After considering her options, she pulled two small daggers from one of her bags, and tucked one into each of her boots. She told herself she wouldn't use them, but that promise didn't make her feel safer.

After sunset, they made their way on foot to the outskirts of the village.

To her relief, the streets were silent. Not even the local taverns and inns, normally abuzz with activity, showed any signs of life.

When they returned to Andra's family home, they found it dark. No lights from candles or a hearth fire shone inside. She worried again about her father and where her mother might be. She shuddered, turning to walk away from the house.

"I was born here," she whispered to Narick. "Whoever has done this is going to pay."

As they headed toward Ternen's home, Andra thought for a moment that she saw a dark form watching them from the shadows, but it vanished before she could be sure.

* * *

Walking lightly, they made their way across the cobbled streets to Ternen's hall and found that the front door remained unlocked. Narick opened it with as little effort as he could, but its old hinges let out an uncomfortable creak that sounded all the louder against the unnatural silence around them. Andra tensed, fearful of being discovered. They paused for a moment, but nothing disturbed the eerie tranquility of their surroundings.

Narick slipped inside, and she followed. They walked across the entrance hall and returned to the room where they'd met Ternen earlier. The door he'd emerged from was now shut, but when Narick tested it, he found it to be unlocked. He pushed it inward and edged his head around to peer in.

"What do you see?" Andra asked in as quiet a voice as she could manage.

"A table and chairs, some scattered scrolls and books. Very disorganized."

"Well, it *is* his study," she replied. "I mean, do you see anything unusual?" She squinted around him to find a room illuminated by what scant moonlight shone through a single large window.

The two crept into the study. As Andra closed the door behind them, she noticed a candle on the table. "Should we risk lighting it?"

"Yes." He took off his cloak and hung it over the window. "Unfortunately, I have nothing with me to create a flame," he said.

Andra drew out her flute and positioned it over the candle wick. She blew four short high notes in a simple rising scale, and a flame ignited.

"I wasn't aware you could affect the elements with your music," he whispered.

"I told you I did learn a few things."

He shook his head and setting the candle on the table, he began searching the parchments spread out before him.

"What are they?" she asked.

"Most of these writings are concerned with business transactions or accounts, tax information, and tariffs. Standard, even dull stuff."

"That's my father's hand, at least on some of them," she offered.

"Nothing here points to anything out of the ordinary."

"What about these books?" She retrieved several volumes from a bookcase by the desk. Bringing them close to the light, and leafing through them, she discovered collections of local history, surveys, and a census. But one was a book of poetry. She read through a number of the poems. Some were poor. Some were awful. Despite their situation, she forced back a chuckle.

"It's Ternen's poetry," she explained. "I've heard he dabbles in it, but it's worse than I would have assumed possible!"

Narick chuckled.

Under better circumstances, she would have reveled in the opportunity to share a laugh with her friend, but the task before them dampened her good humor. Andra's own smile faded as she continued to flip through the pages.

"Wait," she said, her eyes widening. "There's a journal in the second half of the book, dating back to last winter."

Most of the entries concerned business, but by the spring dates, their tone changed considerably. At first, Ternen's writings expressed worry, but soon he began to ramble, like the spoken babble they'd heard from him and her father.

She glanced at Narick. "This might what we're looking for."

Andra read from an entry dated to two moonspans previous. "I make note of our misfortune now, so that if anyone finds this journal, they may know what has befallen us. I have tried to resist him, but he is too powerful, and he is compelling me to do something horrible. I fear my own mind is falling under his control. This sevennight past, I began to introduce the chorlax into the water supplies of our village, may the Land Spirit forgive me! He has forced me to imbibe the wretched drug myself. I do not know how long it will be before I fail and lose my mind and identity to him."

Narick sighed and ran a hand over his face and the top of his head. "I should have guessed it would be something like this."

"What? What's chorlax?" Andra asked, clutching the journal as her throat went dry.

"A mixture of rare herbs meant for calming those who are disturbed or insane. Unless one is a skilled practitioner of the healing arts, its use can be fatal. But in small doses, it makes someone open to suggestion. Continued exposure robs victims of their senses, leaving them empty and without their identities."

A sharp chill shot down Andra's back. "What will happen?" Her voice became carelessly loud.

Narick placed a finger over his lips. "All is not lost. If the influence is removed, those exposed will recover. It may take several days, but fortunately, these small amounts should do no lasting damage. Clearly, whoever is drugging your people keeps the dosage small enough not to kill them."

"So, what should we do?" she pressed.

Narick considered her question. "Based on what Ternen has written here, he's been adding it the well water daily for some time. We need to stop more of it from entering the supply. But we don't know who this 'master' is, or what role he might play. I fear there is far more to this than simply halting the dosage of chorlax. That might be the least of our concerns. What do the later entries say?"

"Most record his worry, but his tone shifts as it goes. At first it sounds like he's resisting, but his attitude becomes more accepting of his situation, until here," she showed him a paragraph written in a particularly shaky hand, "where he speaks of this master almost reverently."

"This is useful," Narick said. "He's only been fully under the influence of chorlax for the last fortnight or so, as has everyone else here. That's not long, and it should make breaking the drug's hold easier. But I still want to know: where has Wyverdorn been during all of this? Does the journal say anything about him?"

She perused the pages again but found nothing. "You don't suppose, well, that Wyverdorn himself is this master?"

"It's an uncomfortable, yet logical conclusion," he said.

Logical, yes, but not in line with what Andra knew about him. Andra recalled meeting Lord Wyverdorn at the age of thirteen when he was in Meln for business. Though reclusive, living with his family in Cernwood, he'd been pleasant enough. Her father once mentioned that sometimes no one in town would hear from him for a moonspan or more.

"It doesn't seem like him, though," she said, setting aside the journal.

"Indeed," Narick said. "He's always been a good man from what I've heard. He has no enmity with the governing council in Tenaeth, or they with him."

"So, something bad has happened to him, too." Andra's heart sank.

"And no one's noticed yet," Narick said.

"That means whoever's behind the drugging probably killed his guards, too. And they are—were—some of the best in the region."

"We don't know their fate yet, and shouldn't guess," Narick cautioned. "For now, we need to find the source of the chorlax poisoning and try to eliminate Ternen's supply, if we can. Let's search this building, and then I'll need you to show me where the village wells are located. All of them."

"I'll try."

She replaced the books they'd pulled from the shelves, while Narick blew out the candle and removed his cloak from the window. As they walked through the room where they'd held their bizarre audience with Ternen, Narick turned his head and held up his hand to Andra. "Someone else is inside."

He motioned to her, and she stepped back to the wall, away from the thin stream of moonlight. She watched the open door leading to the reception room, and waited as Narick crept forward, draping his cloak in his hand. She followed and at his signal, took her flute out of its slender case.

A faint, rhythmic breathing came from the next room, a man's guttural wheeze. The door slid open a little and stopped. After a pause, it slid a little more.

The breathing became louder and more rapid, and its eerie sound made Andra shiver. With shaking hands, she put the flute to her lips and waited. She knew exactly what to do, which song to play, if only she could find the courage.

The door flung open with a bang, and a shadowy figure lurched into the room. Narick swung his cloak at the intruder's feet, wrapping it about his legs like a whip. He gave a sharp tug, and the assailant went down, crashing face-first onto the wooden floor with a loud thud. But the intruder kicked off the cloak and scrambled to his feet in a blink of an eye, clutching a multi-edged dagger glinting in the moonlight. His breathing became louder and more incessant as he lurched for Narick.

Andra blew the first few notes of her song. At once, their opponent rose off the ground. He flailed about awkwardly, kicking the air and grunting in rage. "The Master commands it, strangers! You must know the truth!"

Despite his distorted and gravelly voice, something about it seemed familiar, but she had to keep playing.

Narick landed a series of punches at the man's midsection and legs and ducked under the slashing dagger. A well-placed high kick to the hand sent the weapon sailing away, making their attacker howl even louder.

"Damn it! He's going to wake everyone!" Narick tried to subdue his floating opponent, to knock him unconscious, but each attack only enraged the man even more.

Andra knew Narick held back, not wanting to hurt him seriously. She continued to play, but grew weary and could only take short catch breaths, lest her captive fall from the air.

Narick slapped the man's face hard and coiled his arm around his neck.

"Andra!" he hissed as their assailant struggled against his hold. "Stop playing now!"

She ceased her tune and their foe fell to the floor, face down. Narick jumped on top of the thrashing shadow, holding him in a headlock. He grabbed a handful of hair at the back of the man's head and slammed his forehead into the hardwood floor. He groaned and went limp.

Gasping to catch her breath, Andra rushed over to them. Kneeling beside him, Narick rolled the man over, revealing his face in the faint moonlight. Andra's eyes widened.

"Meix!" she gasped.

"You know him?" Narick asked, catching his breath.

"His father is a tanner. We used to play together as children." The confirmation that her friends and neighbors were under the drug's influence hit her all at once.

Narick retrieved the fallen dagger and examined it. "This type of blade is used by assassins and the Iron Rose. What would a tanner's son be doing with it?"

Andra could offer no answer. "Meix could sometimes be a troublemaker, but he would never harm anyone, let alone try to kill them. He should have recognized me, but he called us 'strangers.'"

"It's clear he's not in possession of his mind." Narick gathered up his cloak. "We shouldn't linger. Both your father and Ternen know we've been here, and whoever is controlling this lad and everyone else might already have learned about us. We won't have time to search the rest of the building. We've already made enough noise to alert the whole village."

"How can we check the wells if we have to leave?"

"That will have to wait, I'm afraid," he said. "We can't do anything else here. There's only one place we can go now."

Andra knew at once what he meant. "Wyverdorn Keep," she said.

"Unfortunately, more answers probably lie there," he answered, keeping an eye on their surroundings. "Let's be off." He made for the exit.

"But we can't go into the woods at night."

He paused, conceding the point. "You're right. It's too risky. We'll make camp outside of Meln and wait for morning."

As he dragged their would-be attacker to the corner, Andra regarded Meix with pity. "Will he be all right?"

"His head will ache, but I promise you I've done no real damage. Far less than what he intended for us, I'm afraid."

They exited the building and made their way across the square.

"Keep a brisk pace," he whispered, "and we can be out of this damned place shortly."

She bristled at his words but knew he meant no true insult to her home. She offered to lead the way.

As they crept back along the silent street, Narick let out a grunt and lurched forward, falling to his knees. Andra gasped as a small, clawed hammer fell to the ground beside him.

"Narick!" she whispered in panic. As she knelt to help him, he gripped the back of his head, blood staining his fingers.

Hearing voices, she turned, shocked by what she saw. At least a dozen villagers shambled toward them, their movements almost rhythmic, as if they shared one mind. She knew some of the faces in the crowd, but gave her attention back to Narick and helped her still-dazed friend to his feet. As she did, a carving knife flew past them, just missing her head and clattering against the wall of a nearby timber-framed building.

"The Master commands you to stay!" one of the villagers called out.

A ghostly chorus echoed, "Stay, stay. The Master commands it! Learn the truth!"

The mindless mob staggered onward with surprising speed. Andra had no time to face them with her flute's magic, and she didn't dare use her kenlim.

She recognized Dalon, the butcher, as the one who'd thrown the blade. Now he held a large meat cleaver, and prepared to throw it.

As Narick regained his senses, Andra made a decision she feared she would later regret.

She steadied herself and drew out one of the daggers from her boot. With Narick safely behind her, she let it fly with a snap of her wrist. It spun through the air and struck Dalon in the thigh. He yelled and fell to his knees, dropping the cleaver.

"I'm so sorry, Dalon," she whispered.

The others lurched past him, oblivious to his pain.

"Run!" she commanded to Narick, and they fled to the empty market square. As they ran, she saw more blood on the back of his neck.

"You're bleeding badly!"

"We have no time to worry about it," he stammered. "To the river!"

They reached the river well before their pursuers. Its waters flowed much higher than usual for this time of year because of summer rains.

"It's not safe to try to swim across," she said, "and we'd have to get past them back there to get to the nearest bridge."

"What do you suggest?"

"I have an idea," she said with a wince, knowing how her friend would react.

"Oh no, no," he protested. "With my head spinning, the last thing I want is to be thrown across the river by your damned flute!"

"We don't have another choice!" She played the notes and lifted both of them off the ground, directing their course to the far side of the river. Behind them, the mumbling and chanting villagers came into view, lurching for the riverbank.

She played with determination and brought them both safely to the south bank.

The villagers howled but didn't try to ford the rapids. Andra saw more familiar faces, friends and neighbors, now blank and lifeless. These were not enemies, but victims.

She and Narick left the river behind and climbed a low hill, out of sight of the mob. At the summit, Narick staggered forward and almost fell.

"Here, let me see," she said, sitting next to him. Her fears were realized upon inspecting it. "It's bad."

With a painful grunt, he slumped forward, his bloodstained fingers still clutching his wound.

"You need a healer."

"I'll survive," he insisted in a weak voice. "A bandage and some hours of deep meditation to block the pain, and I'll be well enough by tomorrow." He swayed back and forth but shook it off. "It's just some dizziness."

She gave him a furious stare. "There will be no meditations, and certainly no journey tomorrow, if we don't heal this now!"

He moved to stand. "I tell you, I'll be—"

"Shut up!" she insisted, forcing him back down with a shove. He conceded and sat again, nearly falling over.

Her hands trembled as she pulled her kenlim from its case on her back. "There is a song to Teuvell for healing. It will ease the pain and stop the bleeding, but you will still need rest for it to heal fully. Not meditation, but proper sleep!" She checked the lyre's tuning and moved closer.

He eyed her with apprehension. "I'm supposed to sit here and let you use the kenlim on me? The same instrument that burned a Gro'ak's head off? I mean, I suppose losing one's head is a unique way to stop the pain."

"Quiet," she scolded, but his reminder made her all the more nervous.

Taking a deep breath to steady herself, she closed her eyes and began gently plucking the first notes of her melody. Narick sat quietly before her, saying nothing but focusing his attention on her work.

"Trust in the Lady," he said. "As I will trust in Enwyonn."

She ignored her fear and played on, forcing herself to hit the right notes and rhythms, and blocking all else out of her mind. As she sang, her voice joined with the melody, the two strands of music wrapping around one another, while the jewel glowed with a soft violet light.

As the song neared its end, she opened her eyes and willed her magic to take shape, for the sound to materialize. She nearly faltered, but despite her uncertainty, she continued.

Narick jerked back as a stream of purple light wafted from the stone and surrounded his head. A moment later, when he realized that he still possessed a head, he exhaled in relief. Andra watched astonished as the light concentrated itself over his wound. Mustering her confidence, she sang with even more conviction.

She neared the end of her song and the light from the jewel began to fade, while the remaining violet swirls about Narick's head dissipated into nothingness. She ended with a long-held note, which dissolved into a whispered prayer. For a moment, she felt as she had in the *Mirithnaa*, when the Lady of Song so lovingly embraced her.

"Now, let me see," she said, moving to inspect him. "That song will eliminate the immediate danger, but you must allow time to heal, you must…"

"What? What is it?" he demanded.

She stuttered for a moment in disbelief. "The wound. It's, it's completely gone. That can't be! This is only a simple healing melody."

Narick ran a hand over the back of his head. "It's still warm, but you're right, there is no trace of injury," he said, stunned. "You did this? Izznil was right after all."

She sank back onto the ground, trying to comprehend what she'd done. What were the possibilities of this new power? What were its limitations? She found herself wanting to explore its potential for the first time since she'd accidentally killed the Gro'ak.

"While I'm most grateful," he interrupted her train of thought, "we cannot go back to the village, and we shouldn't stay exposed out here tonight."

"You're right." She frowned. She'd so wanted to sleep in her own bed tonight.

"We can't even retrieve our horses," he added, "not at the moment. Where do you suggest we go?"

Andra considered their dilemma for a moment. "I have an idea."

Eleven

Dawn came too soon. Dorinen almost always awoke with ease and alertness, but Mylth's magic, though well-intended, made her sluggish. She roused herself and found that she ached, and stiffness plagued her limbs.

Surveying her surroundings, she spied him sitting a short distance away, cross-legged with his eyes shut, as if attempting somehow to recapture a small portion of his *Hyradenn*. So much about him she didn't yet understand, from his magical nature to his contradictory behavior around her, friendly and concerned one moment, distant and rude the next.

Close by, the ashy remains of her horse still smoldered. In contrast, Mylth's own horse stood in silence, as if unaffected by the terror of last night.

Dorinen stood and stretched, making her way over to her packs and provisions. Out of the corner of her eye, she noticed Mylth had now finished his meditation.

"We must leave soon," he said, returning to her. "We have a long distance to travel."

"Good morning to you, as well," she replied with some sarcasm.

"Forgive me," he answered, placing one hand on his chest. "I've been in contemplation since dawn, and my attention was elsewhere. I trust you slept well last night?"

"Yes, it was blissful. I'd nearly forgotten such rest was possible."

"I'm glad you are renewed, but we should depart as soon as you are ready."

"But with only one horse, how can we?" she objected. "We're too much for the one animal to bear, along with our packs." Dorinen furrowed her brow and gestured to their provisions. "Surely, he cannot hold everything."

"I believe I have a solution." Mylth brought forth a velvet pouch from his shoulder bag. "Gather all our supplies together, except our weapons."

Eyeing him with curiosity, she did as he asked.

He opened the pouch and drew out a smaller bag, reaching in with two fingers and pulling out a pinch of greyish-pink sand. He walked over to their possessions and whispered something Dorinen couldn't hear, blowing the sand over the pile. To her astonishment, everything shrank, until all of it could easily be held in one arm. Mylth took a larger sack and placed the shrunken materials inside, tying the bag and securing it to the horse.

Dorinen gawked at the sight, dumbfounded. She'd seen too many bewildering things in recent days to try to accept them all. More and more, she understood why Ramwin insisted this remarkable man join her.

"I can return them to their proper state when we need them," he said, almost like what he'd done was as natural as breathing.

The early morning clouds parted overhead and they mounted the horse, Dorinen seated in front of Mylth, and set off. This arrangement comforted her more than she'd expected, but she found herself still wary about their hostile surroundings.

What else is watching us?

* * *

By midday, cold winds swept across the landscape. Overhead, grey clouds gathered again, blocking out the sun, bringing a chill to the air. As they rode onward, the weather became ever more fierce and unforgiving. Both drew their cloaks about them, but the wind blew right through them, and they offered little protection from the elements.

The undulating hills extended out seemingly forever, the brown and faded brush monotonous and unchanging. They crossed through ponds of stagnant water and passed by occasional outcroppings of large rocks, but these did little to break the sameness of the terrain.

Dorinen kept her face lowered and her hood pulled well over her head. More than once during the morning she found herself drifting off into sleep, the effects of Mylth's spell not yet worn off. Whatever else they might have to endure here, a chance for further rest offered her at least some comfort. The rhythmic motion of the horse began to lull her into sleep again.

Sometime later, they stopped to rest the animal and eat, taking shelter behind a hill, where Mylth restored some of their bread and dried meat to its full size.

"Here," he said, offering it to her. "I'll go and keep watch."

Dorinen watched him, incredulous, as he wandered off without another word. She sat on a large rock and ate alone in silence.

Sooner than she expected, he returned, but he sat with his back to her on another large rock some distance away, taking a small amount of bread and nibbling at it as if it were a nuisance, not a necessity.

She eyed him for a moment, and decided it was best to leave him be.

"It's possible, though rare," he said to her after a long and uncomfortable silence, fixating his attention on the landscape.

Was he even speaking to her?

When she didn't respond, he turned to her. "My parentage," he said. "You asked about my mixed heritage. I'm not the only one who has both Dalaethrian and human blood. I know of at least three others in this time, and there were more long ago."

Dorinen was too startled to answer. Certain she'd offended him by asking, and given the angry and embarrassing exchange the following morning, she hadn't expected him ever to tell her about his family. She moved nearer to him and sat.

"A rare and precious thing indeed, for a human to be the parent of a Dalaethrian child," she said with all sincerity, and perhaps a bit of envy. "Which of them was human?"

"My father," he answered, fixated on the terrain. "He was a nobleman from the Three Kingdoms, in the days when they *were* still kingdoms. At the time, the Dalaethri interacted more often with humankind. It was only later that, like your own people, they retreated from human lands."

"Was it because of the Gharborr War?"

He nodded. "Partially, but the Dalaethri had other reasons. They decided that if they were to survive, they would have to protect themselves. The decision was not made lightly, I can assure you. Contrary what you may have heard, the Dalaethri were and are fond of humanity."

She regarded him with skepticism. "Truly? I was taught the Dalaethri at first welcomed my ancestors into Cernwood, but over time, relations soured between the two peoples, and yours withdrew from contact. The Cernodyn never found out why. As such, I've always been fascinated by them, and wanted to learn more. That's the only reason I asked you."

"In my experience, my kin see humans as something like younger siblings—a bit unruly perhaps—but worthy beings, nonetheless.

Mortals possess a passion and a fire, a creativity and a need to explore and progress beyond themselves. This is both their strength and weakness. It brings great achievement, but also great capacity for destruction. The Dalaethri began to feel there was enough evil in the world already, and humanity's frequent tendency to cause destruction, even if accidentally, meant that we—they—decided to withdraw from most human contact." His expression softened for a moment, though she couldn't read the mood on his face.

"My father loved my mother deeply," he went on, "and respected her people's customs. She raised me, though taught me to respect the ways of humanity as well, and I learned about both of my heritages. Nevertheless, I mostly immersed myself in the culture of the Dalaethri."

"That's quite a gift."

"I suppose. I learned Dalaethrian magical lore, which is different from human magic-casting or the divine workings of the Artisans. As I told you, my craft makes use of natural substances, of elements. Without them, I can do little. And again," he said almost like an afterthought, "since I've been revived sooner than I would prefer, my magic work is not as potent as it would otherwise be."

"But it's better than none at all," she offered.

"Perhaps."

Dorinen pondered the conflict in his words; he seemed not to be sure of where he fit in. Her throat tightened, but she spoke up. "It must be difficult for you, having to live in two worlds."

He turned, and for a moment, said nothing. "I've had a long time to learn how to do so. It's hard indeed to know where I belong, but in some ways, I'm blessed. I've experienced the richness of both peoples."

"Forgive me, but why are you telling me this now?" she asked, though she worried she might offend him again or appear ungracious for his sharing his story.

Mylth managed a slight smile. "We've fought together, protected each other, so you deserve to know. You are brave and kind, Dorinen."

She glanced down, waving away his compliment. "I did what was needed." But inwardly, she enjoyed a moment of satisfaction, briefly darting her eyes back to him.

"No, you've shown great resolve in the challenges you've faced so far," he continued. "You came to me at the request of the Sarvethar, not knowing what awaited you. You've taken on this burden willingly, already seen horrors no one should. It must be overwhelming."

Her momentary pride melted away as his words reminded her of what she'd already faced and barely survived. She shook off a shudder. "Overwhelming is a mild way to state it. I sometimes still wonder if I'm dreaming this whole affair. How can any of it possibly be real?"

He turned his attention back to the horizon. "I truly wish it weren't. Yet, when the Scatterlings attacked, you fought with determination and skill, despite what you might think of yourself. From what you've told me of your encounter with the Vordlai, I'm sure the same could be said of you then. Ramwin chose well in sending you to me, and I'm thankful you are on this journey with me, however it might end."

She relaxed a little more, enjoying the warm comfort of his presence. "I am thankful for you, too." Pointless words that surely sounded foolish as soon as she spoke them. She regretted them at once.

"I know I haven't been a good companion, and I'm sorry," he continued. "I promise, you haven't caused offense to me. My quarrel is with Ramwin."

"What *is* that quarrel?" Dorinen pressed, now less fearful she was intruding. "Why do you bear so much anger toward him? I don't pretend to comprehend his strange ways, but he saved my life, and he is very concerned, enough to risk waking you when there is such enmity between you. He must believe you can stop whatever is happening."

"I don't doubt that," Mylth responded.

"Why?" she asked.

He picked up a small rock and tossed it into the bracken. "Because

I was important in the effort to end the previous manifestation of the Eral-savat."

"What?" She'd not expected that answer. "How?"

He took a deep breath. "The War of Gharborr began as a territorial dispute between nations, but grew into a horrid conflict between the peoples of this world on one side—human, Tveor, and Dalaethrian—and the creatures of the Underplanes on the other. A war across dimensions."

He regarded her again with a disquieted expression. "Despite its power, the Land Spirit is still vulnerable to chaos and disturbances in the balance between order and disorder. Normally, such chaos serves a purpose, allowing for change and growth. But if that balance becomes too upset, whether through the actions of evil men, or by the collective will of the denizens of the Underplanes, terrible destruction can occur."

Dorinen struggled to take it all in. "Why do the Underplanes exist at all? How can the Spirit contain such evil? Cernodyn priests and Shylan Dar monks try to explain it, but their answers always feel riddled with false confidence and wishful thinking."

"Those shadowed realms exist simply because they must," Mylth answered. "In the end, the free choice of every being is its own, even though we are each a part of the whole. The Spirit does not act. It simply is. We must be the doers of all things. The choice is ours. Some choose wisely, some do not."

"Do you mean nothing compels us to do good?" Dorinen pressed.

"Exactly," he responded. "Goodness, truth, justice... none of these can be forced on anyone. If a being doesn't believe such things in its heart, then all the philosophy, proselytizing, cajoling, and punishment in the world cannot make them."

"So why follow the path of goodness at all? Why seek to help and protect others?" Dorinen countered.

"You already know the answer. Look at the situation we now face.

When the balance is tipped too far in favor of chaos, destruction reigns. The fabric of our existence cannot contain such intense forces. When evil intentions are deliberately focused through evil actions, the result is an abomination like the Eral-savat. Balance is the most important factor in universal harmony, not the total elimination of evil."

"So, beings can choose to be evil, as long as there aren't too many of them choosing to do it at any given time," Dorinen answered with a tinge of sarcasm.

"That's a simplification, but yes, essentially you are correct."

"And what happens when too many *do* choose evil?"

"Then the Spirit will strive to restore the balance, though doing so risks creating an even greater chaos."

"Ramwin is a means of its intervention," Dorinen said, realizing a little more of what was at stake.

Mylth stood, and began to pace. "The Sarvethar has many manifestations in this world, and Ramwin is only one of them." He focused on his feet as he spoke.

"It doesn't seem right," she said. "Are we expected to tolerate a certain amount of evil just to make sure that some 'cosmic balance' is maintained? Should I allow a child to drown or not protect an old woman from attack with the idea that it serves some higher purpose? Is this the way of the universe?"

"Of course not," Mylth answered, regarding her and shaking his head. "Chaos and evil are two different concepts. Change and disorder can be good or bad, or anything in between. When your people walked away from the so-called civilized lands, it was a supreme act of free will, of change. From that chaotic act, you created a new order, one suited to your temperament. But you didn't conquer another people to do so, nor did you destroy the forest. Do you understand the difference?"

"I think so." She stood, shaking out some stiffness from the morning's ride. "So, what about Ramwin?"

"Ramwin represents the subversive, even playful, element of the

Land Spirit. As Xalphed said, he is the sense of humor of the cosmos, the divine fool, if you will. He is chaos in human form, but positive chaos, for the good of the world. Though I no longer walk his path, and hold a great deal of personal enmity toward him, I still acknowledge his vital role."

But for all his talking, he'd still avoided her initial question, and now she needed to know. "If he's so important, why do you bear him such ill will?"

The clouds on the northern horizon threatened rain, mirroring the darkening mood she sensed in him.

"We should be on our way soon," he said. "I'd prefer to walk the horse for a while."

* * *

They trudged onward under a light rain, finding muddy paths where they could. Mylth led the horse by the reins, while Dorinen walked ahead of him.

"It began after the human kingdoms went to war," he said, breaking the silence.

"What?" She looked back at him.

"You asked about my quarrel with Ramwin. 'Gharborr,' by the way, means 'devastation' in Old Yrthryrian, and there is no more apt word. Yrthryr claimed ancestral burial grounds in lands held by its neighbor, Escarin. Who knows if that was true? But not even their most skilled diplomats and envoys could resolve the dispute, and small skirmishes quickly flared into full-scale armed conflict."

She waited for him to catch up and then walked alongside him. "Why did Yrthryr do such a thing?"

"Well, despite its fertile lands and wealth, Yrthryr never possessed the political stability of neighboring nations, and its leadership was often in disarray. The noble families who ruled only did so for as long as they could maintain their power. It was simple misfortune that allowed House Keradir—known for being hot-headed and ruthless—to assume control at the time, and their leader was foolish and incompetent."

"Always a terrible pairing," Dorinen remarked.

"Indeed. And since he was determined to enhance his family's glory by defeating his rivals, he picked fights with Yrthryr's neighbors. The situation became worse when his son, Ananbrom, began putting his study of darkened, arcane magic into practice. Sorcery and politics are a dangerous blend."

"Of course. Ramwin told me about him."

"Good. Well, when he resurrected the Arltorath—I assume Ramwin mentioned them too—they took control, and Yrthryr and its people were destroyed in the earth ravage within a moonspan. Everything that House Keradir schemed, fought, and murdered for was gone. Even the land itself. And the Vordlai did much of the initial slaughter. They heralded the coming of the destructive force, and its presence allowed them to kill and feed as they wished. The fools of Keradir realized they were too late in asking other nations for aid, and though the relief forces tried to retreat and regroup, most of them didn't survive. The Vordlai killed them as they fled. They ate my own father alive."

Dorinen stared him in horror, though his own mood didn't change. She shivered at the mention of the Vordlai.

"I was young, only thirty-two springs, barely more than a child in Dalaethrian reckoning. And those of us who survived, together with the Tveor of Stimus-hodd, knew we needed to act if we wished to save ourselves. Our remaining forces battled foes whose minds were enslaved by the Eral-savat, such as Gro'aken and humans who'd been seduced by the power that evil offers. Knowing that arrows and swords would do little against the Vordlai, much less the Eral-savat, a select few of us, human mages and Dalaethrians, called upon our own magical powers.

The Sarvethar revealed himself to us. I implored him, begged him, to intervene.

"But he didn't," Dorinen interjected, crunching browned bracken under her feet.

He shook his head. "I was younger and headstrong and didn't understand. Why reveal himself to us if he wouldn't aid us?"

"So, if he didn't help, how did you defeat the Eral-savat?"

"Ramwin showed me a way through the danger we faced. So, I, other Dalaethrians, and the mages trekked to the Mountains of Sorrow, where we managed to turn the Arltorath's own sorceries against them. We robbed the Eral-savat of enough of its power and we sealed it away, deep beneath the ground where it first erupted. Others among us banished the Arltorath yet again. And Denderath and the human magic casters locked away most of the Vordlai, trapping the few remaining in an eternal sleep."

"Those are the ones in Cernwood?"

He nodded, and Dorinen sensed regret in his expression. "We believed the seals and wards holding them would last forever, but, apparently, we were wrong."

"So." She hesitated. "If you were able to defeat the Eral-savat and lock away the Vordlai, and Ramwin told you how, why do you harbor so much anger against him?"

"Because he cheated, like he always does."

She stopped. "How was that cheating?"

Mylth stopped too, and turned to her, his annoyed expression tinged with spite. "He made us do his work for him. He wouldn't save us from the very evils he allows, so he simply told us how to do it ourselves. It's nothing more than duplicity. More often than not he achieves his goals in violation of the grand cosmic order he claims to uphold."

Frustrated, Dorinen pointed a finger at him. "But you yourself said all beings must choose, that good can't be forced on them. Doing so would make us no better than those that side with evil. He tolerated the outrage for as long as he could, before showing you the way to preserve the balance." She took a hesitant step forward. "You didn't have to do what he told you. You freely chose good over evil, and you won."

Mylth face flashed with anger. "What choice did I have? Any of us? To do nothing meant certain death for all living things in this world."

"And your anger at the idea of that death shows you'd already made the decision to uphold order and goodness long before Ramwin ever appeared to you," she retorted, irritated at his condescending tone. "You knew your way of life was worth preserving. He knew that too, or he wouldn't have chosen you, then as now."

Mylth gave her a dismissive wave, a pained expression on his face.

"There's more. More you're not telling me."

He almost smiled. "I suppose I can hide nothing from you. My mother, Elabryll, journeyed with us to the Mountains of Sorrow. She insisted, saying Ramwin had favored her, as well. I objected, of course, but how could I go against his will, or hers? If we could banish the Arltorath and save everything, so be it. Ramwin actually came to us during our journey, offering no real help, but much foppish banter. Perhaps he was trying to lighten the mood, but he most assuredly didn't. And even without his help, we succeeded in banishing those damned sorcerers again, and in stopping the earth ravage."

"But…"

"But on our return journey, a band of common thieves ambushed us and shot an arrow through my mother's heart."

She drew a sharp breath and released it. "I'm so sorry."

"Her death was pointless." He clenched a fist. "We'd made a perilous journey, faced the Arltorath, sealed away the Eral-savat. We'd won! We'd even saved the lives of those murderers, and they took hers without a moment's thought. There was nothing we could do. What healing magic I possessed could not save her. She died in my arms."

As grief shadowed his face, Dorinen didn't know what to say. She could see his pain, even as he struggled to suppress it. She wanted to comfort him, but didn't know how, or if she should even try.

"That wasn't the end of it, I fear," he continued. "My companion, a Dalaethrian woman, traveled with us too. Kyndaeviel..." His voice softened at her memory.

"That's a beautiful name," Dorinen said.

"Indeed. It means 'beloved of the star-born.' We'd committed our lives to each other."

Dorinen tensed, fearing what he was about to say.

"As I and the others attended to our tasks, she and several magic-casters stayed behind to guard against the Vordlai." He rubbed his temple with his fingers. "As the Eral-savat weakened, the creatures became even more savage, sensing their own destruction. They attacked and devoured everything about them with a mindless fury. They slaughtered Kyndaeviel and her entire company." His voice cracked.

"Before we left for the Mountains, she'd assured me they were doing Ramwin's will. Ramwin's will," he spat. "We all believed we were doing his damned will." He stomped the ground with one foot.

Dorinen noted he didn't cry, wouldn't allow any release of true feelings. How much more did he hide from himself?

He turned again to face her. "Everything I held dear was torn from me. Do you see why I don't care at all for Ramwin and his supposed guidance? And he's doing it again. He's using you, he's using me, and perhaps others, to fight his dirty war for him, because he will not eliminate these foul beings once and for all!"

"But if he can't—"

"He can!"

"But the risk of destroying balance—"

"A risk worth taking. It would be the kind of chaotic act he supposedly represents. And it might do some good for once."

Dorinen paused, a singular memory coming to her. "When I spoke to him, there was something odd about him," she said, "beyond his demeanor. Something almost sad, like he knew he was fading, diminishing. Perhaps this revived Eral-savat exists for many reasons, but maybe it's simply that Ramwin, the Spirit, can no longer hold the evil in check. Maybe allowing for the presence of evil is destroying the Land Spirit. It's sown the seeds of its own destruction, out of a necessary cosmic principle. Maybe that's how the Eral-savat was remade and the Vordlai released."

He shrugged. "It's an interesting notion. There's an ancient legend among the Dalaethri saying the Spirit itself must die in repeated cycles, though its life span is immeasurable to us. From that death, it will be reborn from the darkness, the chaos that comes with its drawing inward."

"Maybe that's what we have to do: stop the chaos and restore order. Whatever opinion you have of him, he chose you again because he knew you're capable of ending this horror before it destroys everything. I assume you're among the last of those who was there at that time?"

"Undoubtedly."

"So, this is why we must find the keep as soon as we can," she said, holding out one hand to him. "Please. I can see now our task is hurting you deeply, reminding you of things you'd rather forget. But you can never forget. Maybe you can't forgive Ramwin, but there's much more to this affair than your quarrel with him. Surely you see that."

"If I didn't," Mylth answered coldly, "I wouldn't even be here talking with you."

Dorinen bristled at his sarcasm. "I'm only trying to help."

"I did not ask for help."

She fumed. "You are not the only one who has suffered loss, Mylth Gwyndon! My parents were murdered too. By the Iron Rose, when I'd passed only five summers. Thieves, like those who killed your mother. My own mother and father were murdered for supplies as they returned to Cernwood from Tenaeth. I watched them die in front of me!"

He looked away, ashamed. "Forgive me, I didn't know."

"When the Vordlai attacked my dwelling, it killed a man dear to me, one who helped raised me after they were gone." She choked back her tears. "That vile thing ripped his heart out. It nearly killed me, and sometimes I wish it had! So you see, I can be a pitiable wretch just as well as you!" She quickened her pace and stormed away.

Later, she noticed he walked no faster, but now watched the horizon and the sun break through the clouds directly overhead, even as rain fell. She slowed and before long, she heard him approaching, though she didn't turn to face him, even as he came to within a short distance behind her.

"I'm sorry," he said after an uncomfortably long silence. "You've only expected me to be civil, and maybe for us to be friends. A reasonable request, if we're going to save our world."

She turned her head a little, but didn't face him. "The great Mylth Gwyndon? Subduer of the Eral-savat and one who dares to speak against the Land Spirit? He's actually deigning to apologize to me?" Her words were more biting than she'd intended, though at the moment, she didn't care.

"I deserved that. But I do sympathize with your loss, and I share it. No matter what I might think of the Sarvethar, I know we must succeed. I would like to be your friend, if you would let me."

Her mood softened a little. "I would like that."

She turned to him, but over his shoulder, she spied a dark shape moving from behind a mound of rocks in the distance. She took a step back and drew her sword. Seeing her, he did the same and spun about.

"Something's out there," she whispered.

Twelve

Andra and Narick set off from the view of Meln, but she couldn't shake the fear that something even more dreadful could yet be waiting for them. The faintest sliver of the moon hung in the sky as they crossed a tall and narrow bridge back to the north side of river, trudging over rolling terrain and along winding paths in the near darkness.

At last, they climbed a small hill, following a narrow path to the top. In the distance, campfires burned like beacons in the night. As they drew closer, Andra worried that whoever had made them might wish her and Narick ill will. But as they approached, she recognized designs on the colorful wooden wagons parked in a large circle around a makeshift camp of tents and other temporary shelters.

"Rajaani!" Andra exclaimed with an excited relief that her hunch had been correct.

These bands of travelers often frequented the wolds north of Meln as they made their annual migration westward to seek winter shelter. But Andra knew that while they weren't hostile to strangers, such travelers often viewed outsiders with some suspicion. The only way to find out if this group of Rajaani would let them stay for the night would be to ask.

As they descended to the bottom of the hill, she felt some trepidation. Without warning, her vision dimmed, and she stopped at once as light-headedness struck her.

"Are you well?" Narick asked. "Has the gem's magic taxed you too much?"

She shook her head, rubbing her forehead, pushing away queasiness. "It's nothing. I'm fine. Come on."

As they neared the settlement, the sounds of singing and hand clapping accompanying a fiddle grew louder. Andra recognized the sharp and rosined sound of the roballa, a bowed instrument she'd had the pleasure of hearing once during her studies, when she'd learned some of the Rajaani's basic customs.

That knowledge gave her enough optimism to forge ahead, with Narick following close behind her. Her confidence faded as two dour-faced men in dark blue leather doublets strode from the camp and blocked their way. One held out his hand for them to stop, and said something in his own language.

"I don't speak the Rajaani tongue, I'm afraid," Narick whispered to Andra.

"I only know a little," she said.

"Why are you here, *jadya?*" the other man demanded, one hand gripping the sword at his belt. Andra knew the word. "Stranger."

"We... we're seeking shelter for the night," Andra said in her own language, deciding that trying to use her limited knowledge of theirs would only make matters worse. "The dark has turned us around, I'm afraid." She hoped to present as innocent and encouraging, but the dour expression on his stubbled face remained unchanged.

"Leave, now. You are not welcome here."

Andra held up her hands. "We mean you no harm, we're simply travelers worried about sleeping in the open countryside at night."

"That is not our concern."

She turned to Narick, letting out a frustrated groan. "What are we going to do?" she whispered.

"I fear we have no choice but to respect their wishes," he said. "We should go find some trees and seek shelter."

A woman's voice spoke in the Rajaani language and they both looked back.

Andra did a double take, beholding the most ravishing young woman she'd ever seen. And Andra had seen quite a few. She wore a plain, white shift, a black vest, and a purple skirt, beautifully-embroidered along the hem with intricate, golden floral patterns. Her long and straight black hair flowed freely about her, while her dark eyes only made her more beguiling to Andra. Did Andra see some recognition in them? Perhaps they'd met before. No, that was impossible; Andra had never met a Rajaani in her life.

Andra's light-headedness returned, and she reached out to Narick to steady herself. The woman locked eyes with her for a little too long, given they'd not met, offering her an inviting smile. Andra's heart raced as her head cleared.

She spoke to the belligerent man, twice more glancing at Andra, though Andra only understood a small portion of the conversation. The man answered in his gruff, unforgiving tone.

"What are they saying?" Narick whispered to her.

"I think the guard said something about some kind of threat?"

"Well, that doesn't bode well for us, does it?"

"Outsiders bring danger in this time!" he protested, this time in Rilnaryan. Andra assumed he now wanted her to understand him. "You know what we've sensed these past many nights."

But the young woman stood firm. "A Shylan Dar monk and an

artisan of Teuvell are hardly our enemies." She also now spoke in the Rilnaryan tongue, turning her attention again to Andra, as she gestured to the instrument case on Andra's back.

Andra shot a nervous glance at Narick, who studied the woman, as if trying to gain the measure of their new advocate.

The guard stepped back with a curt nod. "Fine. If you say we can trust them, we will also trust you."

"I do." She placed her hands over her heart with a slight bow of her head. "Welcome, travelers, be at ease and join us in our gathering. My name is Jeena Karahla."

"I'm Andra... Andra Illindrien, and this is my good friend, Narick Yerral."

"Lady." Narick bowed his head in response.

Jeena pressed her palms together in front of herself, as if in prayer. "Monk of Shylan Dar, Artisan of Teuvell, your presence here honors us."

Narick put both hands before him in the same prayer position. "*Daar mathnon emballh*," he said in solemn tones, speaking the ancient greeting of his order.

"*Emballhi ne mathenonei*," she replied with a bow.

Seeing this, Andra held up her right palm, and recited the greeting of her own temple. "*Thre shiin amqu Teuvell*."

The Rajaani woman stepped forward and placed her palm on Andra's. "*Teuvell shiin persea amqo*." Her hand lingered on Andra's for a bit longer than she expected, and warmth emanated from it. A tingling sensation traveled from her fingers and up Andra's arm, startling her.

Jeena led Andra and Narick past the guards and the wall of wagons into the camp, which grew louder with music and cheerful revelry with each step.

"Visitors are a gift of the Twilight Lady," Jeena said, "though I fear in these times, some"—she motioned to the guards—"have forgotten this. I apologize for their lack of hospitality."

"No, it's fine," Andra said to assure her. "You have no idea who might be out there. But I think we came at just the right time," she added, admiring the streams of garlands arcing between the wagons and breathing in the rich scent of incense and savory spiced dishes cooking nearby.

"Tonight, we honor our Twilight Lady, Koliserr, in the *Lennai parkarra*, the Gratitude of Summertide, mindful that the days begin to shorten, and our journeys will need to end for a time when the cold air comes again."

"Forgive me," Andra said, "but how did you know who we are?"

Jeena chuckled and gestured to her and Narick. "A man wearing the traveling clothes of the Shylan Dar, and a woman with an instrument strapped to her back? One needs no magical talents to make such a guess!"

Andra chuckled as well, placing a hand over her mouth to hide her embarrassment.

Jeena led them past a cluster of fires and waved at a middle-aged man in a white shirt adorned in colorful ribbons as he played his roballa with contagious energy. Several others clapped the rhythm in complex syncopations, alternating with a skill Andra had only seen in the most virtuosic players at her college. A small crowd gathered around, some dancing in time, others shouting enthusiastic calls of appreciation.

Andra couldn't help but sway to the infectious beat.

"Songstress." Jeena interrupted her reverie. "You know well the arts of music and dance, yes?"

"Um," Andra stammered, "I... as well as anyone with my training and skills can, I suppose." She cringed at her reply and cast her eyes downward.

The young Rajaani woman laughed. "I suspect you are far more gifted than you allow for yourself."

A buzzing filled Andra's head, the unsettling feeling coming over her again. She took a deep breath.

"I'm probably wearier than I thought," she said to Narick. "Or maybe it's the gem."

"I'm not so sure," he replied in a whisper. "Maybe it's her."

"Perhaps partaking of a generous meal will help revive you," Jeena said. If she'd heard Narick, she said nothing.

She led them to a larger clearing between tents and carts, where food cooked, and various people busily arranged bowls and plates for those now gathering. Other Rajaani tipped their hats or smiled at the trio as they walked into the open area.

Andra breathed in the scents of fresh-baked bread, steaming vegetables, woodsmoke, and the unmistakable aromas of fresh beer and aged wine being poured from their wooden casks. Clusters of people cheered and clinked mugs together, offering toasts in the Rajaani language and engaging in excited conversation, all while offering the pair a warm welcome. Somewhere in the distance, the roballa player took up the tune again as Andra and Narick accepted two heaping dishes of food and two overflowing mugs of beer with much gratitude.

Jeena, with a modest plate of her own, sat with them on a pair of well-worn wooden benches at the edge of the revelry.

Only as Andra dug into her bowl of vegetable stew did she realize how much hunger gnawed at her. Surely this must have caused her light-headedness. She took a good swig of her beer, delighting in its woody and earthy flavors.

A man with snow white hair and a thick beard came over with a plate of little vegetable rolls drizzled with a vibrant red sauce.

"Welcome, and welcome again!" he said with boisterous enthusiasm, offering the plate to Andra and Narick. "You must try the *saerm*! Cabbage stuffed with uh… how do you say it?" He snapped his fingers. "Onions! And spiced like liquid fire. It scorches the tongue, but it arouses the passions like nothing else. Perfect for a lucky gentleman in your life, yes?"

Andra almost choked on her food and forced back a guffaw. If only he knew.

"You are too kind," she sputtered as she took a piece for herself. She wasn't sure she'd eat it—it might have been a little too much liquid fire for her reeling head—but she knew it would be impolite to refuse.

He beamed at her with a triumphant expression on his face. "Ha! I'll leave you to it."

Relieved she didn't have to actually eat the *saerm* in front of him, she impulsively blew him a kiss as he turned to stroll away.

This brought a series of whistles and cheers, prompting the man to turn about and throw his arms wide. "You see, you young pups? Seventy-one winters and still Ruscan must fight off the ladies! Guard your mothers well tonight!" He bellowed with laughter and a nearby companion clapped him on the back, offering a mug of dark beer, which he drank eagerly as he offered an exaggerated bow to her and wandered off, no doubt in search of others to interrupt with his good-natured teasing.

Andra sank back in mild embarrassment, but the widening smile on her face betrayed her enjoyment of the whole celebration. She also noted Narick, who gave her a little nudge.

"Not one word," she said through gritted teeth.

"Oh, I have many, in fact."

Andra returned her attention to her food, and noticed that Jeena hardly ate, but instead regarded her with a deep, penetrating gaze.

"You have recently been touched by the Spirit," she said with assurance.

Andra's jaw fell, and she quickly gathered it up so as to not show the entire camp her partially-chewed meal. Or make Jeena think she had terrible manners, which would be much worse.

"Y-yes," Andra stammered, swallowing quickly. "Narick told me so, but I don't know what it means."

Jeena made a satisfied sound and her attention stopped for a while on Narick.

"The Sarvethar has manifested to you, I believe?"

Narick shifted uncomfortably before he spoke. "The Sarvethar Ramwin indeed revealed himself to me some days ago, but with each passing sun and moon, I hold onto less of the experience. I can't recall what transpired, other than vaguely."

"You will remember if you need to," Jeena said. "In time, when it is right for you." Her eyes met Andra's. "And you possess a jewel of great power and mystery, yes?"

Andra stared, dumbfounded, unable to comprehend how Jeena could determine so much about her and Narick within only a few moments of their meeting. Finally, she found her words. "I can see how you knew who we were, I mean, it was obvious, now that I think about it. But how do you know about the gem, or the Sarvethar?"

Jeena leaned toward her, as if about to share a secret. "I am of the Ferwareen."

Andra found herself entranced as the young woman's presence, maturity, and demeanor dazzled her. And she was a Ferwar, too? Andra knew of these women who possessed great powers of magic, prophecy, and healing. Some said they were particularly sensitive to the Spirit itself.

"I'm surprised to find one such as you here," Andra replied, though she feared how foolish she must have sounded.

"We travel where we wish," Jeena said, giving Andra no indication that she sounded foolish at all, "and do not band together, save in communion with our Craft Mothers. The Rajaani are my people. My training was completed here, among them."

Narick lowered his voice. "Does that mean you know why we're here?"

Jeena took in a deep breath, her face becoming solemn. "I know there has been disruption in the harmony of the *Kontarr*, the balance," she answered, "and I worry that something terrible is not far from here. While we dance and sing on this holy night, I have also communed with the Twilight Lady to try to learn more."

Jeena's voice almost hypnotized Andra, as if each word held deeper layers of meaning that might only reveal themselves if she meditated on them. An awareness stirred in Andra's heart, a knowing of deeper truths, though she couldn't yet grasp them.

Her trance evaporated as the roballa player strolled to their bench, playing a tune Andra had never heard before. Yet something about it seemed familiar, as if she might have known it in another life.

Putting her mystical musings down to the effects of her now-sated hunger and some strong Rajaani beer, she clapped in rhythm as the fiddler played on.

Soon a group of revelers formed, holding hands in a line, and dancing in unison. As they moved in a slow circle toward the center of the camp, drummers, armed with clay and wooden percussion, stepped to the fore and knelt, taking up the rhythm and giving it more vigor.

A broad smile stretched across Jeena's face, and she stood. "Come," she said with confidence, taking Andra's hand. "Dance with me!"

Andra's heart raced at Jeena's warm touch.

"This should be entertaining," Narick quipped. "Music, you know. Dancing? Not so much."

Andra shot him a mock scowl and, still holding Jeena's hand, followed her into the open area, leaving Narick to his jibes. Musicians and clappers alike encouraged them, while the dancing line continued to add new participants, stepping in rhythm in an ever-growing spiral. Jeena turned to regard her with an inviting raised eyebrow, and Andra couldn't help but laugh. Dancing skills or not, she needed this relief from her cares.

Taking both of Andra's hands, Jeena swayed back and forth to the music and its slow and steady tempo, her gaze wandering to the crowd and back to Andra. Andra allowed herself to be taken by the sounds and senses, and she tried to imitate Jeena's movements as best as she could. It didn't matter to anyone that her attempts weren't perfect, and she soon felt less self-conscious. Or perhaps it was the beer. She even wished she'd sampled the *saerm*.

The revelry continued, and encouraged by the crowd, Andra basked in the uninhibited fun of it all. The music's pace began to grow faster, yet she found herself very much at home here. Jeena slipped an arm around Andra's waist, drawing her close. Andra gasped at her boldness, but allowed herself to go with the mood, wrapping her own arms around her partner. Jeena flashed a large smile and closed her eyes, lost in the sounds of the music and the ever-increasing tempo. Andra followed suit, and the two swayed back and forth.

"You are loved by the Spirit," Jeena said over the din of the revelry.

"What?" Andra opened her eyes, struggling to understand her.

"Within you, there is grace and power."

"I don't..."

A cheer erupted from the crowd as more people joined the line, stepping, skipping, whooping, and laughing.

Jeena moved in to speak in her ear. "I saw much when we met. Ferwareen possess the gift to join in union with the hearts of others, to see the precious part of another, each in our own way. It is a gift we cherish and use with great care."

With these words, the sounds of the music and the raucous crowd faded from Andra's awareness, and she felt as if she were almost floating.

"I know Teuvell speaks and sings through you." Jeena now spoke softly, her voice supplanting the revelry around them. "Have courage in the times to come. You have the strength to prevail, but you must not doubt yourself."

Jeena began to direct them to spin, and Andra could do nothing but follow. She feared she might fall, but as she relaxed, her steps no longer seemed hesitant or awkward. Instead, she moved as if floating through the air. The two spun around one another, and as they sped up, time itself slowed.

Andra dreamily absorbed her surroundings and to her surprise, saw that the crowd had formed a larger ring around them, some swaying, some spinning on their own, some clapping. All the while, the line dance spiraled on. A golden light rose from the earth and encircled both of them. Andra fairly floated, sure that some mystical power directed their movements.

Jeena tilted back her head, bliss illuminating her face. She held Andra tightly, and Andra did the same to her. Andra drifted away again and allowed the sensations of the moment to wash over her. Indeed, she sensed great magic here, a deep communion with the Spirit. Enchanted energy flowed all around her, and back and forth between them. Andra knew only exhilaration, feeling one with creation, experiencing all things as the Spirit did. Jeena became a part of her, as though their souls merged into one. Waves of bliss pulsed through her, as if they were lovers reaching a glorious climax.

Too soon, the music stopped to thunderous cheers and applause. As Andra and Jeena slowed, Andra's euphoria ended, but she'd never been more alive. She opened her eyes to see Jeena's face right in front of hers, their lips tantalizingly close, the warmth of Jeena's breath enticing her. Jeena exhaled with an inviting sigh, leaning in to touch her forehead to Andra's.

As the moment ended, Andra reeled from weakness. "I need to lie down."

Jeena brushed a strand of her hair away from her face and smiled. "Come, let us rest for a while," she said in a heavy breath, motioning to a pale tent near some covered wagons.

Andra agreed and retrieved her lyre and pack. Putting an arm around her waist, Jeena led Andra away from the gathering and the firelight. Andra happened to see Narick across the way, his face illuminated by firelight. He simply bowed his head to her, turned, and disappeared into the crowd.

As she and Jeena made their way to the tent, Ruscan stopped Andra with a hand on her shoulder. "I see I was wrong about the lucky man," he teased, speaking into her ear. "But you'll still need plenty of *saerm*!"

Her cheeks flushed hot and she shot him an annoyed look. He laughed, giving her a gentle pat on the back.

A new song started and the enthusiastic revelers began the celebration again.

"Please, take some refuge from the commotion," Jeena said, opening the tent's flap and gesturing for Andra to enter.

"I could use a bit of quiet right now, honestly," Andra replied, ducking in.

The inside of the tent was lit by a soft orange glow as if from a candle, though Andra saw no source for the light. The two sat on large, comfortable cushions scattered about on a woven rug. Beautifully scented incense, a resin Andra didn't recognize, perfumed the air.

"I was so alive, so fulfilled when we danced," Andra said, still catching her breath, and lying back. "Words can't express what that was like out there. I was surrounded by spiritual power, as odd as that sounds."

"I am not surprised," Jeena said, fiddling with the slender gold chain around her neck. "My dance is my meditation and my magic, and all of my life, it has served me."

"Dance is your Ferwar talent?" Andra asked.

"My *purhan*, yes," Jeena replied. "The Twilight Lady's gift from birth. Through it, I work magic and invoke visions. When I was a little girl, a Craft Mother discovered me. Her name was Ahnji, and she told me she had been guided to my people to find me. She told me dance was the key to many wondrous things like healing, spellcraft, and insights. She trained me for sixteen summers, and I learned to control my dancing, to make magic through moving my body."

"Is Ahnji here, as well?" Andra asked.

Jeena's face tensed. "The Iron Rose killed her two autumns past, when they attacked our company. We drove them off, but not before an arrow took her. Many others also died that night."

On instinct, Andra offered her hand to Jeena, who took it willingly. A mild surge of warmth again ran up her arm, like the welcome caress of heat from a fire on a cold night. "I'm so sorry."

Jeena placed her other hand atop Andra's. "It was meant to be," she answered with a wistful look. "In the days before the attack, she told me her time had come and she would soon pass on. I assumed she meant that she would leave us to go elsewhere. I did not recognize that she would die, but she knew, as I shall also know when it is my time. It is another gift of the Ferwareen."

"A gift many wouldn't wish to have, I'd imagine," Andra said, pondering what such precise foreknowledge might be like. She traced a finger over the scarlet glass beads on Jeena's bracelet.

"Indeed," Jeena answered. "But I know something else for certain."

"Know what?"

"I confess I have perceived you for some time. I have tried find you, but always you have been just beyond my touch. Only now am I sure it was you I have searched for."

"Wait…" Andra sat up. "My dreams, it's been you? When I played my flute in the forest, that was you?"

"Yes, I have been compelled to call to you, seeing you in my mind, yet not knowing your name. But when I saw you earlier, I knew you had come at last, and Koliserr must have answered my prayers."

"I, I don't understand," Andra said, dumbfounded at Jeena's words.

"I do not entirely either, but I know there is a dreadful darkness in this world, spreading far quicker than we fear. I sense evil, horrific danger. It will be here soon, too soon. But I also believe your Lady and mine have brought us together in this time."

Andra desperately wanted Jeena's conviction about them to be true. "So much has happened so quickly," she said, her mind turning again to the day's events. "Meln, my village, is in danger. Something terrible has happened to everyone there."

"They have been drugged," Jeena interjected, "and shadowy beasts haunt the night. But all is not lost, not yet."

Andra slumped forward a little, her stomach tightening. "A half-moon ago, I was a student of music in Tenaeth, with no real cares. I only wanted to go home. Now, my village is possessed, a terrible evil threatens our lands, and I'm told I must do something to help stop it." She teared up. "I'm scared, Jeena. I'm not disciplined like Narick, or even others in my college. What if I can't succeed? What if I fail and all is lost because of me? Why have I been asked to do this?"

Jeena took and held Andra's hand again, stroking it. "I do not yet know why you have been given this task, dear one," she said in a soft and comforting tone, "but I promise you that you can accomplish it. I am certain. The Spirit knows what we do not, and I believe there are others who may yet join you, help you. With the blessings of our Ladies, the power of the many worlds is yours to draw upon."

"It's so difficult to trust."

Jeena wiped a tear from her cheek. "Not all things can be seen or understood by us."

Andra concurred sadly. "I wish I'd paid more attention in my studies. I know so little, and have experienced even less. Most of the time, I was either asleep or suffering from drink woe before a morning lesson! I attended many of those instructions feeling absolutely dreadful."

Jeena burst out laughing. "Now I know why Ramwin the Sarvethar chose you!" Her joke was lost on Andra, but she smiled anyway, happy for the lighter mood. She joined Jeena in sharing a laugh, as welcome a release from the turmoil of the day as their dance.

Andra's laugh turned into a great yawn. She stretched. "I'm exhausted, in body and in heart. What I've seen today has overwhelmed me, and that wonderful dancing has finished me off, I fear. It's hit me all at once. Will you let me sleep awhile? You can wake me later, if you wish," she said. "We can talk more."

In answer, Jeena embraced her. "Sleep now, for as long as you need. Our celebrations go on, and I should attend them. But the night is yet long, so take your rest."

"Thank you." Andra took Jeena's hand again.

Jeena hesitated to leave, a troubled expression on her face.

"What? What is it?" Andra asked.

"Nothing." Jeena shook her head. "It can wait. Rest now." She squeezed Andra's hand and left the tent.

Andra sank back to the cushions, but couldn't relax for some time and found her sleep to be fitful and restless, haunted by disturbing images of her mindless friends and family in Meln. At last she was comforted by the vision of a beautiful face, no longer hidden in mist and shadow, with inviting lips, a warm smile, and soulful, dark eyes.

* * *

Sometime later, Andra awoke to an empty tent.

With a sense of foreboding, she roused herself and, taking her lyre from its case, stepped outside. The fires of the night's summer celebrations burned low, casting only a faint glow across the quiet encampment. Instead of a joyous celebratory cacophony, an eerie silence now reigned. Some of the Rajaani dozed outside, perhaps sleeping off their indulgences, but most had retired to their tents and wagons. A few watchmen here and there tended to various torches and lanterns.

Making her way to the common area where she'd danced with such joy, she saw two individuals standing by the remains of a fire. Recognizing Narick and Jeena, she approached.

"I am sorry I was not with you, but I knew you would awaken soon," Jeena whispered.

"What is it?" Andra asked.

"Something is nearby," Narick whispered.

"Gro'aken?" Andra asked.

He shook his head. "Far worse."

"Worse?" Andra's heart began to race. "You said something earlier, about 'shadowy beasts?'"

An unearthly screech ripped through the night.

"Vordlai!" Narick yelled, assuming a wide stance with his arms outstretched.

That word sent a shockwave of horror through Andra. Trembling, she clasped Jeena's hand, frantically searching the darkness for any signs of the creature. Jeena squeezed her hand hard and didn't let go.

"It is here!" Jeena cried out, pulling Andra close.

They screamed as a massive Vordlai swept into view from the dark above them and tore into a nearby tent, its horrid yellow eyes piercing through the darkness. It emerged holding the body of one of the men who'd been dancing in the line with them earlier in the night, a deep gash across his throat.

The camp broke into chaos, as shouts and panicked screams flooded the air.

"By Enwyonn!" yelled Narick. "How did it get this close without us seeing it?"

Several of the older Rajaani, shocked out of their dozing, rushed for safety, while others brandished weapons and stood close to one another, forming a defensive line.

"Stay back, all of you!" Narick commanded, but his warning came too late, his voice drowned out in the clamor.

Two younger men rushed forward with fierce determination, swords in hand. It was the last action they would ever take.

The creature lunged at them, raking its vicious claws across the stomach of the first. Horror-stricken, the man dropped his weapon and sank to one knee, clutching helplessly with bloody hands at his remaining midsection.

The second of these would-be defenders tripped as he tried to scramble away. With astonishing swiftness, the Vordlai caught the terrified man and lifted him to its jaws. His screams were cut short as the creature bit deep into his neck, snapping his head off and dropping the body to feast on the gory remains.

Chanting in a low voice, Narick launched himself at the beast, landing a kick squarely on the creature's chest, knocking it backward, and dislodging the dead man's head from its mouth. But the Vordlai regained its balance at once. It swiped its deadly claws at Narick, though he leapt out of the way with ease.

Jeena ran toward the creature, and fell into a wide stance, swaying back and forth.

"Jeena!" Andra screamed, her heart jumping to her throat.

Jeena circled her hands around each other. As she stepped to one side and back again, an orange flame appeared in her cupped hands. She blew a sharp breath, and the flame shot forth from her palms, striking half the creature's snarling face. It howled as the fire blackened its tough skin.

Andra stood motionless for a moment, awed by the power Jeena had unleashed.

Several Rajaani archers launched arrows at the beast, but they bounced off the creature's thick hide. It bellowed at them and swatted the air in front of it.

Narick jumped and delivered a powerful kick to the side of the monster's face with his heavy-soled boot. The impact knocked out several of its sharp teeth, and it spat grey blood. It fell and Narick pounded his fists on top of its head. But the creature was far from defeated. It swatted at Narick, knocking him to the ground with a blow harsh enough to stun him.

Andra desperately wanted to do something, anything. Panting, panicking, she nearly dropped her lyre, trying to remember how she'd unleashed its deadly power. *Sing you fool! Invoke the Lady! Do something!*

As she tried to bring a song to mind, the Vordlai lunged to one side of the encampment where a woman shielded her two screaming and crying children. A helpless terror gripped Andra with all the cruelty of the monster's talons. She tried in vain to recall the melody she'd used against the Gro'ak in the Eladran shrine, but in the moment, her mind went blank.

To her horror, Ruscan appeared between the Vordlai and the terrified mother and children, wielding two finely crafted daggers, glinting in the remaining firelight. With a roar he let the first one fly, and it found its mark in one of the creature's eyes. It screamed and stomped to the ground, yanking the blade out with a spurt of grey blood.

"Come to me, you bastard!" Ruscan yelled. Behind him, the woman had time to gather her children and flee.

"Ruscan," Andra whispered. "No!"

The Vordlai lashed out. Ruscan ducked and plunged his second dagger into the creature's chest, but the old man didn't have the strength to force the blade deep into its tough hide.

For one long, awful moment, the two glared at one another, then Ruscan laughed defiantly and spit in the Vordlai's face. The creature's talons dug deep into the old man's chest. Blood spurted from Ruscan's mouth as he swore at the beast, before falling limp. The woman he'd saved let out an agonized scream.

Shocked back into the moment, Andra found her song at last. "*Eiath, eiathann, demma mey, demma than...*" those words that should have summoned a simple wind, but which instead had brought fiery death to a Gro'aken. Would they work now?

As she finished them for a third time, a stream of purple light burst forth from the jewel, striking the Vordlai on the arm and shoulder. The magic did its work, even on the creature's enchanted hide, and tore away layers of its flesh, enough to show this monstrosity could be harmed. It howled as it clutched its charred, smoking limb.

With a renewed sense of confidence, Andra began the song again. Jeena moved beside her, her feet tracing circular patterns on the ground while whirling her hands, again conjuring her Ferwar flame. But the Vordlai propelled itself forward and rose up in front of both of them.

In one terrible moment, it raked its claws across Jeena's neck and shoulder.

"No!" Andra screamed. She dived to push Jeena out of the way as she fell under a shower of blood, sending her lyre tumbling away in the dirt.

Narick jumped on the creature's shoulders, knocking it to the ground, cracking its skull on the hard earth. With a swift punch, he snapped its neck back with a sickening crunch. Several Rajaani fell on it with their weapons, hacking and stabbing with fierce blows, the combined force of their weapons finally silencing the foul beast forever. The attackers scampered away as the Vordlai's body began to crackle and seethe, turning to ash.

Andra hardly noticed, shaking as she cradled Jeena in her arms, desperately trying to stop the bleeding. Tears streamed down her face as Narick made his way to her side.

"The creature's venom has already begun to work," he said in a solemn voice.

Jeena remained surprisingly serene and calm, whispering weakly, "do not weep for me, for I saw this possible future when we danced. I knew my time might be drawing near." A bloody cough interrupted her words, and Andra choked back a sob seeing the agony that gripped her. Stroking Jeena's forehead, she said through her tears, "Listen to me. I nearly lost Narick tonight when my own people attacked us. I might already have lost my family and friends. I will be damned before I lose you, too!"

She turned to Narick. "Get my kenlim and help me get her to her tent."

"Andra..." Narick started, pessimism in his voice.

"Do it!" she commanded, and Narick, taken aback by her forcefulness, did as she asked.

He retrieved her lyre, and they moved the dying woman as carefully as they could to her tent, followed by many grief-stricken onlookers. Inside, Andra and Narick laid her down gently, not allowing anyone else to join them. Making sure Jeena was as comfortable as possible, Andra slid a plush pillow under her head, focused on a single-minded purpose.

"Tell someone to bring water and clean cloths, now!" she commanded Narick, rolling up her sleeves.

Soon, she was washing Jeena's wounds, but no matter how much pressure she applied, she couldn't stop the bleeding. Narick helped where he could, taking the soiled linens and giving her fresh ones.

"Leave us now please," she implored. He hesitated, as if on the verge of saying something.

"Out!" Andra snapped. To her surprise, he bowed his head and left.

Turning her attention back to Jeena, she saw the horror of the creature's wound, three deep gashes pooling with blood. Jeena shivered and convulsed, rolling her eyes back, the venom already nearing her heart.

In a moment of desperation, Andra grasped her kenlim. She wanted to scream in rage, to sob, to do anything to release the agony churning inside her, but she kept her composure and tried to focus. With great effort, she searched deep inside herself and found the song, the healing song of Teuvell. She played the first notes, focused only on their perfect execution. The gem shone with a dim lavender light, but she knew it wouldn't be enough.

"W-what I wanted to say before," Jeena whispered, "but couldn't. I say to you n-now." She coughed more blood.

Andra wiped away tears and stroked Jeena's hair. "Shh! Lie still. I have a healing song, I can—"

"No, please," Jeena implored. "Listen. I will soon perish, but I want to offer you a gift. I have seen into your spirit, Andra Illindrien, and I believe my *mynthari*, my soul-bond, is meant for you. I am fading from this world, so let me join with you in soul, that you might yet have some small part of me remaining."

Andra refused to believe what she heard. "But… the *mynthari*. Isn't it the greatest gift of the Ferwareen? For those who are betrothed, bonded?"

Jeena stroked her cheek. "I suspect you and I have known one another for, f-far longer than this night. I have seen you—I have seen *us*—in my dreams since I was a child. And now you have seen me in yours, of late. I can offer you my gift, but only you can accept." She clenched her teeth and shivered. "I w-would never try to make the ch-choice for you, even if I could. The decision is y-yours, if you will."

"Jeena," she cried, fighting light-headedness as she tried to bring the healing song back to her mind. *Please, Lady!*

As if in response, her head cleared and a plan came to her. "Jeena, I don't have the strength to heal you, not a wound this terrible. But together, by Teuvell and Koliserr, and all that is holy, we might prevail."

Jeena closed her eyes, her breathing shallow.

"Jeena! Look at me, listen to me. I accept your *mynthari*. I choose to bond with you. Let our souls unite, so that the grace of our Ladies' magic can flow through me and be yours, too. Stay with me, please!"

Jeena shuddered and went still.

"No," Andra begged. "Jeena! Jeena!"

Thirteen

Dorinen raced back to the horse to retrieve their bows and quivers, keeping an eye on the rocks. Mylth remained crouched, his sword ready.

"What are they?" she asked, returning and handing Mylth his bow. He didn't answer, instead taking out a small green stone from his shoulder bag. She gave him a questioning glance, but he remained silent. He motioned for her to follow him.

"We know you are there," he called out, startling her. "We will not harm you, and you cannot harm us."

Before she could ask him to explain, three figures in tattered, hooded robes emerged from behind the rock formation, their forms obscured by the rough-spun, dark brown garments clinging to them. As they approached, the one closest to them pulled back his hood.

Dorinen gasped as she beheld a tangle of black vein-like growths covering his ashen face and spreading out along his neck. The same disfigurement covered his hands, and, she assumed, his whole body. The red irises of his bloodshot eyes expressed something like despair. Pity tugged at her heart despite his revolting appearance.

"Please," the exposed intruder said in a raspy voice. "So hungry."

Mylth held out the stone and the intruders shrank back in terror. They yowled and crouched, holding their hands over their haggard faces and swaying back and forth almost in unison, as if partaking in a macabre dance.

"Please," one of them begged. "Some small portion to nourish us!"

"Mylth," she said, empathy weighing on her. "Surely, we have enough rations. Could we not give these poor souls something? Maybe they'll leave, taking whatever pestilence consumes them far away from us."

He shook his head. "No, nothing we could offer will satisfy them."

As the diseased men tried to stand again, Dorinen had no time to ask what he meant.

"Eat!" one of them croaked, holding out its veined hands, as if pleading.

"Give now!" another demanded.

Dorinen flinched and took a step back.

"Give, or we take from you!" the first croaked as he bounded past his companion, shambling instead straight for Dorinen and Mylth's horse. He drew a rusted knife from his belt. "Fresh meat!"

Before Dorinen could even consider her options, she let loose her arrow, the twang of the bowshot piercing the air. The intruder stopped, as if jerked back by an unforgiving rope, her arrow protruding from his neck. He grasped at it, gurgled, choked, and fell to the ground.

She stared in shock. "I, I didn't mean to kill him."

"He gave you no choice." Mylth turned his attention back to the others, holding forth the stone again. "Be gone at once," he said in a commanding voice, "or we kill you all."

Finding her confidence, Dorinen drew another arrow and aimed it at the others.

They scrambled to their feet and ran, disappearing into a cave in the distance.

Dorinen crouched beside the body of her victim and pulled her arrow from his chest. She winced as the sharp edge of the arrowhead grazed her palm.

"Be careful," Mylth warned. "You do not want to come into contact with their blood."

Dorinen froze, examining the light scrape on her skin. "Why? What happens?"

"They are afflicted with Cho Ar Plague. These poor men likely fell ill centuries ago, as the disease swept through these lands from the east."

"Centuries? How are they still alive?"

"The Cho Ar parasite absorbs whatever sustenance its host eats and greatly prolongs the life of its victim to ensure its own survival. The infected will eat anything, particularly raw flesh. Once the parasite has attached itself to its host, the two are inseparable. In time, the victims go insane, with little trace remaining of the people they once were." He looked at the green stone. "This little rock irritates parasites and possessing entities of all kinds, and causes pain to the host. I'm glad I thought to bring it, in case we encountered such dangers."

"Why are they out here?"

"The Council of Tenaeth banished some to these moors on penalty of death. Others exiled themselves here voluntarily to save their communities and loved ones."

She stood, and carefully wiped the arrow. "Surely someone must have devised a remedy by now?"

Mylth shook his head. "Healers and those proficient in magic have tried everything."

"What a horrible fate," she said, certain that death would be preferable to whatever existence those wretched victims endured. She studied her palm again, grateful it seemed to be only a surface scratch.

"Indeed," he said, "but I suppose it's all part of Ramwin's glorious cosmic balance, eh?"

His caustic tone stung Dorinen, but at least she now understood his bitterness. It troubled her even more that she found it difficult to disagree with him. She shuddered. "Mylth, I really want to leave this terrible place."

"Agreed," he said moving to pack. "Let us be off swiftly."

"What of the body?" she asked.

"Let the wind and rain take it, as they will. What is time to the dead?"

* * *

They rode as fast as their horse could carry them, quickly putting distance between themselves and the Cho Ar victims. They pushed on even in darkness.

At midmorn the day after, the northern moors finally gave way to grasslands, leaving all trace of the twisted and forbidding landscape behind. The weight of recent days lifted from Dorinen, like unloading a heavy sack of grain she'd been carrying for far too long.

At sunset, they found a small grove of trees at the base of a hill that afforded good shelter. Leaving Mylth to tend to the horse and make camp, Dorinen searched the area, relieved to see no signs of threat, whether they be Iron Rose brigands, Scatterlings, plague victims, or things even more horrible that she'd not yet considered.

"It's hardly a forest, but I'm afraid it's the best we have right now," Mylth said on her return, as if apologizing.

"No, it's lovely," she answered. "As long as we don't have to cross any more moors."

"Oh, didn't I tell you?" Mylth quipped. "After Crythmarr and the

River Cryth, we must then cross the dreaded Cryth Moors, home of the terrifying Cryth beasts!"

For half a moment she believed him, but his struggle to hide his grin gave him away. She swatted his shoulder lightly with a begrudging smile. "Go collect some kindling!"

With a chuckle, he obeyed and wandered off with haste. She appreciated his little jest and welcomed any sign of him moving beyond his broodiness. But a sharp yawn reminded her that right now, sleep was her first concern.

After a brief meal in front of a small fire, she found herself dozing and lay down on her meager bedroll. She barely noticed him wrapping her cloak about her before she drifted off, feeling more at peace than in some time.

* * *

A loud yell pierced the silence, followed by the sounds of battle, jarring Dorinen awake. She scrambled across the campfire ashes and retrieved her bow and arrows, tightening the string in haste. Mylth started awake, drew his sword, and slung the sack with his magical items over one shoulder, his bow sling over the other.

"It's coming from beyond the hill," she said, pointing as she climbed the ridge. Halfway up, she stopped and listened. "There are four of them, three fighting one."

"You can tell just by listening?"

"Can't you?"

A man screamed. Glancing at each other, they raced to the summit and peered over to see a tree-dotted dale, with forest stretching up the opposite hillside. A thick fog draped the cool morning, hanging over the treetops.

A single Tveor warrior battled two men dressed in black who towered over him, but no matter how many times they tried, they couldn't hit their opponent. As he swung his axe, his well-worn, weathered shirt of chain mail rattled.

Dorinen immediately recognized the symbol on the men's tunics: a rusted flower covered in thorns.

"Iron Rose!" Dorinen cursed, and she readied an arrow, aiming at the one nearest to her.

"Wait!" Mylth said, placing his hand on her arm. "He's already wounded one, badly in my estimation. He may not need us, and we shouldn't announce our presence unless we must." He pointed to a third brigand writhing on the ground near to the skirmish, gripping his bleeding thigh.

"Come to me, you bastards!" their small opponent yelled with such fury that his attackers now held their distance. With a belligerent roar, he charged at the nearer of his two opponents. To Dorinen's surprise, he rolled between the startled man's legs, knocking him off balance and sending him sprawling. He stood at once and as the stunned ruffian scrambled to his feet, the Tveor fighter swung his axe into the man's chest. A muffled cry escaped him as he fell to the ground.

"Two on the ground, and only you're left, scum!" he gloated to the last remaining man, who held his distance and appeared for a moment to consider fleeing. But instead, he shouted out something, perhaps in the Iron Rose's secret cant.

In answer, five more of his cohorts appeared from behind the trees on the hillside. Three pointed crossbows at the Tveor, while the other two brandished swords. The stout warrior scowled and assessed the situation for a moment. Holding forth his axe, he bellowed what sounded like a string of curses in his native language, and charged, perhaps determined to take as many enemies with him as he could.

He never had the chance.

With a sharp whistle in the air, two of the Iron Rose crossbowmen fell, arrows imbedded in their sides. The third fell moments later, stumbling to the ground, dead before he landed. Dorinen and Mylth both prepared to draw new arrows.

The small warrior laughed, and saluted his saviors, still perched at the top of the hill. But he couldn't gloat for long.

The brigand who'd summoned reinforcements swung his sword desperately, but the little warrior buried his weapon in the man's midsection. His opponent lurched backward, before the Tveor drove him into the ground.

"Treacherous Wold Hog!" He pulled his weapon out and turned to face the two remaining Iron Rose soldiers. "So, who's next?"

By now, Dorinen and Mylth had made their way down the hill, seeing no need to hide any longer. Dorinen drew another arrow and prepared to shoot, but to her surprise, she no longer saw a target. The two remaining Iron Rose men were already dead by the small fighter's hands, and only the first one he'd wounded remained alive, still writhing and sobbing on the ground, oblivious to the violence around him.

The Tveor raised his axe and prepared to deliver a killing blow.

"Hold!" Mylth shouted as he effortlessly bounded over the rocks.

The Tveor turned to him. "I'm thankin' you and your friend for the help, stranger, but this ain't your business. This trash doesn't deserve mercy, and I'll not show it!"

"He may have some valuable information," Mylth said, his breathing heavy as he slowed.

Dorinen caught up to him, but held her tongue, unsure of Mylth's intentions.

"Information? About what?" the warrior growled, motioning to the injured man with a dismissive wave.

"About an attack on me and my companion, two nights ago," Mylth lied.

The Tveor stood to one side. "Well, ask him then."

"I must tend to his wound first." Mylth said, searching his shoulder bag.

"You're gonna heal him? You want to hold his hand and tell him a story, too?"

Mylth stared him down with determined resolve. The Tveor swore and stomped away, pausing to tear off part of one of the slain men's tunics to wipe his axe clean.

Dorinen approached him with some trepidation. "Well fought!"

He offered her quick nod, though his face betrayed no friendly sentiments. He removed his one-horned helmet and ran a hand through his dark shoulder-length hair, pausing to rub the balding patch on his forehead. "Well done yourself, lass. And thanks." His eyes narrowed. "But tell me, why's a skilled archer like you taken up with an Iron Rose sympathizer?"

Dorinen guffawed. "Surely you don't believe that! His arrow felled one of your attackers."

He snorted. "Then why is he off curin' that one now, eh?"

"He might be able to help us," Dorinen bluffed. She could only trust that Mylth knew what he was doing.

Mylth sprinkled a pinch of yellow powder over the man's wound and chanted a few words, waving his hand over the gash in a series of circular gestures.

"It's not a powerful healing," he said to them both. "But it's enough to prevent him from bleeding to death, and it will ease the pain."

"Still don't see why he didn't let me finish off the bastard," the Tveor sulked.

Dorinen ignored him and strode over to Mylth, kneeling beside him. "Is he going to be well enough for you to question him?"

"He'll live," Mylth answered, followed shortly by another snort of disapproval from their new friend in the distance. Moving close to her, he said in a quiet voice, "I need to see if he knows anything. If someone has indeed released the Vordlai, they might well have tried to employ a faction of the Iron Rose in some way. They would be quick to ally themselves with anyone who seeks the ruin of the established order and is powerful enough to actually do it."

Their diminutive new friend wandered back to them. "Well? Has he talked yet?" he demanded, stroking his thick, dark beard. He eyed his axe eagerly, swinging it back and forth with his wrist.

Mylth held up a hand. "He will need to rest a bit first. I have worked a small enchantment to help him to sleep."

"Rest?" the little warrior roared in exasperation. "Why don't you just rent a plushy room for him at an inn in Crythmarr? Gah! By the Stone Lord..." He spat and squinted at Mylth with suspicion. He pointed at Mylth's ears, visible through his long hair. "You a pixie?"

"Dalaethrian," Mylth answered with calm, turning his attention to the man's wound again. "Half Dalaethrian, to be precise."

"Oh, aye," the Tveor muttered, "half Dalaethrian and half horse's ass!"

Dorinen tried to cover her laugh with her hand.

"You would know about horses, little friend," Mylth countered, gesturing at the warrior's dented helmet, and its single horn protruding from the front. "Walking around resembling a shrunken, unkempt unicorn."

Dorinen turned away to hide her amusement.

"Mind your words, pixie!" He took a menacing step toward Mylth and made a fist. "Or the half of you that's Dalaethrian'll be separated from the other half by my axe!"

"Ouch!" Dorinen said between chuckles.

"Enough." Mylth stood and extended his hand to the Tveor, who seemed surprised by the seriousness of his tone. "I am Mylth Gwyndon, and my... jovial companion is Dorinen Elqestir. We've come from Tenaeth, and we are on our way to Crythmarr."

The Tveor eyed them both with caution for a moment, as if his pride still smarted from Mylth's insult. But he clasped hands with Mylth, and Dorinen breathed a mild sigh of relief. "I'm Bayark. Bayark Stimus Thunderheart, of Stimus-hodd." He moved to take Dorinen's hand.

She extended hers in response, relieved their confrontation would not boil over.

Bayark eyed her for a moment. "So now, tell me the truth: what's a Cernodyn girl doin' away from Cernwood, much less bein' in Tenaeth, much less bein' out in the Wild with this here pixie?"

She was so shocked by his clever perception that she couldn't conceive of a lie to deny his statement. "H-how could you tell?"

"I ain't stupid, girl!" Bayark snapped. "The Tveor of Stimus-hodd haven't survived where we are for ten centuries without bein' aware of what's goin' on around us, and who's doin' it! Why do you think we're the guardians of the Grey Wolds? 'Cause we're short and precious?"

"We're returning to Cernwood," Mylth offered, ignoring his sarcasm. "We've been conducting diplomatic business in the capital city on behalf of the Cernodyn, and return with news of our success."

"That so?" Bayark answered, a skeptical hand rubbing his chubby nose. "Then how come you're here, when the Cernodyn Dwellin' is that way?" He pointed to the southeast.

"First, we must go to Crythmarr to return some important legal documents," Dorinen interjected, hoping to sound convincing. "Afterward, we will return to my people." She pointed a bit farther south than he'd done, to correct him. "That way."

Bayark squinted with one eye, clearly not convinced. "Long way to go, especially when you just crossed the Buragon Moors. Oh yeah, I can smell it on you. Quite the accomplishment. Not too many can do it. Wouldn't especially want to try myself, and I doubt two 'diplomats' would be so dumb as to have a go on their own." He shook his head. "Lass, you're a poor liar. Honestly, I don't much care what you're doin' out here, but I'm on my way home, once I've stopped in Crythmarr myself. Got waylaid by these bastards."

"Then we may as well make the journey there together," Dorinen said, relieved he didn't press her any more about her unconvincing fabrication. "Safety in numbers."

"Might be a good plan," he conceded.

Mylth's face betrayed his concern. She suspected he didn't at all like the idea of Bayark joining them.

"Ah don't look so worried, pixie!" Bayark laughed. "You can do whatever secret stuff you want, and I like the lass's company. She's got great aim and a good heart, and she's a better woman than you deserve!"

"We're only traveling companions," Mylth objected, stiffening his posture and crossing his arms.

"Sure, and my wife's whiskers are naturally red!" he laughed. "Pixie, you're as bad a liar as she is."

Dorinen face flushed.

"What about slumberin' beauty over there?" Bayark asked after a moment of awkward silence, gesturing to the sleeping Iron Rose man.

"His wound is stable and should heal," Mylth answered. "We can question him in Crythmarr and turn him over to the authorities there."

"Well, I sure ain't carryin' him." Bayark grunted. "I prefer to mete out justice myself, but whatever you want to do, I suppose. So how do you propose to get him there?"

"We have," Dorinen began with confidence, but finished the sentence with hesitation, "a horse."

"One horse between you?" he chuckled. "Yeah, you're 'traveling companions' all right!"

Dorinen took Mylth aside, ignoring Bayark's immature taunts. "He has a point. How are we going to get this man to Crythmarr? And what about Bayark? How will he keep up?"

"Well, you're the one that suggested we travel with him," Mylth said with slight condescension.

"Well, *you* are the one that wants to take this criminal on to Crythmarr!" she shot back, raising her voice.

Another chuckle from Bayark interrupted them. "You're scrappin'! It's how it starts, kids!"

"Look!" Dorinen jabbed an angry finger in Bayark's direction. "I'm getting tired of your opinions, so just keep them to yourself!"

"They wouldn't bother you if they weren't true, lass," Bayark answered in a superior tone. Dorinen scowled.

"Stop, you two." Mylth stepped between them. "I have a solution… at least to the problem of our criminal." He spoke with a knowing raise of his eyebrow. "Let's retrieve our trusted animal."

As Dorinen and Mylth secured their possessions to their horse, Bayark paced with a frustrated frown, making a show of being impatient the whole time, and no doubt still eager to put his axe into the brigand's head. Dorinen kept a watchful eye on him, just in case the temptation became too great.

She already suspected what Mylth intended to do when he knelt next to the sleeping man. Sure enough, he pulled out the tiny pouch of sand and dusted a little over the brigand, who shrank to a fraction of his original size, no more than the length of a man's outstretched hand.

Bayark gasped, his eyes widening. "Where in the name of the Stone Lord did you learn how to do *that*?"

"I've learned many tricks in six centuries of life. Not so bad for a 'kid,' eh?" Mylth's expression betrayed a well-earned smugness as he placed the diminutive man in a burlap sack from the Gorben trading post.

"I didn't know the spell would work on a living creature," Dorinen said, almost as dumbstruck as Bayark appeared.

"Neither did I," Mylth answered with a sly smile.

Bayark burst into raucous laughter, slapping Mylth on the back. "I like you, pixie! Willin' to take a chance!" His happy mood vanished with a furrowed brow. "You're not plannin' on doin' that shrinkin' crap on me are you?"

"What would be point?" Mylth quipped.

Dorinen softly punched Mylth's shoulder as Bayark swore under his breath.

"You can ride on the horse with one of us," Mylth offered.

"I ain't keen on sittin' atop some big beast!" Bayark protested.

"You don't have to come with us at all," Mylth countered.

Bayark considered his options for a moment. Dorinen hoped he'd join them; despite his gruffness, she'd already grown fond of him.

"Well," he said. "I'm eager to get to Crythmarr as soon as possible, and any more Iron Rose bastards about will slow me down if I'm by myself, fun as those scraps are. Fine." He gave his assent and allowed Dorinen—and her only—to help him up onto the animal's back.

"You ridin' with me lass?" he asked.

"Of course." She set herself behind him and took the horse's reins. Mylth bowed to both of them in an exaggerated manner and disappeared over the hill.

"Where's the pixie off to?" Bayark asked.

"Scouting ahead," she answered. "If we find any more regiments of the Iron Rose, we want to avoid them."

Bayark shook his head. "Where's the fun in that? You tall ones are a strange lot!"

* * *

At midday, they arrived at Crythmarr, a large and thriving town that, while not on the scale of Tenaeth, still offered a number of the usual diversions of civilization for the weary traveler, from food and drink to gambling and inns of all kinds. Yet, Dorinen felt no more at ease here than in Tenaeth or Gorben.

"The sooner we can leave, the better," she mumbled, as she led their horse though the bustling streets.

"What?" Bayark asked, ambling alongside her.

"Nothing." She took in her surroundings. "Is there is a place on every street corner to indulge in alcohol?"

"More inns and pubs are packed into its walls than any other town in the north, given its importance for traders and the like," Bayark explained. "I'm proud to have sampled them all in my time. It so happens I'm pretty well known here, which is why we got through the gate just fine."

"And we're grateful," Dorinen said. She didn't want a repeat of the ridiculous spectacle at the walls of Tenaeth.

Mylth kept to himself and walked ahead of them.

Bayark led them through crowded streets to his favorite inn, The Dead Drunkard, which Dorinen found to be as almost as charming as its name. But it seemed clean enough, and inexpensive. She could tolerate it for one night.

Once inside, Bayark made his way to the bar; Dorinen and Mylth took advantage of his preoccupation with the local beer to sneak their small captive upstairs and question him. Closing the door to Mylth's room, they plucked the tiny man from the sack and laid him out on the bed, still unconscious.

Mylth placed one hand over the man's body, nearly covering it completely, and snapped his fingers. The brigand awoke with a jolt. He tried to stand, but fell over on his first attempt.

"Giants!" he yelled in horror. "Where in damnation am I? Where have you taken me? Don't eat me, please! I have gold!"

"We're not going to eat you," Mylth said, glancing at Dorinen with amusement, "and we are not large. You are now small. I can help you return to your original size, but not before you give me some information."

"Information about what?" the shrunken man demanded with folded arms and an absurd defiance, given his harmless stature and now-tiny voice.

Dorinen suppressed a chuckle, as Mylth picked him up by the back of his jerkin. He kicked, shouted, and swung his fists about.

"Surely you and your criminal colleagues have seen some unusual magical activity in this area recently," Mylth said, ignoring the pointless wiggling.

"We don't concern ourselves with the ways of sorcerers and magic casters," the man sneered, "Dalaethrian."

Mylth wasn't fazed by the attempted provocation. "Except when they pay you well," he said.

The man said nothing, instead turning his head away with a scowl and folding his arms again in a huff, throwing a defensive expression.

"You and I both know," Mylth continued, "the Iron Rose wouldn't miss an opportunity to use magic to destroy the government in Tenaeth if they could."

"Those incompetent fools," the little man spat. "We don't need magic to overthrow them, just bloody revolution. Our way, our law will prevail."

Dorinen shook her head at the little man, who at the moment was less threatening than a chittering squirrel. "So, you're telling us that the Iron Rose isn't involved at all?"

"I don't know what you're talking about."

She drew an arrow from the quiver still on her back and flipped it casually between her fingers. She wouldn't even need her bow to end this little wretch's life, only a single, swift stab.

His jaw dropped, and he held out his palms as if hoping to quell his captors' anger. "All right, all right! I've heard rumors that someone powerful, possibly a mage, has offered a certain Iron Rose regiment substantial payments to help secure the mines outside the old keep in Cernwood, and keep intruders away. They can have whatever they extract, so I've heard. I'm not a part of it, sadly, and that's all I know."

Dorinen narrowed her eyes at him and turned to Mylth. "He's telling the truth."

Mylth raised an inquisitive eyebrow.

"I'm good at sensing lies, at least in simple-minded people," she explained. "Their presence alters when they lie, almost like a change in scent. Trust me."

The brigand sneered at Mylth smugly. "See? Now, change me back!" he demanded. "Wait, did she call me 'simple-minded'?"

"I will help you," Mylth said. "But only because, unlike you and the men you work with, I have compassion and honor." He motioned to Dorinen, and she drew her sword.

"But then we will take you to the constabulary," she said, "where you'll answer for attacking the Tveor."

Mylth produced a pinch of the pink powder from its pouch. He spoke some words and blew the sand over the shrunken man, who coughed, spat, and uttered a string of profanities.

But he didn't change size.

"What trick is this?" the man roared, as loudly as his puny voice would allow.

Mylth spoke calmly. "I don't know."

"He's telling the truth, too," Dorinen offered, holding no sympathy for their captive.

"Restore me now!" He shook his fists. "You broke your word," he said, now putting his fists on his hips.

"I always keep my word," Mylth corrected. "But I never gave you my word in the first place. I said I might help you, and I did. I saved your life and taught you a valuable lesson. The counter spell should have worked right away. I'm sorry. It may yet."

"Sorry?" the man ranted, "Restore me, or I'll kill you!"

"And how do you propose to do that?" Mylth asked in a mocking tone. He walked to the door and opened it. "Get out," he ordered, "and we won't send you to the constable."

"Or we'll just step on you," Dorinen added with amusement.

The man bared his teeth in rage, searching about the room, as if weighing his options.

"Get out or we'll have the Tveor deal with you, instead," Dorinen warned in a stern voice.

The diminutive criminal considered his options, cursed, and scrambled out the door. Mylth shut it behind him.

"He'll at least be a novelty on the streets," Mylth said with amusement. "Perhaps he can earn money as a performer."

She eyed him, her suspicion now at a peak. "Your magic didn't fail. I told you. I can sense lies."

"A more fitting punishment than sixty days in a Crythmarr dungeon," Mylth said with a grin. "But as I said, my magic isn't nearly as potent as it should be. He might well recover. Some day."

She laughed and shook her head.

"Besides, we now know that someone with a fair amount of strength and influence is hiring members of the Iron Rose to work mines in the forest and guard the way to the keep."

"Hullo there!" a voice thundered.

Bayark stood in the open doorway, his single-horned helmet tucked under one arm and a large mug of beer in the other hand. He let out a loud belch, prompting Mylth to roll his eyes.

"Sorry to interrupt your dilly-dally, uh, didn't think this'd be the place for it." He belched again, this time covering his mouth. "My apologies, this damned drink gets stronger every time I visit this place. I might try to lug a barrel of it back home." He took another great gulp followed by a satisfied exhale.

"Is there a reason you're here?" Mylth demanded.

"Oh aye," Bayark answered, wiping foam from his beard. "Some funny-dressed man in the tavern downstairs sent me up. Says he needs to speak with you both, right now."

fourteen

Andra clutched her lyre, desperate to focus on her healing song again, but the words eluded her. She shook and wept again, unable to steady her breath.

"Jeena," she whispered, "please."

But Jeena didn't move, and her breathing ceased.

"No," Andra vowed. "I'm not going to let you go!"

With newfound intention, Andra played the healing melody again, allowing the words to come to her in their own time. Little by little, they did and the song began in earnest, its notes cascading and circling about the tent. She became one with her music, until her very essence mingled with the melody and poured out all of the love and nurturing she could offer. She now perceived Jeena's spirit and surrounded it with a warm, caring embrace, bringing it back to its home in Jeena's body.

Violet light burst from the gem and encircled Jeena like a descending sea fog, glowing brightest over her dreadful wounds. It surged through her and began its miraculous healing work from the inside, destroying the beast's venom. The torn flesh closed and healed, soon leaving only the faintest trace that wounds had ever been there at all.

Still Andra played on, lost in the ecstasy of her song and the rapture of healing. At last, the notes faded and she returned to the moment.

Jeena drew in a sharp breath and opened her eyes a little.

Andra let out a tearful gasp. "Oh, thank the Lady!"

Jeena brushed Andra's cheek with her hand. Warmth again emanated from Jeena's palm, calmly radiating over Andra's face. Andra sensed a door opening between them, allowing her soul to accept a great gift. The distance between them dissolved and for a brief time, all separateness fell away, their hearts and souls intertwined in a rapturous, blissful embrace. All too soon, Andra came back to her own body, her own mind.

"Oh, Jeena!" she sniffed as she set aside her lyre and leaned in to kiss Jeena's forehead.

"I had faith in you," Jeena whispered.

Andra let out a mixture of a sob and a laugh. "More than I did in myself."

Jeena tried to say more, but Andra silenced her by placing a finger on Jeena's lips. "You're the one who must rest now. Sleep, precious one. Teuvell and Koliserr have saved you. I promise I will not leave you tonight. I'll watch over you to be sure you are safe." She took Jeena's hands in her own.

Jeena closed her eyes and whispered with a faint smile, "Thank you, my beautiful *mynthari*," before drifting into sleep, her hand still clasping Andra's.

A warm lavender glow lingered in the tent. Andra sat in silence with Jeena, fighting her own fatigue, but making good on her promise to remain with her companion. She stayed awake for as long as possible, but sometime before dawn, she finally gave in to exhaustion and laid down beside Jeena, her arm wrapped around her, knowing they were both safe, both protected, and united as one.

* * *

Andra woke, stiff and aching. To her relief, Jeena still slept peacefully. She gently pulled back a portion of Jeena's chemise to check where she'd been wounded so viciously and saw only a hint on Jeena's brown skin of three scars from the claw marks. She covered her mouth to silence a happy sob.

"Teuvell and Koliserr be praised," she whispered.

Rousing herself, she kissed Jeena's cheek and stole out of the tent.

As day broke over the scarred Rajaani camp, a thick mist hung on the hills, bringing a brisk chill to replace the warmth of the previous night's holiday celebrations. Andra shivered.

She walked through the encampment, and while the morning was calm, the same couldn't be said of its inhabitants. Most of the Rajaani were awake; she doubted if many had even slept following the horrific attack. A mother in a bright red headscarf wrapped her arms around her scared child, two elderly women sobbed together on a short bench, and a trio of younger men argued about something in the Rajaani language. Others wept or held one another; a few sat quietly with haunted expressions.

These were a hardy people; they kept no permanent home by choice. They'd survived long days on back country roads, harsh winters, and attacks from Gro'aken and the Iron Rose, but nothing could have prepared them for the terror of the Vordlai.

Andra stopped and beheld the grief, the suffering, the anguish. Guilt gnawed at her, a dread about her own actions.

Are Narick and I responsible for bringing the creature here? She couldn't bear to answer such a terrible question. *Did I nearly cause Jeena's death?*

She placed a hand over her heart, sensing a warmth and a true belonging. Was it the *mynthari*? Andra wondered how she could possibly be worthy of it, even if their Ladies had saved Jeena's life.

She tried to shove such questions away, but they persisted. Yet, despite her growing remorse, no one acted less than charitable to her, and several greeted her with a tip of a hat, a friendly smile, and even a "good morning" in their language. One even offered her a small basin of water to wash her hands and face. And all this kindness only made her feel worse.

After rinsing off, she found her way to the center of the camp, where she and Jeena had danced with such inhibition. The joy of the experience warmed her now.

A few paces away, she saw Narick, wrapped in his grey cloak, conversing with two older men. When he finished speaking to them, he approached her.

She braced herself for bad news, for disapproval from the Rajaani, for expulsion from the camp, or even that Narick might be cross with her for her aggressive behavior. To her surprise, he greeted her without words, taking her in his arms and holding her. Relief washed over her, and she returned his embrace, burying her head in his chest.

"Did you sleep?" he asked.

"A little. I stayed with Jeena the whole night. I wanted to be sure she was safe."

"My dear friend." He stood back and regarded her, his hands on her shoulders. "You are remarkable, just as I've always suspected."

Andra's face flushed and she fidgeted with a button on her jerkin. "I did what I needed to, I suppose."

"You did far more, I suspect. She offered you her soul-bond, yes?"

She jerked her head up. "You know about that?"

"I surmised it," he replied. "I checked her tent earlier while you slept. A gentle light surrounded you, holding you both as if in a loving embrace. By the grace of the Lady, your command over the gem grows stronger with every use. Teuvell works through you, I'm certain, for I've never seen a healer with that kind of ability. The Shylan Dar *Book of Purgation* tells us no one can survive a wound inflicted by a Vordlai, and yet, Jeena lives and will recover because of you."

Andra stood taller and prouder, even as disbelief still burdened her. "Somehow, I did it. I mean, I called on Teuvell and Koliserr in desperation, and they heard me. Even more, it's like they knew my agony. Their power coursed through me, through my voice, giving the gem its enchantment and burning away the venom. But I also needed Jeena to do it. It's all so strange, I hardly even remember it now."

"But you should feel blessed."

"I do," Andra said, taking his hands, enjoying a momentary relief from the night's horrors. But one question still lurked in the back of her mind. She hesitated and lowered her voice. "Is it possible we lured the creature here?" She feared Narick might confirm her fears.

"I was worried about that, as well," he replied, "but I don't think so. The Vordlai are obviously avoiding Meln and its people. Their master must be compelling them to do so."

"Thank the Lady for that, at least," Andra said.

"But as such, they need to feed, so I suspect it was only a matter of time before an attack like this happened. Whoever drugged your village must possess considerable power over these vile creatures' hungers, so they will be ravenous. It's likely that our arrival in your village yesterday is coincidental to last night's attack."

"I hope you're right," she replied. "Poor Ruscan." She grieved as she spoke his name. "He sacrificed himself to save those children. He was so happy, so funny, so... *alive*."

"It's never easy to accept the emptiness and sense of loss that comes with sudden death. And such a brave man deserves a better fate than being slaughtered by one of those monstrosities. Praise Enwyonn that we destroyed the beast before it could fully sate its hunger."

Andra shuddered at the thought.

They wandered to where the creature had fallen. No trace of it now remained, save scattered piles of ash.

One older man stood nearby, his haunted expression betraying his fear and exhaustion. "Is it truly dead?" he asked in a shaky voice.

"There's nothing here now that can harm anyone, I assure you," Narick said. "Their physical bodies cannot last long without their animating spirits."

"Thank Koliserr," the man replied, as he turned to leave them. "Perhaps we'll sleep tonight."

Narick turned to Andra, placing his hands on her shoulders. "Your courage and selflessness were remarkable, and I'm so proud of you. But my dear friend, this is only the beginning."

She looked away. "I know. Whoever captured my village must also control these beasts. We have to stop him. Stop this from happening again." She gestured to the camp.

"Yes. Even more so now, I see no point in returning to Meln," he said. "The answers we need are at Wyverdorn Keep. My fear is that Lord Wyverdorn has fallen, and the Vordlai are there now, awaiting their chance for freedom. We must destroy them, or at least prevent their return to this world. You've seen what a single one of them can do. Imagine what would happen if dozens escaped."

Andra shivered, fighting back a chilling fear.

"As horrifying as last night was," he continued, "what we'll see will be far worse than anything we have encountered or could imagine. It will be a place of terror and nightmare. What we are about to undertake is a burden so great that it's almost unbearable. I don't know if we will succeed, or even if we can. We may well perish, but we must try. We're the only ones who can act, and we need to do it quickly. There isn't enough time to seek further help. Even the Tveor would be slaughtered if they were to confront a swarm of these creatures."

At once, a memory came back to her. "Wait, Jeena told me last night that there are others who might join us. Ramwin said something similar to you, right?"

"He did, I think, but we can't rely on vague promises of assistance. If such help is out there, we can only pray we'll meet them when the time comes. We must leave soon and make for Cernwood. The Rajaani have kindly offered us provisions and supplies, despite their own losses. The settled peoples of these lands could learn much from them."

Concern nagged Andra. "I'm so worried about Jeena," she said, her eyes drawn again to Jeena's tent.

"You don't need to be. The Ferwareen can take care of themselves. You've given her life back to her, and she will grow strong again, and quickly, I suspect."

"Maybe she can come with us," Andra said, though she doubted it even as she voiced her wish.

"It would be a great advantage," Narick offered, "but I doubt she'll do so. She's still weak, and even if she weren't, she wouldn't leave her people in danger. She is their best protection, their best chance for survival, so she'll stay close by them. They trust her and rely on her. She's needed here."

Andra agreed but wished it could be otherwise. Wrestling with this inner conflict, she walked with Narick back to the central clearing, where a number of the Rajaani tried their best to carry out normal duties: cooking, packing, and tending fires.

"They'll strike the camp and leave today," she said. "They won't risk a second night here."

"Indeed," Narick said, "if for no other reason than fearing more of the creatures might be attracted by the scent of death."

Andra's attention drifted to Jeena's tent, overcome by a sudden urge to return to it.

"She's awake, I know it," she said. "I'll be back soon."

"Of course. Take what time you need."

Her heart racing, a gentle warmth spreading through her chest, Andra hastened back to Jeena's tent and peered inside. Sure enough, the young Rajaani woman was awake, though still in her bed. She held out her arms.

Andra went to her at once, knelt, and embraced her, stroking her head, reveling in the amber scent of her hair. They held each other for a long while before drawing back and regarding one another, smiles hiding their mutual sadness. Andra knew they must part and that neither of them wanted to speak of the night's terrible events.

"You must leave us—me—soon," Jeena said, tracing a finger over Andra's cheek.

Andra nodded and held back tears. "Where will you go?" she asked in a choked voice.

"Farther west, as always," Jeena replied. "It will be safer for us. We will travel well past Wold Lake and spend time in the forests to the north of it, perhaps the whole winter."

"I wish you could come with us, or I could come with you," Andra whispered, her tears finally coming.

Jeena stroked Andra's face and wiped away her tears, even as she clearly struggled to hold back her own. "There are no endings, dearest one. We shall meet again, in body or in spirit, or with luck, both. Lady Teuvell walks with you, sings through you, and embraces you. I have faith you will destroy this terror. I believe in you with all my heart." She took Andra's hand, their fingers interlacing. "*Mar shokara*," she said in barely a whisper.

"Those words," Andra, sitting back with a start. "I've heard them before. In my dream!"

A knowing smile tugged on Jeena's lips. "You truly knew me before we even met."

"What do they mean?"

"'My beauty,' for that is who you are to me now."

Andra let out a breath, half laughing, half crying. "I am your 'beauty.' But I need a name for you. How would I say in your language," she paused, "the 'treasure of my heart'? When I think of you, I feel such warmth there."

"*Mar dhe cortan*," Jeena answered as she caressed Andra's arm with her tender palm.

"You are *mar dhe cortan*." Andra placed her hand over Jeena's heart, then over her own.

Jeena sat up fully and brought her face close to Andra's. They gazed at one another in longing silence, Andra's breathing shallow, her stomach a bundle of nerves.

Jeena leaned in and softly kissed Andra, a moment of bliss that was everything Andra could have hoped for, and one she wished wouldn't end. She could not let Jeena go, returning her kiss with another, soft and warm, delicate and perfect. She delighted in Jeena's lips, as welcome as a hearth fire in winter, as familiar as a lifetime of comfort and refuge.

Jeena began to cry. The two embraced again, Andra luxuriating in the sweetness of her companion's welcoming arms. She felt safe, even home, and they held each other for some time. Andra wanted more than anything to stay here with Jeena, but she knew she couldn't, not now, not yet. She could only wish for better times to come, a yearning that now seemed vanishingly remote.

Her heart heavy, she retrieved her lyre and stood. She beheld Jeena once more, holding back tears. "I must go."

"Yes, you must."

"Farewell, *mar dhe cortan*."

Jeena took her hand again and squeezed it. "Farewell, *mar shokara*. Know that I am with you always."

Andra took Jeena's hand to her lips and kissed it, caressing her fingers and again struggling to let go. With a determined breath, she turned to leave, pausing for a moment to see one last time Jeena's lovely, tear-stained face.

Andra went at once to Narick, who waited at the edge of the camp with their new supplies. He placed a supportive hand on her shoulder, and without another word, they set off for Cernwood. With a heavy heart, she feared she would never see Jeena again, and they would never leave the forest alive.

* * *

Andra and Narick circumvented Meln with a watchful eye and traveled eastward before turning south. After midday, the pair reached the edge of the great forest. All appeared normal, except for an eerie quiet: no birds, no creatures, barely a wind in the leaves.

"This is wrong," she said, considering the silence to be a warning they shouldn't ignore. "And something else is missing."

"What is it?" Narick asked.

"There should be a road here," Andra said. "Into the forest, I mean. It leads to Wyverdorn's keep, but it's just not here. It was, Narick, I know it was! I've been here many times. I even recognize those trees." She gestured to a cluster nearby.

"I don't doubt you," he replied. "I fear that whoever has enslaved your village and unleashed the Vordlai has erased any easy paths to their lair. It might be an illusion, or the landscape might have been altered with some horrific magic. In any case, you'll have to trust your memory to guide us."

"Probably not the best idea. Unless…" She undid the straps on her lyre case and brought out her kenlim. Plucking it, she chanted a short song in the archaic language of Teuvell's elder Artisans. She passed her hand over the gem, and it flashed a violet light for a brief moment. "When we near the keep, it will glow bright."

"How do you know?"

"I don't, really. It's a direction chant, to aid in a journey. I willed the jewel to perform the same function as the song, and I guess I believe it will. Call it instinct?"

"Enwyonn be praised," Narick said.

"Then again, I might just get us completely lost."

Her uncertain mood worsened as they entered the woods. Despite the vibrant greens and shimmering golds cast by sunlight on the lush summer foliage, an unsettling sensation crept over her.

"Everything seems 'heavy,' if that makes sense?"

"I feel it, too," Narick replied. "Some form of darkened magic lies over this place. It's oppressive, like a burden on my shoulders."

Andra led them through the thickening forest, relying only on the gem and her instincts. Despite her sure memory, she found no sign that a road or path had ever been there at all. The gem provided little guidance beyond an occasional faint, ambiguous glow.

Their footsteps snapped fallen branches, and they stumbled over rocks concealed under moss and leaves.

"Nothing like announcing our arrival with a clumsy fanfare to our unwelcoming hosts," Narick complained.

Andra thought for a moment and, handing her lyre to Narick, took her flute from its own slender case, playing a short, lively melody. She confidently stomped on a fallen tree branch, but it made no sound, and she delighted in Narick's surprised expression.

"Another of your talents I didn't know about?" he asked, with barely concealed sarcasm.

She winked at him as she put her flute away. "How did you think I could sneak girls into my room under Wenn's nose all those years?"

Narick chuckled, returning her kenlim, and they continued onward through the dense undergrowth in complete silence.

"The flute's magic silences our footsteps," she whispered, "but does allow us to talk, if we need to."

"We should say little, and not announce our presence," he said. "It's possible we are already being watched."

After some time, Narick cocked his head, and motioned Andra to his side. "I hear movements nearby. To our right."

She stopped and focused, but heard nothing. "Are you sure?"

"Absolutely."

"That's not the direction of the keep," Andra protested. "Maybe we should continue on?"

"But this might be important. Any presence in the forest warrants our attention. We don't know what it is."

"Exactly!" she whispered harshly. "All the more reason to leave it alone and be on our way. What if it's a pack of Vordlai?"

"I don't sense anything of the sort," Narick responded calmly.

"You also didn't sense the Vordlai last night before it struck!" Andra regretted her words at once. Seeing his pained expression, she regretted them even more.

"If we stand here and argue, whatever is there may hear us," he said. "I'd rather see what it is so we can be better prepared if it is an enemy." And with that, he started off.

Andra let out a sigh of exasperation. "This is a bad idea." But she followed along behind him, making sure he didn't step outside of the range of their magical silence.

They passed through a thick clump of trees covered in ferns, and hid themselves behind a large fallen log. In the clearing beyond, the terrain sloped upward to some rocky outcroppings. Several tents and a weatherworn stone cabin stood around the entrance to a mine. Three grubby and hardened men tossed dice on a makeshift table and argued, while a fourth took generous swigs from a wooden cup. Yet another sharpened the point of his spear. They all wore the same black tunics, adorned with a bronze flower on a stem of exaggerated thorns.

"The Iron Rose!" Narick whispered, too loudly for Andra's liking.

She glared at him. "So, do you want to fight all of them at once?"

He almost snarled in annoyance.

"Why would they be here?" she asked, ignoring him. "And what are they doing at Wyverdorn's mine?"

Narick shook his head. "If something has happened to Wyverdorn and his guard, these criminals could be taking advantage of the entrance not being guarded, but I wouldn't be surprised if whoever drugged your village has employed them. Iron Rose factions owe loyalty to no one, not even to each other, and they could easily be hired for the right price. Perhaps the price is the free reign to plunder Wyverdorn's resources, in exchange for watching for intruders. If that's true, their 'master' is likely nothing more than human."

"But who would want to try to control the Vordlai?"

"Someone insane. And powerful. That he might be a mere man doesn't make our task any easier, I'm afraid. If we have to contend with these criminals as well, we're in great danger."

"So let's not 'contend' with them at all!" Andra whispered in anger. "Let's get out of here, now! I told you we should have——"

Andra froze as the edge of a blade pushed against her throat and she glimpsed a dagger also pressed to Narick's neck. Narick could easily take out the man behind him, but Andra knew he wouldn't risk it. She didn't have the skill to do the same to the man behind her.

Exhaling in frustration, Narick held up his hands in surrender. His captor let out a satisfied laugh.

"Turn around slowly. Both of you," a grating voice commanded.

They obeyed, and she saw a balding man with a scar across his forehead point his weapon at Narick's chest. Andra's captor pulled her tight against the rough wool of his tunic as he held the dagger near to her face. It resembled the one Meix carried in Meln, while the edge of the blade shone faintly with something dark and oily. Poison.

All marks of the Iron Rose.

"A Shylan Dar monk, and his pretty young companion. An Artisan, I think," Narick's captor taunted. "Guess your magic silenced more than you bargained for. I can't even hear the sound of my own feet! Maybe next time you'll be more discerning. Nice trick, monkey!"

Narick cursed.

"Moarkh will be pleased," snarled Andra's captor, his revolting breath warming her neck. "And maybe we can please ourselves first."

She recoiled in disgust but held her tongue.

Narick's face was a picture of restrained rage, but she shot him a determined look. They needed to remain calm for the moment.

"You'll do nothing!" the other yelled at him. "Moarkh will want to question them, and maybe the master himself will want to see them."

Narick cast a subtle half-wink at Andra. He was right.

* * *

Their captors led Andra and Narick closer to the mine's entrance and forced them into a supply tent, where another brigand bound their hands behind their backs, before tying them to support poles along the side of the canvas walls.

"We'll take these, thank you." One of the men snatched away Andra's lyre and flute. "Can't have you doing any of that fancy Lady magic on us now, can we?"

"Leave them alone!" Andra demanded, kicking out with her feet.

"I'd watch my tongue, if I were you," he threatened. "Unless you want to lose it."

Clutching her instruments, he stormed out of the tent.

She let out a furious sigh when they were alone. "So, I suppose we won't be leaving anytime soon?" she asked in a sarcastically flowery voice.

"All right! Coming here was a mistake," he conceded. "But at least we now have some important information."

"True," she said. "We've learned the Iron Rose will sell their services to anyone with money. I'm sure the council in Tenaeth would love to know that, though it will be difficult to inform them after our throats have been cut."

"Damn it, this is important!" Narick hissed. "It means the 'master' is indeed human, not some magical creature or half-dead mage. It narrows down the possibilities as to who he might be."

"Who is he, then?" she asked, somewhat apologetically, regretting being flippant.

"I don't know. Not yet."

Andra rolled her eyes. "Well, do tell me when you figure it out."

Narick scoffed. "I don't have time for your childish taunts!"

"Childish? Childish?" She clenched her teeth and growled. "I'm the one who warned you not to go searching after strange sounds. If you'd listened to me, we might have been well on our way to the keep by now."

"And lost a chance to learn who is releasing the Vordlai before we must confront them!"

"What difference does it make?" She now struggled to loosen the rope binding her hands behind her back.

"It might well save our lives. Even if we don't learn their master's identity, we may still be able to discover just what we will face, what is out there."

"We already *know* what's out there, Narick," she snapped bitterly.

Before he could respond, the tent flap opened and in strode a tall man, dressed in the all-black garb of an Iron Rose captain, a black leather patch slung over his left eye.

"A Shylan Dar monk, and a young lady, presumably some kind of Artisan, based on that fancy instrument of yours." He ran one hand through his long, unkempt hair, fingers passing through his coppery red curls. "I am Moarkh, commander of the Blood Spear regiment of the Iron Rose. You're trespassing on Iron Rose territory. Why?"

"This 'territory' belongs to Lord Wyverdorn," Andra snapped, even knowing such an attitude could cost her life.

Moarkh chuckled, almost pleasantly. "The master has seen to that small problem. There's been… a change of ownership."

"Who is your master?" Narick demanded.

"I ask the questions, not you, monk," Moarkh commanded, striking Narick across the face with the back of his gloved hand. Andra winced as the blow left a mark on Narick's cheek.

"Before we decide if we'll cut your throats, you'll tell us why you're here. Say nothing and we might torture you first."

Narick now focused inward, perhaps working to untie the crude knot binding his hands behind his back, something Andra had been unable to do. She swallowed hard, but vowed to herself she wouldn't panic or volunteer any information, no matter what Moarkh threatened. She tried not to show fear, determined not to let her captor see her tremble.

"Why are you here, monk?" Moarkh knelt, jutting his stubbly chin and hardened face directly in front of Narick.

"We're lost," Narick answered, sounding dejected.

"Lost," Moarkh echoed mockingly, pulling back. "A Shylan Dar monk, lost? I don't think so, try again."

"So, how do you account for how easily we were captured?" Narick asked, a defiant sneer on his face. "Do you think if I'd had my wits about me, I would have let those fools take me, or her?" He tilted his head toward Andra. A dangerous ploy; he gambled that Moarkh knew nothing yet of her magical silence.

"Perhaps," Moarkh said, "but it still doesn't explain why you are in Cernwood to begin with. It's more likely your order and Teuvell's whores are eager to discover the master's plans. He told us this might happen."

Andra bristled at his insult. With her lyre, she could tear off his disgusting head.

"I've been authorized to kill any such intruders, not that I need incentive or permission to kill anyone," Moarkh gloated. "Have a care monk," he said with a squint, standing and stepping back. "I know what you're doing. You won't escape. Before you can finish untying yourself, I'll summon ten men here, all with—"

Narick lurched forward, his fist delivering a cracking blow to Moarkh's face, sending him tumbling to the ground, where he lay still.

Freeing himself from the bonds around his legs, Narick moved over to loosen Andra's.

"He knew you were untying yourself?" she said, astonished.

"Of course," Narick said. "No monk could be kept bound for very long by such feeble knots. He mistakenly assumed I needed more time than I did. Besides, he would have killed us, regardless of whether we'd told him anything or not. Now, let's find our things and get out of here."

He peered out of the tent.

"Several of them are roaming about, some moving in and out of the mine entrance." He turned back to her. "There are too many, you'll be seen. I'm not worried about myself, but you're vulnerable."

"Oh, thank you for your confidence."

"Wait here." Held up a hand, clearly in no mood to argue, and she decided not to quarrel with him.

He slipped out for a short time to examine their surroundings, while she watched for more guards. Soon, he returned.

"No one is in the tent, but neither are our possessions. But even I have no way of getting to the stone structure without attracting the attention of at least one of them."

"Even you?" She shook her head.

"If they find I'm free, they might come back for you before I can reach it. I'm not sure what we should—"

A dagger whirled past his head. He spun about as two brigands approached him, short swords drawn.

"I admire your courage," Narick boasted, folding his arms. "It's rare for men to attack a monk of the Shylan Dar willingly, knowing they will die."

His threat stopped them in their tracks. Narick jumped toward them, arcing his hands outward. One fist connected with each man's jaw, and both collapsed to the ground. Narick managed to duck and roll away just in time to avoid the swing of a club behind him. Already another enemy loomed over him, sword above his head, prepared to deal a killing blow. But Narick kicked up, his boot connecting with the man's chest, sending his attacker tumbling to the ground, where he lay, half-conscious.

Andra became distracted watching this skirmish. By the time she saw her own peril, it was too late. "Narick!"

Two more men appeared nearby, crossbows aimed at her. Another emerged from the stone building, his own crossbow pointed at Narick.

"Not a move monk," threated the one nearest to her, "or she dies now. Surrender, and she lives, at least for a while." His comrade joined him in his cruel, pitiless chuckle.

Three more Iron Rose soldiers emerged from the mine, brandishing swords and clubs. Still more exited the other tents, drawn like wasps to honey by the sounds of battle. They joined in the mirth, and the cacophonous chorus of their mocking laughter burned in Andra's ears.

Part II

Fifteen

Mylth shielded his face as the air exploded in a shower of purple lights and smoke. Bayark swore as he was jolted back to sobriety. The haze cleared to reveal Ramwin, leaning against the room's now-closed door, twirling an ornately carved walking stick in one hand and holding his fanciful hat in the other.

Mylth gritted his teeth but said nothing.

"Sorry," he quipped, "but I did need to get your attention rather quickly."

"You already had it by sending us the drunken Bayark," Mylth grumbled. "What do you want, Sarvethar?"

"It's lovely to see you as well, *Shy'nande*," Ramwin said.

"Do not call me that!" Mylth ordered, pointing his finger in warning at his periodic nemesis. "I no longer serve you. I am not your lapdog. What I do here is for the people and the land, not for you."

"Really?" Ramwin asked with a raised eyebrow. "And how do you separate them? The land, its folk, its creatures, me?" He waved his hand to dismiss the matter, striking the floor hard with his stick, making it glow with blue light.

"What in the name of the Stone Lord is goin' on here?" Bayark wiped his beard, dropped his empty mug with a clank, and drew his axe out from its sheath on his back.

"An apt choice of words, my fierce Tveoran warrior," Mylth answered. "Behold, a manifestation of your Stone Lord, such as he is."

Bayark shoved his helmet onto his head and made a fist. "Mind your words, pixie! You're talkin' blasphemy. I can put up with lotsa' things, but I'll not hear the Stone Lord profaned."

"Bayark," Dorinen said, hastening to pat him on the back. "It's true. That which your people recognize in the Land Spirit as the Stone Lord, is incarnate in this being. This is Ramwin Roakthone, one of the Sarvethar's many forms."

"Much as I wish it were otherwise," Mylth muttered with venom.

"I've heard of you," Bayark addressed Ramwin with suspicion, not convinced. "How do I know it's you, eh?"

"You can be assured, my friend, I have no desire to deceive you." Ramwin bowed and held out a hand in a gesture of respect. "I would show you more, but unfortunately, we have more pressing matters to attend to at this moment."

Mylth let out a breath in disgust, eliciting an annoyed frown from Dorinen.

"It *is* him, Bayark, I promise you. He saved my life," she said, turning her attention to Mylth. "Please, both of you, calm your tempers. If they grow any hotter, they'll likely burn the whole inn down."

Bayark kept a wary eye on the Sarvethar, removing his hand from his axe handle, prompting Dorinen to let out a short sigh of relief.

Ramwin smiled at Dorinen and gave her a courteous bow. "My dear, I see you two have become acquainted well enough since we last spoke. He is quite a charmer, to be sure. I think it's the golden hair, or maybe those sweet little pointed ears."

"What do you *want*, Sarvethar?" Mylth demanded again.

"The time is short, shorter than even I anticipated." Ramwin's tone took on a serious and stern tone. "The Vordlai are almost fully awake; their power grows strong, and the one who controls them has nearly succeeded in dissolving the planar barrier."

"Then leave us be so that we can see to the task," Mylth countered. "We have no time for your games!"

"You have no time at all." Ramwin's voice went cold. "By nightfall tomorrow, at the beginning of the darkmoon, the portal will fall, and the Vordlai will be free."

"We must leave at once," Dorinen insisted.

"It's nearly a day's ride to Cernwood at least," Mylth said.

"Then we've lost." Her face fell.

"No," Ramwin offered. "I will take you to the northern edge of Cernwood, but that is as much as I can do."

"Ah yes," Mylth said, bile rising in his throat. "The Spirit must not interfere in the events of the world, except when it decides that's a good idea, but only a little so as not to upset the precious cosmic balance too much, but just enough to give it a nudge. Correct?"

"I do not have time to argue with you," Ramwin shot back with an angry tone making Dorinen take a step back. "You know the ways, *Shy'nande*," Ramwin continued, "and you know it is as it must be. Stop pitying yourself for once and see the greater good."

Giving into his fury, Mylth drew his sword and pointed it at Ramwin.

"No!" Dorinen grabbed his arm to hold him back. "Please, both of you. You must see how important it is for us to succeed. We cannot let these creatures escape." She moved to stand between them, pleading with her eyes.

"Agreed," Mylth said, jaw clenched. "I undertake this task because it must be done. But when it is finished, and it will be, we will settle this quarrel at last!"

Ramwin observed him impassively for a moment, tapping his walking stick with one finger. "Now I see your fire, the fortitude of a true Dalaethrian. Thank you. Your confidence in your success is most welcome." He placed a hand on his chest and bowed.

Mylth remained unmoved by the Sarvethar's flattery, but nevertheless lowered his sword.

"Would someone mind tellin' me what in Ultock's Fiery Forge is goin' on here?" Bayark interjected.

Ramwin struck the floor again with his stick, and a luminous, blue mist surrounded them.

"Have courage and make yourself ready, friend Bayark," Ramwin said. "You are about to help save a world."

* * *

As the mist cleared, Dorinen beheld a canopy of trees surrounding her. She recognized her beloved forest at once, but her stomach churned, her head ached, and she fought against dizziness.

Nearby, sickness overcame Bayark; he rushed into the bushes and vomited with some violence. Dorinen wanted to ignore him, but his expelling made her feel all the more ill. She shook her head to clear it and stood.

Ramwin had taken them to the edge of the great wood in the blink of an eye. The fields and rolling hills marking the beginnings of the Grey Wolds lay to the west.

To her surprise, the Sarvethar seemed the most affected by this remarkable feat. He leaned against a tree, clutching his head before sinking to one knee.

"Ramwin!" She rushed to his side. As she approached, she struggled to comprehend what surely was one of the strangest sights she'd ever seen. He'd become partially transparent, as if made of mist and glass. She knelt and took his hand, but it felt almost insubstantial, like trying to grasp and hold on to a plume of smoke.

"Too close," he whispered through his heavy breathing. "I'm too close to the source of the disruption. I cannot stay here." He doubled over, clutching his belly, and let out a sharp groan.

Dorinen wrapped an arm around him, on the verge of panic. "What do we do?"

"I can only take you this far, the edge of the forest," Ramwin said, panting.

When his gaze met hers again, Dorinen shuddered at the fear in his eyes.

"Find the source of the evil, Dorinen. This is your home. I know you can do it. Seek first the others. You'll find them. But I must leave you now!" He snapped his fingers and disappeared in a flash of white light, slipping through her grasp like sand.

Mylth stood a short distance away. He clasped his hands and bowed his head.

"The Land Spirit is indeed fading," he said. "If I'd not seen it, I wouldn't have believed it. We must stop the dimensional breach without him. He's done all he can for us."

"So, you finally believe he's not playing games?" she snapped.

Mylth didn't answer, but faced the forest, his expression more troubled than she'd ever seen before.

Having left two mugs of The Dead Drunkard's finest ale and some fresh-baked bread as a gift to the forest, Bayark came stumbling back from the bushes, his ruddy complexion now pale. "Where are we?" he asked weakly, wiping his beard.

"Cernwood, to the north of Crythmarr," Dorinen answered.

"How?"

"I told you," she replied with assurance. "That was Ramwin Roakthone, one of the guises of the Sarvethar. He brought us here to complete the task he set us, to save this land, and maybe even himself, from destruction."

Bayark shook his head, confused. "I have no idea what you're goin' on about."

"We must move quickly, and on foot," Mylth interjected. "I suppose our horse will serve as adequate payment for our rooms back at the inn. I'm sorry, Bayark, but there's no time for long explanations. If you choose to join us, we can tell you more along the way."

He scowled. "I was on my way home before I ran into you two! And I ain't interested in whatever magical mess you've got yourselves mixed up with. If I'm where I think I am, I can be in Meln by tonight. Nice meetin' ya both, but don't burst into my affairs again."

"You're a fine warrior," Dorinen said, hoping to appeal to his bravado, "we could use your skills."

"Nope!" Bayark stomped off toward the fields.

"You'll have the chance to kill many vile creatures from the Underplanes, and more of the Iron Rose, maybe a lot of them," she called after him.

Bayark stopped and spun around. "Monsters and Iron Rose, eh?"

"Undoubtedly," Mylth confirmed.

He flashed a wicked smile. "So, how long you think this little trip's gonna take?"

* * *

Before they set off, Dorinen knelt and kissed the ground. She touched the earth with her palms as she visualized drawing the energy of the forest into her body. She'd missed this connection to her home, and communing with the earth felt like a welcoming draught of water quenching the deepest of thirsts. Uttering a silent prayer, she took hold of her bow, and turned to Mylth and Bayark.

"This is my home, and I'll lead us. I can already smell death here.

But there's more, almost like something's calling us. Follow me and stay as close as you can. We cannot dawdle." She plunged at once into the thick forest, disappearing without a sound.

For some time, they traversed through the dense foliage. Bayark swore more than once as he tripped over gnarled roots and knotted branches, struggling to keep up.

"I'm beginning to question the wisdom of asking him to join us," Mylth said with a heavy breath, quickening his stride to come alongside Dorinen. "We're announcing our presence to whatever might be waiting."

"He's an excellent fighter, and we need all the help we can get." She didn't stop, focusing instead on discerning a way forward for them.

"True enough." Mylth glanced back at their new companion. "I've explained to him the events of recent days and what we're trying to do. The more he's heard, the more eager he's become to stay with us."

"Good. Come on!"

She raced ahead but grew ever more frustrated that her companions lagged behind, and she often needed to slow her pace to let them catch up.

When they stopped to rest, though she would have preferred to continue, an unusual scent and a chorus of sounds caught her attention. She held out her hand for Mylth and Bayark to be quiet, and crept off into a dense collection of trees. She stood in silence, listening to harsh and cruel voices, a presence unwelcome in this place. But the hair on the back of her neck stood up as she sensed a greater presence, a loving force, akin to the sensation before meeting Ramwin the first time. "How is that possible?"

She returned to them in haste. "There are others here," she said in a hushed voice. "Not far away, and definitely human. The scent is unmistakable. It's what's been calling me."

"Iron Rose?" Bayark asked, eyebrows raised in anticipation.

"Maybe. But something else. I can't explain it."

"I agree," Mylth agreed. "There is magic, powerful magic, and it's not of the Underplanes. Strangely, I sense the presence of Teuvell."

"Ramwin said to 'seek the others,'" Dorinen said. "If it *is* followers of Teuvell, this could be important. They might be in trouble."

"I agree," Mylth said. "Can you lead us to them?"

She nodded.

"Are we gonna get to split some skulls?" Bayark gripped the handle of his axe as if restraining it from releasing itself.

Dorinen patted his shoulder. "Let's just wait until we see what's there."

* * *

Narick cursed himself for being so reckless. He'd endangered—and probably doomed—his best friend. And now a member of the Iron Rose held a poisoned dagger at her throat again. The man restraining Andra tightened his grip, and she struggled against his grasp.

More Iron Rose guards circled them, taunting and jeering the pair with threats and rude comments.

"Looks like Moarkh will be out for a bit longer." He spoke into her ear, his breath reeking of stale beer. "I'm thinking me and the lads need some of what you have. And I'm thinking it'll be fun to take turns and let your monk friend watch."

"Perhaps he'd like to join in!" one of them shouted, to a chorus of raucous laughter. Narick almost shook with rage and struggled to contain it, drawing on his discipline to stamp out the seething fire burning within. But he remained vigilant, waiting for any chance to take down all of them.

"How about it, monkey?" Andra's captor demanded with a chuckle. "Want to throw away your vow? Why don't you take her right here in front of us, and we might let you both live. Care to show us what you're made of?"

The band laughed again, none louder than the brigand holding Andra. But his laughter came to an abrupt halt with the hiss of an arrow and the sickening crunch of iron piercing bone.

Before the dead man even hit the ground, Narick acted.

A cacophony of shouts and curses flew about the tents. Narick struck out with a series of punches, disarming the shocked crossbowmen and breaking their arms in succession. One of them cried out, discharging his bolt by accident, striking and killing a nearby comrade.

Narick elbowed the man closest to him in the face, knocking him out. The other two, unarmed, backed away in a panicked haste, shoving at each other to try to get away faster.

Two more arrows sailed into the clearing, finding their marks and killing one man each. After this came a great roar. A Tveor wearing a one-horned helmet charged into the camp, swinging his axe and cutting down everyone in his way. Three soldiers fell to his double-bladed weapon, and as each did, he gained more momentum.

Andra ducked and dove to the side. Narick motioned for her to slip away to the stone building, through the chaos of shouts and panicked soldiers. "Hurry! I think your instruments are in there!"

None of the remaining brigands even noticed her.

The little warrior ended another opponent with his axe and called out to Narick. "Well fought! Let's see how many more we can take out, eh?"

Narick ducked as a sword swung at him from behind, kicking backward and pushing the guard's feet out from underneath him. He turned and slammed his fists into the man's head, knocking him out. He saw a brigand bash the Tveor's helmet with a mace, leaving a sizeable dent, but the little warrior hardly noticed and took out his attacker with one mighty swing of his weapon.

Two others—what appeared to be a Dalaethrian and perhaps one of the Cernodyn—rushed toward the Tveor, bows in hand, as frantic guards scrambled to get out of their way. The remaining Iron Rose soldiers made a hasty retreat. The Tveor pointed to Narick, and the two ran to him.

The Dalaethrian waved as he approached. "Shylan Dar monk, we'll exchange introductions later. Where is the devotee of Teuvell? I sense her magic."

Andra ran out of the building, clutching her instruments. "Who are you? How did you find us?"

"No time to talk," the Dalaethrian said. "Let's get away before they can regroup. We've done enough here. Hurry!"

* * *

Andra hastened into the forest along with the others, the Cernodyn woman deftly leading them through the undergrowth and putting distance between them and the remaining Iron Rose soldiers. They stopped at last near a thick tangle of bushes, each pausing to catch their breath.

"We've lost them long ago," the Cernodyn woman said. "We'll be safe here for now."

"How did you find us?" Andra asked, trying to catch her breath, amazed at their change of fortune.

Mylth, Dorinen, and Bayark recounted their stories for Andra and Narick, who responded in kind, trading introductions all around.

"The Sarvethar was with you only a short while ago?' Andra asked, awed the by the idea.

"Indeed," Mylth said.

"But he's ill," she said, struggling to grasp what such a concept might even mean.

"There's more to it, but the sooner we can get to the keep, the better," Mylth answered.

"We seem to have a common objective," Narick said, "though our journey has been by accident and yours by design."

"I'm sure yours was no accident," Dorinen responded.

Narick shrugged. "I suppose I should say that ours was unclear to us until yesterday. When Ramwin revealed himself to me, he said nothing of what you've told me. The keep, the portal, none of it."

"Maybe it wasn't necessary for us to know," Andra offered. "If we'd gone to Meln aware it was under someone's control, we wouldn't have done the things we did. We might not even be here, and we might never have fought the Vordlai in the Rajaani camp." *And I might never have met Jeena.*

"We must trust that what has happened has been for the best," Narick added. "The Spirit works in ways we cannot comprehend fully."

"The Land Spirit seems to be passing away," Mylth said, after a short silence. "Even if we succeed here, I don't know what will happen afterward."

"But surely sealing the portal to the Underplanes will repair whatever damage has been done," Andra countered.

"It's not that simple," Mylth answered, dashing her hopes. "The Eral-savat, the earth ravage, the Vordlai… these are all symptoms of the Spirit's sickness, not the cause. It's possible that were the Land Spirit not weakened, none of these incursions could have happened."

"Do you think whoever this 'master' is, he might have been aware of the Spirit drawing in, and that was how he was able to release the Eral-savat?" Dorinen asked.

"It's highly likely," Narick said. "Our *Book of Syontar* states that the Land Spirit follows cycles, just as the seasons and all living things do. But these cycles span vast amounts of time, and no mortal, or even Dalaethrian, can mark their progress. If such a cycle were coming to an end, it would be a time of terrible danger for all living things. I believe that's happening now."

A sinking feeling gripped Andra. "The Land Spirit will really die?"

"Die, yes, but be reborn again and again, in an endless cycle," Narick answered. "Unless an incursion of the Underplanes prevents it from doing so. This is the great danger we now face. We've arrived at the crisis point in an endless struggle between life and death, and each time, there is a chance the darkness may triumph eternally."

"And each time it happens, living beings must choose to stand against the darkness," Dorinen said, "so that the Spirit can be reborn. That's what Ramwin meant when he spoke to me. My own people have a legend about the land's death, which we see enacted each year in the life cycle of the forest. The Soul of Urkera draws into itself in the autumn, leaving the lands bare through winter. Many beliefs like this exist, all over the world I'd imagine, perhaps a hidden memory of a greater truth."

Narick turned to Andra. "The sealing of the portal, and even the destruction of the Eral-savat will not stop the Spirit's death. Rather, doing so will ensure it can die and be reborn as it must. If evil is allowed to run rampant, the rebirth might not happen."

"Izznil told me the danger is already here," Andra said.

"He saw what was to come, as did the highest seers of my order." Narick placed a comforting hand on her shoulder.

"That's why he gave me this gem." She held up her lyre to show the others. "Somehow it gives me a stronger connection to Teuvell, even as She weakens."

"If a master of your college gave it to you," Mylth said to Andra, "you must have the ability to wield it as he envisioned."

"But what *is* it?" Andra asked.

"I suspect it's a conduit for great power, ancient and rare," he answered, "because I sensed your magic when we were still far from you. You said it gives you a means to channel your Lady Teuvell, yes?"

Andra nodded.

"Then with it," Mylth added, "we may have the power to strengthen the portal."

"But for how long?" Dorinen asked in a weary and despairing voice.

"It might not matter." Mylth turned to her. "The previous seal remained secure and undisturbed for more than five centuries. If we can prevent the portal from opening now, it will weaken the evil's incursion into our world, undoing some of what our enemy has tried to accomplish."

"So," Bayark at last spoke, "we have to go into Wyverdorn's keep, slay as many of those Vordlai beasties as we can, and lock away the rest, and kill this 'master'?"

"Essentially," Narick answered, "though I would prefer we take him alive. My order will be keen to question him. During the War of Gharborr, the Arltorath awakened the Eral-savat when the Spirit was not weakened, but it took all four of them to do so. Now, a single man has been able to raise it. We must discover how he was able to access such power and summon the Eral-savat again. We don't even know his ultimate motive."

"You said that your *Book of Syontar* speaks of the death of the Land Spirit," Mylth said to Narick. "Might someone have gleaned from it at least some clues about when that death would occur? And thus, have set these events in motion?"

"It's possible, though the book reveals nothing of specific times in the Spirit's great cycle," Narick answered. "Someone might have used it as a starting point for further research."

"Who would have access to this book?" Mylth asked.

"There are several copies, undoubtedly in different versions," Narick answered. "Three that I know of in the Shylan Dar Mother House library, two at least in the possession of Teuvell's college."

"I've heard of it," Andra offered, "but we aren't permitted to see it. Too old and fragile, they say."

"Xalphed Gornio probably owns one," Narick went on. "There are also likely a handful in Gavalahorne and throughout the Three Federations. I would imagine some among the Dalaethri would possess a few old copies."

"Quite possibly," Mylth answered.

"So, we're no closer to knowing who might have viewed this book," Andra said. "It could have been anyone in any of those places."

"If it even *has* had an influence," Narick cautioned.

"I suspect it has," Mylth said. "One with access to such a tome, and others, might also have acquired sufficient knowledge to perform the forbidden summoning of the Eral-Savat and to waken the Vordlai. Such power does not come easily. We are dealing with a learned individual who understands much about the ways of magic and the cosmos, and who knew the time of the Spirit's death was near. It's likely they've been planning this loathsome work for many seasons."

"But why hasn't Ramwin told any of you who this person might be?" Andra asked.

"I don't think he knows," Dorinen said.

"Or perhaps in order for us to come to this conclusion and find the answers on our own," Narick said, "and freely choose to act."

Mylth pinched the bridge of his nose. Dorinen seemed annoyed with him and turned away. Something must have happened between them, but Andra decided she shouldn't ask about it.

"Well," Bayark said. "*I* choose to carve up as many of those damned things as I can, and you better keep this 'master' away from me or there won't be enough of him left for you monks to talk to!"

"Master Bayark," Andra said, not wanting to change the subject, but no longer able to hold back from asking, and thinking the mood needed to be lifted a little.

"Ay lass?"

"I'm curious. Your helmet. It's very, well, unusual. Do your people hold the unicorn as a sacred animal?"

Dorinen suppressed a laugh and even Mylth smiled.

Bayark flushed red with irritation. "You tall ones," he grumbled and stomped away, leaving Andra and Narick in a state of bewilderment.

* * *

For much of the afternoon, the five of them pressed on as Dorinen led the way, while Andra kept watch on her gem. The woods grew ever thicker. The sun had moved well past its mid-point in the sky, and the group struggled through the thick foliage and dimming light. Bayark in particular cursed at the difficulty of the terrain, chopping at roots and bushes that presumed to get in his way.

As they progressed, the jewel on Andra's lyre gradually began to glow brighter, confirming Dorinen's hunch that they drew nearer to their goal. The forest, normally teeming with life, had fallen silent, interrupted only by the sounds of their passage.

"I sense a darkening magic nearby," Mylth said in a hushed voice as they passed three trees growing tangled about each other like vipers twisting in a pit.

"I do, too," Dorinen replied, her body stiffening. "This unsettling feeling is like when I faced the Vordlai," she replied. "Only, the sensation is stronger, more intense. And the Spirit isn't here. At all. There's evil everywhere in this forsaken place. Look."

She pointed to another clump of misshapen trees, twisted and gnarled, dulled to shades of grey and charcoal, as if corroding from the inside. A chill spread through her as awful as the Vordlai's venom, the certainty of the danger threatening to engulf her.

"The forest is bending to the will of the Underplanes," Mylth said. "I suspect it will only get worse as we get closer to the keep."

Dorinen trembled in anger. This abominable magic desecrated her beloved woods, warping them to its own disgusting essence. She took a deep breath, mindful of the rage that had consumed her in the aftermath of the Vordlai's attack on the Dwelling. She wanted to let that rage out now, to throw her whole heart into ending whoever had unleashed this atrocity.

"By the soul of Urkera, I *will* destroy you!"

* * *

"We're getting nearer," Andra said, joining Dorinen and Mylth. She stepped in front of the others and paused, the gem glowing warm and bright. Andra sang several notes in a mournful melody. "This way," she said a moment later, pointing in a direction that would take them southward. When the others hesitated, she said with exasperation, "I'm sure!"

"She's right," Dorinen said as they adjusted their course. "My senses are mistaken. I wouldn't have chosen this direction. How is that possible? I've never been wrong like this before."

"The foulness of the magic warping this place is also distorting your perception, slowing our progress" Narick said. "It will deceive and trick us more the closer we get to the evil's source."

Andra tried to ignore the implications of his words, and what they might mean for her home, her family. She turned her attention back to the gem. *Lady, if you can hear me, guide us truly. Help us.*

They pressed forward, confronting an ever-greater thickening of twisted foliage. Both Mylth and Dorinen drew their bows, and Bayark took out his axe.

Andra gripped her lyre, clearing her throat in case she should need to sing again.

The foliage distorted in front of them, degrading from lush greens to sickly greys, faded yellows, and mottled blacks, while its shapes grew ever more jagged and gnarled. Branches trembled and withered, as if autumn and winter collided in a single moment. Yet the trees didn't appear to be dying; instead, they were eroding into twisted, shadowy versions of themselves, grotesque shapes stretching out like the grasping hands of malevolent wraiths.

"If there are trees in the Underplanes, they must resemble these," Mylth said.

"Every step I take makes me more uneasy," Dorinen said with a heavy breath. "I'm not well. Maybe it's what the forest itself is feeling."

The air around them grew damp with a noxious odor of organic decay.

"What's happening?" Andra noticed a grey mist looming above them. The gemstone glowed hot. She saw Dorinen through the gathering murk, but the Cernodyn woman was already reeling, overcome with some sickness. To Andra's surprise, Mylth fell to his knees, his focus fixated on some point in the distance. She shot an alarmed look to Narick, but the monk now stood unmoving, hands clasped and eyes shut, as if in deep meditation.

"What in blazes is goin' on lass?" Bayark demanded in a hoarse voice. In the next instant, a dark fog swirled from the ground to encircle Andra. She struggled to catch her breath, and in a panic, she called out his name.

"Andra, my darling!"

Andra turned, distrusting her ears.

"Thank the Spirit you're here at last," a woman said with a broad smile, standing before Andra and holding her arms wide for an embrace.

Andra drew in a sharp, shocked breath and put a hand over her mouth. "Mother?"

Sixteen

Mylth slumped to his knees in disbelief. "Kyndaeviel?"

A captivating Dalaethrian woman stood before him, holding his attention with her deep green eyes. Flowers adorned her long brown hair, while her golden-trimmed robe flowed around her like rose petals falling in a gentle breeze.

He struggled to speak. "H-How are you here?"

"I've been sent by the Land Spirit to warn you," she said as she held a hand out to him. "The path you take is one of great danger. This is not the place to accomplish what you seek. Leave Cernwood, now."

The touch of her fingers on his cheek sent a shiver down his back. "But, how is this possible? Ramwin himself delivered us here."

"Ramwin was wrong," she said. "His power is weak in this forest, and he did not understand the truth, but now he sees clearly. He can no longer perceive you here, so he has sent my spirit to seek you out."

"Why you? Why now?" Mylth couldn't hold back his tears.

She caressed his face. "Because, my love, you know full well that you would not listen to anyone else, and it is urgent you heed my words."

"I've missed you," he said. "So much."

"As I have you, my love," she replied.

"What should I do?" he asked in a choked voice.

"Hasten to Meln, as soon as you can. You will be safe there. There are those in the village who can help and will give you the guidance you need."

Mylth clasped her hands tightly.

* * *

"Why are you here? How?" Andra stammered as her mother, Lysavell, embraced her. Andra hugged her in return, baffled. "How did you come to be in the forest?"

"The Iron Rose abducted me outside of Meln, but I escaped. I've been wandering alone for a long time, lost and afraid. And yet, I knew in my heart you would find me here. You have so many gifts, my love. I called out for you, and you came!"

Andra broke their embrace. "But I didn't sense you. I think I would have noticed my own mother in the woods!"

"But you did know. Somehow you knew!" Lysavell exclaimed, opening her arms again. "Please, my darling, let's go home now. I'm so tired, and I'm sure your father must be terribly worried about me. You know how he fusses over the slightest thing. I don't wish to keep him waiting any longer."

"You couldn't have known I would be here," Andra protested, stepping back. "You didn't know when I left Tenaeth. And you must have seen what's wrong with the people in Meln! You must have experienced it yourself." As she held up her lyre defensively, the gem glowed a deeper purple, as if in warning. She centered her lyre in front of her, almost as a shield. "Who are you? *What* are you?"

"Andra…"

"Stay away from me." Andra tensed, calling to mind a protection melody.

The woman began to cry. "Please Andra, don't do this! I love you."

Andra wanted so much to believe, to hug her mother again, but her intuition warned her of danger. "Shut your mouth!" Andra yelled. "You are *not* my mother!"

Finding enough composure to play a melodic phrase on her kenlim, Andra sang a short lyric in the language of Teuvell.

The woman claiming to be Lysavell began to shake, first a little and then more violently. She cried out, her voice devolving into a low-pitched growl blending with the sound of the wind blowing through the trees. A black mist seeped from her mouth, ears, eyes, and nose, and her face distorted like a flickering shadow in dim candlelight.

Keeping her concentration on the song, Andra took another step back, repeating the musical phrase over and over. The woman sank to the ground, convulsing.

Andra jumped back with a shriek. And where were her companions? They'd been right here.

"They can't have just disappeared."

She'd been so focused on the shocking sight in front of her that she hadn't realized her companions were missing, even though she'd stood right where they'd been only a few moments before.

"Where are they?" she demanded of the warped entity before her. "What have you done to them? To me? I will kill you if you don't answer!" She focused on the gem and called to mind her deadly song.

The oily black mist seeping from the being swirled about both of them. Andra's head spun with the sound of her mother's voice, calling, beckoning, pleading.

"Get out!" Andra yelled.

As if in response, her dizziness subsided, the mist cleared, and she saw the others, right where they'd been. Her mind raced, searching for an explanation. A few steps away, Narick stood motionless, in deep meditation. Dorinen knelt nearby on her hands and knees, retching. Mylth also knelt on one knee, caressing the air in front of him, his eyes glazed.

"What happened to you, lass?" Bayark demanded. "You just stopped and stood there!"

"What's going on?" she asked him. "With Mylth?"

"The pixie? Want me to knock some sense into him?"

Dorinen coughed loudly, drawing Andra's attention.

"She needs my help," Andra said. "Do something to wake Mylth out of his trance, but be careful."

Bayark clapped his hands together and rubbed his palms. "I know exactly what to do."

* * *

Mylth swooned before Kyndaeviel and covered his mouth to hide his sobs. Her gentle touch sent sensations of yearning and loss rippling through him. He wanted to hold her, to take her in his arms and kiss her, to lose himself in bliss.

Yet, something about this vision unsettled him. An intuition deep within cried out to him, warning of danger amid the swirl of raging emotions. He fought his uncertainty, wanting so badly to be reunited with his long-lost love.

"How am I touching your hand?" he whispered, regaining some sense of rationality. "If you are but spirit, you cannot have physical form."

"Ramwin can accomplish much," she assured him, "even now. You must listen to me, heed my warning."

More doubts crept into Mylth's mind. Her words didn't accord with the Sarvethar's own. "But he wouldn't warn us to flee from Wyverdorn Keep. He could not—"

A tight grip on his shoulders and a sharp shake almost sent him falling over. His head spun and the black haze swirling about him cleared.

"You were gettin' carried away there, pixie," Bayark said. "Luckily, I was here to bring ya back!'

"What did you do?" His head addled with dizziness, Mylth launched himself at Bayark. "Why did you interrupt me?" His would-be opponent stepped out of the way in haste, and Mylth stumbled to the ground, his reflexes still numbed by his confusion.

"What…" He drew in a deep breath, smelling the decaying scent of the forest, trying to remember where he'd been. But disorientation took him once more and he struggled to his feet, striking out again at Bayark.

"Mylth, stop it!" Andra shouted from a short distance away, where she comforted Dorinen as she retched.

"The lass is right, pixie," Bayark declared. "Somethin' strange is goin' on here. Whatever you were seein', it wasn't real. It wasn't right."

Mylth paused for a moment, clutching his throat and breathing deeply. "But she was there. Didn't you see her? She… was so real."

Andra stared at him. "Did you see her too?"

"You saw Kyndaeviel?" Mylth whispered, his body quaking at the mere mention of her name.

"What? Who? No! I mean, my mother. I saw my mother. Except, it wasn't her." Andra continued to stay with Dorinen, who now raised her head, pale and drawn.

Mylth considered going to her, but held back. "What about the monk?" he asked instead, rubbing his head, his clarity at last returning.

Andra glanced over at Narick, who still stood motionless. "If it's a trick of the mind, he can fight as well there as he can with his hands."

Mylth lowered his head to Bayark. "My apologies for lashing out. What did you see?"

Bayark pounded his chest with his fist. "I'm Tveor! We're not affected much by magic spells and mind tricks. You know that, pixie. Got a damned headache right now, though."

Mylth tapped the side of one eyebrow. "Well, one must have a mind to be affected, I suppose."

Bayark scowled at him, rubbing the handle his axe.

* * *

Dorinen shook off her confusion, barely able to stand upright, her head pounding and her stomach churning. Mylth now pushed past Bayark and went to her side, offering his hand to help steady her.

"Are you all right?" he asked.

"The sickness in the forest has been trying to afflict me," she said in a faltering voice, "but I've fought it off for now. I'll be well enough." She doubted her own words despite her assurance. "Thank you," she said to Mylth, leaning against him and appreciative of his support.

He gave her a compassionate embrace with one arm. "I wanted to be sure—"

Narick let out a shocking low-pitched growl that built into a yell. When he opened his eyes, he clenched his fists, poised to strike.

"Narick, what—" Andra started.

The snapping of old tree limbs crackled ahead of them. A swirl of black mist revealed two twisted mockeries of the human form made from barren foliage, like that of late autumn. They shuffled into view, scattering decaying leaves in their wake. Despite lacking anything like a face, pale eyes glowed green under their winding, dead branches and dried, rotting vines.

Dorinen didn't know why, but the sight of them brought a bitter taste to her mouth.

"Mondrytes," Mylth said, taking a deep breath and standing in front of Dorinen, almost protectively. "That's why we were seeing things."

One of the creatures raised its tangled limbs. "Leave this place, or die where you stand," it commanded in a rustling, dry voice.

"No one enters the master's home," the other one rasped.

Andra turned to Narick. "Master?"

Dorinen drew an arrow and kept her focus firmly on these perverse imitations of trees. She'd never seen such terrible creatures in her woods, and a wave of revulsion swept over her, thinking that they might now infest the forest.

As she nocked her arrow, Mylth shot his hand out in front of her.

"Wait! Don't waste it. They have no flesh to wound."

She glared at him in frustration. "Fine, so how do we fight them? And why are they unknown to me?"

"Creating them takes skill with rare elder magicks," Mylth answered. "I'd be surprised if you'd seen one before."

The creatures lumbered toward them, their makeshift legs still rooted to the earth.

"If you lot aren't gonna do somethin' about 'em, I will!" Bayark launched himself at the first Mondryte.

"Bayark, no!" Mylth shouted as Bayark cut his axe deep into its trunk.

As soon as he jerked his weapon free, the tangled twigs and branches twisted and coiled around the massive gash. Within moments, it was as if he'd done nothing at all.

The Mondryte struck out, slamming a gnarled limb into Bayark's face. He staggered back, blood trickling from his mouth, and raised his axe over his head, preparing a second charge. "Come on, you walkin' pile of kindlin'!"

Narick stepped forward and held out his hands between the Mondryte and Bayark.

As the other Mondryte shuffled to Dorinen and Andra, Dorinen ignored Mylth's warning and let loose her arrow. The thing halted for a moment as the arrow struck, but simply pulled it from the tangled roots of its form and discarded it.

"Oh, blood and tree ash!" she swore, throwing off the last of her malaise.

Andra drew out her flute and played four short notes, loud and piercing, in succession. She stood back as her flame flew at the nearest creature; but the fire deflected around it, as if it were made of stone.

Bewildered, her jaw dropped. "What happened?"

"These creatures are enchanted with ancient spells," Mylth answered. "No normal or even magical fire will harm them."

"Then by the Oaks, what do we do?" Dorinen demanded, pulling out another arrow.

As she did so, Narick began a monotone chant. He muttered a few words over and over, and the creatures stopped and turned to him. He chanted louder and with more force, holding out one hand to each of them, while a sound like a strong wind disturbing fallen leaves rustled inside the Mondrytes. They trembled and writhed, as if blown by fierce storm winds, shaking twigs and leaves free from their twisted forms, before crashing to the ground in a rush of hissing foliage and dead, tangled branches.

Narick broke off his chant and stumbled forward. Leaning over, hands on knees, he gasped for air.

"Narick!" Andra ran to him and helped him to stand.

Not knowing what else to do, Dorinen took tentative steps to where the creatures had disintegrated. She poked at the earth with her bow, unsure of what to expect. To her relief, she found nothing more than the damp ground.

"What in damnation happened to you folks?" Bayark bellowed behind her.

"Mondrytes warp the mind," Narick answered, taking deep breaths and rubbing the sides of his head. "In an attempt to guard their specified locations, they create vivid illusions. This is where they are most powerful. Thankfully, their fighting skills cannot match their mental intrusions. I was able to delve inside their limited thoughts and stop them."

Dorinen stamped the ground where they'd stood, perhaps hoping to obliterate any trace of them. Now clear on their purpose, the idea of such monstrosities polluting her home upset her even further.

Narick addressed everyone in turn. "Once I entered into meditation and focused inwardly, I was able to drive them out of your minds and into the open. I also disrupted their bodies, at least for a while. But they will return."

"Yet only Andra and Mylth were charmed," Dorinen said.

Narick nodded. "The Mondrytes made them see what they most wanted to see."

"I saw my mother, alone and lost in the forest," Andra said, her voice shaking. "But I knew something wasn't right, that it wasn't actually her."

Narick put a comforting arm around her shoulder. "I'm so sorry. I'm not surprised they would draw such an image from you."

"But what about the rest of us?" Dorinen asked. "I just fell ill. Why only those two?"

"Possibly because we are the ones who use magic," Mylth said, watching the trees beyond them, as if anticipating more danger. "Enchanted creatures are drawn to us."

Dorinen noted he said nothing about what he'd seen, even as he kept himself turned away from all of them.

"Perhaps," Narick agreed. "But had they succeeded in causing the two of you to depart, they would no doubt have turned their attention to the rest of us. And Dorinen felt their presence before any of us."

"Yes, and I'd rather not repeat it!" Dorinen put her bow back in its sling and swung it onto her back.

"Hm!" Bayark snorted. "I don't like enemies I can't hit! Messin' with your head ain't fair."

"Our enemies are anything but fair," Narick responded. "I suggest we leave this place quickly. These two will reform and there may well be more of them out here."

"Bayark, you're hurt!" Andra exclaimed.

Bayark shook his head and wiped away the blood from his face. "Ah, don't worry about me, lass, he said. "It'll take a lot more than these walkin' leaf piles to lay me to rest, so don't be offerin' to do any fancy magic on me."

Mylth approached Dorinen. "How are you, truly?" he asked.

She studied him, searching for any signs of what he might be feeling. But his face revealed nothing. Further, she didn't know if she wanted his concern or preferred him to leave her alone for now. "The sickness has passed." She focused on the ground and then back on him.

He regarded her for a moment with an expression resembling concern, though Dorinen recognized that whatever he'd seen still haunted him. He turned away.

"Mylth," she called after him, though she kept her distance. "Are *you* well? What did the Mondryte make you see?"

He hesitated. "I was... disoriented, that's all. Come, the monk is right. We must leave." He turned away from her again, perhaps not yet ready to tell her what he'd seen. She feared he might never be.

They pressed on into the old forest, its gnarled trees growing more tangled and misshapen almost with each step. Dorinen continually fought to shake off her disgust at the violation of Cernwood by ignoring as much of her surroundings as possible, something she wasn't accustomed to doing. She wanted to absorb the forest's essence, to breathe its fresh air, to bask in its abundant life and find the path forward. But here, that vitality decayed all around her, clouding her senses and dulling her perception. Her stomach knotted as she struggled with the anger and fear raging within, and most of all, a desire to see justice done.

Ahead of her, Mylth walked with Narick. They seemed to be conferring, but they were out of her earshot. Mylth obviously evaded her question, reverting back to his irritating tendency to keep to himself. What had shaken him so much?

Behind her, Bayark cursed, struggled to keep up again. Yet despite his grumpy nature, she welcomed him in their company.

She found herself walking beside Andra, but they couldn't find words for even a simple conversation, and so carried on in silence for a time, not looking at each other. Perhaps the Mondryte's vision still haunted her. How could those things have so disturbed these two, each so at ease with the powers of magic? That both could be so vulnerable when they were the most magically adept members of this ragged group didn't bode well for whatever lay ahead of them.

* * *

In a dark and forbidding place, a figure sat in mid-air, his legs crossed, his long grey robe hanging loosely about him, hood drawn over his head. Above his outstretched palms, an orb of blood red energy pulsated with light. In it, he witnessed far away things, and what he now saw interested him greatly.

"The Sarvethar has succeeded in gathering new slaves to do its bidding." His eloquent voice resonated off of the frigid stone walls. "Ramwin, you clever old boy. You kept them from my knowledge until now. I would be disappointed if you hadn't, but you could not hide them forever. I've now heard their words and learned much about them. Your power wanes. You cannot intrude here."

He took a deep breath of the damp, subterranean air.

"And what a motley band you send to me. The Dalaethrian who bound the Arltorath and helped seal the ravaged earth so long ago, oh what exquisite irony! A weak and frightened tracker of the Cernodyn. A young singer of Teuvell, capable of nothing but the simplest charms. A crotchety Tveor-at-arms, and most satisfying of all, the monk. When I destroy him, he shall suffer with pain that he never even knew possible. He'll learn the true futility of his wretched order!"

His mouth twisted into a crooked smile, and he beckoned to the darkness with his hand. A growl erupted as a huge Vordlai shuffled into view, larger than most of its kind, its wings folded neatly on its back, even as its yellow eyes shone with a hideous glint in the light of the orb's magical fire.

"Observe, Tarnohken," the figure commanded.

The Vordlai thrust its face close to the orb and squinted against the glow. As it watched the intruders, it let out a series of grunts, and croaked something resembling a laugh. Vapor filled the chilled air as it hissed.

"Yes, my dear," the floating figure said. "You and your kin will feed. The power of the Spirit is strong within them, raw streams of cosmic potency and light. Not only their flesh, but their essences will sustain you for some time."

The creature growled in delight, its grey tongue passing over its fangs eagerly, drool dripping on the stone floor.

And when your purpose is served, I shall feed you all to the Eral-savat.

As if sensing a challenge, the beast eyed him, almost in curiosity.

He diverted the Vordlai's attention by addressing it again. "Now my dear, we will prepare for the arrival of our guests. They must be allowed to enter the lowest levels of the keep. I want them to believe they are succeeding in their noble endeavor, and that their Land Spirit is still with them, even in this appalling place. Our triumph will be so much more satisfying when we destroy what pitiful hopes they've built. I want the Sarvethar to see what happens to his precious fools, to know that at last, he has failed, and to share in every moment of their suffering as they die. This time, the Spirit will not rise again."

He gave the beast a commanding stare.

"Tell your kin to offer only a token resistance to our guests at first. Under no circumstances is the monk to be harmed. I will punish severely any who disobey my commands. I will inflict a pain that not even your infernal kind can comprehend. Am I clear?"

The creature snorted.

"See this as an extended hunt." His tone softened. "Your kind love to taunt your prey, to feed on their fears as well as their forms, yes? So, frighten them, destroy their confidence, break their wills. Imagine how flavorful their flesh and blood will taste when it is permeated with the raw terror of their own annihilation, of the realization that the Land Spirit has died and shall never be reborn, that I have taken its place!"

He pointed upward with a slender finger.

"Once they are in the caves, you will subdue them. I will break their spirits with horrors beyond their imagining, and tomorrow night in Meln, on the eve of the darkmoon, they shall be the first offerings in a bloody harvest of humanity. They and those pathetic villagers will feed you, their deaths will break the portal's seal, and your kin shall walk these lands freely once more."

Tarnohken grunted in approval, leering with anticipation for the delicious ecstasy of the first flow of blood, sweetened by the terror of the victims.

"Go now, my beloved, and inform your kin of what they must do."

The beast bowed its head and lumbered away into the darkness.

The figure dismissed the orb and sat in silence for a time, brooding and contemplating. He descended to the ground, landing gently on his feet. The knowledge that nothing could stop him now, that his years of work and preparation would at last bear fruit, made him do something he'd not done for a long time.

He laughed, a scratchy snigger that blossomed into a full-throated cackle. The joy of the moment filled him and he let out a joyous bellowing from the depths of his twisted soul.

Seventeen

"Our passage has been too easy." Narick confided his concerns to Mylth as they walked ahead of the others. "A token resistance from two Mondrytes can't be all that this 'master' has to set against us."

"Indeed," Mylth answered. "Whoever it is wants us to find the keep. Otherwise, we might even be dead by now."

"Perhaps you underestimate our collective strength, Dalaethrian," Narick countered. "I don't believe we've come this far only to fail. The Spirit is still with us, even in this accursed place."

Mylth scoffed. "The Spirit acts only as it wishes, with little concern for us. Its Sarvethar will do whatever is necessary to preserve its own existence. That we've come this far is as much a testimony to our enemy's lack of concern about us or his ignorance as anything we or the Spirit have done."

Narick bristled. "Harsh words from a *Shy'nande*, especially the one who helped seal away the Eral-savat."

Mylth flinched, like a criminal whose secret had just been revealed.

"You cannot believe I wouldn't know who you are," Narick said with some satisfaction. "You are as much a legend as any from those times. But you don't know who *I* am. I've studied widely. I know the history of these lands, and while you may wish to remain unknown, you can't escape from your past."

"More than you know, monk," Mylth said, not hiding his bitterness.

Narick sensed he shouldn't press the matter further, deciding to change the subject. "What do you know about this keep?"

"Very little. Wyverdorn's great-grandfather built it over a century ago in the last days of Rilnarya's monarchy. The new government allowed him to retain his noble title. In exchange, he offered to protect the region and ensure that trade through Meln and elsewhere wouldn't be disrupted, by the Iron Rose or worse. But why he chose to build over the actual site where the Vordlai slept, I don't know."

"Perhaps it was deliberate," Narick offered. "The current lord may indeed be a good man, but one virtuous man does not an honorable legacy make. Who knows the intentions of his ancestors?"

"It's possible," Mylth said. "Many noble houses resented the end of the monarchy. Perhaps his ancestor's desire to preserve trade routes was merely a cover for more nefarious aims? He might have tried to resurrect the Vordlai himself and failed. What happened to him?"

Narick paused. "I don't recall, but I can't remember anything especially unusual about him or his death. The family has always been reclusive, but that proves nothing."

"Nevertheless, I agree it's odd to accept as mere coincidence that he chose that site, of all places."

"I suppose it doesn't matter," Narick replied. "Assorted madmen have tried to raise evil over the centuries, hoping to control it and subdue it to their wishes. All the more reason why we must stop the Vordlai, strengthen the portal, and find out who is behind it all."

"It won't be easy," Mylth warned. "Even if he is defeated or killed, the Eral-savat won't be undone. Sealing the portal here is only the first step in a much larger task."

"That's what worries me." Narick glanced at Mylth, who fixed his gaze on the distance, and now seemed lost in his own thoughts.

*   *   *

Some distance back, Andra and Dorinen still walked side by side. The silence between them ate at Andra, who found herself fairly bursting to know more about her new companion.

"I wonder what they're talking about so intently," Andra said at last, motioning to Narick and Mylth in an effort to find something, anything, to say.

Dorinen shrugged. "Normally, I could easily hear them, but I'm forcing myself to dull my senses. So, I have no idea."

"Is there anything I can do for you?" Andra asked, wanting to offer some comfort.

Dorinen sighed sadly. "No, thank you. And I haven't been much of a good traveling companion so far, I'm afraid. Please excuse my rudeness."

Andra didn't expect such a candid answer from one who'd been so closed off and focused. "It must be so hard for you to keep yourself centered in the midst of this desecration of your home."

"You're right. This place is violated, degraded. I'm struggling to contain my outrage, and anguish strikes me, almost with each step I take."

"And you have every right to feel that way." Andra wanted to reach out to her but held back.

Dorinen focused ahead of herself again. "My whole life has been so disrupted in such a short time. Everything I took for granted, all I was sure of, has been challenged, tested, swept away, even my belief in myself. I don't know what to think anymore."

Andra commiserated, appreciating that Dorinen shared her worries. "I'm not sure I've ever known what I truly believe, and the last several days haven't done anything to change my opinion, to be honest."

"I understand. I've experienced joy at being in the presence of the Spirit, and the deepest possible horror and fear when that Vordlai nearly killed me. I've met the Sarvethar, but come away not knowing why, maybe even wishing I hadn't. I've yet to discover my place in this affair at all."

Dorinen's words struck a chord of familiarity with Andra, though Andra struggled to know how to respond. "It sounds like we have a lot in common." But her words felt inadequate as soon as she spoke them.

Dorinen turned to her. "In common? You live in the world of cities and people. How could you understand what I've been through?"

Andra drew back, trying not to take offense. "I'm, I'm sorry. I just meant we've both been tested in ways we never thought possible. Others have faith in me, but that's something I don't often have in myself."

Dorinen's expression softened. "But you're an Artisan, yes?"

"Barely. In training." Andra shrugged. "I still have so much to learn."

"But you have your lyre, the glowing gem. You work miracles with your instruments, with your music, yes?"

Andra shook her head, trying to deflect. "That's because of the gem, not me. And every time I call on it, I fear it won't work, or it will work too well and destroy something."

"What is it?"

"I don't know, but it's ancient and powerful." She again recalled the Gro'ak, but tempered her uncertainty with memories of healing Narick and Jeena. "It's only determination, even anger, that's compelled me to keep trying to use it. And when it does what I want, I'm elated, even blessed. But the feeling doesn't last. It's like I constantly need to be reminded of my talents, and the gifts I do have."

"Because you don't yet hold them truly within you," Dorinen said, with sympathy. "I have the same struggle. No matter what anyone says to me about my role here, I've yet to believe it."

"You see," Andra said, "I told you we have things in common."

Andra observed Narick and Mylth, still some distance ahead of them. "They doubt themselves, surely?" She recalled Narick's near breakdown after his encounter with Ramwin, but kept the memory to herself, knowing it wasn't her place to mention it.

"Of course they do," Dorinen said. "Mylth carries great pain within him. He's old and wise. But he torments himself with false beliefs about his failures and regrets for someone he lost a long time ago."

This news surprised Andra. "You worry about him?"

"Perhaps. After the Mondryte possessed him, he became haunted. I think it made him see a Dalaethrian woman killed by the Vordlai during the Gharborr War. He still loves her, and I fear his regret is making him question why he's here, what he can do. Honestly, he could be a liability in the fight ahead, one we cannot afford."

"But it was a trick to weaken him. Those things invaded our memories to draw out the most moving images possible, to make us vulnerable and drive us away from the forest. I saw my mother. She's been missing since before I returned to Meln." Her chin trembled and she clenched her jaw, hoping to force it to stop, with little success.

"Your mother is missing?" Dorinen stopped, giving her a pained expression. "I'm so sorry."

"Thank you. She should have been at home in Meln, but..." Her voice trailed off.

Dorinen laid a comforting hand on Andra's shoulder, and Andra placed her own hand over Dorinen's. "I don't even know if she's alive, and my whole village is under the influence of some kind of drug. Chorlax, Narick called it. We think whoever controls those Mondrytes probably poisoned the village's wells."

Dorinen raised her eyebrows. "That's an unpleasant thought. But perhaps we'll have the chance to find her," she offered.

Andra shook her head. "I don't see how, but thank you again." She let go of Dorinen's hand and took a deep breath. "We're all afraid. We fear failing now."

"More than you know," Dorinen asked.

They walked for a short time, when she turned to Andra again. "May I confess something?"

Andra regarded her with curiosity. "Of course."

Dorinen took a deep breath. "What I've seen so far on this journey has reminded me of how much I fear to care for anyone, and how I often I'm threatened by those outside my own home. My parents were killed when I was a child, and I swore I would never give myself over to anyone again with the same love and devotion. I even kept some distance from those who cared for me in their absence, though I loved them all. And a Vordlai killed one of them."

Andra gasped. "Oh Dorinen, I'm so sorry."

Dorinen took hold of Andra's arm, as they made their way down a gentle slope to a creek and hopped over to the other side. "Thank you. The creature's attack was the beginning of everything that's happened since. I haven't even had time to take it all in, to grieve."

"You will, when our task over," Andra offered, hoping to give her some comfort.

"But when will that be?" Dorinen asked, turning to face her. "Even if we succeed, what's coming afterward will surely be far worse. I'm afraid I'll never see the Dwelling again."

"I suppose we have to take things as they come," Andra said. "I want nothing else than for my family to be safe and my home restored, but those things won't happen, not yet. Even if we save my village from being drugged, the effects will take time to wear off. I'm afraid I won't live to see my people recover. I miss my mother so much, and I dread the idea that she may be lost, that I'll never see her again." Andra's voice trembled as the memory of the Mondryte's vision intruded into her mind again. For a brief time, her mother had seemed so alive, so real.

"Don't give up hope for her yet," Dorinen said.

"I don't want to, but everything worries me so much," Andra answered. "People from my own village could have killed Narick yesterday, and... someone else I've come to care for almost died from a Vordlai attack before this past dawn. I saved them both, but it hasn't made me feel any stronger or more confident."

Dorinen gave her a sympathetic pat on the back. "Don't be harsh with yourself. As if I'm one to talk. I mean, maybe I've been too harsh with myself, too."

"We both have," Andra assured her. "I guess everyone has fears and doubts at times like these."

"Times like these?" Dorinen raised a suspicious eyebrow.

Andra found herself grinning. "You know, the loss of everything and the end of all that is?"

"Oh, is that all? Not the most confidence-building speech, I must say."

Andra chuckled as she warmed to the Cernodyn woman. "Well, I know our situation is far from what we would want, but how about this for encouragement? Somehow, we've all found each other in the middle of terror and chaos, and that's fairly good proof that at least *something* is guiding us. Mind you, I'm saying this for my benefit as much as for yours."

Dorinen covered her mouth and snickered.

"If we can't rely on the Spirit," Andra went on, "we must be each other's strength. We're here now, and we each have our own talents and gifts. I mean, I have my music and... a deep bond with another, but that person is far away now, so I must rely on you all."

"A lover?"

"More, I think. Maybe?" Andra cast her gaze downward, her cheeks warm, her heart warmer.

Dorinen gave her a gentle bump with her elbow and a teasing grin. "You think?"

Andra glanced briefly at her. "It's complicated and new, and confusing."

"Ah, he must be special."

"She." Andra looked down again.

"Oh. Oh! Forgive me. I meant no offense."

"None taken, I promise you." Andra placed a reassuring hand on Dorinen's. "I'm used to others making assumptions."

"Well, it's what lies in one's heart that matters," Dorinen said. "And yours is very much in the right place. If you have a bond with her, she's lucky."

Andra savored these words and for a moment she felt a gentle touch, like a loving caress, in her soul. "We'll see what the future may hold. If there is a future."

"There has to be. We can't allow for any other option. And if there isn't, I shall give the Spirit a good, stern lecture about how to better order the cosmos."

Andra burst out laughing and threw an arm around Dorinen as they walked. "Your words are wise and bold, even if they come from a place of doubt."

"And you are far more confident than you claim to be," Dorinen said, smiling.

"Honestly," Andra said with wince, "much of it's just bluffing."

"Well, I wish I possessed the talent to bluff that you do."

Andra gave her hair an exaggerated flip. "Oh, I'm very good at bluffing! I can teach you how sometime, if you'd like. It's quite the useful skill and has saved my foolish behind more than once. Someday, I'll bring you along to one of my favorite taverns, and you'll see how good at prevarication I can be."

"And I shall take you up on that offer. Just as soon as we prevent the end of all that is and the loss of everything!"

* * *

The robed figure walked in silence. He had much to prepare for his new guests, but first he needed to attend to his practice. Each day, he engaged in physical exertion, and each day, the work became more tedious.

He opened a rotting wooden door at the end of the hallway, and entered a chamber, barren except for a well-worn cushion on the floor, near a brazier burning bright with a golden fire. He sat cross-legged on the cushion, resting his hands on his knees. Taking a breath, he focused and spoke. "Enter."

A door at the opposite end of the chamber swung open, and in stumbled a nervous Gro'ak clutching the hilt of a sword hanging loosely at its belt.

"Good meet, Kuhg," the man said in the Gro'ak language.

"Why is Kuhg here?" the Gro'ak asked.

"Because you've an honored role in my great plan," he replied in his own language.

"Kuhg help you?"

"Indeed. I need you, little friend. I must maintain my skills to ensure that I am strong when the battle truly begins. You understand the importance of being strong."

"Aye," the Gro'ak grunted.

"Good. Now, come close, draw your weapon, and stab me."

Kuhg cocked its head. "Master wishes stabbing?"

"Yes. Stab me. Do not worry. I will be safe."

The Gro'ak drew its dented sword with caution and advanced. It came closer to its seated master, but hesitated.

"Stab me," the man said again, with calm. "It would please me greatly."

The Gro'ak growled and clutched its weapon. It lunged clumsily at the man in grey, aiming its sword at his heart. Still, the man did not move. The blade came to within a breath of his chest, but he swerved away, disappearing into the darkness at the chamber's edge. The Gro'ak stumbled and fell, dropping its sword with a clatter on the stone floor.

"I told you I could not be harmed," the man stated, emerging casually from the shadows. You are doing well. Pick up your sword, and strike at me again."

"Kuhg like not tricks!" The Gro'ak crawled to its feet and retrieved its weapon. "Master is cruel!"

"Indeed."

But the Gro'ak wouldn't move. "Kuhg will not attack. Master will kill Kuhg."

The man observed Kuhg from underneath his hood. He motioned for the Gro'ak to approach. "Come, my little friend. Sit."

Kuhg watched him with suspicion and sat some distance away.

"No, sit near to me," he commanded. He waved his hand, and the Gro'ak was pulled across the chamber to its master's feet.

Annoyed, the man grasped the blade. He snapped it in half with one hand, and Kuhg hissed in shock. He grabbed Kuhg's shirt and lifted the little creature to his face. The Gro'ak squealed and wriggled about in desperation.

With his free hand, the man tapped Kuhg twice at the base of the neck. It clutched at its throat, terror darkening its haggard face. Its breath began to rasp as it struggled for air.

"You will not disobey me again." He dragged his hand across the creature's neck and willed the Gro'ak to breathe once more, before dropping it to the floor, where it took deep, wheezy breaths.

"Look at me," he said to the wretched creature, who now cowered on the stone floor. Kuhg obeyed, whimpering.

He knelt and sighed. "You make me weary."

He placed a hand on the trembling Kuhg's forehead and paused for a moment. With one sharp tap, the Gro'ak fell back, slumping to the floor, dead.

The man stood. "Approach!" he commanded in a loud voice. The same door swung open again, and a Vordlai squeezed through.

"Take it away, and feed if you wish."

The Vordlai scooped up the Gro'ak's body with a hungry growl and left the room, slamming the door behind it.

"No challenge," the man said bitterly.

How he wished to abandon these pathetic exercises and match skills against one of the Vordlai, but he dared not risk such a conflict, not until he knew he controlled them fully.

Still, satisfaction bubbled up in his poisoned soul. "Ramwin's playthings are coming. Best of all, Narick Yerral is among them. He will be a true test, one who might match my own skills, perhaps even surpass them. Killing him would be the final proof of my path, a vindication of all my work."

He returned to the cushion, preparing to meditate on his own power.

"After more than ten winters of preparation, the fools of the Shylan Dar will soon realize the full consequences of their treachery, their betrayal. At last, I have become who I was meant to be."

* * *

Dorinen strode to Mylth and Narick without hesitation and fell into step with them, easily keeping pace. Mylth regarded her with surprise at the boldness of her intrusion.

Narick broke the silence, as if sensing her wishes. "I will leave you to talk," he said, bowing to them both and heading back toward Andra.

She and Mylth walked in uncomfortable silence for a short distance.

"You should know by now you can't deceive me," she said, avoiding eye contact.

He turned his head to offer her an irritated expression.

"The Mondryte," she faced him at last. "It appeared to you as Kyndaeviel and tried to tempt you into leaving the forest, am I right? It played with your emotions, seeing them as a vulnerability, just as Andra beheld her mother, who she fears might be dead."

Mylth didn't respond, perhaps wishing she would leave him be.

"Not speaking of it will not make it better," Dorinen said, allowing him to hear the frustration in her voice. "Those old feelings are a part of you, Mylth. You've pushed them away for so long that they're tearing you apart. I have seen your unrest from the day I first met you. This turmoil controls you. It fosters your anger, even hatred of Ramwin. It makes you act irrationally, and I'm afraid it will endanger us."

"A bold claim." He refused to meet her gaze.

"A true one. She will always be a part of your life and memories, but you must let her rest in peace. If you don't…"

He clenched his jaw. "If I don't?"

"Our enemy may well attack your mind again, pulling out other memories, maybe even turning you against us. I need to know I can rely on you. We all do."

He stopped abruptly. "Do you forget who I am? What the Sarvethar said? Do you think that one such as I could be so easily taken?"

She returned his stare. "'One such as you?' Honestly, I don't know. I just saw a mindless pile of leaves do a fine job of bringing you to your knees."

Mylth scowled and drew away, increasing his pace. "Now you sound like the Sarvethar. Everything is a joke, is it? Perhaps you've spent a little too much time in his warped company. I will watch over myself. I suggest you do the same."

He quickened his pace and left her behind. But as she watched him press ahead, she knew she was right.

* * *

Darkness set in early. Too early. The thick tangle of trees already threatened to shorten the afternoon's light, but the sorcerous gloom of their surroundings made things even more difficult for Dorinen, as she struggled to focus. She imagined seeing signs of deer tracks, or birds taking flight. But when she examined the earth, the foliage, and the branches, none appeared disturbed at all. She stopped and rubbed her temples, her head hurting and her senses dulled yet again.

"Let me try to help," Andra offered, seeing Dorinen's distress. Removing her lyre from its case, she closed her eyes and played a short, melancholy melody. When she finished, the gem started to glow, compelling Dorinen to reach toward it. Instead of heat, Dorinen noticed a calming warmth spreading up her arm, reinvigorating her and suffusing her with refreshment and renewal. The life-giving sensation receded too soon, but the pain in her head had faded, and her perceptions had become sharp once again.

"How?" She shook out her hand.

"I don't know how long it will last," Andra said, "but it should offer you some relief for a while."

Dorinen now possessed enough of her bearings to chart their course, though it pained her even more to move through the scarred landscape of her beloved forest. Mylth returned to her side, and both made ready their bows. Despite her worries about his state of mind, she needed him. Their quarrel would have to wait.

"Somethin' bad's in the air. I can smell it!" Bayark half-whispered.

"For once, I cannot fault your words," Mylth responded. "We face an evil the world has not seen in many centuries."

"Stay close to each other," Dorinen said.

"We must be alert," Narick said. "The Vordlai that attacked the Rajaani camp last night slipped by me, Andra, and their Ferwar. I suspect those who have been awakened can move with enchanted stealth, which means we might have no way of knowing before one of them strikes."

"That would explain how the Vordlai I fought was able to surprise me," Dorinen said. "No creature of our world could have moved so silently that I couldn't have sensed it." She shook away a shiver at the memory of those horrid claws and tried to hide her unease.

"Those already roaming our world might even be able to enter into the Underplanes, but cannot as yet bring back their kin," Mylth answered. "I suspect that will change soon."

"We will not allow it to happen," Dorinen said, tightening her grip on her bow.

"As long as I get to have at 'em, I don't care where they can go!" Bayark said.

"They're unlike any creatures of this world," Dorinen said. "It took all of my strength to inflict any real wounds with my sword." Fear and doubt clawed at her again.

"I trust my blade and my wits," Bayark answered in defiance. "My weapon ain't just a normal axe, though she's a fine one of them."

Dorinen regarded him with curiosity. "What do you mean?"

"This here axe is blessed by the Stone Lord himself, crafted in the sacred forge under Stimus-hodd. That's what I was doin' when you and the pixie crashed into my fun: bringin' her back home. A thief from the stinkin' Iron Rose stole her and took her to Gavalahorne. Figured he'd be able to sell it to some mage out there for a good price. A whole lot of spell-types'd love to know how this beauty was made. I wasn't about to let him get away with it, so I went west, got my weapon back, and ended as many of those scum as I could. That's why they were followin' me. Anyway, like I said, it's blessed. It'll cut anything made of flesh, and I'm bettin' it'll do a whole lotta damage to the magical skins of them Underplane critters as well. They're in for a real surprise!"

Dorinen sniffed the air and stiffened. She held up her hand, bidding the others to be silent, and dashed ahead into the blackening trees, coming soon to where the dying forest gave way to a much larger clearing. She shuddered at what she saw there.

Eighteen

"This is... horrid," Andra said, her voice shaking.

The crumbling stone walls of Wyverdorn Keep stank of death and decay. Withered, brown vines clung to them like grasping bony fingers. The shadows of late afternoon distorted the keep's towers, transforming them into a mimicry of the withering trees around them, further betraying the fate of a place twisted and violated by a dark magic not of this world.

"Lord Wyverdorn's estate was beautiful," she continued. "People always spoke of its elegance. Those were his prized orchards," she gestured to the dead trees before them. The orchards once adorning this place with beauty now withered brown with decay, gnarled and twisted, as dead as the keep itself. Flies swarmed around the remnants of rotting fruits that littered the ground like corpses. "It was all kept perfectly. But this—"

"This is the clear mark of the Underplanes intruding into our world," Mylth said in a solemn tone. "The evil we face here corrupts and ultimately ruins everything it touches. The forest might recover in time if we succeed, but I'm afraid the keep is destroyed."

"What do you suggest we do?" Narick asked.

"The power of this darkened magic grows stronger at night," Mylth said, "especially with the approach of the darkmoon, but we can't wait until morning to act."

Andra took a few breaths to steady herself, the reality that they had no time fully hitting her.

"If, as I suspect," Mylth continued, "we must venture far below this keep, we must be ready for any attacks. We don't yet know how deep into the earth we'll need to go, or indeed, if there is even a way into the lower levels from the keep itself."

"We have to go underground here?" Andra asked, now wanting more than anything to flee from this horrid place.

"Almost certainly," Mylth answered.

"Then let's not wait any longer," Dorinen said, a dogged determination in her voice. "I'll fight beside you and die, if I must, but I will see my home free from this abomination."

Andra swallowed hard but took Dorinen's hand and cleared her throat. "We can accomplish this. I truly believe that."

"We are here at the Spirit's bidding," Narick said, "but you all need to remember: nothing forces us to do what we are called to do. We must enter into this freely and of our own choosing."

While the others agreed, Mylth remained silent and unmoving.

"Well, I can't wait to get in there and start payin' back!" Bayark said, more eager than anyone else.

"You'll have your chance, friend," Narick said.

Andra detected a shadow of resignation in his voice and worried that if he'd already accepted whatever fate awaited them, she and the others might not survive.

"May the Land Spirit sustain us," Narick continued. "May our own strengths be one with it and with each other, may our hearts and minds be at ease in our time of turmoil. May the eternal essence that suffuses us with our very being glow strong from within and light the way along the troubled path we now walk. So may it be, until the light of the Absolute reclaims us all."

"So may it be, until the light of the Absolute reclaims us all," Andra echoed, while the others spoke quietly, perhaps prayers of their own. All save Mylth.

Andra again took in the crumbling walls of the keep, and the remnants of the trees surrounding them. She placed a hand over her mouth, unable to comprehend the shock of this once-lovely place so laid to waste. "This is appalling."

"It is," Narick agreed, "but we've come this far, when we could have been stopped."

A thought came to her. "We've been assuming this so-called master is waiting for us here, but what if he's somewhere else? He's obviously been to Meln and he's threatened Ternen, so why does he have to be here? Maybe this is only one of several places he frequents?" Andra wanted to convince herself as much as the others.

"I would agree if the collapse of the portal were not likely imminent," Narick answered, "but I think as that time approaches, he will want to be here to finish the task of freeing the Vordlai."

"Still, no matter how strong this man is," Mylth said, "he cannot remain in the presence of such darkening magic for too long. Its power will overwhelm and enslave him."

"I doubt anyone could live in this forsaken place for long," Andra added.

"And if he thinks the Vordlai will do his bidding," Mylth said, "he's a fool."

Bayark shuffled from foot to foot. "I don't like this any more than you folks, but aren't we here to stop this rot from happenin' in the first place? Let's go!"

"I agree," Dorinen said. "The time for speculation has ended. We don't have the luxury to concern ourselves with his motives or his location. And the longer we stand here debating it, the more we risk alerting whatever is here to our presence. If, as you say, they don't know already."

She cocked her head and motioned for the others to be silent. Drawing back her arrow, she spun about and let it fly at a crenellation on the left-hand side of the wall. With a cry of shock, a Gro'ak fell dead to the ground.

"We need to find cover, now," she insisted, her voice calm but concerned. A series of distant grunts from another wall confirmed her warning.

The companions hastened through the tangled remains of lifeless trees and repugnant fruit, and drew near the stagnant and rancid moat surrounding the keep's walls.

Dorinen scanned for a means to cross it, but saw only the blackened, collapsed husk of what had been a bridge. "How will we get across?" she asked, keeping an eye on the wall in front of them. "The bridge is ruined."

"I have something better than a bridge," Andra drew out her flute. Narick groaned, drawing questioning looks from the others.

As she played her levitation song, Mylth and then Dorinen floated across the water.

"Andra, what?" Dorinen cried out.

Mylth said nothing, though his face betrayed his shock.

As soon as Andra set them down on the opposite side with an apology, they began scouting their surroundings.

"Now hold on there, lass," Bayark protested as Andra turned to him, pointing a finger at her. "I ain't good with this. I've already had one shock today, gettin' flung all the way from Crythmarr to here in the blink of an eye. Our folk don't like magic, even the nice kind."

"Fine. You can swim," she said with a casual air.

He glanced at the stagnant water and back to Andra. "Be quick about it," he grunted.

She played, and he gripped his stomach in astonishment as he floated effortlessly across, until the midpoint of the journey. Then with a sharp jerk, he suddenly rotated head over heels twice. Panicking, he grabbed his helmet and swore loudly. A moment later, she lowered him to the other side.

"I'm sorry!" Andra called out, genuinely apologetic, but amused. "I must have played a wrong note!"

"Wrong note, my ass!" Bayark roared back to her. "You did that on purpose, girl!"

Andra turned to Narick. "Are you ready?"

"No," he said, folding his arms, "but we have no choice."

"I'll make it quick, I'll—" She dropped her flute as pain seared through her upper left arm.

* * *

The man in grey stood in silence, his hands folded before him. In his mind, he conducted his movements with speed and confidence, his mental discipline honed to perfection. He knew no one could stand against him now; no challenges remained for him in this place.

He'd directed his efforts to controlling the murderous urges of the Vordlai and opening the portal to their realm. He'd bided his time, waiting for the onset of the darkmoon.

"Tomorrow, we will initiate the first slaughter, opening the way and hastening the Spirit's death. At last, the folly of the Shylan Dar monks, the Teuvell Artisans, and so many other believers will be revealed."

Despite his strict mental controls, he found he grew ever more impatient, but he reminded himself that impatience would lead to error.

He turned to a Vordlai lurking in silence nearby.

"For ten turnings, ten passages of the summer, I have waited. One more day, and it shall bear fruit."

The creature snarled.

"How I long to test my skills against you." He observed the infernal horror standing in front of him. "To see if I can evade your deadly claws and break your otherworldly bones. Once you and your vile kind have torn apart these lands and grown bloated from their useless flesh, I shall challenge you, humiliate you, defeat you. Then you will be banished again, this time by my hand."

Drawing his hood closer about his face, he turned and made for the chamber door. A loud growl and the sound of claws shuffling on stone stopped him. Had he less control over his emotions, he would have cheered in glee. His gamble worked.

Without turning, he addressed the creature. "So, you have understood my intention. Good. But now I must destroy you before you can convey my plans to the rest of your foul kin. And I want to do so with my body, not my mind. Only then will I prove my mastery over you all."

Removing his robe, he placed his hands together in front of his chest, still facing away from the Vordlai. He heard the creature advance, snorting and sniffing the air as it stalked him. Yet he stood unmoving, seeking a place of calm deep within himself, hoping to lure the creature closer.

"Take me if you can, Qendurrag," he said, addressing the beast in a taunting voice. "I am defenseless, weak, easy prey. Sink your deadly talons into my beating heart. Feast upon the mortal who would betray you."

The creature needed no more prompting. With swiftness, it lunged, and the man in grey sensed it slashing its claws at his back. They never struck.

Dropping down, he fell forward onto his hands, and kicked back with both feet. He struck the Vordlai's legs; it screeched and tumbled to the floor.

Rolling over, he jumped to his feet. His enemy struggled to stand, its agony only enraging it further.

"Face me with all of your primal fury!" he commanded with amused mockery. "Aim for my heart, try to rip out my throat! I deny your supremacy, I laugh at you and your disgusting appetites. Your kind are worthy only to be my slaves!"

The furious beast charged, swiping at his head. He ducked, but part of its massive body caught him in passing, knocking him to the floor. Stars exploded in his vision, and pain surged through his face as he slammed into cold, hard stone. Blood trickled from his nose.

No matter. He relished feeling more alive now than in ages, and pulled himself to his feet.

Breathing heavily, he lunged at the creature, punching below its ribcage with a potentially killing blow. It spit blood, falling backward with a thunderous noise, crashing to the floor, where it lay convulsing, gasping for air.

Chuckling, he approached. Keeping his distance, he strolled around it, stopping near its head. The Vordlai hissed.

"Perhaps you are easier to kill than the ancient texts suggest," he observed, with a hint of disappointment.

The creature struck in haste, its talons slashing the man's thigh. He cried out and scrambled to move away from the Vordlai's grasp, as blood gushed from the wound. The Vordlai rasped something resembling a laugh.

The man cursed himself for his arrogance. He tried to stand, but his injured leg buckled. The beast's venom had begun to take effect. *You damned fool!*

He reminded himself that he still controlled them, and he'd taunted the creature to attack him. Shuffling away and kneeling, he entered deep inside himself, to a point of mental stillness. Calling on his years of training, he silenced the pain, blocked out the numbness, and willed his injured limb to feel again. He commanded the blood to stop flowing. With his will, he counteracted the toxin and visualized it dissipating. As his mind compelled, so his body obeyed. But his meditation left him vulnerable.

The injured Vordlai pulled itself toward him, stumbling and clutching at its damaged belly. It let out an agonized howl.

It swung.

And missed.

The man in grey ducked to one side, even as his weakened leg threatened to give out underneath him again. He moved in for what needed to be a final attack, launching a sharp kick that caught the beast under its chin. The creature reeled and fell to the hard stone floor. The man jumped on top of it and slammed the heel of his hand into the soft spot under its jaw. Three more hits to the sides of its head, and the Vordlai lay dead. Smoke poured from its leathery flesh, which now crackled and rippled as if seared by flames. The body collapsed in rapid decay, its skin crumbling to ash as a fetid stench arose from the corpse.

His breathing heavy, the man in grey fell to one knee near his fallen opponent. He flashed a grim smile of satisfaction. He'd defeated a Vordlai with his bare hands, finding the answer he sought, the final challenge he needed. His sheer will and determination had defeated this supernatural monstrosity and its deadly venom. No one, not the Vordlai, the Land Spirit in its death, or even the Eral-savat itself would stop him.

"Come to me swiftly, Narick," he whispered in a heavy breath. "Come to me and with your dying breath, learn at last the true value of our art."

* * *

"Andra!" Narick yelled.

A Gro'ak arrow stuck in the mud beside her, having grazed her skin. At once, Narick stood over her, offering himself as a shield. Both Dorinen and Mylth let arrows fly. In an instant, the Gro'ak responsible fell from above them with a squeal. The two kept their arrows taut against their bowstrings as they scouted the wall for more of the creatures, while Bayark swore and threatened violence.

Andra gasped as Narick pressed his fingers against the bleeding wound. With his free hand, he gave her the kenlim. "Heal yourself, quickly! We don't have much time."

"It's so difficult." She tried to ignore the stinging, even as it grew worse. "I need to focus all of my attention on the song."

"You must try," he said. "We have to get across the moat. We're easy targets out here. Dorinen and Mylth can only protect us for so long."

Narick placed a hand on her forehead and chanted in the Shylan Dar language. His warm palm eased Andra's pain and comforted her, allowing her the calm she needed to play. She grimaced as she picked up her instrument, and struggled to concentrate, plucking the wrong strings and singing sour notes. But after several strained efforts, the gem's light shone over her wound, easing the scrape and cooling its throbbing heat.

Another arrow cut through the air beside them, shaking Andra from her song. But she'd done enough to stem the bleeding and the pain, even though a stinging mark still streaked her skin.

Beyond the moat, Dorinen and Mylth felled another Gro'ak archer.

Narick helped her to her feet. "Are you well enough to cross?"

"I am." Though her limbs shook as she stood. She'd try later to heal herself further, but she feared she wouldn't get another chance.

"Take yourself across first," Narick said, "before me."

"Narick, I won't leave you vulnerable to any arrows."

"Do it! Your safety is vital to our survival."

She reluctantly played herself across as quickly as she could manage, before turning her attention to Narick. She lifted him from the ground, but as he landed near to her, a third arrow just missed him and splashed into the water.

Bayark swung his axe and stomped. "Come out, you craven bastards! Is shootin' an unarmed girl your idea of sport? Fight me face to face, weaklings!"

Mylth put a hand on his shoulder. "Quiet! You'll do us no good by announcing our presence to anything else that's not yet aware of it. You'll have your fight soon enough."

"Good!" Bayark shot back, shaking free of his grip with a jerk.

Weapons drawn, the five made their way to the rusted and ruined iron gates of the bar and entered into the keep.

"These inner walls have walkways around them," Mylth observed. "More Gro'aken are likely up there. We shouldn't linger."

They hastened to four stone buildings, arranged in a quadrangle, one larger than the others, and two more like towers, set opposite one another. Andra remembered being here once as a child. These buildings boasted fine stonework and ornament, but now broken windows and splintered doors marred each, betraying signs of struggle and looting. She nearly stumbled over heaps of tattered cloth, a broken bench, and rusting tools littering the ground. In the center of the square, the remnants of a bonfire smoldered. For Andra, the whole scene conjured fears of what might yet happen to her own home.

They approached the embers, and through the ashes and rising wisps of smoke, she made out traces of bodies, charred beyond recognition. She froze and her hand shot to cover her mouth as she gasped.

"This the folks that lived here?" Bayark asked.

Narick shook his head. "I would say these are Gro'aken bones.

Cooked for food. They'll eat their dead out of necessity, if there is nothing else for them to hunt."

Though repulsed, Andra couldn't tear her gaze away, remembering hearing about the Eladran with his heart cut out.

"They've been here for a while," Dorinen said, pacing around the perimeter of the burn.

"Wyverdorn's forces must have fallen some time ago," Narick said.

"Is it possible anyone here might still be alive?" Andra asked him, though she doubted it in the same instant.

"We have no way of knowing what this 'master' intends for them," he answered, "but I wouldn't hold out much hope."

Andra dreaded his words as she again worried about her missing mother, and tried to shove away all harrowing thoughts of what Lysavell's fate might have been.

Seeing her distress. Narick placed a hand on her shoulder. "I'm sorry. And honestly, we have no way yet of knowing for certain the fates of anyone."

Mylth ventured beyond the embers and scanned the buildings. "We must try to find some way to access the tunnels that I believe are under the keep."

"You 'believe' are under the keep?" Bayark asked, raising an annoyed eyebrow. "You mean you're not sure if what we're lookin' for is even down there?"

Mylth paused for a moment. "No."

"Damnation!" Bayark pounded the rotting earth with the end of his axe. "I came all the way out here with you for a fight, pixie. I ain't here for a grand tour of country estates, or to explore the charms of this stupid forest!"

Dorinen glared at him.

At once, Bayark bowed his head to her. "My apologies, lass. I know this is your home. I'd be just as furious as you if mine was under attack."

Dorinen rubbed her forehead. "I'm afraid all of us are on edge now," she said. "But we all want the same thing, even if for different reasons."

Narick pointed to the ruined towers. "I suggest we start searching for entryways, and see what comes of it."

Andra had a sudden insight. "It might not be as difficult as we think, if our enemy actually wants us to be here."

Narick regarded Andra with a disturbing realization on his face. "Which means it's a trap."

Nineteen

The frantic Gro'ak struggled in the Vordlai's deadly grip, dangling by its worn and tattered shirt. Scraps of rusty chainmail, salvaged from some long dead soldier, clattered and clanked around its leathery neck as its captor shambled along an old stone corridor. The little captive panted and shook as they entered the master's octagonal chamber.

The man in grey sat suspended in midair. The Vordlai threw the Gro'ak to the ground at his feet. The Gro'ak whimpered and cowered, fearing it was about to die.

"Jumm-av," the man addressed the Gro'ak in its own guttural language, "Told you I did, let passage for guests into keep. Few arrows shot wide, some warning from wall, no more. Tell me, leader of clan of yours, why you disobey me?"

Jumm-av sputtered and stammered. "Know nothing of what master speaks. Did as asked, no more!"

"The young singer has a hurt, by one of you. Arrow struck her and killed her might have. Lucky you, has she stone of power, and healed herself."

He paused and changed to his own tongue. "The pleasure of inflicting harm upon them belongs to me alone."

"It was mistake! Was not to strike girl! Fool shot arrow and got killed. Got what he deserved. Please, master not to kill Jumm-av?"

"Kill? Oh no!" The master descended to the ground. He knelt and helped the wretched Gro'ak to its feet. "As you rightly say, it was a mistake, and you did not commit the offense yourself. You are so pathetic I actually believe you. A stray arrow, intended to land farther away, hit her by accident. The one who did this is dead. That is good."

Jumm-av breathed a sigh of relief. "Thanks to you, master."

The master leaned closer to the Gro'ak. "Of course, I must ensure you obey me in the future. As the leader, you are responsible for all that your underlings do. You must be an example for their errors." He forcefully took hold of the Gro'ak's arm and held it out.

"Gerinvarg!" he called. The Vordlai lumbered to his side. "Remove this arm, at the elbow. Eat it if you wish."

Jumm-av howled in terror as the Vordlai drooled, flashing its teeth.

The master turned to walk away as the Gro'ak's screams echoed from the chamber and down the old stone hall.

* * *

Andra followed Dorinen's lead and they searched the nearest building, but found only broken furniture and torn garments in the lower rooms. As they emerged outside, dusk had settled and the first few stars already dotted the sky.

"This is getting us nowhere," Andra said in frustration. "What if…"

She held up her lyre and focused on the gem, plucking a simple scale. The strings hummed of their own accord, and the jewel's dim flicker of light expanded to surround her in a shimmering spiral. She felt herself begin to drift away, to be taken far from her surroundings and her waking consciousness.

"What's happening?" she heard Dorinen whisper in an alarmed voice. "What if this alerts more Gro'aken?"

But nothing intruded, and Andra continued.

"Teuvell has her!" Narick exclaimed, as if from a long way off. "Stand back. She's being guided."

If only Andra shared his optimism.

In her trance, she sang a haunting and beautiful song in a language she'd never before heard, her voice echoing off the stone walls. Images of the recent past played out in her mind's eye, before unimaginable horror fell on this keep, this home. She witnessed happiness, laughter, and life. She embraced this place, experiencing its warmth and its love, as well as the sorrow in having those things torn away. But she didn't yield to despair, using her altered state instead to gain insight and knowledge.

And so, clarity came to her. Her visions showed her the way forward, as if offered by the Lady Herself. A certainty of purpose flowed into her along with something more, like a gentle embrace.

The light around her dimmed and faded, and she returned to her waking state. Her head tingled, and she stood in silence for a moment. Narick approached her, while the others stood by with questioning stares.

"Andra?" he asked.

"I've seen it, Narick," she said. "I know where the entrance to the tunnels is!"

"The place we want is under us, right?" Bayark asked.

Andra nodded, her head still in a haze from her vision.

"What do we do?" Dorinen asked.

"First, we need to get into the cellars over there." She pointed to the largest of the buildings, ornate stonework in floral patterns adorning its doorway. "It's Wyverdorn's residence, I think. There's a tunnel under his home. He had it repaired in case of attack, probably so his family could hide, and maybe escape somewhere into the forest. There's a chamber down there somewhere, too, and that's the way in. But it needs something, I can't explain it more clearly. It will require magic. When we get there, I'll need your help, Mylth."

He stepped forward. "Of course, what must we do?"

"I'm not sure, not yet. I saw so much so fast that it's hard to focus and remember it all. I'll have to trust the Lady's guidance."

They made their way to Wyverdorn's residence, which appeared to be in no better condition than the other buildings. Inside, doors were broken, piles of refuse littered rooms and hallways, and foul smells wafted through the air. Andra recoiled and covered her nose.

"The Gro'aken have ransacked and ruined everything," Narick said, kicking a pile of broken wood and loose rocks. "What they haven't stolen they've destroyed."

"Let's check, just in case," Dorinen suggested.

A search of rooms upstairs revealed the same wanton destruction. Once lush velvet chairs lay slashed open, their horsehair stuffing spilling out on to the scarred hardwood floor. A tapestry had been pulled from a bedroom wall and cut in half. Room after room showed only the pitiful remains of what once had been a happy home.

Dorinen stepped back through a splintered door to the main hall. "Vile creatures!" she cursed. "How can they have so little respect for the lives of others? This was a child's room." She threw down a part of a broken doll in disgust.

"It's the way they are, lass," Bayark answered. "There ain't a spot of good in them."

Andra wanted to offer words of comfort to Dorinen, but she held back, as more insights from her vision came to her.

"They're a part of life, like we are," she said at last, hesitating to say more. "I know it sounds strange, but the Lady opened my mind, my heart. We find them horrid, and their actions are repulsive, but they have their place," she continued, a little more confident. "We don't fully understand it, and it's not necessary for us to. The Spirit is even in those things that offend it."

No one else seemed inclined to welcome her point of view, as they turned away and wandered down the hall. No one but Narick.

He motioned to her and took her aside. "You see so much, and your potential is vast. Remember that. I thank Enwyonn for you."

Andra waved him away and didn't answer. While she knew he meant to comfort her, the weight of this growing responsibility made her doubt again if she could ever live up to his praise.

As she stepped with care on squeaky, damaged stairs, Andra had another sudden insight. "I think the entrance to the cellars is in Wyverdorn's study. That way." She gestured toward the main hallway to a room at the end with the door pulled off, lying in front of the entrance.

Inside, book cases lining the walls sat empty and barren, probably once full of bound manuscripts and scrolls, but like everywhere else, nothing of value now remained. One shelf lay splintered on the stone floor.

"There are no other doors." Mylth scanned the room.

"My people are good at findin' hidden entrances," Bayark said. "Let me try."

He pulled back the dusty and dirty carpet. One of the stone slabs on the floor sat slightly out of place. Bayark ran his hands over the slab and yanked it away with a firm tug and a slight grunt of effort, revealing an opening with a ladder emerging from the dark below. "Been used not long ago," he said, sniffing and feeling along the edges of the slab. "Maybe even earlier today."

"There's been a lot of passage through here," Dorinen confirmed as she knelt and examined the entrance. "By humans, but not Vordlai. I don't detect their scent."

"The entrance is too small," Narick said.

"The Vordlai who've attacked must have some other means of leaving the keep," said Mylth. "They can likely reach the surface directly from some point below."

"Never mind, this'll do!" Bayark scrambled into the hole before the others could stop him.

"I suppose we'd better follow him," Narick said with a raised eyebrow. "With his bravery, the Vordlai don't stand a chance."

Andra chuckled, despite a foreboding sense of what might wait for them.

"Come on," Bayark called out. "It ain't far."

Mylth went next, while Andra and Narick climbed down the ladder after him, followed by Dorinen.

"I can't see," Andra protested as she stepped with uncertainty onto the stone floor. She shivered, sensing nothing but the chill of stale, damp air and the faint sound of dripping water echoing in the distance. Even that water sounded strangely devoid of life, as if it, too, were contaminated like the wells in Meln. She hugged herself for warmth as the fresh wound on her arm stung again. Still, she didn't want to waste precious magic now.

A ball of yellow light flared in the darkness a few steps away, above Mylth's hands, casting a ghostly glow across this face.

"No!" Narick waved his hands frantically. "Using magic will only make it easier for our enemies to find us."

"What does it matter?" Dorinen said, hopping off the last rung of the ladder. Andra could barely make out her silhouette, even with Mylth's light. "Whoever is waiting for us already knows we're here. If we must face the Vordlai, I'd like to be able to see them."

Andra found herself disagreeing with Narick, something she didn't like doing. "She's right. I'd rather know what's coming."

Bayark spoke up. "Absolutely! Ain't much fun if you can't see what you're hackin' to bits."

"It seems I'm outnumbered," Narick conceded.

Andra almost felt bad for him and placed a comforting hand on his back. "It's for the best. At this point, we're not trying to hide."

Mylth circled his hands with a flourish, and his glowing orb expanded to illuminate the chamber with the light of half a dozen torches, revealing two passages on opposite sides.

"Which way is it?" Narick asked.

Without hesitation, Andra pointed at the passage to their right, and Mylth directed his lighted orb into it.

Dorinen readied an arrow in her bow. "I'll lead."

She headed down the corridor into a cellar, with a number of small rooms and alcoves, most of which remained largely undisturbed, their wine bottles and crates intact. The tunnel stretched away from them into the vast dark.

"Apparently, this place remains free of ransacking," Narick commented. "The Gro'aken haven't yet discovered the way in here to despoil it."

"Or maybe they weren't allowed to," Andra replied, staying close by him.

"You're probably right," Narick said, "and honestly? That worries me. Our enemy can likely compel all these creatures to do his bidding as he wishes."

While Dorinen moved ahead, Mylth re-joined the others. "Andra," he said, "do you have any sense of where we should be going?"

She concentrated before answering. "The entrance to the lower levels isn't far, I'm pretty sure of it. Dorinen, can you detect anything at all?"

"No," she came back closer to Andra. "In the dark, surrounded by stone, I'm not of much help."

"Mylth?" Andra turned to him.

He closed his eyes, as if trying to tap into their surroundings, but shook his head. "I haven't been awake long enough. My senses are still adjusting, and I don't know exactly what we're seeking. I'm afraid the burden of finding the entrance is yours alone."

Andra exhaled in frustration and tried to focus again on what Teuvell had shown her. "The Lady's vision has already faded from my memory. Something here might even be blocking me from remembering it." She shook off a chill at the idea of their enemy having so much power.

As they edged farther into the darkness, Bayark stopped in front of one old and unremarkable side door and sniffed the air. "We want to be goin' in there."

Andra tugged on the door latch, which hardly budged. "I doubt anyone has opened this door in ages. It won't move."

"Trust me lass, there's somethin' in there we need to see."

"But I don't feel anything, and the gem's not even glowing."

"Just do it, girl. Whatever's in there may help us. And don't be taken in by the lock. It's been altered by magic. It don't fool me, though. This door's been used recently, and that's what's tellin' me it's important."

He turned to Mylth. "Go get Dorinen, pixie. She doesn't need to scout any farther until we know what's in there."

Without a word, Mylth disappeared into the blackness and returned shortly with Dorinen.

"We should take some precautions," Narick warned. "The door may contain magical wards or perhaps be guarded—"

"Bayark, wait!" Andra held out her hands as he swung his axe into the door, splintering it in two. He kicked it in, sending the old latch falling to the floor. He turned to Narick with supremely smug satisfaction. Narick looked as though he wanted to both lecture the Tveor and punch him.

"That's the problem with you Shylan Dar types," Bayark derided. You fight good enough, but you spend far too much time thinkin' about stuff instead of just doin' it!"

"I was simply recommending caution!" Narick barked. "What if it had exploded in your face?"

"I'm still standin' here, ain't I?"

Narick gave him a grudging "hmph."

"Do you need to write a chronicle entry about it first, or can we go in?" Bayark grumped.

Andra offered her best friend an apologetic shrug. "Come on."

Narick rolled his eyes, stepping past Bayark and through the splintered doorway with a slight huff.

"That's more like it!" Bayark barked.

Andra followed.

"See?" Bayark said, striding toward the only thing in the room: a weathered wooden pedestal, atop which rested a well-worn book. "Nothin' to worry about, just some old tome."

"Ah, but books can be the most dangerous things of all," Narick quipped.

"Why is this here?" Andra asked. "It seems very unlikely."

"What have you found?" Mylth stepped in, followed closely by Dorinen, who scanned the small room.

"I'm not sure we should all be in this place," she said. "What if it's a trap?"

"A poor place for a trap, locked behind a door we might have ignored," Narick said. "More likely, it's meant for us."

He examined the book's binding. "It's locked," he said, studying the small latch affixed to a leather strap around it. "And someone apparently didn't want it removed from this room." A tarnished silver chain hooked through the book's spine and attached to the pedestal.

"I can take care of it!" Bayark bounced the handle of his axe against his palm.

Narick gave him a blistering scowl to warn him off, and placed his hand on the lock. With a twist of his fingers, he broke the latch, sending it clanging to the floor.

Bayark gasped as though his bearded jaw might drop to the ground.

Andra watched her friend in amazement. Even after years of friendship, he could still surprise her.

"I could have done the same with the door if you'd not been so impulsive," Narick said smugly. He returned his attention to the book, leafing through the pages. He frowned. Andra knew that face; it meant he'd found something, possibly valuable, possibly unsettling.

Narick glanced up. "It's Wyverdorn's journal."

* * *

In a dark cave, Tarnohken awoke from its sleep, aware of the approaching night. As the time of the portal's opening drew near, its blood lust grew. One more day in this world and its kin would be free.

It dropped to the floor and beheld the others clutching the ceiling with their taloned feet amid the multitude of dripstones hanging like pointed daggers, ready to impale the unwary. Most of its kin still waited in an enchanted sleep, bound by the wretched mortal mage Denderath five centuries ago. Here remained those he could not banish to Torr Hiirgroth. Tarnohken seethed with hatred for that man, for all mortal kind.

It hated the new mortal master as well, who so presumptuously tried to control them. He'd succeeded in awakening a number of the brood, and even allowed a few out to feed, though he could always compel them to come back. That would change. It didn't care how or why the master woke them, but he would regret it. And some of its kin hadn't returned. Tarnohken sensed they were dead, though it didn't know if their deaths were by this mortal's hand or by others; it mattered not. With their release from the Underplanes, Tarnohken would slay this weakling, would feast on his heart. Then, the brood would take revenge on this world.

The beast lumbered out of its cave and through a series of tunnels, entering into a cavern that opened to reveal a ball of grey mist swirling high above. Hundreds of blue lights slowly circled around it, each following their own orbital paths.

As it observed shadowy shapes moving in the haze, distant visions of its kind trapped in Torr Hiirgroth, several of the lights flickered and darkened. Soon these bonds would fail to hold the gate shut, releasing the Vordlai lurking on the other side.

Tarnohken convulsed with blood-hunger as it imagined the feel of torn flesh, and the sweet taste of mortal terror.

* * *

"See?" Bayark announced with triumph, breaking Narick's concentration and further annoying him. "I knew there was somethin' important in here!"

Dorinen regarded the book with a skeptical eye. "It's a little too fortunate that we just happened to find this book."

"Indeed," Narick answered, examining the journal's first few pages, his brows tilting with worry. "Everything about our passage into this place has been far too untroubled."

"But what about the Mondrytes that attacked us, and the arrow that hit me?" Andra protested, rubbing her arm again.

"Only two Mondrytes," Narick reminded her. "Our enemy undoubtedly could have conjured up twenty or more. He could have overwhelmed us, killed us already. And I believe the arrow struck you accidentally. Gro'aken are not so skilled with their bows."

"But why would Teuvell guide me here? Guide us here?" Andra asked.

"The Spirit is doing what it can," Narick replied, "but our challenges are essentially what we would expect if someone were lying in wait for us. Think about it: Dorinen's tracking skills, Bayark sensing this hidden room, my breaking the lock without destroying the book.

Our adversary not only knows we're here, but also has learned about us in preparation for our arrival." He motioned to the book. "And why would Wyverdorn's personal journal be chained to a pedestal in a cellar beneath his residence? It's absurd."

"But how could this 'master' know who we are?" Dorinen asked.

"Maybe there's a traitor among us." Bayark said, his grip on his weapon tightening.

An unpleasant silence ensued, as the companions looked at each other awkwardly. Bayark scowled, Mylth appeared lost in thought, while Andra's eyes widened, and Dorinen seemed troubled, as if in denial. Finally, Narick shook his head.

"No, I'm certain one of us would have sensed if something were amiss before now. I trust all of you."

"Indeed. If we are being watched, it is likely by scrying," Mylth said.

"I've seen that magic at the Temple," Andra said. "The master Artisans believe scrying is invasive and only to be used in the most extreme circumstances, and only by the learned and wise. It's also not an easy enchantment to learn."

Narick considered the situation. "Whoever we're dealing with is allowing us to proceed, perhaps to trick us into believing that stopping him and closing the portal will be a simple task."

"Why?" Dorinen asked. "What purpose would that serve?"

Narick recalled some of his own training. "The Shylan Dar sometimes employ a strategy of catching the opponent unawares," he said. "The idea is to lure one's enemy into a false sense of confidence, and use such assurance against them. It's quite effective and has applications not only in combat, but also in politics, commerce, games, and philosophical debate."

"What are you saying? Who could be doing this?" Andra asked.

Narick shook his head but turned the matter over silently. He did not like his conclusion and tried to dismiss it, even as a bitter sense of betrayal ate at him in the pit of his stomach.

Bayark rubbed his nose and sniffed. "I said it before, I don't care who he is. I just want to stop this! Now can we *please* talk about this journal, considerin' it's why I bashed in the damned door in the first place?"

Narick conceded the point, despite the misgivings eating at him. "You're right. Even if we are being fed this information, there's no reason to ignore it. We might learn things that our foe doesn't intend for us to discover. Let's see what breadcrumbs he's left for us, shall we?"

He flipped through it again. Watery, smeared ink rendered some writing unreadable, while in other sections, only remnants of paper remained where someone had torn out the pages.

"Is there anything useful?" Andra asked. "Maybe we can compare it with what we found in Ternen's journal."

"I see no reference to Meln at all," Narick answered. "There's not much more than scattered sentences, mostly recording personal observations." An intact page caught his eye, and he scanned it.

"This section is dated to almost two moonspans ago. It reads: 'This afternoon I received him in my hall. He was immediately unpleasant, insisting he be granted access to caverns under the keep. I knew nothing about what he was referring to, but he said I was lying. He threatened me and my family, at which point I ordered him escorted back to the forest. I'd assumed that was the end of the matter, until my guards did not return.' The passage ends there."

He turned the page. "There's more. 'Three of my finest soldiers were killed today, presumably by this man. I have hidden my children in the cellar and will send them into the forest if necessary.'"

Narick scanned for the next readable section. "'He forced his way into the keep today with a clan of Gro'aken. My own men were overwhelmed. He entered the cellars before I could get to my children. My wife was with them. He warned me not to interfere or he would kill them all. May the Spirit forgive me. I have allowed myself to be held captive in my own residence while he searches for caverns he is certain lie far beneath us. It's as if he can control my thoughts. He makes me yield to his wishes. I cannot even send for outside help.'" He turned to Andra. "At least now we know Wyverdorn had nothing to do with drugging Meln."

She relaxed a little at his words, but he worried all the more because of the remarkable power their enemy possessed.

He leafed through a few more pages. "This was obviously written in haste. 'I have seen the horrors he has unleashed. He controls them, though I do not know how. He says he will destroy the Land Spirit and reveal the folly of our devotion to it. He says we will worship him. He...' There's nothing else."

The others stared at him in stunned silence. Ignoring them and hungry for answers, he returned to the book. "I suspect this is all our enemy wants us to see. It's enough to confirm that the portal is somewhere below us. We've been given sufficient information to make us want to keep going forward."

"I don't like being toyed with," Mylth said. "Whatever the fate of the Spirit, I won't allow this man to have his way. The Vordlai will not roam freely again."

"Well said, pixie!" Bayark thundered with a stomp of his booted foot.

But Narick wrestled with the determination in his companions' words. In the journal entries and their experiences thus far, he'd found clues that the others wouldn't see or recognize. If his companions understood the full scale of what he suspected, they wouldn't be eager to go forward at all. He resolved to keep his suspicions to himself until proven, although he was sure he now knew the master's identity.

And for the first time in a long while, Narick Yerral was truly afraid.

Twenty

The gem vibrated, catching Andra's attention. "It's, it's never done that before." She held her instrument close and placed her fingers on the jewel's surface. It felt warm to the touch and the tremor intensified with her contact.

"Trust in your instincts," Narick advised. "Let the Lady guide you."

Focusing on the gem, Andra went back into the hall, with Dorinen keeping close by.

She took meditative, deliberate steps, trying to recall elements of her vision, but clear images remained elusive.

She stopped abruptly, and when she placed her palm on the stone wall on her right, her hand passed through easily. The wall shimmered like disturbed water. An astonished Dorinen gasped as her own fingers disappeared into the ripples.

"We need to go this way," Andra told her.

Mylth examined the wall and reached out to it. "A

fairly standard illusion," he said, "but useful for hiding what one doesn't want noticed."

"Mylth and I should go in first," Andra announced.

"I admit I'm not thrilled with the prospect," Mylth said with trepidation, "but I suppose I have to trust you."

"Come on, it will be fine." She took his hand, not at all believing her own words, as together, they stepped through.

The space beyond was not exactly a room, and its size and dimensions shifted constantly. Dim white light emanated from everywhere and nowhere, as if lanterns lined the walls, but there were none to be seen. Andra eyed Mylth. His form elongated, stretched, and contracted, like a reflection in the glass of a warped mirror.

"I don't want to stay in here longer than we have to," she said, queasiness threatening her, like she'd woken up with the worst case of drink woe in her life. And she'd experienced her share of terrible drink woes.

He squinted and turned pale. "This place will play tricks on our minds the longer we remain."

"It's having an effect on me already." She turned and called back to the others. "It's safe to come through, but you might want to close your eyes, to keep from falling sick."

A moment later, the others stood beside her, their own forms undulating and rippling. Bayark indeed kept his eyes shut. Dorinen muttered something about being reminded of Ramwin's dining room, but Andra had no idea what she meant.

"What should we do?" Mylth asked, his voice warped and distant.

Andra tried to trust in the Lady. Did she hear a voice in her head?

"I know this sounds ridiculous," she said, "but picture caverns in your mind. It doesn't matter what kind of caverns, as long as you don't let that image go."

Bayark grumbled. "More magical crap is not what I had in mind for this excursion!"

"Please, trust her." Narick said.

They did what she asked, and she kept a firm grasp on her lyre, concentrating on willing this place to take them away, though her head started to spin. The light around them grew brighter and the distortions became more extreme, the forms of her friends stretching into absurd and impossible lengths. Bayark mumbled something about his unsettled stomach. The air thickened as the light continued to brighten and a low hum grew louder. She wanted to block her ears.

"Everything is so loud," Dorinen whispered.

"Stay with it a little longer," Andra urged.

Just as the sensations became unbearable, the overload ceased and after a flash of bright light, they stood in a large hallway, filled with an eerie green glow. It narrowed in the distance, shrouded in a swirl of mist.

Andra glanced at Narick, stunned that their surroundings had so utterly changed.

"Well done, my friend. Remarkable!" Narick placed a reassuring hand on Andra's shoulder. "It's not what I'd expected, though," he added. "Weren't we searching for caves?"

"This is part of the antechambers," Mylth said as he moved ahead of them, "built above the portal and filled with spells and wards to prevent entry from the outside."

"How far are we from the caverns, assuming they are what we seek?" Narick asked.

"Near enough, I'd guess," Mylth answered.

Dorinen rushed past him and knelt, aiming an arrow into the darkness.

Seeing this, Andra clutched her lyre, prepared to play. "What? What is it?"

"I saw something," Dorinen whispered. "It reminded me of… those horrid eyes."

Mylth drew his own bow out of its sling, while Bayark shoved his way in front of Andra, gripping his axe with both hands. "Watch yourself, lass. Let us lead."

The gem hummed intermittently now, drawing Andra's attention. "That's odd."

"What does it mean?" Narick asked.

"I don't know." Steeling herself with a deep breath, she began to sing the deadly melody, ever fearful she might not be able to control it.

Narick stepped in closer to her, his fists clenched. "Now I fear our task goes from dangerous to nearly impossible."

* * *

Gerinvarg withdrew into the haze the moment the human raised her weapon. The mortal master compelled it only to observe and perhaps to threaten the intruders. But it smelled their flesh, heard their beating hearts, sensed the Spirit's power flowing through them. The temptation to devour them almost made it disregard the command not to attack. Almost.

It knew what the mortal man in grey had done to those who disobeyed him. Somehow, he possessed power far beyond most of his hated kind.

These invaders pursued Gerinvarg as it stole along the hallway. It snarled, the hunter turned hunted, anticipating showing itself to them and delighting in their delicious terror. It reveled in that prospect until a bolt of violet light shot from out of the mist and tore three of its taloned fingers off.

* * *

The Vordlai reeled from the jewel's blast.

Fighting her fear, Andra prepared her melody again, as Dorinen and Mylth let arrows fly at the creature. But singing and unleashing the power of the gem left her weakened, vulnerable.

Lady, please be with me!

Bayark charged forward with a roar, striking his axe into the creature's leg. The beast howled. He struck again, his blessed weapon biting effortlessly into the beast's enchanted hide. It fell to one knee.

Narick delivered a devastating punch to the Vordlai's chin. The creature staggered back with a yelp.

Fighting a new bout of light-headedness, Andra sang and willed magic from the jewel. Its light seared through the haze, burning deep into the creature's shoulder.

As the smoke of its charred flesh whipped at his face, Bayark cursed and swatted at the air, lowering his axe and coughing. The Vordlai struck with fury, catching him in the chest with its vicious claws.

Andra screamed as he fell back with an agonized cry. Mylth pulled him away from the creature in an instant.

Dorinen let loose another arrow and twisted out of harm's way as the enraged creature slashed in her direction. She stumbled, struggling to regain her focus, and backed away.

Before the creature could strike again, Narick punched its throat, snapping the Vordlai's head back with a sickening crack, and by the sound of it, breaking its neck. It flailed its arms about as it fell to the floor, and soon lay still.

At the sight of Bayark on the ground, his blood spilling across the old stone floor, Andra gave in to every awful feeling she'd tried to keep at bay since seeing her people drugged and nearly losing Jeena. Rage and grief threatening to overtake her, she lurched toward the fallen Vordlai and kicked it as hard as she could before drawing her second dagger from her boot, trying to stab it over and over. Most of her blows barely even scratched its skin. Tears streamed down her face as she screamed and swore at it, her hits becoming more forceful, more vicious.

Bayark let out a groan, snapping Andra out of her futile rage and reminding her of what she needed to do. Taking a deep breath, she hastened to him with her lyre, leaving the dead Vordlai smoking and disintegrating behind her.

Mylth pressed with his fingers against the worst of the gashes, giving her a grave expression. "I've used much of my remaining healing mixture, but the wounds still won't close. He's lost a lot of blood."

"Damned thing got me good," he sputtered. "Hope you can do something with that pretty song of yours."

Andra heaved a sigh of relief to hear him alive and complaining. She summoned the healing song to her mind, fending off the memory of Jeena's horrific injury. As she sang, Teuvell's healing energy poured forth, surrounding his wounds, counteracting the venom, and healing the grisly slashes in his chest.

But Andra faltered. She fought to remember the song, as though she were chasing it through a muddy swamp. Did the foul enchantments here block her connection with the Lady? Her *mynthari*? She struggled for her breath, taking in deeper and deeper inhales but finding less and less power to sing. Black spots bubbled at the edges of her vision, and despite her desire to go on, she gave in to a compulsion to stop. She slumped over and laid her lyre aside.

Dorinen knelt beside her, her hands on Andra's shoulders. "What's happening? Are you all right?"

"I've overused Her magic," she said, her head throbbing. "He'll live, but I can't do any more. Not for a while."

"I'll be fine," Bayark declared, but he grunted in pain and faltered as he tried to sit up.

"Sit down!" Andra commanded, fighting her own fatigue to stop him. "You need to rest."

"Rest? Where in damnation do you think we are, girl? We could get another one of those things comin' our way at any moment. I don't intend on bein' on my back when that happens."

"I doubt there will be any more attacks, at least not right away," Narick said, scanning the area ahead of them. "The Vordlai's master was testing us, watching how well we'd fare against it."

"Not well at all, I'd say," Dorinen offered, a frustrated expression on her face as she thrust an arrow back into her quiver.

"On the contrary," Narick said. "We utterly outmatched it. Only as it sensed its own danger did it show any real resistance."

"And it was just because of the thing's stinkin' smoke, that's all," Bayark said. "Never would've got me otherwise."

Andra dragged herself to her feet and staggered away from the others without a word. Narick followed, but when he caught up, she didn't turn to face him. She knew what he would say, but she didn't want to hear it, couldn't make herself believe it.

"Bayark's injury was not your fault," Narick said after a moment's silence.

"Wasn't it?" she shot back. "You heard him. The smoke blinded him. He probably wouldn't have been distracted if the gem hadn't blasted a hole in that thing's shoulder. It seems the only thing I'm good at is undoing the damage I've done by healing those who get hurt from my mistakes. First it was Jeena, now Bayark. Both of them nearly died, Narick. I'm endangering all of our lives."

"We wouldn't have been able to slay the creature without you."

"That's no compensation if it gets someone killed."

"Andra." He placed a hand on her shoulder. "We're all risking death here. Ramwin didn't tell me this would be easy, or without pain and suffering. Bayark is strong. He'll recover much more quickly than you or I could."

"But I can't access the music again, Narick, maybe not for a while." She turned to face him, her guilt gnawing at her as weariness in mind and body threatened again. "We can't just plunge into fights hoping the healing song will be there if we're hurt. I can't help any of us now, and we've barely started."

She leaned on him for support. "I haven't pushed like that before, and I don't know how long I need to wait before I can try again. And this place… it's interfering with what power the gem has. I still don't understand its magic. Izznil didn't give me a scroll of instructions. I don't even know what else it can do besides kill and heal."

"Then we'll have to be considerably more careful from now on," Narick answered, giving her a gentle hug with one arm.

But she saw a familiar expression, furrowed brows and a set jaw, which told her he was keeping something from her.

She looked him straight in the eyes, certain he was hiding something. "You know more than you're saying. Who is he? Who is the master?"

He turned away. "I'm not absolutely sure."

"But you have suspicions."

He bit his lip and sighed. "At this point, even speaking his name is too dangerous, assuming he's who I suspect he is. I'd prefer to wait and hope I'm wrong. But I tell you honestly and in confidence: if I'm correct, I fear none of us will live to see tomorrow."

His words struck her like a slap to the face. She tried to steady the trembling in her jaw, forcing away fears for her mother, her father… for Jeena. "If there's any chance we can survive what's down there, we will, with or without the Lady's aid." But she didn't believe her own words.

"We must try and pray that if we die, the Spirit will have sufficient strength to find others to take our place and finish whatever must be done."

Andra shuddered but held firm, trying to ignore her own fatigue. "There are no others. Even though the Spirit's power is weak here, Teuvell made it clear to me in my vision that no one else can do what we need to do."

He hugged her. "Then we must keep going, no matter what."

* * *

The master sat cross-legged in the air, resting his chin on one hand.

"My dear Gerinvarg. You suffered a violent death, one befitting your savage kind." He dismissed his fiery scrying globe with a sigh. "Four of you miserable wretches have perished since I awoke you. You are not as powerful as the legends describe. Disappointing. Time does have a way of exaggerating one's prowess, I suppose. Still, releasing hundreds of you into this world will serve my purposes just as well. I am encouraged to know that when I have finished, I can indeed banish you all again, or at least sacrifice you to the Eral-savat."

He stroked his chin.

"And you gave them some doubts, some fears. Your kind will feed on those energies, a tantalizing taste of what is to come. It will arouse you, like the touch of an excited lover, the promise of lusts delayed, satiated only by blood. Beautiful creatures, you are, in your own perverse way. Is that why the Spirit could not bear to destroy you so long ago, because of the twisted beauty of pure wickedness and hatred that you embody? Oh Ramwin, perhaps you are darker than you realize!"

He chuckled.

"Now I see the full nature of your slaves. Fools all, but they have fought well enough. I will allow them to enter the caverns. They have earned the right to see what awaits them. I will show them horrors beyond their feeble imaginations, Sarvethar, nightmares that, were they to live, would torment them for the rest of their scarred and ruined lives.

He pressed his palms together and gave a slight bow.

"And I commend you, Narick Yerral, on your ability to solve mysteries. Of course, I wished for you to discover me. But have a care before you utter my name aloud."

His expression softened.

"Ramwin, holy fool, Ramwin. How could you send them to me thinking they would succeed? Only Narick and perhaps Mylth Gwyndon have any sense of what they now face. And only young Andra can seal the portal again, and her powers are already drained with a few simple healings, dulled by the presence of the darkening magics infesting this place."

He gently descended to the floor.

"You have badly underestimated me, Spirit, and as you die, you will know all of the pains and sufferings of this world as your own. As you fade into oblivion, it will be in anguish and regret for the lies you have spread and maintained throughout these endless ages. You have subjected mortal kind to your whims and fancies and made them weak, but I shall make them strong again. Those powerful enough to survive the earth ravage will be liberated, freed from the Spirit, freed to be as gods, a privilege the Dalaethri stole from us eons ago. So, send your pathetic slaves to me. Their deaths will stand as a fitting epitaph to your wretched failures."

He fixated on the darkness in front of him and allowed himself the brief conceit of imagining the glories that would soon be his.

* * *

Narick set aside his preoccupations and spoke to them all. "Be under no illusions. We are walking into a trap, and our enemy holds all the advantages."

"Why are you now such a fatalist, monk?" Mylth asked. "We all know the risks, I more than anyone. No one wants this affair to be over more than I do, but I believe we have at least a chance of succeeding. Your pessimism does us no good."

Narick didn't respond but stared hard at the floor.

"We've waited long enough while you all played bein' my nurse, can we go now?" Bayark ran a hand over the crown of his balding head and growled as he threw on his torn chain mail shirt.

Andra returned to Narick's side, but he didn't speak to her. Together, they stepped into the mists, unable to see more than a short distance ahead. Tension and misgiving, as thick as the haze surrounding them, weighed on his thoughts. Even worse, Narick's own mind became ever more clouded.

"My senses are dulled in this place, even worse than in the forest," Dorinen whispered, as if confirming his own fears. "I can tell something terrible has been here recently, but it's left no trace I can identify. I have no idea what it is."

"We are dealing with tricks of both magic and mind here," Narick said to her.

"What does that mean?"

Before he could answer, the mist dissipated, and the hall opened into a large, circular chamber. Floating high above, wispy strands of ambient lights illuminated a crumbling domed ceiling. Narick stepped over a few torn scraps of clothing and stains on the floor that might be blood, but the vestige of a familiar presence drew his attention. A shudder rushed through him.

"The master must have scried us from here," Narick said.

"There's something else," Mylth said, tilting his head and sniffing the air. "A Vordlai of immense strength and power. The brood ruler, Tarnohken," he said after a moment. "The master must have succeeded in awakening it. We're in terrible danger if he can control it."

"We are indeed," whispered Narick.

He sensed another force. Not magic, but instead the traces of something subtler: mental energy, the unmistakable sign of Shylan Dar practices detectable only by other members of the order. The master undoubtedly knew Narick would discover this psychic echo, and perhaps even left it here on purpose, like an esoteric breadcrumb trail. Bile burned in his throat, for this all but proved Narick's suspicions, confirming his worst fears.

Twenty-One

Two passageways led out of the opposite side of the chamber. Andra preferred the one to the left, without knowing why. "This way."

"I agree," Mylth said, taking a deeper breath. "The air fairly reeks of magic down there."

"Let's get on with it." Bayark hoisted the handle of his axe on his shoulder.

"Something is there," Dorinen offered. "I can't yet tell what."

"Nor I," Narick added, "but I don't like it."

"We have no choice," Andra said with some fatalism. With Mylth behind her, she led them through the narrow stone hall, which soon opened out into a large, nearly square room, adorned with an archway on the opposite wall leading onward into a stretch of inky darkness. A vaporous green glow wafted forward from the impenetrable shadows beyond it.

"Blood and tree ash," Dorinen whispered nearby.

Despite her confidence in this correct path, Andra recoiled at what she saw. Standing on either side of the archway were two life-sized statues of Vordlai, carved from black polished stone. Each held different features and expressions—one a snarl while another screamed, one standing while another knelt—as if they might spring to life at any moment.

Andra lost all faith that she'd made the right choice. "Are they dangerous?"

"If I recall, real Vordlai were bound to these forms," Mylth answered. "Perhaps it was the only means to imprison them."

"But can they do anything?" Narick asked, stepping forward to examine one of the statues, though not touching it.

"I doubt it," Mylth said. "I would imagine that if our enemy knew how to counteract the enchantment, he would have released them from these forms by now. On the other hand, if this place were still truly serving its purpose, I don't think we would have been able to pass from Wyverdorn's cellars into the main hallway at all."

"The caves are in there?" Bayark asked, his eyes brightening.

"So it would seem," Mylth responded.

Andra ignored her fears and tried once again to gain some notion of what they should do. She sensed something past the green glow but had no clear vision of what might lie in wait for them beyond it.

"How far to the caverns?" she asked, shuddering at simply plunging forward into the unknown. Having to pass by those hideous, lifelike statues only made her apprehension worse.

"We have no way of knowing," Mylth answered.

"Andra," Narick said, turning to her, "this won't get any easier, but we're all here. We can rely on each other."

She offered him an accepting nod. "I know. Come on."

Casting a wary and suspicious eye at the statues, she stepped forward, trying yet again to find the Lady in her heart, her mind, anywhere. But she received no response, and the gem felt cold to the touch again.

After twenty paces or so, they approached the source of the light, a glass lantern suspended near the ceiling, but whose glow came from no flame. As she passed through the light, the passage grew darker beyond, and the ground under her feet become more uneven, less hewn.

She shivered as the air chilled her skin. "The caves are near."

"It's a risk, but we must have light," Mylth said. None objected as he conjured his illumination, sending it out before him.

As soon as she could see, Andra wished he couldn't. The cavern ceiling loomed overhead, drip stones threatening her like the sharp incisors of a Vordlai. As in the forest above, no life stirred: no bats fluttered overhead, no vermin crawled along the damp ground, as if the place had been stripped of all life. A single drop of water on the crown of Andra's head nearly made her scream.

The place reeked with fetid smells, making Andra's stomach churn with disgust. She'd never smelled human remains, but something inside her knew that was what now offended her. She again heard the sound of dripping water in the distance, somewhere deep in the darkness from one of the tunnels leading out of the cavern, a pulse that echoed against the stone, like a dying heartbeat.

She took another step and flinched. All manner of soiled and torn garments—from commoners' shifts to soldiers' leather jerkins, to the brocade and embroidered doublets of the wealthy—lay scattered about. Andra imagined the horror of the Vordlai ripping these clothes from their victims. Her mind again turned to her missing mother and her throat tightened. *These could be people from home. What if*—

"Let's keep moving, please," Dorinen said with a shaky voice, tugging at Andra's arm and interrupting her thoughts.

"Prepare yourselves, friends," Mylth said. "We must take great care here."

Andra tried to ignore Mylth's unsettling words, but a faint breeze carried another waft of rotting flesh toward her and she almost retched.

"Andra, do you have any sense of the correct path now?" Dorinen asked.

She shook her head, barely registering the question. In her mind, she fought back the fear that some people from Meln, including her mother, were here. *That clothing, those smells...*

She searched herself for any sign of Teuvell, for a warmth in her heart, for a loving embrace. Nothing but emptiness met her. "No," she answered after a heavy pause. "The Lady isn't here." *Nor is Jeena.*

"From what I know, this darkened magic shouldn't prevent Teuvell from speaking to you," Mylth offered.

Andra knew he was trying to be encouraging, yet his words had the opposite effect. "But with the Spirit fading, Her powers are weak," she said, distraught. "Without Her, I don't know if I can be of any use in sealing the portal. I don't even know if the gem can guide us to it."

"We'll confront that issue when we must," Mylth said. "For now, let's just choose a passageway and keep moving."

"One's probably as bad as any." Bayark tapped his axe handle on the cavern floor and squinted at each tunnel in turn.

"Let's try that one." Andra pointed to the tunnel directly opposite them.

"Any particular reason?" Narick asked as they made for its entrance.

She shrugged. "One's probably as bad as any."

They followed an uneven path, which sloped downward at a steeper grade, and dropped into a second cave. Here, dripstones hung from the ceiling like massive shards of broken glass. Other stones rose up around them, taller than two men, their edges like freshly sharpened butcher's knives. Some were marred with thick, clotted blood.

Andra shrunk back and tried to keep her distance from them, but in such close quarters and so confined, she found it difficult to avoid brushing against them. She resisted the momentary worry that her own clothing would soon join the scattered garments she'd already seen.

"You must resist your fear," Mylth said, as if knowing exactly what she dreaded. "The Vordlai feed on it, as they feed on flesh. Let's not give them any more than they deserve, so we have at least a chance at survival."

Dorinen paused, listening, but all Andra could hear was the echo of the others' footsteps.

"Something's moving, there." Dorinen pointed to a smaller tunnel ahead of them.

"I'm with you lass," Bayark said. "Felt it when we got in here, but I didn't know if it was just me. Glad to know my senses are workin'."

"Vordlai?" Andra asked, tensing.

"No," Dorinen answered, appearing perplexed. "I don't think it's even alive, if that makes any sense."

"It doesn't."

A raspy voice hissed in the darkness, sending a shudder down Andra's back.

"By Urkera, what is that?" Dorinen took a step back.

Bayark swore and swung his axe one time around.

A ghastly and misshapen form emerged into sight, its hideous red eyes flickering in the light of Mylth's orb.

Andra gasped in horror when she beheld its disfigured face, its jaw hanging open, its grey skin rotting around its mouth. Worse, its head dangled from a twisted, broken neck.

Andra flinched, her mind flooded with images of the poor, possessed souls she and Narick had confronted in Meln. She wished what she saw could be anything else.

"Vahn?" she whispered, almost unaware she'd said his name aloud. She stepped back in desperation to Narick, hoping he could explain such a horrid sight. But he said nothing, his open-mouthed expression betraying his own shock and disgust.

Two more shapes lumbered into view behind Vahn.

"The master commands it. Ssoon you shall ssee." Their horrible voices whispered in a chilling cacophony.

The second, the corpse of a woman, seemed to glimpse them from hollow eye sockets as it swung the stumps of its missing arms.

Andra couldn't recognize its identity, but in her revulsion, she couldn't focus.

She tried to deny the horror of these things, but she began to shake, a numbing dread at last claiming her as she froze in place.

Mylth shook Andra's shoulder, bringing her back to the moment. "Fight against being frightened, remember?" He turned to the others. "We must not be afraid! The Vordlai feed on it. Their master might well have sent these things to prey on our fears. Stand strong!"

At his words, Dorinen advanced toward Vahn, and swung her sword into the reanimated corpse. It fell, convulsing and twitching wildly, still uttering the words of its master. Dorinen swung again, but still Vahn hissed as if oblivious to the gaping wound nearly tearing it in half. "Soon you shall ssee, ssoon sshall the truth be revealed…"

"Stop it!" Dorinen commanded. "Silence your cursed voice!" She thrust her sword into its throat, pinning the neck to the ground. The remains of the voice dissolved into little more than a curdling rasp before finally falling silent.

Andra couldn't take her eyes off of Vahn as his corpse ceased to twitch. Narick said nothing but stood by her, one hand on her shoulder, as much for his own reassurance, she suspected, as for hers. He raised a fist.

"Do not engage them," he warned. "We cannot risk you being injured."

Mylth stepped forward and decapitated the armless woman with a single swing of his sword, sending the head flying across the cavern to smash against a cave wall with a sickening, rotting squelch.

Pushing past the others, Bayark charged, cutting the last of the corpses clear through the waist, sending its upper half tumbling to the damp stone. Still, the thing tried to mount a resistance, clutching in futility at his leg, even as it lay in two parts on the floor. Kicking off the grasp with a curse, Bayark swung his axe blade deep into the dead man's chest. And yet, it continued its hideous whisper, "The masster commandss it, witnesss…" for a few moments more before falling silent. Even the battle-hardened Bayark flinched and stepped back, unnerved by the sight.

"That was… Jarew," Andra whimpered, holding a hand over her mouth. Whenever she'd accompany her father to see Hamm, the local blacksmith, to shoe the family horses, his son Jarew always greeted them with a warm welcome. "He, he was so young, too young." Her legs threatened to fail under her, and she reached for Narick to steady herself.

"May the Spirit rest his soul." He whispered a prayer in the Shylan Dar tongue, before clenching his teeth and shaking his head to one side with a sharp jerk.

"What is it?" she asked, holding tight to him.

"I'm sorry, Andra," Narick said, making a pained face, "I need a moment alone." He clutched his head with one hand.

"Narick, tell me what's happening!"

"Please!" He waved her away and set off to stand several paces away.

"Where are you going?" she insisted. "What if more of those things come through?"

He ignored her, but she wanted to go after him, hurt that he would say nothing to her.

Dorinen came to Andra and put a hand on her back. "Is he all right?"

Andra shook her head, still observing him. "I don't know." She turned to Dorinen. "Something's wrong, but I don't dare interfere. He's struggling with something inside, and I can't risk interrupting him."

"Is it because of those… people? The dead ones?"

"I don't think so." Andra peered over her shoulder to see Mylth and Bayark inspecting the corpses.

"Their words. They reminded me of everyone back in Meln," Andra said, hugging her lyre close. "Is… is this what will happen to them?"

She turned back to see Narick approaching them, shaking his head. "Forgive me."

"What?" she asked again, with a dry mouth and growing despair. "Narick, what was that?"

He waved away her concern. "I prefer not to say, not now. But to answer your question, you needn't worry about your fellow Melnians, at least not yet. The people in your village are drugged, but very much alive. The master has simply imbued these corpses with his own rhetoric. Mylth is right. He sent them to frighten us."

"Well, he did a damned good job," Bayark said, kicking the half-corpse at his feet. "When we get this sack of dung in our sights, he'll regret what he's done to those poor folks. It's bad enough to kill 'em, but to make a mockery of their bodies is somethin' I'll not stand for!"

"Their whole purpose was to repulse us and make us fear, to weaken our resolve," Dorinen said, shaking her head as she viewed their remains.

"Indeed," Mylth said, coming near her. "But we reacted as we needed to." He turned to the others. "These poor people were already dead. Ending the desecration of their bodies was an act of mercy." His expression softened. "Not that it makes our task any easier, I know. But even if more of them wait for us, we must push past them as quickly as we can, show our enemy that his cruel conjurations will not work."

"I wish I had your assurance and confidence," Andra said.

"I've had many centuries to learn," he responded, "and yet I doubt myself, far more often than I should."

"As far as I'm concerned, the sooner we can get to the cause of this, the better," Bayark said.

"I fear we might soon get our wish in that regard," Narick said, his back stiff, his attention now fixed on the cavern floor.

Andra observed him, his expression, his stance, his labored voice. She knew he wrestled internally with great turmoil, with something tearing at him. She worried that it now grew stronger with each passing moment.

* * *

Andra followed behind Mylth, while Dorinen led the way through the short tunnel and into another cavern, this one larger than the previous one.

"*Lethnai e'anshiel*," he whispered, surveying the cave.

Andra turned to him. "What does that mean?"

"Memories," he answered. "Bad ones. As if no time has passed at all."

He let his illumination float out to light the space around them.

"By the Earth Heart," Dorinen whispered.

Andra took a sharp inhale of breath and tried to shake off a chill as she beheld the horror confronting them. The remains of the Vordlai's frenzied feedings lay scattered about the cavern: corpses devoured or half eaten, but set about in a grotesque mockery of life. One legless corpse lay nearby on the cavern floor as if sleeping, the back of its head supported by its hands. A ghastly grin distorted the face of another victim, even though its flesh had been torn from its body. Other bodies were even less complete, but the Vordlai's work, displaying a sadistic sense of humor, resided in the desecration of each of their victims. Mylth knelt to examine one, but turned away in disgust.

"How?" Dorinen exclaimed. "How can they be so perverse?"

"There is nothing I can say to ease your pain," Mylth answered. "But in seeing it, I find some solace for my own sorrow."

One figure caught Andra's attention, lying prone on its back. With a sharp intake of air, she stepped away from the others, but weakness already began to claim her. A sickness surged in her stomach. It couldn't be real, it must not. But the waistcoat, the torn crimson skirt with silver thread flowers, the tangle of bark-brown hair, the golden hairpin Andra had given her mother for her fiftieth birthday—the one she'd loved so much—now lying bent on the cavern floor... all revealed a grisly, horrific truth.

"No, please. Lady Teuvell, no..."

Andra rushed to the half-devoured corpse. She stared, transfixed with horror, at what remained of her mother, feeling her own sanity slipping away. Her scream tore through the cavern, her sobs becoming spasmodic, so hard that she could barely breathe as she fell to her knees, dizzy, faint, nauseated. She wanted the blackness to surround her and take her away.

She felt Bayark beside her, holding her in his arms as she sobbed and yelled, pounding the cavern floor in futile fury. She barely noticed when he covered her mother's remains with a nearby piece of her tattered dress and uttered something in his own language. She looked at him through swollen eyes, not able to form words.

"Andra." Dorinen placed a gentle hand on her shoulder.

But where was Narick? Where was her dearest friend? Why didn't he comfort her?

Bayark took her hand. "I'm so sorry, lass, from the bottom of my heart. She should be buried in your home. We can't take her with us, but we can give her a proper remembrance here and now, maybe with fire. I'll be damned if those beasts get the rest of her."

"I don't think that's wise," Mylth said, approaching them. "We shouldn't fill these tunnels with smoke."

"Shut up, pixie!" Bayark yelled, pointing a finger at him. "I'm talkin' about respect for the dead. This dear lady deserves better than her fate! If she can't be buried, a flame's better to keep them damned things away." He turned back to Andra. "If it's all right with you."

She nodded weakly, but his offer made no difference to her at all. None of this could be real. A fog descended over her mind, and she drifted into a haze of denial. Trapped in a horrid daydream, she slipped back and forth between some imagined better outcome and the nightmare now confronting her. But even as grief and rage threatened to consume her, she understood that burning the rest of her mother's body would at least give the woman a reverent end and keep the Vordlai from further despoiling it.

Mylth started to protest, but Dorinen stopped him. "I'm not sure it matters at this point whether we light a small fire. They already know we're here."

He conceded the point. "But I should conjure a magical fire, if you would permit me, Andra. It will burn hotter and give off no smoke."

"Lass?" Bayark gently rubbed Andra's shoulder. "Honestly, I've had about enough damned magic for one day."

"No, it's, it's all right," Andra muttered. She wanted to cry more, to scream again, but nothing came to her. She didn't even know how she could form words at all.

Mylth produced the flame and lit Lysavell's tattered clothes alight. Bayark stood over her, reciting prayers. Andra slumped on the cavern floor in numb disbelief. Where was Narick?

Dorinen wrapped both arms around her and rested her head on Andra's. Andra held Dorinen's arms in return and they watched the flames grow. In only a few moments, the enchanted fire began to consume what was left of her mother's remains.

Andra finally glanced over at Narick, who throughout this ordeal stood to the side, his eyes again closed. Hurt and confused, she sobbed again. *Why won't he come to me?*

"We should leave now," Dorinen suggested to Andra with another hug.

Bayark motioned for Andra to follow him. She rose, needing Dorinen to help her stand. They made for the far opening, but Andra kept staring over her shoulder, watching the flames, even after entering the tunnel. She was leaving a part of herself behind, perhaps the best part. Whatever remaining naïve notions she'd held about the world now burned to ash with the remainder of her mother's body.

* * *

Narick.

An all-too familiar voice sounded in his thoughts. He focused on keeping it at bay, on shutting the entrance into his mind that his enemy now tried to force open. Keeping pace with the others, he went further inward, calling on his reserves of strength. He was able to hide his inner conflict from them for now, but for how much longer? Worse, he hated not being able to comfort his friend, and could only hope she would eventually forgive him.

Hasten to me, my favorite. It's time for you to learn the truth.

With each word, Narick's resistance wavered. He fought the urge to cry out, to lash out, to give in to his anger, his sense of betrayal. Cold and heat churned within him in equal measure, like the feverish chills of a winter illness. Sweat formed on his brow, the effort to stave off the mental assault taking its toll. This trial was meant for him alone, and he knew the time approached when he would have to confront his foe. And when that happened, he didn't know if he would be up to the task.

* * *

Helping her through another tunnel, Dorinen supported Andra with one arm and held Andra's hand with her own, the only gestures she could give her new friend for now. She hated not being able to offer more comfort, more assurance.

After several paces, Dorinen slowed and sniffed the air, smelling more than the decay of this place. She'd been so concerned for Andra that she hadn't been paying enough attention. With a quick inhale, dread set in, and she knew exactly what came for them. "There's heavy movement against the cavern floors, the stink of Vordlai in the distance behind us," she announced, still holding Andra's hand. "There are four of them. We're being chased!"

A horrid screech ripped through the air, echoing through the tunnel.

"Run!" she shouted, urging Andra on, pulling at her hand. "We can't fight them in here!"

The companions broke into a sprint, struggling to navigate the uneven tunnel floor. As he ran, Narick began to chant out loud, his rhythmic verse keeping time with his pace as he charged forward.

Dorinen helped Andra as best as she could. Andra's movements appeared more reflexive than conscious; she moved only because Dorinen assisted her, even forced her to. More than once, Dorinen needed to catch her as she stumbled, and now she worried that Andra would simply give up.

"We'll make our stand there!" Mylth yelled, pointing to the tunnel opening ahead of them. The others quickened their pace.

Guttural snarls and the sounds of heavy breathing filled the dark air. Dorinen could almost feel the creatures' foul breath and forced herself not give in to the terror, the awful memories. Could she, could any of them, outrun these horrors?

Mylth rushed ahead, followed by Dorinen and a stumbling Andra. Narick dashed into the cavern, chanting with ferocity, Bayark close behind him. Dorinen scanned their surroundings to see a large cavern with a high ceiling, taller than many trees in Cernwood. White balls of lights floated far above, pulsing between the sharp, menacing dripstones.

Their attempted escape came to an abrupt halt at the edge of a broad and deep chasm bisecting the whole of the floor in the middle of the cavern. They backed away in haste, but what she saw on the far side chilled her to the bone.

Three Vordlai and a fourth of enormous size howled, their cries almost deafening. They spread their wings and flew over the chasm, landing no more than twenty paces away.

The horrific cries of Vordlai so near shocked Andra into regaining her senses. She clutched at her kenlim and stood straight, even as Dorinen steadied her.

Bayark came to a halt, gripping his weapon with both hands and staring all around. "We got trouble!"

Dorinen could see the first of their monstrous pursuers emerging from the tunnel behind them. She turned around to see the other four Vordlai advancing. "We've got *real* trouble!"

* * *

Extending its wings in a show of strength, the largest of the creatures stomped toward Mylth. He faced the beast, knowing with awful certainty that his beloved's murderer stood before him. Memories surged through him, and he barely had the foresight to retreat from the creature's advance. The savage attack on the Dalaethri, the shredded body of Kyndaeviel, the utter destruction left in their wake. Five hundred years hadn't dulled the intensity of his misery, his heartbreak, and seeing these hateful things now brought it all back to him. But forcing away those horrid memories, he focused on the task at hand.

As the creature approached, he took a strand of a gnarled root from one of the pouches in his shoulder bag and placed it in his mouth. He'd used this herb many times, but never on something so large. Nevertheless, he chewed it into a pulp and spit it out, the sting of its acids working over his tongue, absorbing and infusing him with its power. This rare plant could be both dangerous and useful for those who knew its properties, which he certainly did.

"Behold me, abomination!" Mylth shouted, in a melodious voice, overtones sounding around him, bouncing off the cavern walls in ghostly echoes. "It was I who helped banish the Eral-Savat and who was among those who locked away your vile kind centuries ago. You were not worthy to face us then, and you are not worthy now! You are nothing but a reminder of all that is pathetic, all that is vile filth. We are your superiors and always shall be!"

The creature snarled.

"I deny you!" His voice grew in intensity as he strode forward, sword in hand.

"Mylth," Dorinen demanded. "What are you doing? Don't—"

He motioned for her to stay in place. "I deny the fear! I deny all you seek to find within me! You are nothing in the sight of the Absolute!"

The Vordlai hissed at him, now stomping in place.

Mylth raised his voice. "Long have I waited to confront you, you wretched nightmare! Long have I burned with the desire to spill *your* blood, to see *you* writhe in pain. Denderath should have killed you centuries ago!"

It flinched as the name of that hated magic-caster seemed to burn in its ears, but still, it did not attack.

"See me for what I am!" he bellowed. "I am Mylth Gwyndon, a *Shy'nande* of the Land Spirit, one of the chosen of the Sarvethar. You are nothing to me!"

He raised his sword and charged at the massive beast, who offered him no resistance, now stunned by his voice. Mylth cut deep across the creature's midsection. It doubled over, but with a defiant howl, it regained its senses, and lashed out at him. He blocked the claw with his hilt, but the blow knocked him off balance and he staggered backward, just beyond the creature's deadly claws.

"Fight them!" he yelled to the others, as he regained his balance. "My enchantment won't last long. Fight your fear and deny them!"

Needing no further prompting, Bayark chopped savagely into the Vordlai nearest him, bringing it down with repeated strikes of his axe. The beast began to disintegrate into ash before he'd finished.

Dorinen cut across a Vordlai's face, splitting wide its mouth and severing its tongue. She struck again and again at the staggering creature, dashing out of harm's way as it tried in vain to counterattack.

The remaining creatures held their ground, hesitant at having seen their kin fall so easily. Mylth risked that they wouldn't be accustomed to such resistance, and his gamble paid off. Only the largest of the Vordlai succeeded in shaking off the belittling enchantment of his voice. Pulling itself to its feet, it howled again, but while Mylth kept his concentration on this largest of the beasts, it turned its attention to Andra.

* * *

The chaos of the moment allowed Andra to shake off her numbness and shock, at least a little. She needed to help her friends, but she faltered, certain she could no longer rely on the gem's channeled magic. She fretted, searching in desperation for other options. Her flute could do little against such creatures. But even as she despaired, she heard a faint voice in her mind, a whisper calling to her.

"Andra..."

Narick opened his eyes with a vigorous shake of his head, and in an instant moved to stand next to her, his hands raised, vigilant for any attacks that might come. But she stepped away from him, trying to hear this new voice more clearly. Confused, he started after her, but she waved him away, resentful that he'd ignored her before, but also needing to discover whomever now called to her.

She began to walk, taking deliberate steps, focusing on the pace and rhythm, and steadying her breathing, fixated on finding the source of the mysterious voice.

"Lady Teuvell?"

Nothing else mattered in the moment. Was Teuvell speaking to her, even here? She recited a prayer-song, one of the first ones she'd ever learned, hoping to find the Lady and allow Her power again to course through the gem.

Somewhere behind her, through her singing and her own meditative trance, she heard Narick call for her. "Andra! Keep away from the fighting!"

She ignored him, placing one foot in front of the other in an even rhythm, searching for the source. Besides, Narick had ignored her earlier, leaving her without his usually comforting presence. She made him wait for her response while she tried to commune with the only power that could help her to close the portal and banish the creatures attacking her and her friends.

Narick yelled something at her, knocking her from her deep concentration. Before she could be angry at him, the largest Vordlai lunged and swiped at her. She shrieked, but it missed, instead slamming into her with such force that she flew into the air.

She hit the ground hard, gasping for breath.

The last thing she saw was Narick's horrified face as she rolled toward the chasm and tumbled over the edge.

Twenty-Two

Narick dropped to his knees, mouth open in shock. He couldn't speak, couldn't do anything as the chaos churned around him: the great Vordlai stunned on the ground, the remaining creatures slowly circling them all. He could only think of Andra, tumbling into the dark. He slouched forward, burning with anguish and regret, ready to abandon all remaining hope.

Bayark swore in his native tongue, his voice blazing with fury. Dorinen screamed Andra's name, while Mylth grasped her jerkin to hold her back from running to the chasm's edge. His concentration faltered with Andra's fall and the creatures' growls now grew ever louder, grunting in a cruel and mocking laughter, as his enchantment failed in full.

Dorinen drew closer to Mylth, and they circled back-to-back, while Bayark ran to Narick and forcefully dragged the monk to his feet. Narick staggered to the others and stood with them as the Vordlai closed in. But in his heart, Narick knew they were finished.

The largest Vordlai stirred and rose to its feet, its brutish visage betraying a feral and bloodthirsty rage. It let out an ear-piercing squawk.

"If we're to die here," Bayark shouted, "let's do honor to Andra and slay as many as we can!" He held his weapon in defiance and began a war song. Dorinen uttered an oath aloud, while Mylth gripped his sword and stood silent, drawing inward, perhaps to recapture the magic of his voice spell.

Forcing himself to suppress his shock, Narick began a calming chant, focusing on the true danger lying in wait beyond these blood-mad creatures. The pain returned to his head, pushing at his thoughts, prodding and invading, like a hot knife. And he knew without a doubt its source.

Confirming his fear, a cold, and self-satisfied laugh echoed through the cavern. The Vordlai recoiled at the sound and halted. Even the largest one paused, coming to stillness and bowing its head, as if compelled to go to sleep.

A figure in grey now appeared on the far side of the chasm, his hood drawn over his head. The voluminous sleeves of the robe hid his hands between his folded arms.

Narick had trained for years, refining his calm and resolve to repress fear in the face of unspeakable dangers. But none of those dangers were so powerful as the man who faced him from across the void.

"Welcome slaves of the Spirit," this intruder said in a calm and emotionless voice. "You've offered a fine resistance, more than I honestly would have expected. The Sarvethar did as much as he could, I suppose, but I'm sorry to say that now your endeavor is ended."

He gestured with his head to the Vordlai. "These creatures are loyal to me, you see. I can speak directly to their minds. As for the ones that pursued you here, I only just awoke them from their ancient sleep in stone. They watched as you passed them by and were drawn by the scent of old flesh burning, the sound of vibrant hearts beating."

"And after all this time," Narick called out, "you're even more haughty. More disturbed."

"Oh, my dear Narick," said the man who must surely be the master, astonishing the others, "you should not be so uncharitable to me. You have not even told your friends who I am. Please, do reveal it to them. They are so curious to know."

Narick's skin crawled at hearing the voice he'd resisted for so long.

"Narick, who is this?" Dorinen demanded.

"I will not utter your name!" Narick spat, ignoring her. "Do you think me such a credulous fool? Do you know how difficult it was for me to be free of you?"

"I am so sorry, my former friend," the master responded in a mocking tone, "but you chose your place. You could have joined me."

"Joined you in your madness?" Narick yelled, his remaining calm once again coming unraveled. "I would rather have died. All of us would! Your arrogance has only grown. Calling yourself 'master'?"

"I do not control what small-minded fools name me." He shook his hands free of his robe.

Narick flinched, fearing he prepared to attack, but the man simply placed them together, fingertips touching.

"No," Narick shot back, "you prefer to rob them of their wills and of their souls!"

His adversary chuckled and gracefully floated across the chasm, landing some ten paces away. The Vordlai retreated from the four companions and made their way to his side, the largest licking a wound on its arm.

"I showed them the truth, Narick, the truth hidden by the Land Spirit since time began, the truth of mortal slavery to the Spirit's whims and wishes." He wandered closer to Mylth, reaching out a hand toward him. "But you would know of this, wouldn't you, Mylth Gwyndon?"

Mylth tightened his grip on his sword. At the same time, Dorinen stepped closer to Mylth, holding her bow close, one hand near the arrow quiver on her back.

The master turned his attention back to Narick. "Since you will not speak my name, dear Narick, I shall have to. It's common courtesy after all. They have fought admirably and at least deserve to know who has defeated them."

He addressed the others with a condescending jeer. "Your friend has been keeping secrets from you, I fear. He has known, or at least suspected, that I am responsible for these events for some time. Oh, it is not because he is deceptive, I assure you. You see, he and I once shared a most special bond."

He pulled back his hood. His once short, pitch-black hair now grew scraggly and grey over his ears from his bald head, just dusting his angular shoulders. His grey eyes burned into Narick's, and within them, Narick could see none of the compassion or humanity that he should have possessed.

"I am Kuurm Adath, formerly of the Shylan Dar order. Narick was once one of my *Kai Erodh*, my students, in fact my most promising one."

Narick stiffened, defiant, hating even the sound of that cursed title.

Mylth glared at Narick, in astonished anger. "You were his *student*? And you said nothing?"

"I needed to be certain," Narick answered, his upper body tensing. "If I had opened myself further, or named him, he might have become even more powerful! Would that have been preferable?"

Mylth scowled. "But you didn't even tell us you knew him, and quite well, it seems!"

"Narick," Dorinen protested. "We had a right to know. All our lives might depend on it."

"I agree, I don't like this, monk," Bayark added. "We trusted you."

Kuurm chuckled and cast his gaze over all of them in a maddening mixture of admiration and contempt. "I hate to interrupt your little argument, but I do want to commend Narick for his restraint." He gave Narick an exaggerated bow. "It must have pained you to keep such a secret from your new friends... my name echoing in your mind as you fought so valiantly to push me out."

"Unlike *you*," Narick hissed, trying hard now not to give into his barely-suppressed outrage. "I stayed true to my training, the training I received after the order banished you."

The day flashed into his memory, ten winters ago, when House Master Kervalian and the elders ordered Kuurm to leave the Mother House and never return. Narick was twenty-two springs old, and only halfway through his studies. When the senior brothers severed the teacher's psychic ties to his pupils, Narick felt as though a part of his very soul had been torn away. Or perhaps it was more like the sawing off of a gangrenous limb, now that he knew what his former master had become.

"Oh, Narick." Kuurm placed his palms over his heart and almost pouted, mocking Narick's sense of betrayal. "I may have been banished, yes, but you know our *Chaar* can never fully be sundered."

"What do you mean your *Chaar*?" Mylth almost growled. "Does that mean you're still connected?"

Kuurm's upper lip lifted into a self-satisfied sneer. "We'd be even more so if my dear student would simply utter my name."

"*Former* student," Narick growled.

Kuurm scoffed. "All the pain of our psychic separation could have been healed with two little words, our *Chaar* fully restored to what it once was."

"Never. Not after all your mad ravings about the Spirit."

"The Spirit enslaves us all, Narick."

"The Spirit *is* us, you reckless fool!" Narick shot back.

"That is only what your superiors deceive you into believing," Kuurm said, his voice once again calm and even. "I have severed all connections with that vile entity, and yet I live. I did not cease to exist."

"You cannot sever all connections," Mylth spoke up, turning his attention back to their captor. "At your core, you are made of the Spirit, like all the rest of us."

"Ah yes, lessons in cosmology from the half-breed of the Dalaethri." Kuurm rolled his eyes. "It is your vile kind who robbed humans of our true place in this world. *We* should have been the immortals, not you decadent outsiders who pander to every wish of your vain Spirit. You do nothing, you accomplish nothing, and you diminish the glory that should be ours by your existence. That the nobler blood of humankind also courses in your veins, Mylth Gwyndon, is the true abomination. You do not deserve such a gift."

Mylth lunged at Kurrm, but Bayark caught him by the arm. "Not now, not yet," he said.

"I've had enough of standing around and talking," Dorinen muttered. Before anyone could stop her, she loosed an arrow at Kuurm. With an arc of his hand, Kuurm deflected it to the farthest wall, where it crashed and splintered against the floor.

"Do not attempt that again, Dorinen of the Cernodyn," he warned, "or I shall send the next one back into your heart."

Dorinen shrank back, casting a glance of disbelief at Narick, though he kept his focus on their adversary.

Clasping his hands together behind his back, Kuurm took a few steps toward Narick. "It is truly a pity your young friend took a little tumble over the edge."

Narick bristled with anger at the mention of Andra.

"She possessed great power, and it is a shame she devoted herself to that whore Teuvell. If she'd but seen the truth, she could have known true glory, true purpose."

"What truth, you mad dog?" Bayark slammed his axe handle on the ground. "Her mama's ashes are back in that cavern. If it weren't for your guard mongrels there, I'd split your miserable skull wide open!"

"I've no doubt you would enjoy that immensely, you filthy creature, but you shall never have the chance. You and your feculent kind shall also fall to the powers I have unleashed."

"You are indeed mad, Kuurm." Mylth. "I have seen the destructive power of the Eral-savat. You have not. It will consume you and everything it touches. What could you possibly seek to accomplish by raising it? You will destroy the lands you seek to gain for yourself."

Kuurm darted an accusatory stare at Mylth. "Do you think I want to rule over kingdoms? Territories?" he asked. "Such pathetic gains are but the preserve of weak monarchs and petty governors, with their brutish and infantile fantasies. What I desire is to create a fundamental shift in the cosmic order. One that will make the deserving who they were destined to be, before the Land Spirit ensnared their souls and imprisoned them."

His expression softened with reminiscence.

"You see, Kervalian and the other masters expelled me from the Shylan Dar because I discovered a secret, a dangerous secret, one that most within the order knew nothing of. Through my passionate pursuit of knowledge, I found the truth they did not want me, or anyone else, to learn. Ten summers ago, I discovered that within our lifetimes, the Spirit would perish."

* * *

Andra's head ached. She groaned and opened her eyes, touching her forehead and wincing at a stinging cut. Pain throbbed in her sides with each breath. As she tried to sit up, her fingers found nothing. By some miracle, she hadn't plummeted to her death, but instead landed on a narrow ledge at least two men's height below from where she'd tumbled. With a gasp, she pushed herself back, away from the yawning blackness below. She could just see that part of the ledge sloped down into the chasm itself, creating a pathway. A wave of dizziness threatened to send her falling over again, but with a deep breath, she steadied herself.

In the faint light from above, she noticed her kenlim beside her, but something was wrong. Perhaps the blow to her head, or the impact of the fall made the lyre appear distorted and twisted. When she picked up the instrument, its strings twanged and snapped. Its body, made of the finest cherry wood, now lay split in half, the gem still affixed to its soundboard.

Andra struggled against the despondent tears threatening to cloud her sight. What could she do to close the portal with a broken kenlim, and trapped here in the darkness with no way to escape?

Even if she could connect with the power of Teuvell in this Spirit-forsaken place, she had no chance now. No means of channeling the jewel's volatile power meant no way to invoke the spirit of the Lady to protect herself or her friends.

The others. Where were the others?

Light flickered far above her, accompanied by faint and unintelligible talking. She wanted to stand, to return to them, but this ledge trapped her, pinned her to the damp, rocky ground. The horror of it all—her mother, the Vordlai, her beloved instrument broken—rendered her immobile.

But someone again whispered her name. "Andra…"

"Who's there?" She sat forward. "Lady Teuvell, is it you?"

"Andra…"

"Show yourself to me, please!" she demanded, desperately needing to know who could find her deep in this terrible place.

"Do not be afraid, *mar shokara*."

Andra's eyes widened. "Jeena?" A tingling ran through her arms and into her chest.

Surely, she only imagined Jeena's voice, her injured head playing tricks on her and making her hear the one person who she wanted with her more than anyone.

Yet the voice sounded so real. As though whoever spoke it were only a few paces away.

"Jeena, if you're here, please, please answer me. Please come to me!"

Swirling, multi-colored lights danced before Andra, and a form emerged from the luminance. Jeena, exactly as Andra remembered her, floated beyond the limit of the ledge, beautiful, radiant, and life affirming. Shining in the dark, she smiled warmly and drifted to Andra, her arms held open.

Andra didn't know if she was hallucinating and for the moment, didn't care. The comforting sight of her soul bond gave her everything she could need. She wanted to wrap herself in Jeena's loving embrace, but as she reached out, their hands passed through one another, just as in her dreams and visions.

She slouched back, losing heart. "Are you even real? Why can we not touch?" she asked.

"This is my *liskja*, my spirit, which knows no bounds, dear one."

Andra still couldn't believe. "How can you speak to me here, but I can't even find Teuvell?"

"We are soul-bonded, *mar shokara*," Jeena said. "We can find each other, across distance and time. The power of the Underplanes is too strong for your Lady to reach you, and the Land Spirit ever weakens. But I am here. And through me, Teuvell and Koliserr can embrace you. As the grace of your Lady flowed into me and saved me, now let the grace of mine be yours."

"Where are you? I wish you were truly here now."

Jeena tried to stroke Andra's cheek, but Andra only felt a faint warmth. "My people are now a full day's journey to the west and I am with them. I must keep them safe, but I am also here with you."

"But what do I do now?" Andra asked, despairing despite Jeena's comforting presence. "My lyre is broken, and its magic doesn't work here. I'm separated from my friends. I don't even know if they're still alive. And, my mother. She's, she's…" Andra's voice shook and she wept again.

"Let your tears flow," Jeena said. "It will take much time for you to be whole again."

After allowing herself to cry for a time in grief and helplessness, Andra took a deep breath. "How can I do alone what we all came here to do?"

"You can, my darling, and you are not alone. I will help you. I came to you because I knew you were in great danger. Together we can still seal the portal."

"You know about it?"

Jeena placed a hand over her heart. "Now that we are bonded, I know what you know. In time, you shall also know what I know."

Andra marveled at Jeena's knowledge. She couldn't yet imagine the wisdom Jeena must possess. "Does that mean you can guide me to the portal?"

"Indeed, with our talents combined, we might yet find it."

"Talents," Andra echoed with sarcasm. "I have no talents, except for endangering others and nearly getting myself killed."

"Oh, *mar shokara*. You are deeply loved by Teuvell, by the Spirit. The Lady sings through your voice. I knew it when first I beheld you. You are blessed in more ways than you could ever know."

"Blessed? My whole village is in danger, and I've lost my mother." An awful feeling of despair settled in the pit of her stomach.

"I do understand how you feel," Jeena replied, caressing the air around Andra's face. "When I lost my dearest Craft Mother, Ahnji, my heart broke. She and your mother were taken by a terrible evil, but we survive. We must if the Spirit itself is to live again. It needs us, Andra, it needs you. You cannot yet know how special, how important you are, but I see. You are precious, to me and to the Spirit."

Andra pointed to where she'd fallen from. "We should try to get back to them, my friends. If they live, they might need us!"

Jeena hesitated. "No, no, we must not. There is much danger, and we cannot reveal to our enemy that you yet live. Secrecy will be to our advantage."

"But they'll think I'm dead. Narick, the others…" The realization devastated her.

"I am sorry, my dear, but staying hidden will keep you safer."

"I suppose." Andra sighed and hugged herself, warmed by Jeena's presence, but thwarted by being unable to touch her. "Please, tell me what we need to do."

"The portal is not far. Concentrate with me and allow the magic to guide you." She rose and began to move, swaying side to side. "You must join me."

Andra stood, finding that her ankle ached from her fall. She rubbed it, swearing to herself.

Jeena came close. "Are you well?"

"I'll be fine, thank you." If only she could throw her arms around Jeena and never let go.

"Now, we must leave this place," Jeena said.

"But I can barely see anything." Andra squinted into the darkness.

"Follow your senses through the blackness, and we shall find what we seek."

Andra collected her beloved, broken instrument, holding it with a heavy heart. Her most treasured possession lay ruined in her hands. She cradled the shattered pieces close. "How can I do anything now?"

Jeena floated near to her. "Your song will not fail you, not with me here. You can still work wonders."

Andra regarded her with skepticism and placed the ruined lyre in its leather case, slinging it back over her shoulder. "If only I'd not been carrying it when I fell."

Guided by Jeena's spirit light, the two descended down the slope to the chasm floor far below the blackness.

* * *

Narick seethed at the presence of his former master, his arrogance, his mockery. Dorinen and Bayark said nothing, while Mylth quietly observed their enemy, perhaps measuring each word for its truth or falsehood.

"I can see you're all quite surprised," Kuurm said to his unwilling guests. "Sit, please, and allow me to enlighten you."

The snarls of the Vordlai indicted that this was no request.

"Do it," Narick said, fearful that his former master would force them if they did not comply. With grumbles and protests, his companions settled in on the cave floor.

Kuurm began to pace back and forth. "Ancient legends spoke of the death and rebirth of the Land Spirit, but most people came to dismiss such tales as folklore or mythic tutorials, celebrated as mere symbols of the cycles of life, seasons, and years. Few ever realized that the legends spoke of true events. But our elders knew. They've known for a long time, perhaps always."

Narick struggled with how this could be so, and fought against Kuurm's words and his own disbelief.

Perhaps spying on Narick's thoughts, Kuurm continued. "The elders didn't want us to discover the truth, Narick. They hid it from us. Forbid us from knowing it. It is a pity you could never read the original *Book of Syontar*. Did you even know there was an original? That the one we perused in our studies was censored?"

"What is this heap of Wold Hog dung on about?" Bayark grumbled.

"It's true," Kuurm continued, ignoring the insult. "The elders of our order knew about the impending demise of the Spirit, and that with the Spirit's death came the possibility of the annihilation of all life with it."

"What?" Dorinen gasped and shot an accusative glare at Narick, as if he'd somehow known. He shook his head, appalled at how Kuurm's revelations made sense.

Kuurm began to meander in a circle around them. "Perhaps the Spirit would be reborn as well, but were we to merely accept the possibility of our own oblivion?" Kuurm stopped in front of Narick, glaring at him, steepling his fingers. "Are we all to die without a choice? Is this the infinite love of the Spirit?"

"You understand very little of the Spirit's love," Narick said.

"Indeed?" Kuurm raised his eyebrows. "Then explain to me why our elders did not let us know the truth. Well, they promised each other not to tell anyone beneath them, the monks and students like us. They claimed to have shared with us everything they knew. But they lied. They had been lying to us the entire time."

He sneered, and Narick clenched his jaw, struggling to restrain his anger, his all-consuming desire to lash out at his former master and beat him to death. But with the Vordlai so close, he didn't dare make the first move.

"I later discovered that some of the elder Ferwareen witches knew," Kuurm continued, "and perhaps a few of the great magic-casters in the west, but the common people? Even our glorious leaders? They were kept ignorant."

He paced in front of them, hands again clasped behind his back.

"I argued passionately with the order's senior monks, telling them we should let the people know, let them decide for themselves how they would respond, how they would live. But they told me, in private, that this cosmic death was part of an inevitable cycle, and while there was indeed danger, the greater portion of people could never know about it, lest they give in to fear and succumb to the influence of the

Underplanes, and so prevent the Spirit's rebirth. We would all just have to perish and be reborn with the Spirit, if such was its will. Or not."

He stopped and regarded them with disdain, as if they were also complicit in keeping this enormous secret.

"And what did the elders give me for my courage to stand against this conspiracy? They denounced me, silenced me, disgraced me, expelled me from the order, banished me to the Wild. They severed my psychic connection with my students, which was as painful for me as it was for you, Narick, I assure you. They lied to you in saying that I practiced the cursed magic of the Underplanes." His flashed a wicked grin. "At the time, at least, I did not."

Kuurm's words unsettled Narick further. He believed in the order; he'd committed to it for twelve winters. If Kuurm spoke truly, everything he knew might be wrong, shattered, in disarray. What else were his masters hiding from him and his fellow monks? He tried to dismiss such a disquieting notion.

Kuurm paced again, his hands folded in his voluminous sleeves. "The elders placed an agonizing psychic block in my mind. I could not speak of my experiences, for to utter such words caused great pains to tear through my body that would have killed me if I persisted. They assumed this would prevent me from ever rising against them. They should have taken my life instead." He stopped and winced. "Even now, the pain can return if I say too much."

"You know they would never do that. Murder is not our way," Narick said, though he now desired to kill this man in violation of his own vow. The irony of it struck him.

"A weakness that will bring about the order's doom," Kuurm said, taunting. "In fleeing from my banishment, I did the only thing I could do: I studied more. I traveled west to Gavalahorne and learned what I could from the Darrowrath, the aphotic mages, there. I uncovered what I could from their ancient magical works and intuited the rest. I even began working magic of my own. I continued to develop my martial skills, my mental prowess. The order could not take away from me those things I'd already learned."

He took a few steps toward Mylth and Dorinen.

"And I discovered the lost writings of Ananbrom of House Keradir."

"What?" Mylth gasped.

"Oh yes, *Shy'nande*, they have survived. Not the originals, of course, but faithful copies, made some time after the Gharborr conflict. Certain, shall we say, secretive sorcerers who did not wish their actions to be noticed, held them in private collections. Through those works, I saw a means of reclaiming justice for us all and finally putting an end to the deceptions that the Spirit forced on this world. Many would die, but if we were doomed anyway, this might at least offer a chance for the strong to triumph, free from the Land Spirit's control. I resolved to release the powers of Torr Hiirgroth, hastening the Spirit's death and preventing its rebirth."

"You cannot prevent the rebirth," Mylth protested.

"Can I not?" Kuurm asked with mock ignorance. "Well, I learned the means by which Ananbrom raised the ancient Arltorath. And so, in the Mountains of Sorrow, I located their cursed tombs and awoke their energies, freeing them, but I bound them at once within the darkness of the Eral-savat, which still slowly fed on the souls of those that perished during the war."

"You awoke them?" Mylth demanded.

"Oh yes," Kuurm boasted. "They wait, trapped within the Eral-savat even now, their own considerable power giving force to the eruption now ravaging Yrthryr once more. Perhaps I'll release them at some point to wander this world… or perhaps not."

"You lie!" Narick snapped. "No one has such power."

Kuurm turned to him. "Oh, I could not have done so, but for the weakening of the Land Spirit. I also learned of this wretched place, where Denderath banished the Vordlai. With the Spirit dying, it was an easy matter to release some of those creatures still sleeping on this plane." He almost started to laugh, though his face fell into a cold expression.

"But now, the time approaches when the portal to Torr Hiirgroth can truly be opened. I have held the Vordlai in check through my will." He motioned to the creatures standing about them, their restraint proof enough of his boast. "But they grow stronger each day. Tomorrow night, we will return to Meln. The drugged fools there shall willingly lay down their lives."

He fixed his mocking stare on Narick. "Your young musician friend, isn't she from Meln? By the way, where *is* she? I'd hoped she might rejoin us by now. Alas, she must have slipped a bit too far."

He flashed a satisfied smile, which only made Narick want to break his neck.

Kuurm held his hands out, as if in supplication or prayer. "It will be a grand sacrifice, a harvest of blood, if you will. The Vordlai will devour the villagers, and the dark energies I raise shall be enough to destroy the portal. Their foul kin will be free to roam these lands again, and I shall not stop them. The mass murder of the weak will strengthen the Eral-savat, and the fury of the earth ravage shall tear across the north, hastening the Spirit to an early death. There will be no rebirth, no reestablishment of the old way. When the Land Spirit has died, my power will increase tenfold."

Dorinen shot alarmed glances at both Bayark and Mylth. Bayark placed a comforting hand on her arm, while Mylth's narrowed eyes once more bored into Narick.

"And then what, you fool?" Narick demanded. "What will be left for you?"

Kuurm remained silent, which only made Narick want to tear into his old teacher with every combat technique he knew.

"I can sense exactly what you desire, Narick," Kuurm taunted. He held his arms out in a show of capitulation. "You may strike at me any time you choose."

Mylth spoke. "You are mad, Kuurm. Even if you succeed, the Vordlai will overwhelm you as soon as they are freed. You cannot possibly contain the power of the Eral-savat. No mortal can, even if the Spirit *is* near death. The powers of Torr Hiirgroth have twisted your mind, used you to gain an advantage in their eternal war with the Spirit. You believe that you use them, but they use you, and as soon as your purpose here is completed, they will destroy you."

Kuurm sneered at him. "And you would know all about them, wouldn't you, Dalaethrian? Remember what Tarnohken did to your beloved?"

Mylth rose to his feet, pointing his sword at Kuurm.

"Mylth, no!" Dorinen implored, standing and reaching for his arm.

"Don't," Narick implored, knowing full well what might happen.

Kuurm didn't give them the satisfaction of a reaction, but merely gestured to Tarnohken. "Do you know exactly what this magnificent creature did to your fair Kyndaeviel? Shall I tell you how it tore her apart slowly, so that she did not die immediately, and how it feasted on her beating heart? How did devotion to the Land Spirit save her? I can see you already doubt. You have blamed Ramwin for centuries for her death and your mother's. Admit it! You know I am right! You know you are a slave to this Spirit and must act according to its desires."

Mylth remained silent, hand shaking as his grip tightened on his weapon. Yet Narick shared his obvious concern that Kuurm spoke truthfully.

"Don't listen to him, Mylth," Dorinen pleaded, laying a hand on his forearm. "His words are deceit. He's trying to seduce you with hate. Fight it, as you told us to do!"

"Ah, Dorinen, dear Dorinen." Kuurm directed his attention to her.

She also kept her hand ready on the hilt of her sword, so focused on him that she hardly even blinked. A growl tugged at her lips, an anger Narick understood all too well.

"So much like his lost Kyndaeviel you are, which is the only reason he keeps you close. You remind him of her, and he grasps at anything to recapture that time of bliss, anything to lessen the pain he has carried for so long. He knows he has served a lie, but you can make him forget it, at least for a while. You are a comfortable illusion to him, nothing more."

Scowling, Mylth raised his sword to strike.

"Woah, pixie!" Bayark grabbed hold of him around the waist and held him back, as two Vordlai shuffled protectively in front of Kuurm.

"You speak vile falsehoods," Dorinen countered.

"A naïve child such as you could never understand deception," Kuurm answered, as he pushed past the beasts, oblivious to Mylth's threat. "Even after all you have suffered in your young life, you still hold to the perversity of the Urkera, when anything you value can be taken from you in an instant, without the slightest concern of the Spirit."

Dorinen shook her head and regarded him with disdain. Narick knew that Kuurm's taunts rang terribly true for her, just as they were now becoming for him.

Kuurm spoke again, drawing Narick's attention. "Observe."

With a wave of his hand, one of the Vordlai flew swiftly into a tunnel on the opposite side of the chasm.

* * *

The Vordlai returned, clutching a pale, middle-aged woman in its clawed hands. Her body hung limp.

"Brynna!" Dorinen cried, her heart pounding with the awful recognition.

"Dori?" the woman rasped weakly, her voice shaking with fear.

"Brynna," Dorinen whispered. "Don't move!"

"What's happening, Dori? Help me, please."

Dorinen instinctively pulled another arrow from her quiver, but Kuurm's hand, held up in warning, stopped her.

"Ah, so you do know each other." Kuurm raised an eyebrow in a show of genuine surprise, but his voice couldn't hide his derision.

Indeed, when the Vordlai attacked the Dwelling, Dorinen watched helplessly as it grabbed Brynna and others and vanished into the forest.

"Oh, there were two creatures," Kuurm said, bringing her back to the moment. "But I only allowed one to attack."

Dorinen took a step back. "What?"

"I found it prudent not to let them fall into too much of a frenzy," Kuurm went on. "So, one creature took some of your people as captives, while the other remained behind in case it was pursued. That one was meant to take you, as well."

"And yet here I stand." She lifted herself up in defiance.

"Only because of Ramwin's interference," he snapped. "In any case, after the first Vordlai seized her, it brought her here. I've had others be conducted to this place, from the keep above and from Meln, so I decided to add some of your people to my little collection," Kuurm explained with a chuckle. "But this one has been of no use, numbed by petty fears and offering nothing of value to tell me, so she may as well serve a new purpose now."

He motioned for the Vordlai to bring the woman near to him. Dorinen drew back the sinew of her bow, aiming for the creature.

Kuurm observed Dorinen with merciless eyes. "If you release your arrow, I promise you the creature shall tear her apart"

Dorinen paused and lowered her bow. Gritting her teeth, she desperately weighed her options to free her friend.

"Now, ask your Urkera to intervene." Kuurm's venomous voice interrupted her frantic planning. "Pray for it to spare her, as Ramwin saved you. If the Earth Heart is truly a part of you and her, it should not let such an injustice fall upon the innocent. Beg your wretched Land Spirit to save her life!"

Dorinen shook her head, determined to counter him, but grappling with her own doubts. "The Spirit does not—"

"The Spirit does not listen!" Kuurm's cold expression erupted with rage. "It cares not! Anything that I choose to do now is of my own will, anything you choose is of your own will. We do not have to rely on the whim of some far-away cosmic principle!" He threw out his hands. "Do you still not see? Without the deceptions of the Spirit to tame us, we shall define our own destinies, claim our own power!"

"No!" she shouted. "You're wrong. The Spirit is good and sustains us. When we are hurt, it is hurt. When we feel love and joy, it revels with us! We already control our own destinies, and with the Spirit within us, we have more power than you shall ever know!"

"Perhaps," he answered, "but your so-called power cannot prevent this." He slashed his hand through the air.

Dorinen cried out in horror as the creature plunged its claws into Brynna's chest. Blood poured from her mouth, and she choked and gurgled before falling lifeless out of its grasp.

* * *

Narick barely restrained himself. He resisted the impulse to rush to his foe and fight, for doing so would likely get his friends killed all at once.

Bayark, however, was not so reticent. "I've had enough of this!" he roared. "Your magical mind games don't work on me, monk! You're gonna die, if I have to fight everything in the Underplanes to get to you!" He dashed forward, past one of the Vordlai, axe poised to strike.

With barely a twitch of his hand, Kuurm sent Bayark flying, knocking him to the side of the cavern in a crackle of white sparks and light. His weapon flew from his hands as he slammed into the ground, and though he made a feeble effort to rise, he collapsed, unmoving.

"Bayark!" Dorinen shouted.

"Now," Kuurm said, turning to the others. "I grow weary of justification. You see the truth of my words, and I shall leave you to ponder them until tomorrow night."

Kuurm flicked his wrist again, this time at Mylth and Dorinen, and they doubled over, clutching their bellies. The wind knocked from them, they mustered no resistance at all as two Vordlai lumbered up behind them and twisted their arms behind their backs.

Narick watched helplessly as the Vordlai vanished into another of the cavern's exits, carrying his friends in their sinewy arms.

The Vordlai who'd killed Brynna carried her body away. Tarnohken bowed slightly to Kuurm and left by another passage, followed by the remaining creatures.

Kuurm turned to Narick, like a wolf stalking its prey. "Now, my favorite *Kai Erodh*. Let us see how well you have honed your skills in the time that we have been apart."

Twenty-Three

The faint white light from the cavern far above disappeared by the time Andra and Jeena found the bottom of the near pitch-black chasm, though the glow of Jeena's spirit led Andra along safely. But Andra struggled to breathe, her ribs aching from her fall. She stepped on a sharp stone and cried out, stumbling and cursing. Her sore ankle buckled beneath her weight with a sharp and splitting pain.

Jeena came near to her at once. "My poor dear. Give me your hand."

"But I can't touch you." Andra wanted nothing more than to be able to take Jeena's hand.

"Trust me."

Andra did as she asked, expecting to feel only the damp air of this cursed place above her palm. But as Jeena began to sway, drawing circles in the darkness with her other hand, heat emanated from her spirit, swirling into Andra's arm and through her entire body.

In a moment, the warmth dissipated, and so did the

suffocating ache in Andra's ribs and the stabbing sensation in her foot. She took a deep, invigorating breath. "The pain… it's nearly gone! Thank you, thank you so much."

"Alas, I cannot rid you of it entirely," Jeena said with regret, "but it should ease your burden for a while."

For a brief, excruciating moment, Andra desired only to throw her arms around Jeena in gratitude. But knowing she couldn't, she asked, "How will we find the portal? What must we do if we find it?"

Jeena focused on the tunnel ahead of them. "I do not know exactly. We must trust in our intuitions to guide us. All I know is that we need to continue on this path." She pointed.

"I sense something, too," Andra replied, "though maybe it's just what I'm experiencing through you."

"It is both," Jeena said. "But do not underestimate your own potential. We will succeed, *mar shokara*," she added with a confident and caring smile. "We will succeed."

* * *

Deception. The word burned in Narick's mind. Was Kuurm telling the truth? Had his Shylan Dar superiors known and refused to share such astonishing and world-changing information?

Narick stood in silence, observing his opponent with the attention of a stag eyeing its rival. Kuurm threw off his robe, revealing loose black trousers and a grey shirt. He uttered a guttural chant, barely audible, and focused his intensity directly on Narick. He circled his hands around each other, and bright lightning swirled about them, crackling and sparking.

Kuurm's tactics had succeeded. Narick's friends were dead, captured, demoralized, defeated. They'd been worn down by this renegade monk, who knew how to probe their deepest fears and steal the hope from their hearts.

Though loath to admit it, Narick found Kuurm to be almost perfect in his way, a mad genius whose troubling half-truths, along with his untold powers of discipline and forbidden magic, now brought defeat and despair to the five companions, the Sarvethar's so-called appointed.

He turned over many jumbled observations as he eyed his enemy. He'd devoted his adult life to the order, believed in its principles as a guardian of knowledge, advisor to rulers, and protector of those in need. Yet Kuurm, with his words of sweet poison, had undone it all. Narick knew he should ignore Kuurm's claims, knew that Kuurm planned to wear away his faith and his conviction, his belief in himself. And yet, the possibility remained, enticing him with its promise of blissful despair, of surrender to the darkness.

He took a wider stance and chanted over and over a traditional preparation for combat: "*Charaan noth, charaan dier, shylan noth, shylan gredh.*"

Kuurm chuckled with a cruel delight. "Oh, yes, please do prepare yourself! Let us first spar not in our minds, but in our bodies."

Narick held his ground, setting aside the debate raging inside him. He would deal with the implications of Kuurm's revelations later. Now, he gave himself over to this moment, this challenge. He could not defeat his former master without greater preparation. All he could do was try to hold his ground and devise a way of escaping to find Dorinen and Mylth, if they still lived. Bayark hadn't moved since he fell; Narick feared he might be dead already. Worse, he needed to force thoughts of Andra's terrible fate from his mind. They would only overwhelm him with despair, and Kuurm knew it.

Instead, he found his inner balance and concentrated on his strength, letting the power of his mind rise within him. He spoke no more words to his enemy; he would not risk uttering Kuurm's name. If their psychic link were reforged, his former master could dominate him completely and drive him mad. He'd resisted Kuurm's mental assaults through his directed meditation, and he would fight off his physical assault with equal conviction.

Both held their ground, not willing to make the first move and leave themselves vulnerable.

"Good. Very good," Kuurm said. "You do not rush into battle, not even with my provocation, or with all that you have seen and heard. You wait, you observe, and you let your opponent make the first move, and perhaps the first mistake. You have learned. Unfortunately for you, I have learned more!"

He launched himself at Narick, landing within striking distance. Narick sought to press the advantage and struck with the flat of his palm. Kuurm dodged and missed the brunt of the attack, and kicked out in an arc, connecting with Narick's left leg.

Narick stumbled, but quickly regained his stance, just in time to parry Kuurm's punch with his arm. As their limbs connected, waves of lightning shot from Kuurm's fist and stung Narick's flesh. He recoiled in pain, his arm tingling. Kuurm responded with a hit to Narick's exposed midsection. The force sent another jolt of burning energy through him, like a flame ripping through his chest. He yelled in pain but held his ground.

Kuurm jumped back several steps to momentarily regard his younger opponent, catching his breath. "Yes, this is what I have craved! One worthy of my skills, a true foe! It will be a pity to strike you down."

Narick blocked out the pain of Kuurm's punch.

"There is more, much more," Kuurm said. "I could not speak of it in front of the Vordlai, of course. But when they have finished ravaging these lands and feeding as they wish, I shall cast their bloated bodies into the Eral-savat, and that, dear Narick, shall be the end. The concentration of such chaos in one place on this plane will disrupt the cosmic order such that the Spirit will not be able to regenerate itself."

He turned to regard the cavern.

"Then, I will draw the Arltorath out from the Eral-savat, banishing them, as you and your canny friends did centuries ago, but not before using their strengths to my advantage. I shall forge a new cosmic order. I will be the artificer of a new world where the strong shall be free to attain unlimited power!"

"You're insane!" Narick yelled. "In your boasting, you've shown me your mad plan has no influence over me. I won't be a part of it, and nothing you can say will change that. If you sought my devotion, you have failed utterly."

"I seek only to destroy you, fool!" Kuurm spat. "I knew you would never betray your wretched principles and false vows. This is a test for *me*. You shall die here, while your friends shall die with the coming of the darkmoon. Consider yourself fortunate you will not be rent apart by the Vordlai's talons. Perhaps in its death throes, the Spirit blesses you one last time, and Enwyonn grants you a dignified death!"

He swung his hand in an arc and an invisible force knocked Narick off his feet. He hit the ground hard, and an explosion of stars preceded a rush of pain to his face, while blood trickled from his nose.

Rousing himself, he saw Kuurm standing some distance away, his smug expression taunting and gloating. Yet Narick resisted any gut reactions that might lead to impulsiveness and error. He breathed deeply and again drew inward. It was time for a mental offensive of his own.

* * *

Andra and Jeena pressed on through the tunnel for a short time before entering a cavern at the bottom of a massive chasm. Far above, a globe made of grey mists swirled, lights circling around it, each on their own orbit like a multitude of tiny stars.

Andra felt something within her, something true and right. "This must be it!"

"It is," Jeena responded with encouragement. Andra's confidence began to return. Jeena's trust in her hadn't been misplaced after all. Maybe she wasn't so useless. A sudden spark of inspiration came to her.

"My flute!" Andra said. She exhaled in relief when she discovered it remained undamaged in the case at her belt. "Can you follow me there?"

"Of course. The soul goes where it wishes, *mar shokara*!"

"Let's see the portal up close." Andra commenced her levitation song straightaway, thankful that at least this simple magic apparently couldn't be exhausted, couldn't fail her. She floated upwards with ease. Before long, she and Jeena were near to the misty portal, and Andra set herself down on a nearby ledge. Jeena floated to her.

Andra gazed in wonder at the whirling lights. "They're so beautiful."

But her mood darkened as soon as she saw what lay beyond them, locked away in another world. Shadowy, twisted shapes prowled and paced, while the faint, ravenous growls of Vordlai echoed from their accursed realm.

Andra peered into portal again, following one light on its tiny orbit. It blinked and went dark. Another soon did the same. From beyond, a Vordlai hissed, and this time, it sounded closer, hungrier.

A sickening dread twisted her belly, and she turned to Jeena. "Why are they disappearing?"

"This is a gate to Torr Hiirgroth, to the Underplanes," Jeena said, apprehension in her voice. "Those lights hold it in place. But as Denderath's enchantment weakens, the lights go out, and the portal weakens too."

"How do we stop it?"

Jeena's face betrayed her helplessness. "I do not know. Not yet."

A clawed hand swiped dangerously close to the barrier between the planes. Andra and Jeena watched, horrified as another light flickered and went out.

* * *

Narick stood in silence, betraying no sign of the pain Kuurm inflicted. He focused not on his enemy's movements and strategies, but on his own presence.

"Do you try to make me impatient, Narick?" Kuurm asked in a sarcastic tone, pacing back and forth. "I will not be drawn in by you. I can attack you as easily from here as I can if I were a step away from you. How else do you think I was able to assault your mental defenses long before now?"

"You said you wanted a physical fight," Narick grunted.

"I've changed my mind. As you can see, my power has grown in ways that our pathetic order could never allow. They keep you impotent and weak, Narick, just as mortal kind has been degraded under the control of the Spirit. But I grow stronger with each day. I see what we can truly accomplish, what we can finally become!"

Kuurm punched the air in front of him and a bolt of lightning shot from his hand. Narick whirled, barely evading the blast. A second bolt forced him to dive to the ground, but he came to his feet in an instant, launching himself at Kuurm.

As Narick's feet hit the ground, he thrust his arms forward, focusing all of his attention on the tips of his fingers. Psychic energy surged through them, exploding outward. The impact of the blast caught the older monk full in the chest. Narick gambled that the suddenness and boldness of the maneuver would surprise his foe, catching him off guard.

The force threw Kuurm back to the chasm's edge, but at the last moment, he adjusted to his momentum and threw himself into the air, landing on the cavern floor. He let out mocking chuckle.

Narick sank to one knee and breathed heavily, his arms and chest throbbing. The effort took a tremendous toll on his body, painfully reminding him of why he never used it. Kuurm, however, seemed to have mastered it with no detrimental effects. In his despair, Narick still admired the man's remarkable abilities, which only made him doubt again that he could win. But he brushed the doubts away.

"You see the futility of your efforts" Kuurm held out his arms wide. "One surge of psychic energy and you are already exhausted. You have not learned, dear Narick, to direct this energy wisely, to let it flow through you, to prevent it from entangling with your own strengths. You must distance your body and spirit from such an attack or you will quickly render yourself useless. But of course, since the technique is so rarely employed by the Shylan Dar, how could you be expected to be familiar with its proper use? Clearly, they teach you nothing of true value."

"Oh, I have learned much of value."

"Have you? Such psychic attack is a rare and dangerous discipline," Kuurm continued, "and few have the proper training to use it. It is, I believe, too dangerous for most to employ." He smirked. "Most."

Narick's mind burned with questions. Who among his elders decided who would learn these techniques and who would not? How had they chosen who to train in the deadly art? And why did his training now feel so inadequate?

As if in answer, Kuurm announced, "You have been betrayed, my friend, given the rudiments of a power beyond your imagination, only to be left unfulfilled, and poorly instructed in its proper use. However, I shall be delighted to teach you exactly what this exquisite energy can do!"

Kuurm raised his hands for another strike but turned his head, as if he'd heard a distracting noise. He stood too far away for Narick to attack him physically, and Narick was too drained to risk another psychic assault, so all he could do was watch, confused. *Is this some new strategy?*

"Ah," Kuurm said to no one in particular, "so there is more to your companions' resolve than I'd presumed. No matter, I will attend to it. Now…"

He thrust out one hand and swept it in a jerking motion toward himself. Narick yelled as he was pulled through the air, as if blown by a great gust of wind, and thrown to the ground at his enemy's feet.

"Shall we continue?" Kuurm taunted.

* * *

Dorinen ached and only now could breathe with ease again. Her forehead burned, but she didn't know why. Her arms and hands throbbed. Looking around, she found herself in a large pit the depth of perhaps two men in height. A faint yellow light from somewhere beyond her view barely illuminated her surroundings, though the pit's far corner remained shrouded in darkness.

She felt around for her bow and sword and found them lying nearby. For a moment, she wondered why, but realized that being armed against Kuurm probably made little difference.

She rolled over to see Mylth slumped next to him, barely visible in the dim light shining beyond them. She touched his shoulder, and he took her hand.

"A poor end for the would-be saviors of this world," he said, his voice resigned. "Thrown into a pit, with no idea where we are."

"You have no magic that can aid us now?"

"Nothing of much use, I'm afraid. I know an enchantment that will bring out someone's greatest fears, but Kuurm, the Vordlai? They thrive on fear. And I didn't have time to prepare for every possibility. I'm simply not at full strength."

Dorinen painfully dragged herself into a sitting position. "Then if we are to die, let's do so side by side," she answered. "I will not let them kill me tomorrow. I'll die fighting."

Mylth gave her hand a gentle squeeze. "As will I. Maybe we can still delay the opening of the portal, even if only for a short time. Perhaps the Spirit will find some other way to close it."

"I didn't think I'd hear you say something so wishful, yet so bleak," she said, hesitant to speak her next words. "Were you aware of the Spirit's death all along? Is that part of why you've carried such bitterness with you all this time?"

Mylth shook his head, almost apologetically. "No, I promise you, I didn't. But perhaps I've sensed it without knowing. Some Dalaethrians might have deeper ties to the Spirit that they haven't revealed, even to me. I am a half-breed after all, and probably resented by many among them."

"Cease such shameful talk. They're *your* people, too," Dorinen admonished. "It's right for you to embrace that heritage. I suspect there is more Dalaethrian in you than you admit."

"And yet, Kuurm's words stung me." He let go of her hand.

"Kuurm speaks lies," Dorinen said, bitterness welling up in her throat. "He's distorting the truth, bending it to suit his own hateful views."

"Can you be so sure?" Mylth countered. "Do any of us really know the Spirit's motivations? I don't. I've carried grief and anger for so long that I've ignored such important questions. I've thought the Spirit to be self-motivated, but only in relation to my own suffering. Small minded, I admit, but true." He fixed his gaze on her. "Is Kuurm right, Dorinen? Has the Spirit used us, deceived us?"

Dorinen didn't know how to answer. All she could do was hope he was wrong. With a painful groan, she pulled herself over to him, and lay her head on his shoulder, an action that surprised even her. More surprising, he placed his arm around her. In this forsaken place, she welcomed his caring gesture, his warmth, his presence, all of which soothed her mind and eased her pain.

They were silent for a while, and she recalled Kuurm's words about Mylth's fallen beloved. She broached the subject. "Those terrible things he said about Kyndaeviel—"

"He said them to hurt me," he interrupted, "to inflict pain deeper than physical wounds. But I've grieved for her too long. I have carried the burden of loss for centuries. It's time for me to let her truly rest. We may only have a short time left to live, but I need to be at peace."

The sound of a rustling movement nearby startled her. She sat forward.

"Can you see anything?" she asked.

He squinted toward the far end of the cavern. "We're not alone." He held one hand to his ear to listen with more intent.

In the shadows, someone stirred and stood.

"Who are you?" a man's voice sounded, deep but weak.

Dorinen took hold of her sword.

Mylth put a hand on her arm before she could draw the weapon from its sheath. "He's human," Mylth whispered.

"And he could still want to kill us," she warned.

Mylth turned to her. "If he's trapped here, I doubt he can do us much harm." Before she could object, he raised his voice. "I am Mylth Gwyndon, *Shy'nande* of the Land Spirit."

"Hm. Fancy that," the man grunted. "Strange place for you to be, eh?"

Despite Mylth's warning, she now drew her sword, and held it close.

"Why are you here?" the man asked.

"My companion and I are trying to stop the opening of the portal," Mylth continued, "and prevent Kuurm Adath from bringing great destruction."

"Not doing so well, I see?" the figure answered. "But at least you're alive, that's something. I wouldn't have thought anyone could do much down here. That bastard Kuurm has seen to it."

"Who are you?" Dorinen asked, squinting, but still unable to make out details in his dark shape.

The man sighed. "Honestly, it doesn't matter anymore. None of it. But you were fair enough to reveal yourselves to me, so I owe you no less. I am Lord Wyverdorn."

* * *

"The portal is failing!" Jeena cried. "The Vordlai must have found a way to hasten the process."

"They're doing this themselves?" Andra asked, backing away from the ledge as her short-lived hopefulness faded.

"They do not need that man, Kuurm," Jeena answered in sudden realization. "They are breaking through the seal from the other side! These creatures have used the fool all along. They have drawn on his power to enhance their own."

"We have to stop it from opening!" Andra insisted, her heart racing, her dread mounting. "We must do something, anything!"

"Stay calm, *mar shokara*. Come to me and hold out your hand."

Taking a deep breath, Andra did so and at once, a surge of tingling energy flowed through her.

"Now, sing as I dance!" Jeena commanded.

"But my lyre is ruined."

"Just sing! Anything! Sing with your whole heart and mind, with your soul and your body, sing to She who inspires you and gives you life."

Andra began a hymn to Teuvell, while Jeena joined in, swaying her head from side to side. She increased her pace, forcing Andra to keep up.

"I feel the jewel, it heightens our power. Put your attention on the portal!" Jeena shouted, "use the music and the dance to strengthen it."

Strands of melody became threads of light and circled about the swirling mists of the portal. As they spun, they multiplied, and the speed of their orbits increased with each passing.

Andra sang loudly and triumphantly, rejoicing in the power of the Lady coursing through her, a gift from her soul-bond. Her confidence soared and victory seemed within their grasp.

"We're doing it, Jeena! We're—"

A horrific screech shattered her concentration.

Andra reeled and staggered, barely able to prevent herself from tumbling over the edge. Jeena spun away in the air, disoriented, spiraling randomly, as if no longer in control of her own spirit.

Andra screamed as she saw three pairs of yellow eyes piercing the darkness behind her, three hungry Vordlai looming over her.

Twenty-four

The dim light revealed a shell of a man, wan and haggard. His once-fine doublet hung off of him like a sack, and strings of dirty hair matted his equally filthy face.

"How do you still live?" Dorinen asked in disbelief.

Lord Wyverdorn shrugged. "Apparently, Kuurm thinks I'm better alive than dead. At least for now."

"Are you alone?" she asked.

"No, there are three others, my captain Shelberran and two soldiers, Gontar and Wayden." He gestured behind him, to the darkest end of the cave.

"How long have you been here?" Mylth asked.

Wyverdorn paused. "Perhaps a moonspan? It could have been half that… or two. With no sunlight in here, who can tell? We get scraps of food thrown to us once in a while, and foul water in a waterskin. We relieve ourselves in the corner," he pointed behind them, "in case you're wondering about the stench. But however long it's been, that damnable monk showed up at my keep one day, demanding access to these caverns. I told him I knew nothing of any caves, which was true. He insisted, and I refused."

"But he forced his way in, didn't he?" Dorinen asked. "We found your journal. We read what he did to you. To your people."

Wyverdorn's face slumped with regret. "Indeed. He captured my mind. And my poor guards stood no chance against his martial skills. I've never seen anything like it, certainly not from a Shylan Dar monk."

"He's no Shylan Dar monk," Mylth spat. "Not anymore. The order expelled him ten summers ago."

"And he's used the time since to make himself into the monster he is now," Dorinen added.

"Ah well, that at least explains something," Wyverdorn said, brushing his dirty hair away from his face. "Whatever he is now, he loves to talk. When I asked him how he knew about the caverns, he told me everything. Not even my own father knew about them, but somehow, he did."

"Did he tell you why your great-grandfather chose to build his home here?" she asked.

Wyverdorn nodded his weary head. "I already knew he resented being stripped of many of his powers and titles. To be honest, most of the other nobles did, too. How could they not? But I didn't know he felt so betrayed and spurned that he sought out one of those renegade cults in Gavalahorne, in an effort to regain some of his lost power. Apparently, they instructed him to build here. For the rest of his days, he led a dual life, secretly devoting himself to raising the powers of the Underplanes."

"Blood and tree ash," Dorinen whispered. This evil had been rotting in her home for far longer than she'd been alive.

"But before he could succeed," Wyverdorn went on, "the Rilnaryan Wardens found the cult and destroyed them. He never told his son, or grandson—my father. Honestly, I would have been happy to die having never learned of it. Thanks to Kuurm, now I must carry this weight, knowing my ancestor sought to bring those creatures back, and for what? Spite? Revenge?"

"His misdeeds are not yours," Dorinen said in a meager attempt to comfort him. "These forces work by way of deceit and trickery, seducing and warping those who align themselves with them. Even the most steady-minded are hardly strong enough to resist."

"Then what is the point?" Wyverdorn asked, thrusting out his upturned palms. "I'll tell you truly. More than once, I've considered ending my life, but I couldn't do it. I didn't have the courage. I even asked Shelberran here to put me out of my misery, but he refused."

A groggy man joined Wyverdorn, rubbing his eyes, as if trying to emerge from a perpetual deep sleep. His leather doublet showed more wear than his master's, his longer hair even stringier as he pushed it aside.

Wyverdorn patted him on the back. "I imagine soon enough Kuurm will kill me, so I'll find peace at last. But he's kept us alive to witness that damned slaughter of his. Or be part of it."

"And your family?" Dorinen didn't want to know the answer.

"Gone," he answered with a choked voice. "I've no one left. Well, I have a younger sister, who tired of noble life and left the keep ten springs ago to find her own way. It seems that she had the right idea and saved herself from," he gestured, "this."

"All isn't lost," Dorinen said, even as she contended with her own defeatism. "Mylth and I, along with some others, have killed several Vordlai this night. They're not invulnerable. If we can escape, we might yet stop Kuurm from opening the portal and dooming the Land Spirit, even if we lose our own lives in the fight."

"That would be a cause worth dying for," Shelberran said, his voice hoarse and thin. "But we're weak. I doubt I'd be much more than a liability in battle." He pointed to the entrance to the cavern. "Kuurm has a Vordlai standing guard up there. How would we fight it? We're all injured and exhausted."

Mylth retrieved his shoulder bag from the damp cave floor. "We might not have to."

* * *

Still dazed, Narick acted without thinking, lashing out with a powerful slap across his former master's face. Kuurm's head snapped to one side, and he spat blood as he stumbled to the ground.

Narick pressed the advantage and fell with his elbow hard on Kuurm's chest, knocking the air from him. Kuurm tried to mount a counterattack, but Narick would not relent, striking Kuurm's face with a vicious punch, and again, and a third time. Kuurm frantically attempted to fend off the blows.

Narick intended on killing him then and there, but at the last, he held back. Did he fear to deliver the killing blow, or was he prolonging the attack to make his old master suffer as much as possible?

Kuurm thrust both fists forward to punch Narick's chest, releasing a blast of dark energy. Though much weaker than his mentor's first attack, it was enough to throw the younger monk off. Kuurm kicked at Narick's abdomen, knocking the breath from him and sending him sprawling backward, dangerously close to the chasm's edge. Kuurm didn't hesitate. Pulling himself to his feet, he delivered a sharp kick to Narick's side, sending him to the precipice.

Narick lay prone and dazed, trying to fight the blackness closing in on him, even as he heard mocking laughter and the sound of his old master coming to stand beside him.

"A fine effort, Narick Yerral," he said. "You have been a most worthy opponent. The fools of Shylan Dar have not totally failed. But I have seen enough and am weary. Farewell, my most excellent *Kai Erodh*, and may your dying Spirit grant you some peace before I slay it."

Kuurm slid his foot under Narick and prepared to kick him into the blackness of the chasm.

* * *

The three Vordlai advanced on Andra. Their guttural rumblings grew into loud snarls, as if sensing the presence of the Spirit within her and Jeena and hungering to feed off that primal power. Their maws snapped with a cacophonous babble, an otherworldly language of evil and predation.

Her heart in her throat, Andra did the only thing she could. She stumbled to the edge and put her flute to her lips. And she jumped.

Jeena screamed. As Andra fell, she played an airy, ethereal tune, slowing her descent until she landed gently on the floor of the cavern.

Above, the Vordlai spread their wings to give chase, but the opening around the portal was too small for them to take flight. They shrieked in rage, thrashing and howling.

Andra despaired at the portals' fading lights as Jeena rushed down to join her. "We were so close," Andra lamented. "We almost did it."

Jeena tried to console her, though her ghostly hand passed through Andra's arm. "We have not yet lost. We have contained the portal for a while longer. If our magic did not work, those Vordlai would not have been so eager to stop us. What we did before we can do again, and we have gained more time. Teuvell and Koliserr will be with us. With you."

Though encouraged, Andra wrestled with her doubts. "Maybe if we can find the others, if they still live, we can return with them and finish what we began."

A troubled expression came over Jeena's face.

"What is it?" Andra asked, alarmed.

"I must leave you," Jeena said, her face forlorn.

"No!" Andra cried. "Jeena, why?"

"I am so sorry. My people are in danger again and need me. But I promise you, I will return as soon as I can. Please forgive me. I do not want to go!"

"Jeena, I'm scared. I can't do this without you," Andra pleaded.

"You will not be alone. You will always feel me, in here." She put a hand to her heart. "Be brave, *mar shokara*. I am with you. I promise I shall come back for you!"

Jeena tried to touch Andra's face and Andra felt a faint warmth on her cheek. With a sob of heartbroken regret, Jeena faded.

Andra stood alone, cold and afraid in the darkness. She wrapped her arms around her chest. The monstrous Vordlai still perched far above her, their hungry growls echoing down the chasm as they threatened her with brutal, ravenous eyes.

* * *

Mylth and Dorinen helped Wyverdorn, Shelberran, and the two weak and weary guards gather their weapons.

"How do you plan on getting past that creature?" Shelberran asked as he fastened his sword to his belt.

Mylth held the velvet pouch of sand. "Don't worry," he said, followed by a sly glance at Dorinen. "We'll take care of it. I have enough left." He assumed.

Gathering their meager possessions, he and Dorinen climbed up the side of the pit as quietly as they could. Dorinen pulled herself over the edge, lying low. Mylth joined her, pouch in hand.

The creature slouched motionless at the far end of the cavern, its back turned to them.

"We need to draw it closer," Mylth whispered.

Dorinen aimed an arrow and let it fly. As it clattered against the stone, the creature whirled, screeched, and lurched at them with astonishing speed. Mylth whispered an incantation, and before the Vordlai could strike, he blew a puff of sand toward it. The Vordlai slid to a stop, brushing at its face, squinting and swatting at the tiny granules swirling around it.

Then it began to shrink, so small that it became barely taller than

Dorinen's boots. It glowered at Dorinen and Mylth with a yelp, and flew off in what seemed to be both fear and perhaps even embarrassment.

"Let that be a warning to Kuurm: we're not so easily defeated," Mylth said with smugness. "We'll have some advantage in morale, at least for a while."

As they helped Wyverdorn and his beleaguered men from the pit, Wyverdorn regarded them with a mixture of amusement and respect. "Perhaps there is an escape from this madness, after all."

"But before we discover the way out, we need to find the portal," Dorinen said. "Do you know where it is?"

Wyverdorn shook his head. "I know nothing about it, other than it exists, but I do know the Vordlai and Kuurm himself have used a tunnel somewhere that wends its way up to the surface."

"We're not leaving here until we find the others and close the portal," Dorinen insisted.

"If they're still alive," Mylth said. The fear of failing again weighed on him.

"Let us hope they are," Wyverdorn offered. "What must we do to close the portal?"

"I don't know the exact means by which Denderath sealed it," Mylth said, "so I cannot use the same method now." In fact, he hadn't given as much thought to closing the portal as to getting here in the first place.

"Well, first, we should go back to the cavern where we faced Kuurm," Dorinen said. "It's dangerous, but it's probably our best chance for starting out."

Wyverdorn rolled back his shoulders and let out a deep breath. "Then let us waste no more time. May Kuurm and his vile creatures suffer for what they have done to me and my family."

Mylth closed his eyes. *And for what they might yet do to the world and the Land Spirit.*

* * *

Narick groaned as Kuurm forced his foot underneath Narick's back. He knew what his master intended, and even in his half-conscious state, he tried to fight back. But his body wouldn't respond, now far too weak from physical exertion and repeated psychic assaults. So, he fought back with his only remaining weapon: his mind.

Directing his attention inward and forcing himself to focus, he took in as deep a breath as he could, and his head started to clear. He found his energetic center, his senses heightening, his awareness sharpening. He knew what he must do; he had no choice. Exhaling sharply, he said as loudly as his voice would allow: "Kuurm Adath!"

As he'd anticipated, the utterance caught Kuurm completely off-guard.

At once, strands of mental energy wove together like the threads on a loom, the psychic link between student and master intertwining and reconnecting. Narick feared he would vomit as these energies coursed through him, binding him once more to this hated man, changing everything about his life and his practice in one awful instant.

In Narick's mind, Kuurm now stood before him, as clear as he'd been in the cavern. But here, they faced one another in a Shylan Dar training room, its cold, forbidding stone walls bringing back to him many memories of grueling tests, of bodily and mental pain.

Kuurm scowled at Narick, letting out a thin and wispy chuckle. "Well played, Narick, and quite bold. A daring move worthy of my former pupil. The risk you take in reforging our link is great, the act of a desperate man. You've detained me for a moment, but I shall destroy you, just as I defeated you in our many sparring matches long ago."

"Destroy me, and I'll take you with me!" Narick threatened, lowering his stance and bringing up his open hands to shield his face.

"You have neither the strength nor the power, although, I do commend you on your show of bravado. Perhaps the order is not as weak and simpering as I have assumed."

"I assure you, when the need arises, we can be as deadly as you now fancy yourself to be." Narick retorted, clenching his fists.

"But you couldn't kill me when you had the chance, fool!" Kuurm spat back. "You hesitated when my fate was in your hands. Your pathetic insistence on mercy prevented you from making the kill."

"You're wrong, Kuurm. I held back because I wanted to hurt you as much as possible before I finished you, an exercise in ego that I won't repeat!"

"Indeed, you shall not!" Kuurm taunted.

With his mind, Narick projected a bolt of energy, like a wave of scorching air. It seared through his opponent and would have cut Kuurm's real body in half. But here, in this psychic space the two shared once more, the image of Kuurm merely shimmered like water in its wake. His efforts hadn't been enough. Indeed, his master staggered back but collected himself.

"You arrogant fool," Kuurm whispered. Breathing deeply. "This last battle will be one of wills after all, and I am certain you do not possess my hatred or my drive to accomplish what I have set out to do."

Kuurm launched a psychic wave of his own, more intense than Narick's.

Narick deflected the attack, crossing his wrists in front of his chest, absorbing the heat into his hands. With an arc of one arm, he whirled a pulse of energy at Kuurm like a thrown dagger. Kuurm ducked, but not quickly enough. He cried out as the force spun through him.

Narick didn't hesitate. This time, he wouldn't fall victim to the self-serving satisfaction of humiliating his opponent for the mere sake of being able to do so. He launched himself at his enemy, tackling the weakened Kuurm, twisting his arm around Kuurm's neck and head, pinning him to the floor. Narick began to squeeze, focusing his mind on crushing him in this realm, and choking the life out of Kuurm's physical body.

But Kuurm fought back. Sparks exploded around Narick's face, inflicting a stinging, psychic pain and making his mind-body convulse, but he held on. Calling on his training and discipline, he tried to block out the searing needle-like stabs engulfing his cheeks and neck, and tightened his grip.

His old master struggled beneath his grasp, but Narick finally gained the advantage.

"It… will not end like this!" Kuurm gasped for breath.

Grasping Narick's head with both hands, he uttered a short chant that Narick didn't recognize. Streams of lightning shot through Narick, exploding out of his ears, eyes, and mouth. He screamed as the agonizing surge ripped through his mind and he let Kuurm go as he collapsed.

At once, Narick awoke on the cavern floor, oddly energized, yet still reeling. His ears rang and his mouth burned, but through his blurry vision, he strove to focus on his foe.

Nearby, Kuurm slumped to his knees, gasping for breath.

With his former master so vulnerable, Narick wanted nothing more to rush him, to finish him. But as he tried to stand, his legs faltered, unable to carry his own weight. This mental battle had left his body too weak to mount an attack. Kuurm regarded him with a contemptuous glare for a moment, as he struggled to sit up. "This is a fight neither of us can continue. It will kill me, even if I finish you. And I am not ready to die yet." He smirked and bowed his head, as a voice sounded in Narick's mind.

I salute you, Narick, Kuurm intoned with mock respect. *I have underestimated you and the power of your decaying Land Spirit. But in the end, I shall triumph. I have waited more than ten summers and can wait a short while more. Even if I cannot open the portal to the Underplanes myself, it will eventually fail of its own accord.*

Narick again tried to drag himself to his feet, watching helplessly as Kuurm staggered to the edge of the cliff.

Kuurm turned to him and raised one hand, almost as if waving goodbye. "We will meet again, my *Kai Erodh*." With a single step, he fell backward into the chasm.

Finding his own footing, Narick scrambled to the edge and watched as crackling lightning pulsed and burst around his former master, swirling lights engulfing his body. With a blinding flash, he vanished.

Narick heaved and gasped for air, staggering away from the rocky cliff edge. He could hardly believe it; he'd defeated his master. Further, he fended off attacks from the most dangerous man ever to wear a Shylan Dar robe.

Uttering a silent prayer of thanks to Enwyonn, he slumped to the floor, exhaustion overtaking him at last.

Twenty-five

The three Vordlai perching on the ledge high above Andra growled. Knowing she was safe for the moment didn't stop her from giving in to despair and helplessness. With her kenlim broken, she couldn't summon the gem's powers, and being so deep underground, she stood little chance of channeling the Lady's energies. She whispered again for Jeena, hoping the young Ferwar would hear her and return. She called to her, sang her name, pleaded in her mind, but after several desperate attempts, she heard nothing in response. Her stomach twisted; something terrible must have happened for Jeena to leave so quickly and not respond.

Even worse, the portal's lights began to fade again, with ravenous Vordlai waiting on the other side, eager to break through. Only the Spirit knew how long their repair would hold.

She slumped against the cold, stone wall and resigned herself to being truly trapped in this unforgiving place. As she traced her fingers over the facets of the jewel in her broken instrument, she again considered the powerful artefact.

Why would Izznil give it to me only for it to be rendered useless?

She paused for a moment, and a realization struck her. The gem needed music, yes, but did it need to be from the lyre?

"Jeena told me to sing anyway, and that worked. What if I sing to it?"

She'd assumed her voice only augmented the lyre's power and needed accompaniment. After all, Izznil never told her to affix it to her instrument; it just felt right. But her voice was a powerful instrument, too.

Andra took a deep breath, trying to calm herself.

This might work. And if so, maybe I can contact Jeena, wherever she is, and together we can channel Teuvell and mend the portal for good!

A shrill screech sounded above her. She screamed as she saw a Vordlai, no taller than a riding boot, flying straight toward her.

* * *

Narick opened his eyes, surprised that he even could. How long had he been here? Why hadn't the Vordlai taken his injured body and devoured him by now? Lying on his back, he tried moving his feet and clenching his fists. His head throbbed as he reflected on his ordeal. What of the others? What of Andra? The sickening realization that she'd fallen came back to him all at once.

As tears filled his eyes, he noticed Dorinen's compassionate face to his left. Mylth stood close by.

"Am I dead?" he asked, unsettled at the sight.

"You're quite alive," she said, kneeling next to him. "What happened? Are you all right?"

He groaned as he sat up, aches and pains coursing through his body. "I've been beaten, burned, and kicked. I feel like a novice on his first day of Shylan Dar combat training. Otherwise, not so bad, all things considered."

Dorinen chuckled, but her face fell. "Where's Kuurm?" she asked.

"Gone," Narick replied, stretching out his arms and shaking his hands.

"Dead?" she asked, her expression brightening.

Narick shook his head. "We fought, first physically, and then psychically. My tolerance for pain was greater than he anticipated." His stomach knotted. "But I needed to re-forge my psychic link with him."

"What?" Dorinen drew back.

"It was the only way I could win," Narick answered with deep regret. "He's tremendously powerful. I don't know how I survived. I can only thank Enwyonn."

"And what does his defeat mean for us now?" Mylth asked, peering over the edge of the cliff.

Narick did the same and shook his head. "I don't know. Not yet. There was no other choice. He knew if he stayed here and killed me, he would also likely die, so he threw himself over the ledge and used some magic or psychic power to teleport himself away. All I know is that he still lives."

"Where has he gone?" Mylth pressed.

"I wish I knew. But wherever he is, he's here." Narick touched his forehead, where Kuurm's voice still echoed, each time sending a throbbing, tingling pain through Narick's skull and down his spine.

"But we've stopped him for now, yes?" Dorinen asked, her voice brightening.

Narick nodded. "We've bought ourselves some time, but I don't know how much good it will do."

"That's something," Dorinen said. "It's all we have at the moment. Especially now that it's just the three of us. Plus our new friends."

"New friends?"

"We found Lord Wyverdorn," Dorinen said.

"What?"

"It's true," the older man shuffled forward from the shadows, even as his guards remained behind him. "Apparently, I'm better known than I thought. And not dead, for now."

"I'm glad to hear of it, my lord," Narick said, but at once, his mood darkened again. He glanced around the cavern. "Bayark was here when we fought, but not now. And Andra is… gone." He fought back more tears. "We'll have to find a way to reseal the portal ourselves. If we don't, the Vordlai will escape, and all will truly be lost."

"Do not give up hope, yet, monk," Mylth said, his face brightening. "Come look at this."

Mylth motioned Dorinen to the edge and pointed to where Andra fell. "It's not a sheer drop. See those shelves of rock? It's possible one of them caught Andra before she could tumble farther."

"But what if she's hurt?" Dorinen asked. "She could be down there in the dark and—"

She didn't say more, but Narick knew that Andra might be injured, even dying. Still, he shook the idea away. "No," he said, the signs that his young friend still lived giving him much needed resolve. "She's alive. And we need to find her."

* * *

Andra nearly stumbled over. The Vordlai swooping down on her was no less hideous for its diminutive size, and apparently just as deadly. It burned with hate and it flashed its fangs in a menacing snarl. She ducked and narrowly avoided the creature's deadly claws as it passed over her. It soared into the air again, and turned, preparing for another dive.

In desperation, she dropped her broken kenlim, drew out her flute, placed it to her lips, and forced herself to stand still, though her hands shook as the creature approached. Closer and closer it flew, screeching again. She wanted to scream and run, but she stood her ground, her heart beating furiously, yet trying to present herself as an easy kill. The creature spread its arms wide, its talons poised.

At the last instant, Andra blew four sharp notes. Fire shot from the instrument and struck it directly in the face. It howled and swung wildly as the magical flames seared its visage and burned out its eyes. She dove to one side as it crashed into the chasm wall next to her, falling to the ground and twitching violently, clutching at its head in agony.

She jumped back, terrified, shaking. She almost drew her dagger to finish it off, but remembered the danger and held back. Overhead, the three Vordlai must have seen what had happened; she could hear them hissing angrily.

Keeping watch on the fallen creature, she picked up her broken lyre and scrambled away. It didn't follow her; it no longer even seemed aware of her presence. Quickening her pace, she wouldn't turn her back on it, even though she nearly tripped twice. She backed away into the tunnel, clutching her flute and the pieces of her lyre as her only protection. It still sputtered and thrashed about, while above, the awful sounds of its larger kin echoed down.

Andra wanted anything but to be here. She wanted Jeena. She wanted Narick. She wanted her mother. She wanted to be home. She turned over the day's dreadful events in her mind, and struggled to absorb them in any meaningful way. Narick had warned her truly; this place was worse than they could have imagined. Dizziness claimed her again, and she shivered.

Collapsing to the ground against a tunnel wall, out of sight of the creatures above, she could still hear their horrid baying. As she wrapped her arms around herself, she prayed she would not die here, abandoned, alone, and forgotten. Only then did she wince at the sting on her forearm, noticing her torn shirt and a line of blood across the skin, undoubtedly a Vordlai scratch.

* * *

Narick groaned as he struggled to his feet, even as Dorinen tried to stop him from moving. "No," he insisted, now determined. "If there's a chance that Andra is alive, we must find her."

"You're barely even well enough to move, much less strong enough try to descend into the chasm," Dorinen admonished.

"I will not stay here if she lives!" he barked at her. He softened his voice. "Dorinen, please. There will be time enough for me to rest if we survive this madness. But if we are meant to die, I will not lie here like a helpless victim."

Dorinen accepted the futility of trying to prevent him from searching for his best friend. "Who am I to demand anything of you?" she conceded. "I'd behave the same way."

She and Mylth helped him to his feet.

"Is it possible we can locate her by some magic?" Dorinen asked Mylth.

"No," he answered. "Most of what I have left is forceful in nature, battle-oriented. I anticipated great resistance."

"Well, you haven't used much of it in that regard," Narick said, annoyed.

"There hasn't been time," Mylth answered. "Forgive me, but when flesh-hungry beasts are rushing at one, it does tend to distract from proper spell preparation. My sword was more effective than magic under the frenzied circumstances. Frankly, seeing the kind of psychic assaults that your order advocates, I'm glad I can choose between one and the other. The blend apparently drives men mad."

"Kuurm was the first and the last!" Narick shot back. "He didn't use his training the way the order teaches. He is a renegade and an outcast."

"Banished to the Wild, yes?" Mylth responded. "An effective punishment, obviously. It gave him all the time he needed to set this disaster in motion. Well done."

"Watch your tongue, Dalaethrian!" the monk growled.

"I will not," Mylth said, taking a few steps closer. "Your order is responsible for allowing Kuurm to return, and if we survive, I will see to it that the Shylan Dar are held accountable to the governing bodies in Tenaeth."

"And who are you to judge? Someone who forsook the honored title of *Shy'nande* and rejected the Spirit long ago out of self-pity? Hardly the caliber of man to point accusing fingers." Secretly, though, he shared Mylth's opinion.

"Stop it, both of you!" Dorinen demanded. "There will be no more of this! Andra, and perhaps Bayark, are still alive. We'll find them and the portal, and seal it. We *will* accomplish what we came here to do, provided you two cease squabbling like children. Now, can we please decide what to do next?"

Narick examined where Andra had fallen. The drop opened onto a ledge that sloped away. From there, a clear path led downward. He heaved a great sigh of relief.

They made their way onto the ledge, helping Wyverdorn and his men in their turn. Once there, they discovered signs of displacement and a fall.

Dorinen picked up a rock the size of her fist. She turned it over in her hand. "Andra has been here. This was disturbed only a short while ago. Her trail leads away."

Narick pushed past Mylth; he wouldn't wait another moment. With a single-minded purpose, he limped into the darkness, ignoring the protests of his pain-wracked body.

* * *

"Oh no, oh dearest Lady, no!" Andra cried. "Please don't let me perish here, alone in this awful place." Shaking, she sat against the tunnel wall, and tried to calm herself. "I have to heal myself, I have to… I have to find Jeena." Andra tried to shut out everything confronting her: panic, terror, despair. She needed one thing: to locate her soul bond. Placing her shaking hand over the gem, she closed her eyes.

"Lady of song, Lady of life," she began, her voice uneven and quivering. "Lady of all that is good and brings delight. Hear me in this cursed place. Bring Jeena Karahla to me, when it is right for her. Let the bond that unites our souls grow stronger. Let it transcend time and distance. Help me in my need, dearest Lady."

The gem grew warm under her touch, and she opened her eyes to see a gentle glow begin within its heart. She hummed her favorite melody, a song of love and longing, bringing her attention back to the Rajaani woman who'd captivated her in such a short time. She stopped and listened to her voice echoing off the stone walls.

"Andra," a voice sounded.

"Jeena!" she whispered.

"Yes, *mar shokara*, I promised you I would return!" Jeena's *liskja* appeared, radiant and soothing.

"I was afraid you were gone forever," Andra cried, reaching for her, even as her hands passed helplessly through Jeena's spirit once again. She stamped the ground with her foot and swore.

"I would not leave you for long, dear one."

"Jeena, I, I'm injured. A Vordlai—a small one—struck me." She held out her forearm to reveal in Jeena's light the ugly scratch stretching from her wrist halfway to her elbow.

"Dearest Twilight Lady, no!" Jeena gasped, moving in to see. "How do you feel?"

Andra paused and took a deep breath. "Fine. So far, I mean." Her answer surprised her.

"There is no numbing, no weakness, no sickness? Believe me, I know."

"No," Andra answered. "Was it too small to have venom?" She could only hope.

"I think those creatures are deadly, no matter their size," Jeena said. "I have never heard tell of any without such a horrid weapon."

"But if it hasn't harmed me, what does that mean?" Andra desperately wanted an answer.

"I do not know. We can only thank your Lady and mine that you are safe. But you must tell me if anything begins to afflict you."

"Of course." Andra heaved a sigh and relaxed a little. "Where did you go? Why did you leave?" she asked.

"Gro'aken attacked my people in the wolds."

"What? How?" Ashamed at her selfishness, Andra at once regretted wanting Jeena to be here. "Tveor protect the wolds," she countered. "The Gro'aken can't intrude there." She seethed at thinking of her home so endangered.

"And yet, one of the Vordlai also found my people, and our enemy subdued your village," Jeena said. "Those things should not have happened, either. The presence of so much evil is ominous."

"Are you well, at least?" Andra asked.

"I am. Our best warriors killed several Gro'aken and chased the rest away, but we are fearful, especially now. We will leave the Grey Wolds tomorrow and journey toward Wold Lake. Danger lurks everywhere, and I fear no one will be safe until we can stop this madness."

Andra had heard enough. Whatever might happen, she was going to put an end to the nightmare of the Vordlai. Determination rushed back to her, remembering how she might use the gem. "I think I know what to do," she said.

* * *

Dorinen kept a short distance behind Narick while he pressed onward, annoyed at his insistence on leading them, despite his ordeal. Must she always to defer to those around her who knew no better and couldn't match her skills? At the bottom of the chasm, he stumbled on a rock and struggled to regain his balance.

Exasperated, she would have no more of his stubbornness. "Enough. You will follow me."

He conceded at last that he was too weak. Her bow in hand, she set off in front of them, leaving the light of the cavern behind and entering into a tunnel. She moved quickly, her keen vision limited here, but good enough to avoid jagged rocks and muddy puddles. After scouting father ahead, she heard… singing?

"Andra?"

She stopped to sniff the air.

"I smell humans… and Vordlai," she whispered. That the Vordlai may have trapped Andra alarmed her, and she hurried ahead, her arrow ready. She heard the voices of two women in the distance. One was recognizably Andra's. But who was the other voice, and why by the Five Hallowed Oaks would someone else be down here?

She raced ahead with anticipation, and around the corner, found Andra sitting with the ghostly form of a beautiful young woman with long black hair, dressed in Rajaani clothing.

"Andra!" Dorinen gasped. Tearful relief and joy came over her, and she laughed.

"Dorinen!" Andra sprang up and ran to her friend. The two hugged in a tight embrace.

"We were so afraid you'd died from the fall," Dorinen said.

"And I thought you'd all been killed by Vordlai. Where are the others? Is Narick…"

"He's alive, hurt but alive. He fought Kuurm."

Andra furrowed her brow. "Who's Kuurm?"

"The 'master' who's behind all of this," Dorinen explained. "He's Narick's former teacher. It's a long story, apparently."

"Narick defeated him?" Andra asked, her expression brightening.

Dorinen nodded. "But he's not dead. He fled, and we must still seal the portal."

Andra took a hesitant step forward. "Jeena and I have an idea."

"Oh, thank Urkera. Wait… Jeena?"

The Rajaani woman floated toward them. Dorinen took a step back, despite Andra's assurance. She'd already seen too much magic to trust anyone right away.

"This is Jeena Karahla, of the Rajaani travelers, the people I spoke of before," Andra said.

"Be welcome," Dorinen said, still not understanding what she was seeing.

"It's also a long story," Andra added.

* * *

Andra's attention diverted to the figures emerging from the darkness. When she saw Narick, battered but alive, damaged but victorious, she ran and wrapped her arms around him, holding tight and burying her head in his chest, giving in to sobs of happiness.

Tears also rolled down his face. "I feared you were lost," he managed to say. "When you fell over the edge, a part of me died."

Touched by his heartfelt words, Andra let go of some of her confusion and upset. "But Jeena found me and saved me," she answered.

He took a step back, surprised. She motioned with her chin behind her, to where the spirit of the Ferwar woman hovered. Jeena smiled and waved to Narick with a wink.

"Our soul-bond," Andra explained. "Jeena can appear to me, even from far away, and so the Lady can work through us."

"Enwyonn be praised!" Narick hugged her again.

She looked around in haste. "Where's Bayark?"

Narick shook his head. "Sadly, I don't know. We'd hoped we might find him with you, but he's nowhere to be seen."

Mylth next emerged from the darkness, followed with Wyverdorn and his guards. Mylth saw Jeena and bowed his head slightly. "Well met, Sister of the Ferwar," he said with respect.

"And you as well, *Shy'nande*," she answered, placing her palms together and bowing her head.

Mylth regarded her with surprise. "Narick knew, and so do you. I'm beginning to think I've no private life at all. I'm sorry to tell you that while I may have been a *Shy'nande* once, during the Gharborr War, I left that life long ago."

"Ah, but you are a *Shy'nande* forever," Jeena said. "You cannot resign from it as you would some government post. It is in your blood, in your soul. You may have left the Sarvethar behind, but it has not left you, which is why you are here now. We cannot complete our task without you. The Spirit knows this. It's why you were woken."

"We wouldn't have found Andra or this place had it not been for you," Dorinen added, placing a hand his arm.

Mylth sighed. "You're right. I cannot abandon my fate, much as I'd like to. But that doesn't mean I have to like it."

He introduced Wyverdorn and the others, while Andra told them of the nearby portal.

"Be careful," she said as they made for the cavern, "there's a small Vordlai there. I injured it, badly, but it may still be dangerous."

"Damnation! It didn't occur to me the creature I shrank would pose a threat to anyone else," Mylth said.

Andra stared at him in astonishment. "*You* did that?"

"Indeed. It's my fault, I'm afraid. I'm sorry."

They returned to where she'd fought off the Vordlai, but it was gone. Andra would have panicked had her friends not been with her.

Far above them, the grey mists of the portal caught her attention. "The lights are fading again," she said. *If only we'd not failed earlier.* "The Vordlai have been destroying the portal from their own side."

"The fool!" Narick spat. "I told him he couldn't control them. Part of me wishes the creatures had escaped and torn him to shreds."

"Andra," Dorinen said motioning to Andra's arm, "that's quite the tear on your sleeve. How did it happen?"

Narick came to her. "That's a Vordlai scratch," he said in a halting voice.

Andra inspected her arm again. "It was the small one. When it flung itself at me, I consumed it with flame, but it managed to strike out at me."

"How are you?" Narick pressed, his brow furrowed with concern.

"Strangely, well enough, certainly not sick," Andra said. "It hardly even hurts now."

"Such a deep scratch should have been enough to infect you," Narick said, placing a steadying hand on her shoulder. "Yet you feel nothing?"

"Not a thing." She shook her head, still puzzled. "What does it mean?"

"I don't know," Narick said, "but pay attention to yourself. If anything troubles you, let me know at once."

"Jeena said the same thing. I will." His words made her mindful of every sensation, and she forced herself to try not to imagine the worst.

"I believe there is something greater at work here," Jeena said with assurance. "Be strong, my dear. The Lady yet protects you."

Andra wanted to reply, but with a rush of wind from behind them, a clawed hand ripped through the air from the darkness. It struck at Gontar, severing his head from his body in a single swipe.

Andra screamed.

A shower of blood sprayed over Wyverdorn, Shelberran, and Wayden, the closest to their luckless companion. They scrambled some distance away, almost tripping over one another in the effort. In a moment, two Vordlai emerged from the tunnel, one holding Gontar's head and biting into it like an apple.

Andra cowed behind Narick, her breathing shallow. Jeena moved in close beside her, while Dorinen hastened to Mylth's side, as Wyverdorn and his men moved closer.

Snarls and hisses echoed from behind them. Two more beasts emerged from the opposite tunnel, two sets of glowing yellow eyes piercing the darkness, two gaping maws drooling. One larger than the rest carried in its clawed hand the corpse of the small Vordlai, now lifeless and crushed. It tossed the body aside with a snort.

"That is Tarnohken," Mylth said gravely. "Whom I know all too well."

Louder, more insistent growls sounded above them near the portal, and three Vordlai leered over the chasm's edge.

Andra swallowed hard. "We're surrounded."

Twenty-Six

The companions pressed their backs against each other in a protective circle, weapons drawn against the Vordlai closing in on them. Andra stayed at Narick's side, while Mylth and Dorinen, along with Wyverdorn and his two men, closed the gap with their backs, ensuring no corner, no crevice, no shadow would escape anyone's view. Jeena hovered above them, turning about in every direction, keeping a watchful eye on all the creatures.

Andra tried to control her shaking, while Narick leaned close to her. "No matter what happens here, Andra, you and Jeena must seal the portal."

Andra stepped back. "You mean I need to leave you? No! I won't. Not now!"

"Don't be foolish! If you die, all is lost. Use your flute to fly away from us. Go!"

"But there are three more Vordlai near the ledge, there," she protested, pointing upward. "And I can't stay in the air, because I'll run out of breath. And if I have to play the flute, I won't be able to sing."

"Do whatever you must." He sounded desperate. "We're expendable. You two are not!"

Andra wanted to argue, but in her heart, she knew he spoke a terrible truth. Nothing else mattered but closing the portal. No one else mattered.

Jeena came to Andra and placed a spirit hand over hers. "You do not need to approach the portal this time, not with Mylth here." She turned to him. "Listen to me, both of you. Come."

Andra and Mylth drew back to Jeena's *liskja* as their friends stepped outward to surround them in a circle.

"Concentrate on the portal, as we did before," Jeena explained to Andra, pointing at Andra's ruined lyre. "Your jewel. It is the key."

Andra rested her fingertips on the gem.

"Now *Shy'nande*," Jeena said. "Protect us!"

Mylth furrowed his brow in confusion. "How?"

"Use whatever magic you have left to keep the creatures away from us," she answered. "They fear you far more than you realize. Even the simplest of tricks can give them pause. Show them what you are, show them your courage, and let them see your heart. Speak to them with the voice. Command them to retreat."

Mylth shook his head and took a deep breath. "I'll do my best to keep them at bay." Searching around in his shoulder bag, he pulled out a piece of the same root he'd used before. Knowing its effects wouldn't last long, he chewed it with vigor, spit it out, and spoke.

"Behold!" he commanded in a mellifluous voice. Whispers and choruses encircled the cavern, echoing off its walls.

Andra took in his eerie utterances with astonishment. How unlike the Lady's magic this arcane Dalaethrian spell-work could be! She found herself fascinated.

"Your destroyers stand before you," Mylth continued. "You failed to kill us at Kuurm's command, and you will fail now. I deny your terror! We will not cower!"

Mylth's voice took on a life of its own. As he spoke, his words formed tendrils of mist and smoke that swirled about the creatures' heads. They stopped in mid-step and swatted the air in front of them. As the beasts faltered, Mylth pulled out a small, roughly-hewn wooden cube from his shoulder sack. "Everyone, close your eyes!"

He uttered something Andra couldn't hear before throwing it at the two Vordlai nearest Wyverdorn and his men.

The wood exploded in a brilliant flash, and the creatures shrieked, covering their faces with their grasping hands.

Taking her chance, Jeena soared up to the gate, as the Vordlai on the ledge hissed at her.

"The portal is almost open!" she cried.

Indeed, the tiny orbiting lights began to extinguish rapidly. Andra gasped as a clawed hand thrust forth from the mists, its fingers grasping at the empty cavern air.

Jeena shouted, "We must act quickly! They are breaking free! *Shy'nande*, please, keep them away from Andra!"

Mylth hurled another block of light-wood at the largest Vordlai. It burst in front of the creature, who recoiled in pain. He'd gained them a little more time and began a chant of his own.

Inhaling the cold air, Andra placed her hand on the gem and opened her mouth to sing. Her voice faltered, but grew stronger and more confident with each line. She could do nothing now but trust, believe. Soaring high above her, Jeena began her ecstatic *purhan* dance to the rhythm of Andra's song, calling on Koliserr as she spun and directed magic into the gem far below.

A second claw darted out from the mists.

Soft, golden light coursed through Jeena and washed over Andra like a warm wave of summer ocean water, joining with the beauty of her voice. Andra held the broken lyre above her with both hands and sang now with her whole heart. Her fears diminished as her melody echoed through the chasm.

The gem glowed in violet brilliance, fed by Jeena's channeling of a hallowed magic and Andra lending it her voice. As the stone pulsed, its light burned and flickered like an evening star, ever brighter, as if the Land Spirit itself resided within is shimmering facets.

Andra sang, her view of the Vordlai and the cavern falling away; even Jeena's image faded. Only she remained alone with her music, just like that night in the Temple after her graduation ceremony. The Lady embraced her with Her all-encompassing love and warmth, and for the first time since she'd left Tenaeth, Andra felt truly at peace. Her vision returned and she became aware of her surroundings once more, even as she sang on, wild, uninhibited, free from fear and despair.

The Vordlai recoiled at the sound of her lovely melody, howling and pawing at their ears. All the while, Mylth's dreamlike words filled the cavern, denying the creatures' terror and demeaning their very nature. The beasts stumbled and flailed.

Above them, a third Vordlai claw swiped out from the portal, with only a handful of the protective orbs remaining.

As Andra directed her intention, a column of brilliant purple light burst from the gem, hurtling toward Jeena, who caught it as she spun in the air, and mingled her golden luminance with its violet fires. A great sphere of multi-colored magical energy began to swirl and twist between her palms. The enchantment burst from her hands, as if alive and sentient. It soared upward to the portal and surrounded it, enveloped it. The Vordlai hovering on the ledge screeched as Andra's song and Mylth's chanting, combined with Jeena's dance, empowered the ancient seal once again.

New lights flickered to life, their rapid orbits fully containing the portal as they multiplied. The mists now transformed from dull grey to bright blue, revitalized, invigorated, and rich with the power of the Spirit.

Still, the Vordlai clawed through, growling and snarling in ravenous desperation. But the portal began to close. The gaps sealed, one by one, trapping the Vordlai's twisted arms. The creatures screamed in agony as the lights severed their arms from their bodies, launching the liberated limbs to the farthest corners of the cavern.

And still Jeena whirled, directing their combined energies into the portal, letting Teuvell and Koliserr work through them. The light around the portal burned stronger, accompanied by a deafening roar, and as the Vordlai on the upper ledge howled, its brightness spread out to them. They tried to flee, but in a flash like a wave crashing to the shore, it engulfed them, incinerating their bodies. Soon, nothing remained of them but clouds of dispersing ash, drifting down in feather-light cascades.

Andra ceased her song as the luminance of their efforts faded, and only the portal now remained: swirling blue mists surrounded by countless circling lights, shining brilliantly in the darkness; the barrier was made anew. Andra cried out with a sob of excitement and Jeena shouted for joy as she dove back toward the chasm floor.

But the bestial screams of the remaining Vordlai shocked Andra out of her momentary celebration.

Four Vordlai had fallen to their knees, wailing and screeching in ear-piercing tones.

"My voice will no longer work on them," Mylth warned. "The creatures have no minds left that can even be affected by it. They are weak and vulnerable, fight them now!"

Wyverdorn, Shelberran, and Wayden set upon one of the beasts, while Narick made for another.

"Narick, no!" Andra begged for him to hold his place, but he ignored her.

Despite his weakened condition, Narick launched himself at the nearest creature, landing an elbow in the side of its head. It reeled but managed to backhand the monk in his face. The force of the blow knocked him to the ground, hard.

Andra cried out as she confronted the Vordlai. "Help me, Jeena!" she pleaded, though the Ferwar was already ahead of her. Jeena blew on her palms and a beam of light burst from them. To Andra's shock, it entered the jewel and tore out of it again as blue flames ripped through the creature's skin, burning a hole straight through its arm and piercing its wing. It screamed and collapsed to the ground, whimpering pathetically. Jeena finished it off with another blast.

* * *

Wyverdorn cursed as his men struggled with the Vordlai nearest to them. They were too weak to fight with any effectiveness, but with the others so preoccupied, fight they must. They made cautious swipes at their foe, but their weapons did little damage. The creature toyed with them, leering and hissing, as if it knew it could tear them apart at any moment.

It charged, catching Wayden by surprise and tripping him. Wyverdorn gasped in horror as it scooped Wayden up in its claws and dug his heart out of his chest. Swallowing its gruesome prize in one gulp, and casting the body to one side, the Vordlai turned its attention to the remaining two men.

He and Shelberran scrambled away, when they heard a bellow from behind the beast just before it screamed. The Vordlai crashed to the ground, an ornate black battle-axe embedded in the back of its head.

The Tveor warrior who delivered the deadly throw jumped into view, and yanked the weapon from the creature's skull. His one-horned helmet flew from his head to clatter against the stone floor in the darkness.

"Just in time!" the one called they'd called Bayark yelled as he pulled back his weapon and swung once more. The battle-mad Tveor laid into his enemy again and again, hacking wherever he could. At last, he stood over it, and with a great chop, severed its head. He held it up, bellowing with laughter even as it began to disintegrate into ash in his hand.

"Glad I came to and found my way down into this damned tunnel!"

* * *

Dorinen wanted to run to Bayark, but couldn't take time to rejoice in his return, for she found herself confronting Tarnohken. The creature flicked its tongue back and forth, as if inviting a fight, while she fought the trembling in her legs, calling on whatever bravery she might have left. "You'll find me a far more dangerous enemy than most!" she warned, clutching her sword in front of her as a threat.

Taking a chance, and evading a strike, she swung the blade. Her sword ripped across its midsection, tearing open the wound from Mylth's earlier attack. She whipped her sword around and plunged it deep into the creature's exposed gut. Ignoring her own peril, grasping the hilt with both hands, she forced it toward the creature's heart. She managed to contort her body to one side, but she was an instant too late. The creature's claw caught her near her elbow, tearing through her shirt and cutting deep.

She cried out, and panic filled her as she twisted out of the way and dove for safety. The Vordlai pressed the attack, towering over her with a bestial chortle, ready to strike.

Mylth shouted a challenge as the creature turned to face its new foe. His ancient blade cut deeply into Tarnohken's side, knocking it off balance. Dorinen seized the opportunity and kicked hard at its shin, while lashing out with her sword and cutting a deep gash across its neck.

Mylth did not relent and brandished his weapon again. For the briefest moment, Tarnohken snarled at him with savage hatred. Mylth's blade cut into its skull, cleaving it in two. Its hideous eyes went wide, and as the light from those eyes faded, it began to crumble away.

Dorinen took deep breaths, the gash in her arm already numbing with the creature's poison.

One Vordlai remained near where the brood leader had fallen, though it held its ground. At first it prepared to flee, but then it snarled with something like delight.

"Uh, I don't want to spoil this happy reunion," Bayark called out, "but we've got big problems!"

From behind him, more dark shapes lumbered into view from the tunnel.

Mylth turned about to face them. "Damn it! How many?"

"From the sound of growls and feet hitting the ground, I'd guess at least six," Dorinen said with a labored breath. She could no longer feel the hilt of her sword against her palm. "We can't fight them all," she said to Mylth. "We have to run."

"Run into the tunnel?" he countered. "We don't even know where it goes!"

"We don't have a choice," she said, "I won't survive if I have fight them. I've been struck. I need Andra's healing!"

* * *

A chill shot through Mylth. Fury took him, and he whirled to confront the Vordlai nearest to them. In the ancient Dalaethrian language, he roared the words for the deadliest magic he possessed. Bolts of fire surged from his fingertips, striking the creature in the chest and burning through its hide. It clawed at the wound, slowing enough for Mylth to stagger away, but he fought against disorientation and blurred vision, having overextended himself with a dangerous and draining casting. He struggled now to regain his senses.

"Run!" he shouted, doubling over and gasping for breath. "Flee into the tunnel!"

Andra helped Narick to his feet and half-carried him. Wyverdorn and Shelberran followed, stumbling as they ran. Bayark covered them, swinging his axe back and forth to hold their pursuers at bay. Jeena circled about the creatures, trying to confuse and irritate them to slow them down further.

Mylth and Dorinen led the way, pushing into the unknown darkness of the tunnel ahead. Dorinen's breathing sounded labored and difficult, and he knew the extra effort she needed to flee would only make matters worse.

"I can't... feel my fingertips," she stammered.

He helped her retain her grip on her sword, and forced away his own rising tide of panic. "Shut the wound out of your mind and focus on what lies in front of us," he advised.

But even if they escaped from these creatures, where would they go? And what if more Vordlai lay ahead of them?

* * *

Andra struggled under Narick's weight. Shelberran offered to help prop him up, even as he, too, labored to keep the monk on his feet.

She shrieked when a Vordlai emerged out of a side tunnel just as they fled by it. Bayark swung at it with his axe, enough to slow the creature as it keeled over. Behind, other Vordlai stumbled into it and fell. Enraged, they turned on their kin and tore it to shreds.

The companions kept up their pace, even as Andra tried to stay on her feet, her heart beating furiously and her head pounding in pain.

Jeena came to her at once. "Be strong, *mar shokara*. You will prevail!"

As long as Jeena was beside her, fear wouldn't take hold of her.

*   *   *

Dorinen saw the passage begin to slope upwards ahead of her. She held her hand out to motion Mylth to slow as she sniffed the air, still certain of her senses even as the venom chilled her. She inhaled again. The scent was unmistakable. Green, like moss on a dewy morning. "Wait! That's the scent of the forest. Is this how the Vordlai enter Cernwood?"

"It might be" he answered in a heavy voice. "Hurry!"

She lurched forward and he reached out to support her. Mylth caught her by her wounded arm, and she yelped.

"You need to wrap it," he insisted. "You'll bleed to death if we keep going."

"We can't let them get to the surface," she panted. "Even with the portal sealed, there are still enough of them to devastate the surrounding lands. Kuurm could still succeed."

The tunnel widened and took a sharp turn upwards, but the cool air of the forest brushed against her cheeks. Dragging herself forward, she saw an opening in the distance above. The pre-dawn sky beckoned them, but the tunnel leading to the surface became too steep for them to keep running. They would have to climb.

"Oh, blood and tree ash!"

Mylth scanned the tunnel behind them. "Andra and the others are close." He turned to Dorinen and placed a gentle hand on her good arm. "The Vordlai will not escape, but you will."

"What do you mean?" she asked, shaking as weakness at last began to take her.

"Get yourself and Andra to the surface. Have her see to your wound right away."

The numbness brought her confusion. "What are—"

"Go!" he yelled, starting back down the passageway.

Ignoring his command, Dorinen followed him, even as her body began to fail her. She couldn't leave without him, not after all they'd been through.

"Dorinen, please," he said as he turned to face her, his face pained.

"What are you going to do?"

Andra, Shelberran, and Narick came to them.

"Get to the surface. Climb!" Mylth pointed to the exit.

"Go," Dorinen confirmed. "That's the way out."

"What about you?" Andra asked.

"We'll be along shortly," Dorinen answered. "Go!"

They trudged forward to face the grueling task awaiting them. Jeena soared past Dorinen and Mylth and urged on Andra and the others.

Bayark and Wyverdorn followed close behind, having put some distance between themselves and their hideous pursuers. Bayark ran onward, but Wyverdorn paused to catch his breath, telling the small warrior he would catch up.

Mylth searched his shoulder bag, pulling out and unwrapping two small glass vials of liquid. "I'd hoped these would not be necessary," he said in a grave tone, holding one in each hand, suspiciously far apart.

Dorinen's eyes narrowed. "What do you mean?"

"Stay back," he said, a hollow desperation in his expression. "Separately, they are harmless, but mixed together, they will explode."

She understood. But she didn't want to believe it. "You don't mean to…"

"It's the only way, Dorinen. The blast will collapse the tunnel, killing the Vordlai."

"And you, too!" She grabbed at one of the vials, but he stopped her, pulling away.

"Dorinen, please," he said, the fire nearly gone from his voice. "I've fought this damned war before, and if my time is finished, this is as good a way as any to meet my end. Andra and Jeena can save you."

"No, I will not leave you! Not now! Not when we've nearly won.

Not when we... if you are to die here, then I will die with you, but I won't leave you behind!" She tugged at his jerkin, knowing with appalling certainty that his mind was made up.

With apologetic anguish, Mylth pulled free of her and turned to hurry back down the passage. He never got to take the first step.

Lord Wyverdorn hit Mylth on the back of the head with his sword hilt. As Mylth groaned and slumped to the ground, Dorinen retrieved the two vials from his hands before they could roll onto the tunnel floor and break.

Wyverdorn snatched them from her at once. "I heard everything. Now, take him and get out of here!" he demanded. "If anyone should face these creatures, it's me. I've nothing left, but you have a greater war to fight. Go... live! Win this! For us, for this world!"

"Thank you." Dorinen grasped his hand, kneeling to help the dazed Mylth to his feet. With effort, and the effects of the venom weighing on her, she pulled him up the passage.

* * *

Every muscle in Andra's body ached as she scrambled to the surface, struggling under Narick's weight, even with Shelberran's help. Above, stars lingered in the lavender sky, a beautiful sight she never thought she'd see again.

Jeena stayed with them and tried to focus her energies into their efforts, but Andra saw her fatigue.

"I am drained," she said with such regret that Andra's heart nearly broke. "Soon I must return to my body."

Pain and exhaustion wracked Andra's limbs, but Jeena's encouragement gave her and Shelberran the push they needed. They hauled themselves and the wounded monk out of the tunnel and onto the blessed earth of the forest, savoring a first precious smell of damp, fresh, morning air.

* * *

Back in the tunnel, Wyverdorn whispered prayers to the Spirit.

"May the desecration of this forest by my ancestor be forgiven and washed away. May my family rest in peace, and may these vile creatures be destroyed."

He heard their breathing and their foul hisses echoing in the distance. Pinpoints of yellow light, eyes reflecting pure evil, loomed before him.

Wyverdorn stood still as the Vordlai closed in. As they shuffled toward him, they scratched their claws at the sides of the narrowing tunnel, snarling with mad rage.

Still, he waited.

"Yes, believe you've won," he whispered. "Believe that the last man of Wyverdorn Keep is about to fall and become a part of your damnable feast. Come on, you bastards. Come to your miserable fate!"

They were almost to him now, drooling, panting, growling. The first cried out with the ecstasy of the hunt, arms raised to rip him wide open.

Wyverdorn shouted out in defiance and smashed the two vials together.

* * *

Dorinen faltered, the venom making her shiver and tremble. She grew weaker with each passing moment, fearful her arms and legs would fail her, as her ears rang and her vision began to blur.

Through her haze, she could see Bayark close above them. He offered a hand to lift Mylth up.

"Come on, pixie. You're enough of a burden on her as it is!"

Mylth groaned.

The tunnel around them shook, followed by a low rumbling

that burst into a roar. Smoke drifted past them, and above her, Bayark wrestled with Mylth, dragging him along with one arm as he sought finger holds with the other. He glanced back down the passage. "What in damnation's goin' on?"

Dorinen didn't have the strength to explain but motioned with her chin for him to hurry. The smoke thickened, blotting out the sky. Bayark cursed but found the exit, throwing Mylth over as thick black fumes poured out of the opening.

Dorinen coughed and the smoke stung her throat. She almost lost her grip and fell, but Bayark grasped hold of her hand. As he hoisted her over the edge, she rolled to her side. He peered back down into the passage. His eyes widened.

"Oh, Ultock's co—"

He yanked Dorinen away from the edge just as a giant fireball exploded out of the tunnel and high into the morning sky, scattering ash all about. They coughed, sputtered, and gagged, shielding themselves from falling cinders and flames. Thick, black smoke bellowed out of the ground, which convulsed violently as sections of the tunnel beneath them collapsed.

* * *

Desperately searching the chaos of her smoke-filled surroundings, Andra called out to Jeena, and at once, Jeena came to her side. Her *liskja* now faded in and out. She tried to touch Andra's face, but once more, she could not.

"You're still here," Andra said, grasping for a hand she knew she couldn't take.

"I am weary. I must go soon. I have stayed too long." She glimpsed something past Andra with a surprised expression.

"There are people—in the distance."

Indeed, Andra could see shapes, distorted in the haze, but heading toward them. As they drew near, Andra keeled over, dizzy and seized by a fit of coughing. She nearly collided with a dirt-encrusted black boot where her face hit the grassy ground. She now strained to see Jeena, looking weary, helpless, and afraid.

Andra heard the scrape of a blade against a leather scabbard and felt a cold point against her throat. Seeing its owner, she shivered in recognition and the sight brought her back to her senses.

A man, his black tunic adorned with a thorny, bronze-colored flower, his stringy red hair and eye patch unmistakable, loomed over her.

"Well… what a pleasant surprise!" Moarkh said with satisfaction.

Twenty-Seven

Moarkh pressed the sword point against Andra's neck. She swallowed hard.

As the smoke around her dissipated, she saw that she and her companions had escaped into a small forest clearing. Its trees grew in twisted and grotesque shapes, spiraling upward like the arms of tormented wraiths.

"Seems like we meet again, little songbird," Moarkh taunted. "I would congratulate your monk friend on his daring attack yesterday, but he appears to be lost to the world at the moment." He chuckled, rubbing his cheek, still swollen from Narick's strike.

Beside her, Narick lay unconscious, and Shelberran slumped on the ground. Mylth shifted, drifting in and out of awareness. Dorinen lay beside him, shivering and panting. But Bayark and Wyverdorn were nowhere to be seen. Even Jeena, beside her only a moment before, had disappeared. Through the haze, four other Iron Rose soldiers sneered at their easy catch.

"We don't normally come to this part of the forest," Moarkh continued. "It's reserved for our… employer. Be assured, we didn't follow you into the keep only because the master wouldn't have liked that. But he'll certainly want to know why something's exploded in his domain. Imagine our delight in finding you here!"

"Pathetic lot," one of the others said with a sneer. "In no condition to resist us."

"Indeed," Moarkh said, still eyeing Andra and shifting the position on his sword, bringing it ever closer to her neck. "And as such, they will all die, slowly and painfully."

Andra flinched, trying to ease herself away from the tip of Moarkh's blade. As she edged backward, one of the men behind Moarkh stiffened and let out a muffled cry. Andra watched in disbelief as Jeena passed right through his body, leaving pulses of white light surging all over him. He twitched and fell forward, screaming as the lights burned outward to his skin.

Moarkh swung around. Now Andra seized her chance.

She kicked Moarkh's legs out from underneath him, and staggered away, the effort sending stabbing pains pounding through her feet and legs. Moarkh cursed, dragging himself to his feet to pursue her.

Another Iron Rose soldier yelled out, followed by the sickening sound of blade through flesh. Andra shot a quick glance behind her.

"I've had enough of you scum!" Bayark roared, yanking his axe free from the man's back. He whirled about to parry a sword swing overhead from another of their foes, the sharp clang of metal biting through the morning calm.

Andra stumbled on through the haze. She coughed and wheezed in the still-smoky air, desperate to escape as Moarkh chased after her. He tackled her and rolled her onto her back. Forcing himself on top of her, he drew out a dagger and raised it over her head.

He screamed and dropped his weapon as Jeena's *liskja* surged through his arm. Her enchanted fire surged outward from inside his hand, working its way to the surface of the skin, blackening it and filling Andra's nose with the sickening stench of charred flesh. He clutched at it in agony, howls trailing into whimpers.

Andra took advantage of the distraction and delivered as hard a punch as she could to his throat. He choked, falling away in a dull thud. Her hand throbbing, she worked her way free from his weight, kicked him in the side, and ran to Jeena, who reeled and swayed, fading in and out.

"Jeena, what's wrong?"

"I've used too much power, *mar shokara*," she whispered. "I cannot stay here. I must return to my body, or I will die."

Indeed, Andra could feel the effects of Jeena's exertion in her own body, a weight in her chest, like something being pulled away. She wanted to touch Jeena, but she could only stare helplessly.

Near them, Bayark sparred with another brigand, as they circled each other in the haze. Bayark ducked from the man's swing and lunged forward. He slammed into his opponent, knocking him to the ground. Before the soldier could recover, the Tveor brought down the axe into his chest. The man grasped at the air once and fell limp.

Holding his ruined hand, Moarkh staggered away, calling for his remaining men as he fled into the forest.

Bayark started after them, but Andra, reeling from fatigue, called out, "Bayark, let them go! We need to help the others."

Reluctantly, he heeded her plea, and returned to her, helping her to her feet. He eyed Jeena with caution, but Andra had no time explain.

"Jeena, we have to help Dorinen," Andra said. "She's been struck by a Vordlai. Please, I need your help. I know you're weak, but anything you can offer…"

Jeena held out one hand, as her image faded in and out again. "I will do what I can."

Through the clearing smoke, they found Dorinen and Mylth together. Dorinen shook convulsively, her breathing shallow and her eyes rolling back. Mylth lay beside her, a welt on the back of his head crusted with blood. He let out a pained, weak groan. Andra would have to tend to him later.

Dorinen's skin displayed a sickly greyish color, and Andra feared the poison had already found her heart. If she didn't act soon, her friend would die.

Andra drew on her remaining strength. Exhausted, reeling from pain, she began her healing song one more time, holding tightly onto the gem in her broken instrument. Her voice, hoarse and straining, could barely hold the melody. The words failed her, and her body begged her to give in. but she forced herself through it all and set her intention on her task, refusing to give up. Not now.

Jeena danced, her usually graceful, deliberate movements uneven and uncontrolled. Slowly, the fire of the Lady and the blessing of Koliserr honored Jeena once more, and a golden glow enveloped her *liskja*, blending with the strands of Andra's song.

Bliss and despair mingled within Andra, but she pressed on, refusing to let her friend perish. *Please Lady, I cannot do this without you!*

Bayark knelt beside Dorinen and held her hand. "Come on girl, hang on! These two lasses'll fix you. Don't you leave us now." Tears streamed down his cheeks. "Damn it, don't!"

Violet light swirled over Dorinen, bathing her in its warm and hallowed radiance. She cried out and arched her back as the healing magic did its work, burning away the Vordlai's venom, stopping the bleeding, and threading together her torn skin. She relaxed again and slumped to one side, breathing softly.

Andra gasped for air, knowing she and Jeena could no longer sustain their efforts. She slumped back, spent, the work done.

Dorinen opened her eyes a little. Andra stroked her cheek, and Dorinen offered her a weak smile in return.

"You'll be all right, thank Teuvell," Andra said, wiping tears away. Through the smoke, she glimpsed the sky, hopeful the Lady might somehow be watching her in that miraculous moment. She let out a sob that dissolved into a brief laugh.

"Thank you." Dorinen took hold of Andra's hand. "For this. And the portal. You saved us all."

"I only did what I could," Andra said, struggling to feel worthy of her friend's high praise. "And I needed Jeena."

"You did much more," Dorinen whispered. "Where's Mylth?"

"Right here beside you," Andra said, motioning to him.

Dorinen edged her way over to him, and placed her head on his shoulder.

Andra turned back to Jeena, her *liskja* dissipating.

"I must return to my body at once," she whispered.

Andra nodded. "Go. And thank you. For everything. I can never repay you."

Jeena placed her hands over her heart. "There is nothing to repay. Farewell for now. I will always be with you, *mar shokara*. I swear it."

"Be safe, *mar dhe cortan*. Be well. I am with you, too." She reached out to touch the air where Jeena's hand lingered.

Then Jeena faded away.

* * *

Light shone through Andra's bedroom window on an unusually cool morning. She lay in her own bed, in her own home, though sleep seemed fleeting, while fatigue and restlessness still plagued her. Yet her bed, the familiar aromas of her home, even the worn old wooden ceiling beams overhead, all provided some sense of comfort and relief, if not normalcy.

Three days had passed since she and her friends, battered and near death, crawled out of those horrific caverns. With Dorinen's life saved, they'd found their way out of the forest over the course of the day and arrived back at Meln late that night, exhausted, injured, depleted.

Now, with Ternen not forced to contaminate their waters with chorlax, and Kuurm's psychic controls removed, some of the more strong-willed villagers had begun to regain their sense of identity, Ternen and Andra's father among them. That offered her some relief, at least.

After she got out of bed, washed, and dressed, she peered into the room next to hers where Narick still slept. She thanked Teuvell that he lived. His injuries were severe, but he remained strong in mind and body. Indeed, his recovery had been far more rapid than it should have been, a testimony to his training and discipline.

Her father gained back his wits little by little, remembering more each day, though she still hadn't told him about her mother. He needed to be in a better state before she could find the strength to have such a difficult conversation with him.

She remained too weak to use the gem for anyone else yet, only attending to herself a little. She looked again at the fading pink line on her arm, mystified over how she'd escaped the Vordlai's deadly venom. She couldn't bear to dwell on what might have happened. Worse, she wondered whether her wounds of heart and mind would ever heal, even if her strength returned in full.

Jeena occupied her thoughts, and Andra prayed for her safety. She missed Jeena with her whole being and longed for her. Try as she might, Andra couldn't contact her, not since they'd parted. Yet, Jeena's presence warmed her heart, lifting her spirits with a certainty that their bond remained.

She went downstairs and into the sitting room, where she lit a fire in the hearth, its warmth filling her with a sense of safety and comfort. As the flames grew, she curled up in a nearby chair, drawing her knees to her chin and wrapping her arms around them.

A little while later, the door latch clicking drew her attention. Bayark smiled warmly as he entered, greeting her and sitting on the floor in front of her. She still found it odd to see him without his armor and his funny helmet, now lost in the chasm.

"How're you feelin'?" he asked.

"Well enough, I suppose," she answered. "But I don't sleep well, and visions of those terrible things keep haunting my dreams."

He took her hand with a strong and reassuring squeeze. "You miss your mama." For all his fierceness, he also could be remarkably gentle.

She closed her eyes, tears welling up, and nodded.

"You hear me," he said. "She's in a good place now. She didn't die for no reason. Because of you—her daughter—this world's been saved from a horrible fate. What you and your lass did down there, that took the work of the most powerful magic-casters in these lands, centuries ago, to do. You've made her proud, I know you have."

His kind words comforted her, if only for the moment.

* * *

Dorinen sat by the river outside the village, watching the current. She breathed in the soothing smell of the damp, early morning air. It was a colder day, but the natural world always nourished her, always brought her back to herself and gave her strength. She spoke a quiet prayer of thanks to Urkera that she'd survived, had not died in a lightless chasm, and lived to see a beautiful morning like this once again. The Spirit had embraced her and all her companions and was good after all. Indeed, as she'd suspected from the moment he uttered his venomous words, Kuurm had lied.

A hand gently touched her shoulder. She turned to see Mylth kneeling beside her. She'd heard him long before his approach, of course. He sat, and she leaned into him, placing her hand over his.

"Am I forgiven?" he asked.

"For what?"

"For my rash actions in the tunnel. I was arrogant and thought nothing of the consequences. I nearly killed myself, and in doing so, may as well have killed you." He gazed out over the river. "I am sorry. When Tarnohken struck you, I was horrified that this beast was going to take someone… important from me a second time. All I could see was the need to kill the Vordlai, all of them, even if doing so meant my own death."

She turned to face him. He seemed more troubled over losing her than at his own determination to sacrifice himself for everyone. "You are a *Shy'nande*. Your first duty is to the Spirit, no matter what it may require. It was a desperate action in desperate circumstances. You did what you felt you needed to do."

He picked up a small stone and tossed it into the flowing water. "I don't know if I want or even deserve that title," he said. "Ramwin and I have much wrong between us. Kuurm's anger toward the Spirit in many ways parallels my own, and that frightens me in a way I didn't know was possible. The evil he's unleashed through his resentment and bitterness has shown me just how dangerous a path I've walked in rejecting my heritage, my duties. I'm grateful I haven't fallen as he has."

Warmed by his vulnerability, she drew closer. "You won't. I know it in my heart. Kuurm Adath may be a man wronged, and perhaps the Shylan Dar were unwise, even foolish, in their decisions about him, but that cannot excuse his actions. Kuurm is evil in his heart, and probably always has been. No one with any love of life could unleash the monstrous forces he has and still count themselves as fully human. His heart belongs to the Underplanes, and yours—"

"Belongs here, in this world," he interrupted with a smile. "I know that now."

* * *

The five companions met together that afternoon, convening in the sitting room of Andra's home. Her father rested upstairs, affording them an opportunity to speak in private. Andra served them Meln's famous Starberry herbal brew, with all the comfort that such a normal, simple, and homey pleasure could bring after the horrors they'd witnessed and endured. They talked of simple things for a while, each wanting to preserve this peaceful moment for as long as they could. But at some point, they fell silent.

"What of the Vordlai now?" Andra asked at last, knowing the topic couldn't be avoided. She stared at the floor, hoping no one would answer.

"The ones that pursued us are dead, buried in rubble," Mylth said. "Kuurm probably opened that tunnel for them to begin with, so we simply resealed it. Most within the caverns still slept, and any others awakened will quickly turn on each other without Kuurm to control them. Regardless, they are trapped, once again."

Narick sipped his brew. "When we faced them in the caverns, why didn't they hide from our awareness as effectively as they seemed to be able to on the surface?"

"My guess is that Kuurm compelled them not to do so in his presence, to prevent treachery," Mylth answered. "And when the portal was resealed, any further powers they might have drawn from Torr Hiirgroth were lost to them, luckily for us."

"Bayark," Dorinen asked. "I've been wondering, how did you find us?"

"Hm, well, when I came to, all was quiet," he said. "I couldn't see straight, couldn't think, so I picked myself up and staggered out of the cavern. You must have been lyin' nearby, monk. Sorry I didn't see you. I finally found a tunnel that sloped down, and as my head cleared, I heard a big commotion. After that, we know what happened."

"All this tells me we've been favored," Narick said. "We must not diminish the magnitude of our victory. The Spirit has not abandoned us, even as it grows weaker. Unfortunately, darker times still lie ahead."

Bayark snorted. "Thanks for the encouragement, monk. Been readin' your chronicles for inspiration again?"

Narick almost laughed. "I didn't mean my words to sound like a monastic lecture, but the seriousness of what we face is all too dire. Kuurm still lives. I feel it. We are again connected in our minds, and I can sense his presence, much as I loathe it. He's far from here now, but he's not finished. He will strike again. As we near the time when the Spirit draws into itself, he will move to extinguish it forever, even without the Vordlai at his side."

Andra wrestled with her many fears as she pondered the implications of Narick's words. "When will it happen? The drawing in?"

Narick shook his head. "Perhaps Kuurm himself doesn't know the exact day, perhaps the Spirit dies at the time of its own choosing. But we don't have long. I would guess two fortnights, more or less."

"By the Lady, that's… very soon," Andra said, hugging herself again, the enormity of what they faced threatening to engulf her once more.

"What will happen when it does die?" Dorinen asked the question none of them wanted to.

"No one knows," Mylth answered. "The Dalaethri have legends about this cyclic event, but such stories are shrouded in myth and symbolism. It hasn't occurred since beyond our reckoning. Even immortals forget, I fear. We don't know exactly what the signs will be, but we've all seen what the denizens of the Underplanes will do to try to gain the advantage. This is a dangerous time of incredible cosmic significance, a struggle between powers far beyond any of us. We will never understand all of the complexities. And yet, almost no one in the wider world knows about it."

"But the Spirit still needs us, yes?" Andra asked, longing for any words of comfort.

"Indeed," Mylth answered. "I'm more certain of it than I have been since my awakening."

"Jeena told me the Gro'aken attacked her people at the edge of the Grey Wolds," Andra said. "Gro'aken haven't entered the wolds before. At least not for centuries."

"Damn right!" Bayark growled. "If they're here now, they've gotten past us. Somethin' is helpin' them out, but we'll get 'em."

"What are we going to do?" Andra asked.

"I'm headin' for home," Bayark said, "like I wanted to do before all of this cosmic crap started. If my people don't know what's happenin' yet because of some perverse magic, they've gotta be warned."

"A sound plan," Mylth said. "We should leave for Stimus-hodd as soon as possible. There, we can decide our best course of action."

"We?" Bayark asked.

"Yes. The Eral-savat grows in strength each day," Mylth answered. "It may yet be confined to Yrthryr, but it must be contained. If it is able to send forth bands of Gro'aken under its control to attack human settlements in the Grey Wolds, its influence has already spread beyond the wastes. It might have summoned other creatures to do its bidding. Since we are the ones who closed the portal, we must continue with the task. While we have needed these few days to rest, the time draws near when we should depart."

"There must be others more capable of stopping the Eral-savat," Dorinen said. "We barely survived. Surely, Ramwin will now decide on someone else?"

"*We* are the ones the Sarvethar selected," Narick said, "and we're all alive. Remarkably, we have passed through the trials in those caverns and sit here as victors. That's what's important. Perhaps there will be others who will join us, like Jeena, but I believe the task will ultimately fall to us, to you." He looked at Andra.

She took a sharp inhale. "And what happens if we do stop the Eral-savat? Afterwards, I mean."

"My greatest concern is the Arltorath," Mylth said. "Since Kuurm has somehow trapped them inside the Eral-savat to increase its power, we must deal with them if they can free themselves from it, lest they escape and seek to interfere with the Spirit's rebirth in their own way. They must be bound to their tombs again in the Mountains of Sorrow, as they were five hundred years ago. The task of banishing them is something I will have to undertake."

Dorinen placed a hand on his arm.

"And Kuurm?" Andra asked.

"We have no choice but to wait and see what he'll do next," Narick answered. "For now, I am blocking his mind from my own, but I cannot say how long I'll be able to do so."

"Then it's settled," Dorinen said with a heavy sigh, "We must leave as soon as we can for Stimus-hodd."

Mylth placed one hand over hers. "Be encouraged," he said, as much to all of them as to her. "In this room, in this moment, the Land Spirit still lives, and the bonds we've forged together from the horrors we've endured will sustain us. Nothing can change that, whatever fate may yet decree."

Narick gave a satisfied nod in agreement as he took Andra's hand. "In this moment, we are at peace. Enwyonn be praised."

She smiled at him in return, then at all of them, the warmth in her heart mirroring the golden glow of the hearth. "And for that, I'm so thankful. When we're ready, we'll set off, and may the Lady be with us all."

Glossary

A Guide to Terms, Peoples, and Places

Arltorath: Four ancient and evil sorcerers of immense power, who cannot be killed, only contained. Their origin and true identity remain a mystery.

Artisans: Devotees of Lady Teuvell, gifted in music, poetry, art, dance, and other forms of artistic expression. They channel the Lady's magic through their arts.

Ashyzym: The capital city of the southern land of Maradhoor.

Ayssa: A female incarnation of the Land Spirit revered in the lands of Maradhoor and beyond.

Book of Syontar: A holy book of the Shylan Dar monks that tells of the cycles of the Land Spirit. Only redacted copies are believed to survive.

Cernodyn: The people of the great forest of Cernwood, who care for the woods and help maintain them.

Chaar: A special psychic bond between a Shylan Dar master and one or more of his students.

Cho Ar: A parasitic infection that extends the host's life immeasurably but drives them mad and instills in them an endless, ravenous hunger. There is no known cure.

Chorlax: An intoxicating compound of herbs that can be used for many purposes, not all of them beneficial.

Daatha: The ruling council of the Cernodyn.

Dalaethri: An ancient, immortal people who are rarely seen in the current age. Steeped in magic and history, they were the first higher beings to have emerged from the light of the Land Spirit.

Darrowrath: Human practitioners of darkened and forbidden magic. They mainly reside in the western land of Gavalahorne and seek to overthrow the last remaining monarchy there and impose themselves as rulers.

Doa: A manifestation of the Land Spirit in the lands to the west, over the great ocean.

Eladra: A manifestation of the Land Spirit that advocates for pacifism and contemplation. Her houses are open to all, and Her devotees live simple, communal lives.

Enanim: A people small of stature, related to the Tveor, but less rugged than their cousins, and more given to lives of the mind and the arts.

Enwyonn: A manifestation of the Land Spirit revered by the monks of Shylan Dar. He is known as a patron of learning, as well as physical and mental disciplines.

Eral-savat: An ancient, hateful, amorphous entity trapped deep underground that slowly devours the souls of the living to sustain itself. Those spirits trapped in its endless dark might linger in that state for thousands of years as it slowly consumes them.

Ferwareen: Women from any culture around the world who are born with special talents, powers, and magical abilities. They are identified at a young age by other Ferwareen who become their Craft Mothers and guide them to develop their skills. Singular Ferwar.

Gro'aken: Cannibalistic creatures, humanoid, short of stature, known for their greed and brutal social groups. Cowardly, but in larger numbers they can be dangerous.

Hyradenn: A deep, meditative state that each Dalaethri enters into once every hundred years. They will stay in this state for a hundred years to rejuvenate themselves, and so are effectively immortal.

Iron Rose: A loose federation of quasi-military, criminal enterprises that attract outlaws, thieves, murderers, and brigands of all sorts. They work to undermine social norms, enrich themselves, and terrorize others into submission.

Jadya: An outsider to the Rajaani people, not one of them, and someone viewed with suspicion.

Kai Erodh: A student in the Shylan Dar order, who is exalted by his master for his skills and learning.

Kenlim: A type of small lyre (with seven to nine strings) used by the Artisans in composition and singing, especially to work magic.

Koliserr: The Twilight Lady of the Rajaani people, a manifestation of the Land Spirit that is unique to them. She encourages strength and courage, as well as justice.

Kontarr: In Rajaani belief, the balance of life, both mundane and magical. The cosmic order that maintains all things.

Kyrminion: An ancient people from the southern lands who have both human and dragon manifestations. No one is sure which came first, not even the Kyrminion themselves.

Land Spirit: A name given to the great sustaining force of the cosmos, commonly called the Spirit and sometimes the Absolute. It encompasses all things and imbues them with essence and life. It is envisioned in many aspects (Enwyonn, Teuvell, Eladra, and more), and can also incarnate as a Sarvethar (see below), a living being often attuned to the particular culture where the Spirit chooses to manifest.

Lennai parkarra: The Gratitude of Summertide, a Rajaani festival of prayer and thanks for the warm days that remain, while being conscious of the cold weather to come. A quiet day that is followed by a lavish and often raucous evening celebration.

Liskja: A Rajaani word for the soul.

Maradhoor: A great land across the southern sea from Rilnarya, home to the Kyrminion and many unknown wonders.

Mirithnaa: The Hall of Song at Teuvell's temple and college in Tenaeth. Where the Artisans hold ceremonies and rituals.

Mountains of Sorrow: A vast mountain range far to the north, home of many Gro'aken and other unpleasant creatures. Also, the site of a crucial magic-working five centuries past.

Mynthari: A special spiritual connection, a bond at the soul level that a Ferwar may offer to another once in her life. Most often reserved for spouses and partners.

Purhan: The special talent that each Ferwar possesses from birth, which their Craft Mother helps them to develop.

Rajaani: A semi-nomadic people originally from eastern lands, who now travel with the seasons and wander over a large range of the world. They are deeply in tune with nature and its cycles, and retain certain magical knowledge long forgotten by those in more settled societies.

Ramwin Roakthone: A main Sarvethar (incarnation, see below) of the Land Spirit. Ramwin is known for his perplexing, irritating, and comical nature, often playing the fool and the fop to the bewilderment of those who meet him. A symbol of cosmic joy and delightful chaos.

Roballa: A Rajaani bowed instrument; small, portable, and joyous.

Rowana: A female version of Ramwin, rather like his twin sister. The Spirit might choose either of these forms at any given time, or even switch back and forth between them.

Sarvethar: A name for an incarnation of the Land Spirit. Ramwin and Rowana are two examples, but many others have revealed themselves throughout the world.

Shylan Dar: An ancient monastic order, reserved for men. The monks focus on learning and scholarship, as well as martial arts and psychic abilities. Their knowledge is matched only by their combat skills, and they are frequent advisors to the ruling council of Tenaeth and to governments of other countries.

Shy'nande: A name for an exalted living being, often Dalaethrian, who is in the service to the Spirit or its incarnations, carrying out its will at crucial times.

Stimus-hodd: The great fortress of the Tveor (see below) in the northwestern Grey Wolds.

Stone Lord: A manifestation of the Land Spirit revered by the Tveor.

Tenaeth: The capitol city of Rilnarya, a center for trade and government. Home to the temple and college of Teuvell, as well as an important Daughter House of the Shylan Dar Monastery.

Teuvell: A manifestation of the Land Spirit revered by the Artisans. Sometimes called the Lady of Song, or often just the Lady, She is a patron of music, art, dance, and other creative ventures, as well as love and pleasure. The Artisans bring Her magic into the world through their efforts.

Torr Hiirgroth: A realm that is part of the Underplanes (see below). It is the original home of the Vordlai and various other foul creatures that forever try to cross into the mortal world, but they are held in check by powerful magic and the will of the Land Spirit.

Tveor: A hardy people, short in stature, who live in the northern lands. One of their fortresses, Stimus-hodd, acts as a central protector of the northern regions.

Ultock: A hero from Tveor history and myth. He championed strength, honor, justice, smithing, and fine crafts.

Underplanes: A series of realms outside of the visible world, most often populated by creatures and beings that are hostile to the Spirit and to mortals. It's not known how many of these planes exist.

Urkera: A manifestation of the Land Spirit for the Cernodyn, who see in Her the very soul of the forest of Cernwood. She encompasses the woods and all the life within it.

Vordlai: Large, humanoid creatures with bat-like faces, sharp fangs, and enormous wings. Their talons contain a deadly venom that paralyzes their victims and stops their hearts. They are denizens of Torr Hiirgroth and have been locked out of the mortal world for ages beyond counting.

War of Gharborr: A deadly northern conflict five centuries previous that left the land devastated, saw the unleashing of horrific creatures from the Underplanes, and set in motion the events now unfolding.

Yrthryr: The location of the War of Gharborr, a terrible conflict that started small and grew to horrific proportions before it could be stopped. The war utterly destroyed it.

The Bleeding Earth
Book 2 of The Dark Renewal

Andra and her new friends have only just begun their efforts, and now their focus must shift to the seemingly impossible task of confronting and stopping the Eral-savat, the world-shattering horror that is spreading in Yrthryr to the north.

Seeking refuge in the great Tveor fortress, they soon discover that not all is not as it appears, for members of the Shylan Dar, the Artisans, and the Eladrans might actively be working against them. But for what purpose?

And as Kuurm hides, waiting and preparing for the inevitable end, a new horror descends on the Grey Wolds, nightmarish shape-shifting creatures leading bands of Gro'aken on a mission of conquest and destruction.

Andra and her companions must trust in each other to put an end to the earth ravage once and for all, and save the world from certain destruction. But what if the Eral-savat cannot be sealed away again?

Coming in late 2025

Music for The Forbidden Summoning

As if Tim didn't have enough to do already, he has composed and recorded a short album of music inspired by scenes and settings in *The Forbidden Summoning*, using orchestral and ambient sounds to create a unique soundtrack and listening experience!

Gathering Darkness brings his book to life in musical form. To hear how he envisions his world and story, visit the album's Bandcamp page, where you can purchase and then either download the recording or stream it:

https://eidolorous.bandcamp.com/album/gathering-darkness

Tim plans on creating a new recording for each of the four books in the series, to give readers something truly different and immersive!

Acknowledgements

This book began in my mind decades ago, or at least some of the characters did. The story started to take shape in the late 1990s, but I abandoned it because life and other things got in the way. However, in recent years, I dusted off the old files and began to think seriously about how it could come to life. It needed a lot of work! Happily, I felt that I was in the right place to do that work and shape the book into what I wanted it to be.

I grew up reading classic fantasies in the 1970s and 80s, by authors such as J.R.R. Tolkien, Terry Brooks, Michael Moorcock, Anne McCaffrey, Gene Wolf, and others. I wanted to create a story and a world that were a kind of homage to those wonderful tales that kept me enthralled for so many hours, but tweaked and sculpted here and there to bring it to modern readers.

Originally this series was planned as a trilogy, but I found that the characters and events had much more to say, and so the series, *The Dark Renewal*, has expanded to four books. I have plans for additional books set in the world, but they will be separate stories, related but not essential reads, unless you want to...

The task of bringing this book together into something I could be proud of has had a lot of help along the way. I am especially indebted to my wonderful partner and editor, Abigail Keyes, who pored through the manuscript and was merciless in her recommendations for improvement, and boy, were those good recommendations! The book is what it is now thanks to her careful readings and constructive criticisms.

Thanks also to my agent, Maryan Karinch, for continuing to believe in me and my unusual work, ever since she took me on and sold my classical music book of the bizarre to a New York publisher all those years ago. Thanks to Armin Lear/Thousand Acres, for being a home for innovative and unusual books, both fiction and non-fiction.

I had a number of beta readers who have read the manuscript and given their thoughts and support, and I am very thankful to them all: Jacob Heringman, Bill Stewart, Douglas Gueydan, Annie Valdes, Skip Lacaze, Paula Ashton, and Cybele Baker. Thanks for being my initial test audience!

Special thanks to Daniël Hasenbos for his amazing map of my world. He took my simple line drawing and turned it into something truly special. *https://danielsmaps.com/*

Special thanks also to Piere d'Arterie for his beautiful cover design: *https://www.instagram.com/piere_d_arterie*

Many, many thanks to Laura de Antonio Gomez for her stunning front cover painting. When I saw her work online, I just knew she was the right artist for the project. I look forward to seeing how she brings my future books to life! *https://ldeagart.carrd.co/*

And of course, thanks always to Freya, for ongoing inspiration.

About the Author

Tim Rayborn has written a large number of books over the past several years (about fifty and counting!). He lived in England for several years and has a PhD from the University of Leeds, which he likes to pretend means that he knows what he's talking about. His generous output of written material covers such diverse topics as music, the arts, history, the strange and bizarre, fantasy and sci-fi, and general knowledge. He's already planning on writing more books, whether anyone wants him to or not.

He's also an internationally acclaimed musician. He plays dozens of unusual instruments that quite a few people of have never heard of and often can't pronounce, including medieval instrument reconstructions and folk instruments from Northern Europe, the Balkans, and the Middle East.

He has appeared on over forty recordings, and his musical wanderings and tours have taken him across the US, all over Europe, to Canada and Australia, and to such romantic locations as Marrakech, Istanbul, Renaissance chateaux, medieval Italian hill towns, and high school gymnasiums.

He currently lives in Washington State, surrounded by many books and instruments, and is rather enthusiastic about good wines and cooking excellent food.

Find Tim online at multiple websites:

https://timrayborn.com/
https://eidolorous.bandcamp.com/
https://timrayborn.bandcamp.com/
https://www.instgram.com/rayborn.esoterica/
http://www.threads.net/@rayborn.esoterica
https://www.facebook.com/TimRaybornMusicandWriting
https://bsky.app/profile/timrayborn.bsky.social

Also by Tim Rayborn from
Armin Lear / Thousand Acres

Qwyrk Tales

Welcome to a whole new world…

Well, all right, more like part of an old one. Join the (mis)adventures of Qwyrk, a Shadow tasked with keeping an eye on the comings and goings of everyday people and protecting them from supernatural incursions, quite often with considerable inconvenience and annoyance to herself. Bloody hell.

Tagging along with her in this effort and in solving the magical mysteries at hand is a group of misfits, who are friends, foils, and much more. Together, they must confront the many dangers at the edge of reality in modern northern England, a land of shadows, ancient sorcery, strange creatures, mysterious entities of all kinds, appallingly bad sonnets and songs, tacky nightclub attire, queer romance, true love, British humor, an abundance of sarcasm, and even elves… though they are a bit silly.

*"Charming and funny, the characters are delightful.
I wouldn't have missed it for anything."*
~ Peter S. Beagle, author of The Last Unicorn

*"Fans of Pratchett, Beagle, and de Lint will absolutely
feel at home in this story! Such a fun read."*
~ Laura Tempest Zakroff, author of Weave the Liminal

"The action is fun and unpredictable, the characters multifaceted, and the plot evolves some satisfyingly unexpected twists that will keep fans engrossed."
~ D. Donovan, Midwest Book Review

The complete four-book series of comical, modern English urban fantasy stories is available to order online and at bookstores worldwide!
Qwyrk: 978-1736298817 / Lluck: 978-1737276296
Chantz: 978-1956450606 / Faytte: 978-1956450767
https://timrayborn.com/qwyrk-tales/